Advance prais

"Gripping, chilling, and emotio... masterful blend of suspense a... ...ve always been a fan of Darlene Turner and now s...e s moved on to my 'must read' list with this book. Do yourself a favor and don't miss this one!"
—Lynette Eason, award-winning and bestselling author
of the Lake City Heroes series

"Turner's *Echoes of Darkness* has it all: a sinister plot, past trauma, and intriguing characters. I couldn't put it down. Highly recommended!"
—Colleen Coble, *USA TODAY* and *Publishers Weekly* bestselling author

"This read is a battle between darkness and light, and readers will want to hang on for a ride filled with action, agonizing moments, and that spark of hope we all are looking for! Pop a bag of popcorn and settle in. You won't be moving from your spot until you've read this one cover to cover!"
—Jaime Jo Wright, Christy Award–winning author
of *The House on Foster Hill* and *The Vanishing at Castle Moreau*

"In *Echoes of Darkness*, Darlene Turner delves into the depths of human evil while illuminating the transformative beauty of God's light and forgiveness. Oaklynn and Caleb are both scarred souls who must confront the darkness of their past and find the courage to trust and love again. With chilling suspense, heartfelt romance, and a powerful message of redemption, this is a story that lingers in your heart and mind long after the final page."
—Lynn H. Blackburn, award-winning and bestselling author
of the Gossamer Falls series

"Ms. Turner knows exactly how to deliver a fast-paced, high-stakes suspense that will have you on the edge of your seat! *Echoes of Darkness* is an intense, harrowing, and exciting ride. Clear your schedule and grab this book!"
—Natalie Walters, award-winning and bestselling author
of the SNAP Agency and Harbored Secret series

"The daughter of a serial killer and a hero with a dark secret? Yes, please! Hold on tight for the twists and turns in Oaklynn and Caleb's story. If you enjoy a little creep to your suspense, you'll love Darlene L. Turner's *Echoes of Darkness*."
—Sami A. Abrams, award-winning and bestselling author

"Heroine Oaklynn Brock has every reason to run from her past, but her work as a constable means she can't escape her family's deadly legacy. This is a twisty, turny, edge of your seat suspense with plenty of surprises. Strong characters, relentless action, and a beautiful romance will keep you turning the pages of this faith filled adventure."
—Dana Mentink, *USA TODAY* bestselling author

Also by Darlene L. Turner

Love Inspired Suspense

Crisis Rescue Team

Fatal Forensic Investigation
Explosive Christmas Showdown
Mountain Abduction Rescue
Buried Grave Secrets
Yukon Wilderness Evidence
K-9 Ranch Protection

For additional books by Darlene L. Turner,
visit her website, www.darlenelturner.com.

ECHOES OF DARKNESS

DARLENE L. TURNER

Danielle,
    Thanks for being
on my team!
            Blessings,
            Darlene ♡

Rom 13:12b

LOVE INSPIRED

Stories to uplift and inspire

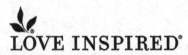

LOVE INSPIRED®

Stories to uplift and inspire

Recycling programs for this product may not exist in your area.

ISBN-13: 978-1-335-08050-9

Echoes of Darkness

Love Inspired
22 Adelaide St. West, 41st Floor
Toronto, Ontario M5H 4E3, Canada
www.LoveInspired.com

Printed in U.S.A.

For Mom and Dad.
I miss you.

Acknowledgments

Writing a book has so many layers, and *Echoes of Darkness*
wouldn't exist without many incredible people in my corner.

Jeff, my handsome PR guy. I'm not kidding when I say that you
need to retire and become my full-time marketing person.
You are my rock and biggest cheerleader. I couldn't do this writing journey
without your continued support. Thank you for encouraging me
to follow my dreams. I love you.

Sue Steeves (aka Sissy), thank you for cheering me on and believing in me
even when I didn't. You bless my life, and I praise God for you!

My family, thank you for loving me through every twist and turn
of my writing journey.

My agent, Tamela Hancock Murray, you are my champion.
I appreciate you believing in my stories and for always having my back.

Tina James, my amazing editor. Thank you for helping me make this story
stronger. Your sharp eye and gentle guidance are gifts from God.

My Fab Four, Suspense Squad and beta readers,
I couldn't have done this without each of you. Sorry if I scared some of you
with this story! Remember, we're God's light in a world of darkness.
This little light of mine...we're shining it brightly!

Darlene's Border Patrol, thank you for reading, reviewing
and spreading the word about my books. You are treasures.

Jessica R. Patch, thank you for answering so many of my questions.
I appreciate you!

Brent Nolan, John Evers, crimescenewriters and many others who helped
me with questions on police procedures, guns, drugs and lots more.
Anything I embellished for fiction is totally on me.

The team at Harlequin, you are amazing. Your covers are gorgeous
and you nailed *Echoes of Darkness*. Thank you for everything you do
for us authors. I love writing for you!

To the authors who've endorsed this book, thank you
for taking the time to read my story. Your kind words are such a gift.
I'm blessed to have you in my life.

Readers, where would I be without you?
Thank you for reading my stories and cheering me on.

Finally, but most importantly, to Jesus, my Lord and Savior. Thank You for
giving me Your story to share. I want to speak for You and be Your light.
May You have all the glory. I love You.

Chapter One

Suicide Slayer Dead. Constable Oaklynn Brock's coffee mug slipped from her fingers and smashed to the floor as she read the newspaper article on her cell phone. The serial killer's picture graced the front cover, sending her heart rate into overdrive. Bile crawled up the back of her throat. *Breathe, Oaklynn, breathe.* Voices filtered into Kenorapeake Falls Police Department's briefing room, or as the constables liked to call it—the bullpen. Her sergeant's words commending the group on their recent successful hostage takedown faded into the background. Could it be true? The monster was dead?

Oaklynn didn't wish death upon anyone, but relief flooded through every muscle in her body with the report of the man's demise. His killings had made national headlines over the years, and news of his death probably made most Canadians cheer. But for her, his brutal slayings hit too close to home. In more ways than one.

Today—fifteen years to the day of his arrest—Dr. Aaron Crowder's penetrating stare still affected her emotions, but she couldn't look away. His dark chocolate eyes had charmed his victims, drawing them in like flies to a sticky trap. Yes, even in death, he continued to haunt her life. *Just when I thought I put you in the rearview mirror, you creep into my brain.* She rubbed her sweaty hands on her uniform slacks as memories from the day the picture was taken flooded her mind. Oaklynn had turned twelve, and the hospital was honoring the doctor's recent life-changing neurosurgery. He had insisted she attend. After shaving, he splashed on his favorite cologne and the putrid, spicy scent had sickened her as his smell remained everywhere.

She held her breath as if the aroma still lingered in the air. It had also remained in her childhood room long after he'd left in the middle of the night.

Oaklynn placed her hand on her chest to silence her rapid heartbeat and the protruding memories of his touch. *He can't hurt you any longer.*

"Did you see this?" Constable Eldon Spearing raised his cell phone, revealing the online article in the *Kenorapeake Falls Tribune*. "Kind of ironic that the Suicide Slayer hung himself, don't you think?"

His question brought her back to the present, and she straightened to prepare for the rest of their morning briefing. She stuffed her phone into her vest pocket and turned to clean up her mess, but her leader beat her to the punch.

Staff Sergeant Rick Rollins crouched in front of Oaklynn and picked up the coffee mug pieces. "You okay?" His whispered question revealed his concern. "I know the article has hit social media."

She pursed her lips. "I'll be fine. He died years ago to me."

Other than her friend, forensic crime scene investigator Chloe Olson, the sergeant was the only additional person in Kenorapeake Falls who knew her connection to the killer, and she wanted to keep it that way. Once she had graduated from police college, she'd been stationed in Toronto, allowing her to hide among the vast population. But after she helped take down a major drug ring a year ago, social media plastered her picture. She requested to be transferred to Kenorapeake Falls, Ontario—a small city with a population of forty thousand. Enough people to hide among, but not too small that everyone knew her business. The perfect fit. More importantly, farther away from *him* and his crimes. Her request had been granted, and she transferred to the area six months ago.

"Tell me. What cereal does a serial killer eat for breakfast?" Eldon laughed at his own joke.

Constable Nika Crabb plunked herself next to Oaklynn and snickered. "Not sure I want to know."

Sergeant Rollins finished cleaning Oaklynn's spilled coffee and moved to the front of the room. "Okay, let's get to it."

"But seriously, what was this guy..." Eldon scanned the paper and tapped on the name "... Aaron Crowder's... MO?"

Oaklynn gripped her armrests until her knuckles turned white. *Can we change the subject?*

Sergeant Rollins avoided eye contact with Oaklynn, obviously not wanting to draw attention her way. "From what I understand, he murdered eight women before his arrest. He made his kills appear like suicides, but the coroner discovered the truth quickly. Once the media caught wind of the serial killer, they deemed him the Suicide Slayer."

"Says here when asked why he killed, he only replied 'because I could.'" Eldon tossed his phone on the table. "Sick that a doctor would kill. Don't they take an oath to save lives?"

Oaklynn shuddered as her past threatened to overtake her life once again. *God, if You're out there like Mama always said, please help this conversation end.*

"The article mentions his own daughter turned him in after she found his trophies." Nika whistled. "Wow. She was only fifteen. Brave girl."

The sergeant cleared his throat. "Okay, let's—"

Their radios screeched throughout the room, announcing an attack at a church on the edge of town.

"Spearing and Brock, you meet the paramedics at the scene." He paused. "Constable Brock, take the lead on this one."

Oaklynn didn't miss normally happy-go-lucky Constable Spearing's expression turn to one of contempt. He outranked her by six months and never let her forget it.

Great. Now she'd have to deal with Eldon. She ignored him and snatched her winter bomber coat from the back of her chair. "Meet you there."

Oaklynn raced from the building, the bitter January wind biting at her exposed cheeks. She ignored the chill as she hustled to her police-issued Charger and hopped inside. She started the engine and flipped on her lights and siren before speeding from the parking lot.

The cruiser swerved on the early morning snow-covered roads. January in Canada could be challenging, especially in the northern regions. Most people hated this time of year, but not Oaklynn. Fresh-fallen snow gave her a sense of renewal. Hope. And she could use lots of hope after this morning's news. *Why did you kill yourself now after all these years?* She set aside the question and concentrated on the route to take to the scene. She had a job to do, and she'd focus on the case. Not the past.

Seven minutes later, she drove into the church parking lot. Fire trucks and an ambulance had already arrived.

Eldon pulled in behind her and jumped out of his vehicle, holding yellow police tape.

The scurry of activity drew a large crowd even in the brisk early morning hours. Great. That's all they needed. She put on her tuque and gloves, exiting her Charger. She adjusted her duty belt as she walked forward.

Oaklynn raised her hands. "Folks, we need you to stand back while we investigate." She turned her back to the crowd and studied the scene.

Two paramedics hovered over the victim lying on the church property under a snow-covered balsam fir close to the visitor parking area. Did that mean the victim was still alive?

She headed toward the duo. "Morning. You guys got here quick. What's the situation?"

The brown-haired male paramedic eased from his squatted position. "Deep cuts on her upper arm. I'm afraid we weren't able to save her." He raised his hand in greeting. "We haven't met. I'm Jayson Scott. You are?"

"Constable Oaklynn Brock." She nodded. "Good to meet you." She turned to his coworker. "I haven't met you either. Are you both new to the area?"

"I'm Andy Vicks. I transferred here a few weeks ago. Jayson has been here forever."

He scowled. "Are you saying I'm old?"

"Naw, but you're getting there." He slapped him on the back.

Jayson chuckled. "You start the paperwork. I'll brief the constables."

Andy nodded and walked toward their ambulance.

"Constable Brock, you look familiar. Are you sure we haven't met?" Jayson's gaze caught hers and held.

She cringed and drew her hat down farther, as if trying to hide her identity. It was a frequent question even after she'd grown up and changed her hair color to blond. Anything to escape her past. "I don't believe so."

Jayson scratched his head. "Well, it's nice to meet you."

Eldon approached the group. "Boss, finished moving the crowd back."

Oaklynn winced at his sarcastic use of the word *boss*. She disregarded him and positioned herself closer to the body for a better view. "You said cuts to her upper arm?"

"Yes, why?"

Oaklynn froze. Same MO as the Suicide Slayer. Coincidence? Was this a suicide or something else? They'd had two other recent deaths deemed suicides over the past four weeks—one of them being the mayor's daughter. The man had refused to believe the coroner's findings, but nothing pointed to anything sinister. "Possible suicide?"

The paramedic shrugged. "Not for me to decide. I'll leave the manner of death to the coroner."

Eldon kneeled beside the body. "Wait, that's now three suicides. Sounds like the Suicide Slayer's MO."

The paramedic stuffed discarded gauze into his bag's pocket. "I heard about that serial killer. Didn't he hang himself?"

Oaklynn popped to her feet and swayed.

Jayson caught her by the arm. "Steady there."

She raised her hands and retreated from his hold. "I'm good, thanks. Got up too fast." She noticed a small rectangular piece of paper lying beside the female victim's hand. "Eldon, what's that?"

Before the constable could retrieve the item, a gust of wind whipped it upward.

Oaklynn chased the object and snatched it in midair. She read the embossed, bold lettering.

The Light Paragons—join us and spread God's light.

"What is it?" Eldon inched closer to Oaklynn.

"Looks like a business card for some type of religious organization. The Light Paragons." She retrieved an evidence bag from her pocket and dropped it inside.

Jayson picked up his medical bag. "I've heard of them. Apparently, they've been working to help clean up our community. You know...a goodwill organization. We'll leave once the coroner arrives and takes possession of her body." He hurried to his partner.

Oaklynn handed the bagged card to Eldon. "Can you find out where Chloe and her forensic team are? And call the coroner."

"On it."

Oaklynn's radio crackled.

"Constable Brock, I wanted to give you the heads-up. Mayor Stevens has dispatched the Canadian Watchers Squad to your location," Sergeant Rollins said.

"What?" Oaklynn suppressed the urge to exhale audibly. She'd heard of this new unit formed by a billionaire. "Why?"

"Because he feels his daughter was murdered. That her supposed suicide was made to look like—"

"The Suicide Slayer." Oaklynn finished his statement. "Do you think we have a copycat on our hands?"

The idea sent trepidation coursing through her iced veins.

"Don't go there, Oaklynn. Mayor Stevens doesn't like that we aren't looking harder into Emily's death. He's bypassed our help and went directly to the CWS unit."

A blue truck sped into the parking lot, its tires slipping on the snow-covered icy pavement.

"I believe they're here now. Who are they sending?"

"Caleb Greene."

Oaklynn flinched. *Great, not him.* Caleb had never forgiven her for breaking up with his buddy, Wil Howard, four months ago. Oaklynn knew it was a mistake to get involved with Wil, but she had a hard time resisting her fellow constable's charm. After a couple of months, she realized she had too much baggage and too many secrets to pursue a relationship. It wasn't fair to Wil, so she gave him the it's-not-you-it's-me speech, attempting to break it off gently. Two days later, he took his own life. Even though she hadn't killed the man, the guilt over his death consumed her. She'd secretly donated to a fund to help stop cop suicides, but it didn't ease the shame. Desperate to find out more about Wil's frame of mind, Oaklynn had talked to his partner and discovered Wil had confessed how the brutal cases he'd worked on haunted him. His partner hadn't realized how far gone he'd been until it was too late.

She clutched her radio tighter. "Why him?"

"He's ex-military. Plus, he has both a psychology background and experience with cults. The mayor believes a religious organization brainwashed his daughter."

Another gust of wind stung Oaklynn's face and stole her breath as she pictured the card they discovered. Had this young female also become entangled with a cult? Were The Light Paragons not what they seemed? A car door slammed, and she peered back at the parking lot.

A hulk of a man wearing a blue parka and gray cargo pants stepped out from his vehicle and glanced in her direction. He hesitated when their eyes met.

His wrenched expression revealed he wasn't happy to see her either.

Oaklynn's stomach lurched as if warning of the conflict to come.

Caleb Greene stopped in his tracks at the sight of the blonde constable heading in his direction. Her makeup-free face didn't hide her undeniable beauty. However, she was the catalyst that launched his buddy's final hours. Caleb hadn't realized how far on the edge Wil had been, and Oaklynn's rejection had been the final straw. Caleb had found his friend's body. A scene he'd never forget. Past anger toward Oaklynn resurfaced and Caleb gritted his teeth. *Lord, why did it have to be her?*

Forgive.

The word struck him like a load of bricks falling on his head. Wil had told him Oaklynn harbored secrets. Did she still? Caleb didn't blame Oaklynn any longer for Wil's death. He blamed himself. He should have seen the signs of the darkness holding Wil hostage. Law enforcement deals with so much death and evil in the world. Wil once shared with him he found it hard to compartmentalize. *It's always around me, bro. I can't escape.* Why hadn't these words triggered something in Caleb?

You know why. Caleb had been going through a divorce and

dealing with his five-year-old daughter's death. He was wrapped up in his own baggage and failed to see his friend's pain.

Caleb zipped his parka closer to his neck and rolled his shoulders, determination setting in. He had a job to do, and he'd put the past where it belonged. Would Oaklynn?

He plodded through the snow and held out his hand. "Constable Brock. How are you?"

Something flashed in her brown eyes, but he failed to label the emotion. Annoyance, perhaps.

She cleared her throat and returned the handshake. "Caleb, I'm a little confused about why you're here."

So, his presence *did* annoy her. "I'm part of the Canadian Watchers Squad now, and Mayor Stevens hired us to help with your investigation."

She crossed her arms. "But you're not law enforcement. Protecting the citizens of this community is KFPD's job."

"Well, CWS was dispatched to work with you, and I'm sure you'll get a call soon verifying that fact. We're only here to consult." Caleb braced himself for the resistance he guessed would come next. Their newly formed team had taken flak from law enforcement in a couple recent cases. Caleb's adoptive father—billionaire Maxwell Greene—had assembled the CWS to work alongside the police, not against them. Caleb prayed the community and officers would soon realize that the CWS wasn't trying to encroach on their territory.

Plus, the mayor had called Caleb personally and shared his concerns that his daughter had gotten caught up in a cult growing across the province—The Light Paragons. Caleb's father chose him for the mission because of Caleb's experience with cults. He knew the dark intricacies of how cults worked because he had once belonged to one—brainwashed at fifteen into an evil Caleb would never forget. He only escaped their clutches with Maxwell Greene's help, and the power of God. A few weeks later, Caleb was living at the man's mansion along with other kids who had run away from their foster parents. Maxwell had a tenderness for those children who found themselves lost in the system.

Oaklynn's cell phone chimed, and she checked her screen, then grimaced. "Mayor Stevens, how can I help you?"

Silence.

Her eyes widened seconds later. "Yes, sir." A pause. "Understood, sir. We'll do everything we can." She ended the call. "Well, not only did my sergeant tell me you were coming, but now the mayor has called me himself, demanding I work with you. He wants us to uncover his daughter's killer and protect his community."

Caleb withheld the told-you-so remark threatening to tumble from his mouth. "Listen, I'm not here to infringe on your jurisdiction. I only want to help." He took a notebook out of his pocket. "Okay, then, let's get to business. Tell me about this victim."

"I realize the mayor ordered me to work with you, but first I want more information about your Canadian Watchers Squad. What exactly do you do?"

Fair question and one he'd been asked more than once since his adoptive father formed this special squad a year ago. "Have you heard of Maxwell Greene?"

"The billionaire? Hasn't everyone? He owns multiple businesses. Why?" She clipped her cell phone back onto her duty belt.

"He's my adoptive father. To make a long story short, his wife and family were all killed by a major crime boss, except for one daughter, Mikaela Cox."

"I've met her, and her daughter Lilly, on a call." Her jaw dropped. "Wait, she's Maxwell's daughter?"

Caleb remembered how Mic had spoken fondly of Oaklynn when she helped Mic out with an intruder. "Correct. Mikaela doesn't like to advertise her family roots."

Darkness clouded Oaklynn's pretty eyes as an emotion flashed across her face.

Fear?

Odd. More secrets? He disregarded her emotions and continued. "Anyway, Dad was supposed to die that day too as the crime boss ordered a hit on the entire family from his prison cell after Dad helped police bring the man down. Mic was only five." The killers had brutally tortured the family before the police finally broke through the barrier the assassins had used to block their entry. "The crime boss got away with everything after he paid off a judge. Police were helpless, and Dad struggled to forgive them."

"So, what does all this have to do with the CWS?"

"Maxwell loves kids, so he opened his enormous ranch to foster children. He rescued each of us from the system and eventually adopted us. Years later, after being frustrated with how law enforcement hands are tied, he formed the CWS. 'To go where no one else will.'" Caleb air-quoted his last sentence—the unit's motto. "There are six of us with unique abilities and we live in different areas of Canada, but still work as one team."

A coroner's van drove into the lot and two individuals exited, moving to the rear doors.

"Looks like Dr. Patterson is here." Oaklynn peeked over her shoulder, then back to him. "So, how can you help our team? What are your skills?"

Caleb had met Oaklynn a few times while she dated Wil, but Caleb had never gotten to know her well. "I'm trained in special forces, so my military background of tactics will be an asset to the case. I know how to enter precarious situations in stealth mode. Plus, I have a degree in psychology." He contemplated how much more he should share. He decided to go with truthful but vague. "I'm familiar with cults, and Mayor Stevens feels his daughter got mixed up in one. I'm here to find out."

"How do you know so much about cults?"

Heat rose in Caleb as floaters flickered in his vision. He unzipped his jacket to embrace the coolness before responding. It
had been fifteen years since Maxwell had hauled him from the
depths of hell, but it still felt like yesterday. Visions of young
girls being mutilated in front of his eyes filled his mind, and
Caleb drew in a ragged breath. *God, protect me from evil.* "That's
a story for another day, but I know how cult leaders think."

Oaklynn's face softened. "But how did you find out about
this death so quickly?"

"Let's just say our team is good at what they do." Caleb eyed
the scene. The coroner kneeled beside the victim, examining
the female as a growing crowd circled the snowy area, grief
and confusion etched on each of their contorted faces. "Perhaps
we can work with the mayor and set up a town-hall meeting
to address the situation. I want to help the community with
their fears."

"We can do that, but I need to talk to Dr. Patterson first."
Oaklynn adjusted her ponytail under her tuque.

"Understood."

They approached the quirky-looking coroner.

His tweed fedora slipped as he glanced in their direction,
exposing his gray hair. His round-wired glasses had steamed
from his surgical mask. He stood and drew it down. "Who do
we have here?"

"Dr. Patterson, this is Caleb Greene." Oaklynn gestured toward Caleb. "He's here on the mayor's request from the Watcher
team."

Caleb thrust out his gloved hand. "Nice to meet you, sir."

Dr. Patterson adjusted his winter coat and shook Caleb's
hand. "Welcome. Always good to have more eyes on our cases."

Caleb circled the girl's body and studied her face. The teen
couldn't be any older than seventeen. *Lord, why?* "What can you
tell us about her?" Remorse hit him over the grief this teen-

ager's parents would go through. A parent should never have to bury their own child.

Oaklynn knelt beside the teen.

Dr. Patterson took off his glasses and pinched the bridge of his nose. "Cuts on her upper arm severed the brachial artery, causing her to bleed out." He rolled the body slightly. "What do we have here?" He reached under and held up a flip cell phone.

"I'll take that." A woman dressed in full protection gear marched over and held out an evidence bag. Another constable followed at her heels.

"Oh, hey, Chloe. Good, you're here." Oaklynn pushed herself to her feet. "Maybe the phone has something to help identify her." She pointed to the snow around the body. "Wait. Where's all the blood? If she bled out here, there would be more of it."

Chloe nodded. "Good question. Perhaps she cut herself somewhere else and walked here."

Caleb pointed to the ground. "But there's no blood trail confirming that scenario."

"It snowed a good eight inches overnight and probably hid it." Chloe addressed Caleb. "You must be the Watcher Sergeant Rollins told me about. I'm Chloe Olson, lead forensic investigator."

"And I'm Constable Eldon Spearing. Low man on the proverbial totem pole." The younger man folded his arms. "What brings you here, Watcher?"

"Caleb Greene. Nice to meet you both." He understood their frustration. After all, Kenorapeake Falls was their jurisdiction. "Mayor called me in to help."

Spearing tipped his chin toward Caleb. "You okay with this, boss lady?"

Dr. Patterson dipped his head and continued his preliminary examination.

"Eldon, please don't call me that. We're a team," Oaklynn said, observing the coroner.

Caleb overlooked their obvious feud and flipped a page in his notebook. "The other two victims that were deemed a suicide…where were they found?"

"The mayor's daughter was discovered near the bleachers at the local high school," Oaklynn said. "Her wrists were cut. A male was found at his home, sitting in a rocker next to his fireplace with a gunshot wound to the head."

"So two females, one male."

She nodded.

"Any common denominators?"

Spearing cocked his head. "Other than them taking their own lives?"

"Any suicide notes?" Something didn't add up. Caleb's spidey senses tingled. He had learned in his stint with the military task force to listen to his gut. At all times. He still applied the same philosophy since joining CWS. Maybe Mayor Stevens was right.

Something sinister was happening in his small city of Kenorapeake Falls.

A news van drove into the parking lot. A male reporter and a cameraman exited the vehicle and ran in their direction. Great, so much for keeping this death a secret from the public.

Caleb gestured toward the duo. "Umm…we need to contain the scene."

"Let me take care of this." Oaklynn stomped over to the reporter and raised her hands in a stop position. "Darius, not now. We can't comment on an ongoing investigation."

"Constable Brock, good to see you again." He signaled to his cameraman and stuck a microphone in her face. "Is this another suicide?"

"No comment."

Darius moved to Caleb's side. "Hey, you're part of Maxwell

Greene's Watcher Squad. I recently wrote an article on your team. What are you doing here?"

"I'm here to help—"

Oaklynn placed her hand on the top of the microphone. "He also has no comment." Her eyes flashed annoyance.

Oops.

"Darius, do I need to have you arrested? Please leave." She covered the camera lens.

"Fine, but we'll find out eventually." The reporter and cameraman walked to the edge of the church property.

Oaklynn and Caleb returned to the young girl's body.

Caleb knelt beside the teen. "Such a waste."

"Well, I'll be." Dr. Patterson scooped his magnifying glass from his bag.

"What did you find?" Oaklynn asked.

The coroner hovered the device over the girl's neck. "Bruising. Time to get her to the morgue for a full examination, but this odd bruising and the lack of blood beneath and around the body leads me to believe this girl may not have killed herself." Dr. Patterson zipped up the body bag.

The finality of the zipping sound sent a tremor through Caleb's body, elevating his guard and skyrocketing him back to the accident scene of his daughter's death. He closed his eyes to shut out the event, but even after eighteen months, it remained forever etched in his memory.

"Constable Brock, I'll be in touch in a few hours." Dr. Patterson snapped his fingers to get his assistant's attention. The pair loaded the body into the back of their van and drove away.

"It's looking like these suicides may not have been what they 'appeared to be.'" Constable Spearing motioned air quotes around his statement. "This sounds like a repeat of the Suicide Slayer. A copycat?"

Caleb didn't miss Oaklynn's slight inhale and sudden rigid body language.

Spearing scanned the property, resting his hand on his holstered weapon. "And if it is a copycat, the killer is here, because Aaron Crowder confessed to watching the crime scene when the police found *his* bodies."

Caleb's acute senses catapulted into overdrive at the idea of a potential killer lurking in the crowd. Prickles wormed up his back, cementing him in place.

He scrutinized the faces, studying each closely.

Could there really be a Suicide Slayer copycat among them?

He found her. Finally. After all these years. He rubbed his hands together, excitement invigorating his chilled body as he ogled the pretty officer.

Where have you been hiding?

The January wind howled and slithered its way down his neck, but he didn't care as he lurked among the crowd gathered in the church parking lot. Perhaps the nip in the air would cool the heat burning within his soul. He couldn't believe the blessing God had given him this morning.

A gift from the heavens.

He shoved his hands in his pockets to curb the desire to reach out and caress her beautiful face. *Patience. That's what he taught you. Patience.*

Later.

For now, he'd get back to work. *Now that I found you, you can't hide. Not anymore.*

He hopped into his vehicle and started the engine.

"About time you came back. Where were you?" The man tapped the dashboard.

"None of your business." He flattened his lips and drove down the street, leaving the gruesome scene behind him. He hated killing the young girl, but he couldn't avoid it.

Missy was about to betray their flock, and he wouldn't let that happen. Not with the elite disciple's position on the line.

The Queen Bee had promised him he'd have it if he kept the others in check.

And so far, he'd done that. The Suicide Slayer had taught him well. Not even that coroner knew the truth.

Yes, he'd fooled everyone. He resisted the urge to pump his fist in the air. The victory would have to wait. Maybe when he was home, he'd have a whiskey in honor of his kills—and this morning's find.

"That cop sure is pretty. Don't ya think?"

The irritating man's question broke his concentration. He chewed the inside of his mouth to silence the rage threatening to erupt. How dare he talk about his Lynny like that. "I hadn't noticed."

A lie.

But necessary.

He brought his focus back to the road. Wet snow splattered his windshield. When the tires slid, he cursed and gripped the steering wheel tighter. He hated this time of year. It brought back too many memories.

Memories of his mother's slap across his six-year-old face before sending him outside in the frigid winter temperatures without a coat for one hour. His lesson for disobeying her. How could any mother hate their child so much?

Each time he'd run into the barn and stay until she rang the bell, indicating his hour of penitence was over. Those days still haunted him. Hatred and love intermingled and had escalated with each flick of her abusive hand.

It was why he'd had a kinship to Aaron, for his mother was the same. Cold. Harsh. Venomous.

"Watch out!" The passenger gripped the armrest.

A car horn thrust him back to the present, and he swerved to miss the oncoming vehicle.

"Dude, you trying to kill us?"

He wanted to slap the man beside him, but once again he

chewed the inside of his mouth and thought back to the woman he just found. He subdued his smile at the constable's secret. *I'll be silent—for now.*

No question about it—Constable Oaklynn Brock was indeed Lynn Jenna Crowder.

Daughter of the infamous Suicide Slayer—his hero.

Sure, she'd changed her hair color, but it was her.

You look prettier as a blonde. Good choice, Lynny.

Aaron had shared the nickname his wife had given Lynn. The Protégé liked it better than the new name she'd given herself—Oaklynn.

From now on, you're Lynny to me.

You're beautiful. Pleasure twirled inside his stomach as goose bumps danced across his skin. His senses stimulated, and he trembled, licking his lips.

You will be mine.

Chapter Two

Oaklynn swallowed the scream threatening to break free. Terror parched her throat. *Breathe.* Her knees buckled, but she shifted her stance to steady herself. Being the infamous Suicide Slayer's daughter proved to be a hard past to erase. Even after his arrest, Oaklynn couldn't escape the glances and whispers when she'd entered her high school classes. Everyone, including her best friend, had cut off all communication, as if her father's crimes were *her* fault. Little did they realize it was Oaklynn herself who'd provided the evidence to convict the serial killer after she discovered his secret when she was a teenager.

After helping the police with her father's case, Oaklynn packed her bags and moved to her aunt's house. But it hadn't helped. The press still found them and hounded them during the trial. After her father was convicted, Aunt Sue suggested they move farther away. At eighteen, Oaklynn took her mother's maiden name and expunged her identity from being tied to her father.

Even though she changed her identity, the monster still

haunted her dreams. Ugliness had seized her soul when her father stole everything good in her life, including her precious mother. She squared her shoulders. Oaklynn wouldn't let him take over again.

She was more than a serial killer's daughter.

Was Eldon right and did they have a copycat on their hands? Her father had bragged about all the fan mail he'd received in jail. Even after she'd severed all ties with her father and changed her name, he'd still found her. When she received his first letter, she immediately threw it away. But her curiosity had tackled her and his magnetism drew her like sea turtles to the ocean. She'd snatched the letter from the trash and tore it open. Others followed the first, but she never replied. Apparently, she couldn't outrun his clutches, even from the grave. *I can't go through this again.*

"Constable Brock, did you hear me?" Caleb's voice filtered through her tunnel-like trance.

Her hand eased to her sidearm, grounding her in the present. She switched back into police mode and silenced thoughts of her father. Time to do her job. If someone was mimicking his killings, she had an advantage.

She knew how serial killers thought because she had lived with one.

Oaklynn turned to Caleb. "I'm sorry. What did you say?"

"Was asking your thoughts on Constable Spearing's idea." His eyes locked with hers.

Was he reading her mind? Some days, she failed to stay out of the darkness as questions plagued her. Was she like her father? Would she become like him? She never thought that would be the case until...

A scene invaded her vision. Her team had entered a pedophile's hideout and found a young girl cowering on a bed. The man stood to the side, hands on his belt buckle. Images of her father entering her room late at night bull-rushed her, and she raised her weapon, ready to save the girl from the man's hostile acts—ready to make him pay. Then her gaze shifted to the girl, and Oaklynn froze. She wouldn't kill the man in front of the child. Oaklynn wasn't like her father. Thankfully, her partner quickly subdued the assailant, but her dark thoughts planted doubts in her mind. That night Oaklynn spent hours on the phone with her aunt—the only person who truly understood the horror Oaklynn went through. Aunt Sue had urged her to give her life over to God once and for all, but something held Oaklynn back.

Eldon shook her shoulder. "Get with it, boss."

Oaklynn recoiled, her pulse elevating. "Please don't touch me."

He raised his hands. "Sorry."

"Just contemplating your idea." Half-truth. She directed her answer toward Caleb. "I guess anything's possible. How about we gather this crowd and let you talk to them since you have a psychology background? Perhaps you can get a read off them."

Eldon arched a brow, giving her an are-you-kidding look.

Caleb kicked at a chunk of snow-covered ice. "You don't agree, Constable Spearing?"

Seemed the Watcher *was* good at reading people.

"I'm a hands-on type of guy. None of this psycho-analyzing stuff." Eldon turned to Oaklynn. "Talk to you for a sec?"

"Sure."

"I'm gonna go speak with the crowd." Caleb tugged his tuque farther onto his head and trudged over to the onlookers.

Eldon hesitated, waiting for Caleb to reach the group. "Are we really letting the Watcher in on this case? You don't think we have enough smarts to handle a crowd?"

She didn't miss his menacing expression as his eyes flashed contempt. "Eldon, unfortunately, my hands are tied. The mayor is calling the shots on this one." She followed Caleb's movements as he passed through the crowd. His gentle gestures spoke volumes. He cared.

Right now she must contain the Eldon situation. She tapped her chin, pondering a solution. "Wait. How about you return to the station and speak to the sergeant? Get him to pull the mayor's daughter's file and the other suicides we had recently. Scene photos, victim backgrounds, coroner reports. Everything. We'll look closer."

His eyes brightened. "Copy that. What are you going to do?"

"Watcher Greene and I will talk to the crowd. See what we can ascertain." She gestured toward Caleb. "Let's use his skills to our advantage, okay?"

"Agreed, but don't let him take over." He grazed Oaklynn's arm. "I know his type." He winked before dashing toward his cruiser.

What did that mean? Was Eldon flirting with her? Oaklynn trembled, but not from the cold. The constable's personality sent Oaklynn's fight-or-flight receptors into overdrive. Her father tainted her from ever surrendering her trust to another man again. She'd seen what he did to her mother—even though he denied it.

Aaron Crowder murdered his own wife. At age five, Oaklynn had the flu and in the middle of the night wanted her mother's tender care, so she stumbled out of bed and wandered into their room. Her father sat on the bed watching his wife as blood oozed from her wrist. Oaklynn yelled at him, and he quickly placed his hands over the wound, claiming he was trying to save his wife as she'd tried to kill herself. She died seconds later.

Oaklynn believed his lie until she turned fifteen when she found what her mother had hidden inside Oaklynn's secret spot in her room—a cubbyhole inside her closet where she had hidden her favorite items. For years Oaklynn failed to see what Jenna Crowder had shoved into a stuffed kangaroo's pouch.

A stash of money, along with two US passports—one for Oaklynn and one for her mother—and an envelope addressed to Oaklynn. She had ripped it open and read her mother's words.

My sweet Lynny,
Right now I'm sitting in your cubby hole writing to you. To hide from him. If you're reading this, it means I've failed. I tried to get us out of the country—away from him, because I know what he does to you. I'm sorry I couldn't stop him. He threatened to kill both of us if I tried to leave with you, but I found someone who can help. There's something else you need to know. I have a secret to…he's coming. I have to go, but I'll tell you later.

That's where the letter stopped. Her mother never finished her note. Oaklynn guessed she was preparing for them to leave, but her father caught her, then killed her.

Oaklynn suspected her father of something sinister and her mother's words proved her suspicions. It was the beginning of the end. She searched for answers and finally got them when she discovered his secret. One question still haunted Oaklynn.

What else had her mother been trying to tell her? That her father was a killer, or something else? Whatever it was, the secret had died with Jenna Crowder.

"Constable Brock!" Caleb's voice thrust her from the memory. "Over here."

She jogged to his side. "What is it?"

He faced a young woman. "Please tell Constable Brock what you told me."

The strawberry blonde bit her lip. "I'm scared they'll find out."

"They?" Oaklynn probed.

The girl's bright blue eyes widened, and once again she chewed on her lip.

"What's your name, sweetheart?" Oaklynn had to keep the frightened girl as calm as possible to gain her trust.

"Kimi," she whispered.

Caleb leaned closer. "Kimi, do you want to go inside to talk, away from the others?"

The girl looked left, then right.

Her twisted expression revealed her terror-stricken state. What warranted the obvious fear consuming the young lady?

"You can trust us," Oaklynn said. "We won't let anything happen to you."

"Promise?"

Could she? Protecting people was her job, and Oaklynn excelled at it. Her experiences had made her who she was today. "I promise."

Caleb's knit eyebrows revealed he didn't agree with her making such a commitment.

Oaklynn tugged at her coat and steeled her jaw. She would do everything in her power to keep Kimi safe. The girl reminded Oaklynn of herself at age seventeen. She'd already been living with Aunt Sue for a couple of years, but every news report mentioning her father put her into a pit of horror, not knowing if he'd get out of jail and come after her. After all, she had betrayed him. Aunt Sue was there for her. Kimi obviously needed someone too.

Multiple conversations competed for Oaklynn's attention, but she focused on the young girl in front of her. "Kimi, please let me help you. Who are you scared of?"

Shouts erupted to the trio's right. A scuffle broke out among the onlookers as a bright yellow van, plastered with paintings of flowers, drove into the parking lot, honking. Spreading Peace to Our Communities appeared in bold, red lettering across the side. The panel door slid open.

Kimi gulped. "I have to go. We're not supposed to leave the flock." She glanced over her shoulder at the van, then removed an item from her pocket, shoving it into Oaklynn's hand. "I can't escape. Missy tried. She's dead." She raced toward the van and climbed into the side.

The other onlookers scrambled away like bees from a disturbed nest. What about the van scared everyone, and why hadn't Oaklynn seen the vehicle before? She memorized the plate number.

"Wait!" she yelled, running forward.

Caleb jerked her back. "Don't. You'll put her in more danger."

"What? How?"

"Trust me. We'll get to her another way. They're always lurking." He gestured at the van as it sped back onto the road. "The followers will strike anywhere, anytime."

"How do you know this?"

Caleb took off his tuque and wiped his forehead. "Because I was once one of them."

A spark of fear and anger ignited in his green eyes.

Oaklynn read the card Kimi had shoved into her hand. "The Light Paragons again. You were part of them?"

"Not them, but another cult. I know how they think, and it's not pretty."

Something like my dear old dad.

"Well, we need to look into them. I'm guessing the Missy she referred to is our victim from this morning." Oaklynn turned the card over. A scribbled sentence sent Oaklynn's emotions reeling.

Help me escape their evil.

Oaklynn's chest tightened and she thrust the card toward Caleb. "She's in danger. We need to get her out."

He read the sentence, his eyes narrowing. "We can't just barrel into their compound. Cult followers don't take kindly to outsiders."

She grimaced. "By outsiders, you mean cops."

"Unfortunately, yes."

Oaklynn scanned the area. "Well, it seems the van scared everyone off. Did you get anything from the others?"

"No. I can tell they're tight-lipped, though. They know something, but are afraid to say."

"I don't understand why I'm not aware of The Light Paragons." She withdrew her notepad. "But I memorized the plate number and will check out the ownership. Maybe that will give us a clue."

"Are we done here? I need to check in with my sister."

She jotted down the plate number and stuffed her notebook into her pocket. "Let's meet at the station in an hour. We could use your expertise on cults in our discussion."

"Sounds good. I'll—"

Oaklynn's cell phone dinged with a text. She retrieved it and swiped the screen.

I know you're his daughter. Are you like him?

She sucked in a ragged breath. Her knees buckled as terror turned her veins to ice. Who was this and how did they know?

Caleb wrapped his arm around her waist. "Whoa. I've got you."

Recurring questions lodged in Oaklynn's mind, plaguing her.

Does evil pass through a family's bloodline? Could she have that gene? Could she take a life so easily, like her father?

Caleb shifted his grip on Oaklynn, leaning her against him for support. He didn't miss the flash of terror that passed over her pretty face as soon as she'd read the text. "What is it?"

She stiffened in his arms and retreated from his hold. "I'm good. Sorry, it's nothing."

He pursed his lips. "I don't believe you. Remember, I'm

good at reading body language, and I can tell you're fibbing. Something in the text frightened you. Big-time."

He should know. He recognized the emotions still engraved on her face. Horror. Alarm. Panic.

All rolled into one.

The expression—*been there, done that, bought the T-shirt*—ran through his mind. He wanted to help her, but would she let him after the accusations he sent her way after Wil's death?

He inched closer to the rattled constable. "Oaklynn, please let me help."

"I'm fine. I have to wrap things up here and check with the officers canvassing the area. See you back at the station." She plodded over to another constable.

He blew out a breath and crossed the parking lot to his blue truck. Why was he surprised? Trust had always been something he wrestled with. *Lord, I sense her darkness. Help me be a light.* He started the engine and hit the button to dial his sister over the Bluetooth.

"Hey, Caleb." Mic's weakened voice revealed her tired state.

"What's wrong?" He tapped the console, waiting for her reply.

"Just Lilly problems. She's been keeping lots of secrets lately."

Caleb hung his head, his chest tightening. "Like what?"

"I discovered she stole money from my wallet and lied about it. She's been hanging around a rough crowd. I don't like it." Silence was followed by a sniffle. "Anyway, what do you need?"

Caleb's chin jerked upward, and he breathed in deeply. He shifted the gear into Drive. "Do me a favor, Mic. I need your skills. See what you can find out about the new cult called The Light Paragons."

Silence.

Caleb made a right turn out of the church parking lot. "Mic?"

"Please stay away from cults. That scares me, bro. Especially after what one did to you." Her voice quivered.

Me too. Could he go back into the world that almost took his life?

God's got you in His hands. Let Him be your light.

Words Maxwell Greene often said to his children.

He strangled his grip on the steering wheel, offsetting his elevating panic into his fingers. "Don't worry, sis. This time I have something I didn't back then—a powerful team at my disposal. Help me find out more about the cult."

Mikaela Cox's white-hat hacker skills added an advantage to the team. She was good at what she did.

"I'll call you when I find something. Where are you headed now?"

"To the KFPD station. We're looking into the suicides. Something tells me we won't like what we discover." He hesitated. Should he ask another question on his mind? He had to know. "Mic, can you also do some hunting on Constable Oaklynn Brock?"

"Um—why? You're working with her?"

"Yes, and I need more details about her past. Wil always said she held secrets. I sense they're still there."

"You're psychoanalyzing again, aren't you? You can't fix everyone, bro."

Caleb pictured his sister's face. She was probably chewing on her lower lip as she pondered the situation. Her habit when nervous or thinking. "Can't help it. The military taught me to always get intel on the players, and if I'm going to help the mayor and this community, I need to know everything about everyone. She's hiding something huge. I can feel it."

"She won't like it."

Truth, Mic. Truth. "Nope. Gotta run. Love ya."

"Ditto."

He ended the call and turned toward his favorite Kenora-peake Falls bakery, Penny's Café—a place he visited every time he was in town. Perhaps treats would help soften the tension he guessed would follow him into the KFPD station—their territory.

An hour later, Caleb took a bite of his apple fritter. The gooey goodness melted in his mouth. He couldn't resist the sweet delight.

He observed the KFPD bullpen. Five rows of three-person tables lined the room. A leaderboard containing pictures of the suicide victims and the crime scenes sat at the front.

Caleb counted five officers, including Oaklynn, who had gathered to get direction from their sergeant on the current situation.

Oaklynn sat beside him, arms folded, jaw tight.

Caleb struggled to ignore her powerful presence. They didn't get along in the past, but could they put their differences aside and work together?

Staff Sergeant Rollins banged on the podium. "Let's get started."

The buzz in the room silenced.

Rollins relocated to Caleb's side. "First, thanks to Watcher Caleb Greene for providing such delicious goodies. Not that we police officers need treats to survive. Bad stereotype. But the sugar rush is out of this world."

"Sure is. But, Watcher, I'm trying to keep my figure." Constable Spearing patted his belly.

The group chuckled.

Even Oaklynn grinned at her colleague's comment.

Caleb nodded. "Good to know. Next time I'll bring you carrot sticks."

Rollins walked to the front of the room. "Caleb, we're curious. Can you tell us about the Canadian Watchers Squad? It's not the average unit."

Caleb expected the question. He rose to his feet. "CWS was founded to help support communities by providing unique assistance alongside local law enforcement because sometimes we can go where you can't."

Constable Dalton huffed. "You don't think we can do our jobs?"

Caleb raised his hands. "Of course you can. I'm only here to consult." He turned to Rollins. "But just to let you know—"

A slender brunette sauntered into the room. "Sorry I'm late. I was running down a lead on the recent bank robberies." She hesitated beside Caleb. "And who are you, handsome?" She held out her hand. "I'm Nika Crabb."

"Caleb Greene. Good to meet you."

"Constable Crabb, take a seat," Sergeant Rollins said. "Caleb was telling us about the Canadian Watchers Squad. Caleb, how many are on your team?"

The officer plunked herself beside Oaklynn.

"Six."

"Tell us about them." Rollins leaned against the board.

"We have a white-hat hacker, sniper, criminologist, survivalist, firefighter turned preacher, and me. We also have other specialized abilities. Mine are psychology and tactical. I used to be in an elite military special ops unit." Caleb walked to the board and pointed at the business card pinned beside the latest victim's picture. "I also have a background in cults. That's why the mayor called me in."

"Cults?" Constable Crabb's voice raised in pitch. "Why do you think we're dealing with a cult?"

He tapped the card. "The mayor believes his daughter got messed up with The Light Paragons. He also feels his daughter did not commit suicide and, from what we saw today at the scene, I agree."

Crabb turned to Oaklynn. "Tell us what happened."

The sergeant gestured to the podium. "Constable Brock, please come to the front and fill everyone in."

Oaklynn placed her hands on the table and pushed herself

to her feet, then joined Caleb. "We believe the victim's name was Missy, but we don't have a positive ID yet. She had multiple cuts on her upper arm, but the coroner found bruising on her neck. We also found the cult's card in her possession." She tapped Missy's picture. "I'm guessing it wasn't suicide."

"So, are the other two recent suicides suspicious too?" Crabb asked.

"Possibly." Oaklynn relayed the rest of today's events, including their conversation with Kimi and the message on the card. "Missy was alive when the paramedics arrived, but died shortly after. We're hoping we get something off the phone found under Missy's body."

"Who called in the attack?"

Constable Spearing raised his right hand. "Dalton, I can answer that. Church office manager found the victim when she arrived at work. I spoke to her, but she knew nothing."

"I'm concerned about Kimi," Oaklynn said. "She ran off when this van appeared out of nowhere."

Caleb sensed her shift in demeanor. She still felt frustrated at him for impeding her pursuit. "Did you get a hit on the plates?"

She drew out her notepad from her vest pocket. "Yes, the van is registered to a Kassandra Nason. Guidance counselor at KFHS."

"Get in touch with her. Find out about The Light Paragons." Rollins pointed to the other two victims. "Okay, so we now have two fatal cuts and a self-inflicted gunshot wound."

"*Supposed* self-inflicted GSW," Oaklynn added before tucking her notebook away. "I'm not so sure anymore and want to get Dr. Patterson to look closer at these two."

Constable Spearing hopped to his feet, his chair screeching on the floor. "I still feel we have a Suicide Slayer copycat on our hands. I've been reviewing Aaron Crowder's case and these deaths are eerily close, if not the same, to how he staged his victims."

Oaklynn shifted her stance.

Caleb noted a flash of panic cross over her face, disappearing as quickly as it came.

Something about the Suicide Slayer's case had her riled. He'd seen the same expression back at the crime scene. *Lord, there's that darkness again. I want to help her.*

A question rose.

Did she realize she needed help? When he was deep inside the cult and in an evil place, he denied needing any type of guidance. He was that far gone.

"But his victims were all females, right?" Crabb asked. "We have two females, one male. If this person is copying the Suicide Slayer, he—or she—has changed the MO."

"That's not uncommon. He's putting his own stamp on his victims." Caleb inched closer to Oaklynn, attempting to provide some sort of support.

"Didn't someone write his story?" Crabb tapped on her phone. "Yes, here it is. *Inside the Suicide Slayer's Mind* by Freda Corbet. Perhaps someone should talk to her. She lives on the edge of town."

"Agreed," Caleb said. "She would have had to speak with him many times to write the book. Maybe Aaron Crowder got inside *her* head. It's difficult to wipe your mind after being so close to evil."

Caleb didn't miss Oaklynn's softened gulp of air.

Rollins cleared his throat. "Okay, that's it for now. I'll hand out your assignments shortly. Folks, I don't need to remind you, but it sounds like these suicides may all be murders. Time to stop whatever is happening before we lose more lives. Dismissed."

Oaklynn's cell phone rang, and she fished it from her pocket. "It's the coroner." She gestured Rollins to join them at the board, then put the doctor on speaker. "Dr. Patterson, I'm here with Caleb and Sergeant Rollins. What have you found?"

"Something unusual." He drew in an audible breath. "The victim swallowed an SD card from a camera. Seemed this young lady wanted to hide something from her killer. Friends, my conclusion is she was definitely murdered. Plus, you need to get here right away. Someone stole our victim's body."

What? Way to bury the lead, Dr. Patterson.

Oaklynn's eyes widened, horror etched on her face.

Their case just took a drastic, deadly turn.

Chapter Three

Oaklynn choked her grip on the Charger's steering wheel as questions invaded her mind. Why would anyone steal Missy's body? What pictures on the SD card warranted her death? And—was there really a copycat killer out there mimicking her father? She drove into the hospital parking lot and cut the engine. Right now, she also had to deal with the man beside her. Her boss had insisted she and Caleb travel together to visit Dr. Patterson. Perhaps to present a unified front? Seemed the mayor was pressuring the sergeant to find his daughter's killer.

Caleb placed his gloved hand on top of hers. "I realize it's been a shock seeing me again. I'm sensing some tension between us. Is everything okay?"

Oaklynn returned her hand to the wheel. "Where have you been? Someone told me you moved away from the area."

He leaned back in the seat and looked out the window. "Had to deal with some stuff, so my dad helped me find a secluded place a few towns over."

"Are you referring to Wil's death?" She adjusted her ponytail.

"That and more. God and I had long conversations while I secluded myself."

"God? You believe in an unseen entity in this dark world?" Even after her aunt's plea to go to church with her, Oaklynn failed to see how God could help. He didn't save her mother, or stop her father from becoming a monster and entering Oaklynn's bedroom in the middle of the night. No, she wouldn't put her faith in a God who allowed all the wickedness she'd endured.

"God changed my life. What about you?"

"I'd rather not talk about it." She gripped the door handle, softening her attitude. "Sorry I'm uptight. I just want to find Missy's killer. Shall we?"

She didn't wait for a reply, but left her Charger and marched toward the entrance. Time to concentrate on finding those responsible for the suicide deaths.

Oaklynn clenched her hands into fists. She hated the foul mood invading her normally cheerful demeanor. She finally had some peace in her life...until she'd seen her father's face plastered in the *Tribune*'s online article. News of his death plummeted her back into the abyss.

Caleb's presence only added to the darkness.

You caused Wil's death. You and your secrets.

Caleb's words tumbled into her mind. Oaklynn hadn't blamed him for uttering the two sentences at Wil's funeral. She felt responsible for his death. She didn't want to deal with that—and her father's evilness—all over again.

"Let me get the door." Caleb hit the entrance's open button.

"Thanks." She entered. "The morgue is on the lower level."

"Bodies in the basement." Caleb chuckled. "How fitting."

Was he trying to lighten her darkened mood?

She stole a glimpse of the handsome Watcher. He'd grown a short, trimmed beard since she'd last seen him—and she liked it. His moss green eyes made her heart skip a beat. She looked away.

Don't go there. Remember your baggage. A man would never love you when they found out you're a monster's daughter.

"Yep. Not my favorite place. This way." Oaklynn hustled around a corner and almost bumped into a scurry of nurses.

They stopped talking to stare at the muscular man at Oaklynn's side.

She understood. He *was* easy on the eyes.

Oaklynn set aside the thought, bypassed the women, and headed toward the elevators. She poked the down button, sneaking a peek at the nurses.

Caleb still held their focus.

Oaklynn gestured toward them. "Looks like you have some admirers."

He flattened his lips and grunted, "Not interested."

What had caused his sudden shift in disposition?

There's a story behind those piercing eyes. Perhaps he held secrets too.

The elevator doors opened, interrupting thoughts of Caleb.

She stepped inside, leaving the gawking nurses behind, and pushed the button that would take them into the dungeon of Kenorapeake Falls Community Hospital.

Moments later, the pungent formaldehyde odor assaulted her nose as soon as the doors slid open. She had associated the stench with death, especially after living in the shadows of a serial killer.

It soured her stomach, and she fished out a stick of cinnamon gum, stuffing it into her mouth to offset both the memories and the scent.

"Got another one of those?" Caleb held out his hand.

"You hate that smell too?" She passed him one.

"Yep. Thanks. Shall we get this over with?" He unwrapped the gum and crammed it into his mouth.

Seemed the tough ex-military man didn't like the morgue either. She silenced a chuckle and turned toward Dr. Patterson's morgue—or *sanctuary*—as he called it. He had told her once he felt at home among the dead and admitted talking to his "friends."

It was why he excelled at his job. He dug deep as he examined them. How did he miss that the first two victims weren't suicides?

If that was indeed the case.

Oaklynn approached the morgue and pressed the button, staring at the No Admittance sign. The hospital sealed the floor off to the public and only those inside could let anyone in. Dr. Patterson kept the code from everyone, except for his staff. She peered at the tiny camera above the door and waved.

The door buzzed, and she tugged it open.

The duo walked down the corridor, passing the refrigerated area where Dr. Patterson kept the bodies. Oaklynn shivered. Not only from the dampness, but the atmosphere. Senseless deaths. *God, why do You allow evil?*

Oaklynn pushed away the question and knocked to enter Dr. Patterson's examining room. She learned the hard way six months ago, when she first transferred to Kenorapeake Falls and had to visit the peculiar coroner on a case involving a young mother's murder, not to barge inside. He'd yelled at her for interrupting his work.

"Come in."

Oaklynn and Caleb entered Dr. Patterson's sanctuary.

The coroner set aside his instruments, peeled off his gloves, and chucked them into the trash can. "I can't believe someone got into my morgue. No one has access here except for me and a few others."

Dr. Patterson pointed to Caleb. "Why is the Watcher here?"

"You'll have to take that one up with the mayor." Oaklynn retrieved her notebook, wanting to get to business and escape the creepy basement. "Tell us what happened."

The gray-haired sixty-year-old removed his round-rimmed

wire glasses and wiped them before putting them back on. "I had just finished sewing up Missy's—"

"Wait, you identified her?"

"Not officially, Constable Brock. I like to name the ones on my table."

Oaklynn's gaze popped to Caleb's.

His wrinkled forehead revealed his confusion too.

The coroner hadn't been present when Kimi said the name Missy. How had he known? Coincidence? Of all the names to choose, why had he picked that one? Suspicion prickled the back of Oaklynn's neck, but Dr. Patterson had never given her or the police department any reason to question his character.

Until now.

"What made you pick the name Missy?" Caleb obviously also suspected the coroner's name choice.

"She reminded me of a gal I went to school with many eons ago. That's all." The doctor pushed his glasses farther up the bridge of his nose. "I found the SD card and sewed her up. Right after, the fire alarm blasted, so my crew and I locked the area down and left." He frowned. "Firefighters deemed it a false alarm. Once they gave us the all clear to come back inside, we discovered the victim's body was gone."

"Someone deliberately pulled the alarm in order to get you out of the morgue to steal her body. What time was this?" Oaklynn clicked her pen.

"Two hours ago."

"What? Why didn't you call us right away? I need to get forensics here." Oaklynn checked her smartwatch and scribbled "1300 hours" in her notebook.

"I hate having my morgue overloaded with the living."

"Did you check video footage?"

"Of course. Security informed me only snowy images appeared during that time frame." He picked up a nearby rag and wiped the counter. "I searched for Missy, but her body and the rolling table were both gone."

To call the coroner a neat freak would be an understatement. The department recognized his OCD nature. Most officers made fun of him, but Oaklynn respected the man.

She hated the uncertainty of his latest actions creeping into her mind. So much for fingerprints. The coroner had wiped away any viable evidence. Oaklynn gritted her teeth. "Well, I still need Chloe to come here."

His jaw locked, then softened as he hung his head. "Okay, Chloe can come, but no one else."

Oaklynn made the call, requesting Chloe come to the morgue. After she finished, she addressed the coroner. "Where is this SD card?"

Dr. Patterson shuffled over to a corner desk, unlocked a drawer, and brought out a bag, holding it up. "I'm afraid it's damaged. I doubt your digital team can get anything off it." He handed it to her.

"I know someone who can," Caleb said.

Oaklynn examined the card. "Who?"

"Mikaela. She's not only a hacker, but is a technology whiz. You'd be amazed at what she can find." He pointed to the bag. "If there are pictures on there, she'll find them."

"Forensics won't like it." Oaklynn passed him the card. "However, I don't want the mayor breathing down my neck. Call Mic."

An alarm pierced the morgue's floor.

Dr. Patterson latched on to Oaklynn's arm. "I gave my staff an extra-long lunch break and the alarm resets after each person enters. Someone has breached the floor."

The panic in his voice elevated her guard, and she rested her hand on her weapon. "I'll check it out. Stay here."

"I'm coming with you." Caleb grabbed the door handle.

"No, you're not armed. Besides, I need you to protect Dr. Patterson." She didn't wait for a response, but left the room.

A shadow passed the refrigerated room moments after the door slammed shut.

Oaklynn's nerves jittered as she unholstered her weapon and inched around the corner, raising her Glock.

And came to a standstill.

The corridor was empty. Only the putrid, spicy scent she remembered from her childhood remained. Her father's cologne permeated the area, thrusting her backward in time. Her cell phone dinged a text. She unhooked it from her duty belt and swiped the screen.

Do you like it? It was your father's fave and now mine.

Oaklynn leaned against the wall as her stomach contents threatened to expel.

This couldn't be happening. Questions haunted her.

How had this person known about her father's cologne?

Was this supposed copycat someone from her past?

He peeked around the corner and stole a glimpse of the beautiful daughter of his hero—the Suicide Slayer. His rapid heartbeat thrashed in his head and he longed to draw her into his arms. Hold her tight. Smell her. Caress her skin. He imagined it to be smooth like silk. She'd been right under his nose the entire time. After tricking his forensic artist friend into doing an age progression sketch using the picture of Lynny at age fifteen that Aaron Crowder had sent him, the Protégé studied her face—long and hard.

He couldn't believe it when he saw her at the church's property earlier. Over the past few hours, he hadn't been able to get her off his mind. He had to get closer to her.

His fingers trembled as a plan formed. He'd have fun with her. Play a game. And then—

The Protégé would do the Suicide Slayer's bidding.

A final gift to his hero. A memorial.

He dug his nails into his palms and squeezed. First, he must watch the Watcher. *You think you can help our community? Think again, Watcher.*

From the first newspaper article written years ago revealing that the suicide deaths in Ontario were in fact murders, he'd analyzed the Suicide Slayer's kills, MO, and signature. He was surprised to discover he'd met Aaron Crowder before. The man had quickly gained admirers on social media and gaming sites. After the serial killer's arrest, he'd written to him in prison, reminding him of where they'd met. He shared his respect and his desire to learn from him.

To become him.

To his surprise, his hero wrote him back and nicknamed him the Protégé. They became pen pals and he learned everything he could about Aaron's life and family—the daughter who betrayed him. Aaron confessed how he'd been toying with her, writing to her at her aunt Sue's. He wanted to cast doubts in her head, but then lost her trail.

The Protégé resisted the urge to reach out and touch Oaklynn's hair. Even though she held it back in a ponytail, he didn't miss the shimmer of her golden-vanilla locks. He fantasized about what kind of shampoo she used. He'd get closer soon and catch her scent. Right now, in the darkness, he must keep his distance.

His game for her took shape in his mind. He'd mess with her. Make her believe she was exactly like her father, and the Protégé knew how to accomplish his goal.

Yes, she would become one of them. The Light Paragons' Queen Bee would be pleased. To bring a constable into the fold—into the light—would be the ultimate holy grail. He'd also gain the position of elite disciple faster now. The three victims had wanted out of their group, so he killed them. He skulked among the fold like a wolf in a henhouse. *Once you're in, you stay.* He pictured the gift he'd left on Missy and resisted the urge to chuckle out loud.

The prize was within sight. The Suicide Slayer would be so proud of his Protégé.

He silently pumped his fist in the air and crept back into the shadows.

Footfalls pounded outside Dr. Patterson's examination room and Caleb snatched a scalpel from the doctor's table. Despite being fully trained and able to handle himself, he didn't want to take any chances. He turned to the coroner. "Stay in the corner." Caleb rushed to the right of the entrance and raised the knife.

The door creaked open.

He lunged forward, scalpel raised.

"It's me!" Oaklynn yelled.

Caleb set the weapon back on the table. "Sorry, thought you were the suspect. Any sign of them?"

Her face blanched before she composed herself.

"What is it, Oaklynn?"

"Suspect is gone, but Dr. Patterson, I think we should check your refrigerated room. The door closed as I came around the corner. I believe someone may have just been in there. Where's your assistant?"

The coroner pushed his glasses farther up his nose. "Dr. Hancock had an appointment and left earlier. Why?"

Oaklynn chewed on her bottom lip. "Just considering all possibilities." She waved them into the hallway. "We need to get into that room."

Caleb followed them into the hallway.

She stopped in the corridor. "Do you smell that?"

Caleb drew in a long breath. "What?"

She rubbed her temples. "Never mind. Dr. Patterson, can you open the door?"

He obeyed, and the group entered the cold morgue.

Chills attacked Caleb. "What are we looking for?"

Oaklynn tapped the handle of a steel container. "Anything out of the ordinary."

"Wait! That gurney shouldn't be in here." Dr. Patterson opened the last container and slid out the corpse. He drew back the sheet. "This is Missy."

"What?" Oaklynn and Caleb said, simultaneously.

Caleb inched closer to the body, ignoring the room's odor. "Why would the suspect steal her, only to return her?"

"Yikes. This is why." Dr. Patterson pointed to Missy's abdominal area. "Someone pried out my stitches. Crudely, I'd add. He was looking for the SD card."

Oaklynn inched closer. "So, he knew she swallowed it? How?"

Caleb's pulse zinged as a realization pummeled his gut. "He was stalking Missy." Was the killer connected to The Light Paragons? "From my cult experience, followers or disciples watch each other closely for signs of betrayal or for escapees. Maybe she gave the killer concern, and he followed her."

Oaklynn raised a brow. "How do you know that?"

"Because I once did it." He rubbed his beard. "Stalked a member, I mean."

"When was this?"

"I was fifteen and in deep." Caleb pointed to etchings on Missy's stomach. "Wait, what's that?"

Dr. Patterson brought out a magnifying glass from his lab coat's pocket and held it close. "Well, I'll be. That was not there before. It says 'I'm back. SS.'" Dr. Patterson peeked over the top of his glasses. "What's that mean?"

Oaklynn stumbled backward, tripping over the gurney.

Caleb wrapped his arm around her waist, preventing a fall. "You okay?"

She cleared her throat and recoiled from his hold. "Fine."

Once again, she lied, holding her secrets close.

He hated secrets.

Even though he had plenty of his own.

The buzzer sounded from the corridor.

"That's probably Chloe." Oaklynn unclipped her cell phone and snapped pictures of the message on Missy's stomach. "She'll want to see this too, Dr. Patterson." She checked her watch. "Caleb, we need to talk to Ms. Nason before she leaves the high school. I'll update Chloe, and then we can go."

Thirty minutes later, Caleb turned to Oaklynn as they walked into Kenorapeake Falls High School. "Can you let me take the lead on this one? She's a counselor, so I believe we think on the same level."

Oaklynn tilted her head. "What are you saying?"

"Sorry, that came out wrong. I only mean because she probably also has a psychology background."

"I'm teasing. I figured that's what you meant. Of course you can." Her lips curved upward, her smile traveling to her gorgeous brown eyes.

His breath hitched. No wonder Wil fell hard for this woman. Her mesmerizing expression would capture any man's attention.

He cleared his throat and gestured toward the school's office. "Shall we?"

"Yes, but I reserve the right to interject."

He nodded and followed her to the reception desk.

Oaklynn raised her badge. "Good afternoon. Sorry we're here at the end of your school day, but we have urgent business with Kassandra Nason. We don't have an appointment. I'm guessing that won't be an issue?"

Impressive. The more time he spent with Oaklynn, the more he liked her. Her strong nature left a mark on everyone around her, including him. She was chipping away at the opinion he'd formed of her.

The woman placed a call to the guidance counselor, inquiring about her schedule. "Got it. Thanks, Ms. Nason." She dropped the receiver back into the cradle. "She only has a few minutes before her next appointment. Her office is down the hall to the right."

"Thank you." Oaklynn turned to him and pointed. "After you."

Caleb approached the office and knocked. "Ms. Nason?"

The slender woman closed her laptop and stood. "Good afternoon." She stuffed the device into a briefcase. "I'm afraid I only have five minutes. How can I help you?"

Caleb introduced both Oaklynn and himself. He noted immediately the guidance counselor's need to flee their presence. Did she indeed have a meeting or just wanted to get away from them? He'd appeal to her on similar ground. "We appreciate and respect your time, so I'll get right to the point. Do you own a yellow '77 Chevy van?" He spieled off the license plate number.

Her eyes narrowed for a split second before she picked up her cell phone, tucking it into her briefcase's side pocket. "That old thing? I gifted it to my sister, Victoria. Why do you ask?"

"What's Victoria's last name?"

"Dutton."

Caleb wasn't buying her story. Something about her body language needled his senses. "Why didn't you change the ownership?"

She lifted an overcoat off a rack, wiggling her arms into the sleeves. "Because I just never got around to it. Again, why do you ask?" She snatched her purse from the desk.

Caleb snuck a peek at Oaklynn.

She dipped her head in acknowledgment. "It was last seen at a crime scene."

Kassandra lost her grip on her bag, and it thudded on the

floor. "Does this have anything to do with that stupid Paragon of Light—or whatever it's called?"

"You mean The Light Paragons?" Caleb noted her nervousness. "Is your sister a member?"

"I believe so." Kassandra scooped her purse from the floor, placing the strap more firmly on her shoulder. "I warned her against getting mixed up with them."

"Them?" Oaklynn took a step toward the woman. "Can you give us additional information?"

"I'm late for a meeting. If you have more questions, make an appointment." She sailed by them and left the room, leaving a trail of pungent perfume in her wake.

"That went well. Not." Caleb cupped his hand on Oaklynn's elbow, nudging her toward the exit.

"Yep. Other than she claims her sister owns the van." Oaklynn pushed the outer office door open and held it for him. "It's getting late. How about we head back to the station? I want to finish my reports before shift ends."

Caleb drove into the driveway of his sister's quaint bungalow an hour later. He was thankful Mic lived in town, so he wouldn't have to drive to his home an hour away from Kenorapeake Falls. He loved spending time with her and his niece, Lilly.

Snow had buried his sister's front lawn, but her contractor had already cleared the driveway. Caleb hit the garage door opener and pulled his truck inside.

Caleb's cell phone chirped multiple messages. Probably his father looking for an update. He exhaled. The long day caught up to him and he wanted to unwind for a bit before heading to bed. Missy's lifeless eyes haunted him. He vowed to give her justice. Vowed to find the supposed Suicide Slayer copycat. Vowed to stop this cult before it sunk its claws deeper into the community.

His German shepherd barked. Caleb unlocked the door and entered his sister's home. The dog greeted him, wagging his tail.

"Hey, buddy." He petted the retired K-9. Briggs had seen many ops missions in the past few years, but a bullet in his leg left him with a slight limp. And out of a job. And it was all Caleb's fault. He should have trusted his K-9's instincts that day instead of his own. After the dog's injury and the trauma of the failed op, Caleb applied to leave the military. He adopted Briggs. Caleb had seen enough death to last a lifetime, and he couldn't leave his dog with someone else. Their bond was too strong. Caleb had struggled being away from his wife and daughter too. It had been time to move on—even if the military tried their darnedest to keep him.

Briggs circled around his feet and whined as if sensing his master's anxiety.

Caleb rubbed his ears. "You're a good boy."

Mic appeared around the corner, her hair disheveled and eyes wide. "You're home. Good."

"I need your help with something else." He handed her the bagged SD card.

"What's this?" Mic eyed the item. "Well, I know what it is, but why am I looking at it?"

"It came from inside a dead girl's stomach."

"Eww." She dangled it loosely between her fingers. "Let me guess. It's damaged and you want your sister to use her superpowers?"

"Something like that. We need to know what's on it, Mic. The girl died trying to keep it a secret." He suppressed a sigh. "How about I fix you and Lilly some of my famous fish and chips?"

"You mean the frozen kind?" Mic chuckled and stuffed the bag into her pocket. "Lilly's staying overnight at her friend's place."

"Well, I'm starved." He gestured toward Briggs. "Let me feed him first."

An hour after supper, Mic retreated to her computer cave to work on restoring the card. He pictured her fingers flying across her keyboard as she observed her multiple monitors.

Caleb rubbed his neck and nabbed a soda from the fridge, then plunked into a recliner. He spotted the television but refused to turn it on. The day's events stirred his emotions and adding senseless crime shows into the mix wouldn't help. Instead, he reached for the local newspaper and settled in for the rest of the evening. He turned to the article about the infamous Suicide Slayer. Something about the killer spooked Oaklynn, and Caleb wanted to learn more about the man.

A thump sounded outside.

Caleb jerked in the chair, his paper falling to the floor. He had nodded off, and darkness now blanketed the room. He flicked his wrist to bring his smartwatch to life. Eleven thirty. He'd been out for hours. Apparently, the day's events had taxed him more than he thought.

Briggs barked and trotted to the patio door, his claws clicking on the hardwood.

Caleb snapped to attention. The K-9 still had his keen sense. Briggs wouldn't act like this for nothing.

Something was wrong.

Caleb hustled to his sister's locked gun cabinet and punched in the code. He withdrew the shotgun and buckshot. He loaded the chamber. After snagging a flashlight from the kitchen drawer and putting on his coat, he flicked on the outside light. He flung open the door, raising his weapon. "Who's there? I'm armed. Show yourself."

Briggs trotted outside and barked.

Caleb stepped onto the deck and scanned the yard, the vein over his temple pulsating.

Nothing.

Briggs barked again.

"What is it, boy?"

The dog growled.

Caleb shined the flashlight on the location Briggs circled. The beam caught the object of the K-9's distress. Caleb approached slowly and stopped at the sight before him.

A blonde doll lay by the tree. Its severed head sat beside it with a note pinned to the doll's black dress.

Go home, Watcher. Or she dies.

He flashed his light on the reddened ground and choked in a breath.

Blood had turned the snow crimson.

A gust of wind whipped around the house's corner, stinging his face and sending a wave of terror throughout his body. His chest tightened as a question ripped through his brain.

Which *she* was the note referring to? Lilly, Mic or Oaklynn?

A coyote howled in the distance, as if responding to Caleb's unspoken question.

Tension strangled his muscles as his heartbeat ratcheted up and he puffed out a ragged breath.

Briggs barked.

Caleb pivoted and scanned his sister's property line.

A shadow skulked along the fence.

Caleb's tactical skills emerged, and he tightened his grip on the shotgun, raising it with determination fresh on his mind.

He wouldn't lose another loved one. He'd protect the *she* even if it cost him his own life.

Chapter Four

"Am I overthinking the situation?" Oaklynn sat at her farmhouse's kitchen table, nursing a cup of hot chocolate. The snow had intensified throughout the day, turning the slippery roads into a sloppy mess. Her muscles relaxed when she reached her home on the city's outskirts. She preferred to be away from watchful eyes, so she'd chosen a place in the country. A farmhouse without animals. Except for the newly acquired Bengal kittens she'd saved from the side of the road.

The smell of peanut butter cookies filled the room, and Oaklynn inhaled. She'd baked as soon as she got home to unwind from her stressful day. Talks of a copycat brought back too many memories. Too many wounds and secrets she tried hard to keep buried. Baking always helped soothe her troubled spirit.

She smiled as she pictured her mother handing her five-year-old daughter a spoon of chocolate-chip cookie dough. *It will be our little secret. Don't tell Daddy. He wouldn't like it.*

Even though Oaklynn didn't understand, she'd nodded as she licked the spoon. After all, there were a few secrets she and her mother had kept from the man. Like their special hiding spot in Lynny's room.

Oaklynn snatched a cookie and stuffed it into her mouth, returning her focus to her friend.

"Only you can decide that." Chloe warmed her hands on her mug, then reached for a handful of marshmallows as a disheveled auburn curl bounced forward. "Did you really smell your father's cologne?"

Oaklynn puffed out a sharp breath and slumped backward. She had shared all the day's activities with her friend. "Maybe all the talk of dear old Dad has overloaded my hyperactive imagination."

"But you didn't imagine the text. Do you have any idea who this person is? Someone from your childhood?"

Oaklynn squeezed the bridge of her nose, searching her past. After her mother's death when Oaklynn was five, many of her memories blurred even to the point where she had lapses of unaccounted time. Why, she didn't know. Her father had withdrawn, and no one visited their home much after the funeral. Occasionally, her aunt Sue would come and check on her, but her visits always ended up with her father and aunt fighting. "No one. My father kept to himself, mostly. Except for the times he prowled for his next victim."

Chloe's face twisted into a contorted mess. "What was it like being his daughter?"

"I'm afraid we don't have that kind of time for me to explain." More importantly, how could she answer her friend without admitting her deepest fear?

A fear she refused to say out loud.

That she could be like her father.

Her friend sipped her hot chocolate as her eyes remained on Oaklynn's face. "I'm sorry. I shouldn't have asked." Chloe set her mug down. "Give me your phone."

Oaklynn hesitated. "What are you going to do?"

"Get our digital team to check it." Chloe reached across the table and wiggled her fingers. "Come on. Hand it over. You can live without a cell phone for one night. You have a police radio and a landline."

Oaklynn shouldn't have told her friend about the text, but Chloe had sensed Oaklynn's shift in mood when Chloe came to the farm. She guessed something was up, and Oaklynn crumbled, letting it all out like an inflated balloon pricked with a pin. The day's events swooshed out.

"Let me text Aunt Sue first." She tapped in a quick goodnight message to her aunt before sliding the phone across the table.

"I just want to ensure it's hacker-free. Won't take them long." Chloe pocketed the phone. "Has Dr. Patterson ruled Missy's death a murder yet?"

"Not officially. He's reexamining the body. Thankfully, he removed the SD card earlier or it would have been stolen. I just don't understand how the person knew it was there."

"Good question." Chloe worried her lip. "Why didn't you give it to digital forensics? Are you sure you trust Mikaela Cox?"

"We don't have a choice. The mayor is calling the shots on this case and he was concerned about the time. We need answers fast. Besides, I've met Mic. She had reported a break-in a few weeks ago, but nothing materialized."

"Is she as good as Caleb says?"

"I guess we'll see." Oaklynn stuffed another cookie into her mouth.

The redhead's eyes sparkled. "Well, at least her brother is easy on the eyes. Maybe you should get to know him better."

Oaklynn played with the buttons on her sweater. No denying that fact. *Don't go there.* She would never open her heart again. The pain was too hard. "He is handsome, but you remember what happened with Wil? I can't go through that again." She swirled the spoon in her hot chocolate.

Chloe rested her hand on top of Oaklynn's. "Time to move on. His death wasn't your fault."

Oaklynn yanked her hand away and stood. "Wasn't it?" Truth be told, she found it hard to forget her father's evil touch and when Wil first kissed her, she froze. It was the beginning of the end of their relationship.

How could Oaklynn ever get close to a man after what her father did to her? The ugliness of his fingers slithering over her body lingered. Even though she had tried to scrub it away with abrasive bodywashes, his touch remained tattooed on her skin, and ruined any hopes of her falling in love. If love was like what Aaron Crowder showed Oaklynn's mother, she didn't want it.

Love was too dark. Too evil.

Time to change the subject.

Oaklynn walked to the kitchen window and snuck a peek through the blinds. Ice pellets clanged on the glass. "Chloe, it's late, and the snow has changed to freezing rain. You need to stay overnight. I have extra pajamas."

Chloe grinned. "Awesome. A sleepover. Just what every girl needs."

Two of Oaklynn's five Bengal kittens trotted into the room with their tails high in the air, meowing in unison.

"Frodo and Sam want their second supper." Oaklynn chuckled.

Chloe's eyes brightened. "Now, that's a perfect way to unwind. How about a *Lord of the Rings* marathon?"

Oaklynn walked to the cupboard and took out her kitten's food, shaking the container. The other three Bengals dashed into the room. "As much as I'd love to, it's a little late for those movies. We both have to work tomorrow."

Although Oaklynn doubted she'd get much sleep tonight.

Not with a Suicide Slayer copycat on the loose.

Caleb trudged through the snow, but the ice pellets had formed a crusty layer, making it difficult to gain speed. He followed the perpetrator's tracks, being careful not to step in them. He eased the gate open, raising his weapon and flashlight in sync. Briggs barked and scrambled around him. Caleb followed, his senses on high alert. The retired K-9's sharpness was still intact.

"What do you see, Briggs?"

Caleb circled the beam over the property, but nothing materialized. Whoever—or whatever—lurked earlier had vanished.

But something had caught his dog's attention.

Briggs ran down the quiet street and stopped.

He'd lost the scent.

Caleb scanned the area. The footprints ended where tire tracks left a U-turn indentation. The perp had parked their car near the intersection.

They were gone.

Caleb whipped out his cell phone. He called 911 and stated the situation, requesting assistance. The operator indicated a cruiser was in the area and she'd redirect the officer to Caleb's location.

Dare he call Oaklynn? Would she be asleep at this hour? He barely knew her, but something told him she'd want to know since he guessed the attack was both related to her case and directed at her. Caleb keyed in her number, but it went to voicemail. He tried the second number she'd given him.

She answered on the first ring. "What's going on, Caleb?"

Her crisp, clear voice told him she'd been awake.

"How long will it take you to get here?" He explained the situation and gave her Mic's address.

"The roads are dicey, so probably thirty minutes. Chloe is here. We'll see you soon." She ended the call.

Caleb rubbed Briggs's head. "Good job, bud."

Sirens pierced the brisk night. Seconds later, flashing lights illuminated the street. Doors opened and residents stepped onto their porches.

He waved his arms. "Stay inside, folks. Lock your doors. Police will keep you informed." His voice boomed in the still night air.

Their porch lights revealed the frowns on their faces.

Great, his sister would never forgive him for creating havoc on her street. Mic had tried to keep a low profile, especially after the break-in at her home. It drew unwanted attention to her. Even though she and Maxwell were close, she still struggled with the attack that occurred years ago. The attack leaving her entire family dead, except for Maxwell Greene and herself.

It was why she never left her home. Her husband, Leo, had brought her out a bit when they met on an online dating site. Then the unspeakable happened. Leo and Mic had gone to a movie and were walking back to their car when a mugger tried to rob them at gunpoint. Leo had stepped in to intervene, but was shot in the process. After that tragedy, her fears had resurfaced, undoing everything Leo had accomplished.

This new violation would drive her farther into the cocoon she'd created for herself—and Lilly wouldn't be able to handle the isolation.

No wonder the girl had been acting up recently. Teenagers needed to be among friends, but her mother's fear wedged a wall between them when she refused to let her daughter stray far from the house.

And Caleb was concerned the wall would become impenetrable if the two didn't deal with it soon.

A cruiser parked in front of him, and Constable Dalton got out. "Watcher Greene, good to see you again." He stuck out his gloved hand.

Caleb nodded and returned the gesture. "It's just Caleb. You're still on shift?"

"Working a double. Can you tell me what happened?"

"Suspect fled in a car parked there." Caleb pointed to where

Briggs sat. "My dog lost the scent." He explained the situation, adding that both Oaklynn and Chloe were on their way.

Dalton gestured toward Mic's opened gate in the distance. "I'll check it out."

"I need to update my sister." Caleb threw up a prayer, asking God to prepare Mic for yet another intrusion in her already tumultuous world.

Oaklynn and Chloe made their way through the crusty snow forty minutes later. A forensic van arrived and stopped behind Oaklynn's Jeep Cherokee.

Caleb observed the pretty constable.

Her long blond hair danced in the winter breeze. She drew out a tuque from her pocket and stuffed it on her head, ducking under the caution tape before approaching the disfigured doll.

The back porch light illuminated the menacing scene. Her eyes settled on the decapitated doll among the bloodied snow and she halted before advancing closer. She leaned over and read the note. Her saucer-eyed expression revealed her trepidation.

Caleb seized her arm to steady her. "I'm guessing from the blond hair, the *her* they're referring to is you. Correct? What reason would they have of targeting you?"

Oaklynn cleared her throat, recomposing herself. She shrugged and moved away from his touch. "No idea."

Liar.

This pretty officer held a secret…not that he didn't have a skeleton in his own closet.

Would she trust him enough to share hers?

Before it was too late?

Oaklynn curbed the angst coursing through her veins and squatted, shining her Maglite closer. The doll wore a black dress, and crimson blotches splattered its body. Its tangled blond hair held the same red residue. Blood, or something else? Chloe would find out. Who would do such a heinous disfigurement to a child's toy?

Oaklynn examined the note. No way to identify the author since they'd used newspaper cutout letters. Perhaps Chloe would find fingerprints.

Somehow Oaklynn doubted it. Was this related to Missy's death and the others? Did the note refer to Oaklynn?

If so, how do they know who I am?

She'd covered her tracks and deleted her old Facebook account back when she started receiving threats. However, she failed to get all newspaper articles about that night removed from social media. Her former self was still out there.

Oaklynn hoped her change of hair coloring would help conceal her real identity. She'd been careful not to post pictures of herself after she and Aunt Sue moved away. Her new friends teased her about not getting into the current century and being on social media, but Oaklynn refused to be thrust back into the limelight. Sure, she no longer looked like the frightened teenager from the past, but dangerous people were still out there looking for the Suicide Slayer's daughter. Her father's "followers" had vowed revenge after he'd been convicted, and they blamed her for betraying their hero. It was why she had put in for a transfer from Toronto.

She couldn't take the chance.

Would she ever get out from under her father's shadow? Even in his death?

Chloe kneeled beside her and leaned closer. "You okay?"

"Of course. This has to be a coincidence, right?" *Doubtful. You don't believe in those, remember?* Oaklynn chewed the inside of her mouth and kept her head bowed. She wouldn't even let Chloe see the fear raging inside.

Chloe dropped the note in an evidence bag. "I don't think you believe that. Someone is targeting you."

The question was…who and why so soon after her father killed himself?

Oaklynn stood and brushed snow from her jeans as if clearing her mind of the past.

A German shepherd barked and trotted toward her, taking her off guard. "Hey there, fella. What's your name?"

Caleb tousled the dog's fir. "Oaklynn, meet Briggs. My retired K-9."

She took off her gloves and held her fingers out.

Briggs licked them, his tail wagging.

"Such a cutie. What retired him?"

"Shot in the leg. He's recovered nicely but has a slight limp. All of his senses are still top-notch. He was the one who alerted to the prowler."

"Smart boy." Oaklynn ruffled Briggs's ears. "Did you work with him in the military?"

Caleb's gaze shifted to Chloe and the forensics unit, but not before she caught an emotion clouding his eyes. Remorse?

"I'd rather not talk about it," he said.

Did the handsome Watcher carry a secret too?

Chloe approached, interrupting Oaklynn's unspoken question. "Oaklynn, you need to see this. There's a newspaper date on the back of this note." She handed Oaklynn the clear evidence bag.

Lack of sleep caused buzzing in her brain and robbed her keen cop sense. *Focus.* She flashed her Maglite's beam on the paper and peered at the date.

Every muscle in her body locked.

The clipped newspaper date was from fifteen years ago.

The day of her father's arrest.

Was someone toying with her, or was this just a coincidence? Somehow, she doubted the latter.

A chill snaked down her spine, coiling around each vertebrae.

Someone in Kenorapeake Falls definitely knew Oaklynn's identity.

How long before they exposed her secret?

Chapter Five

Caleb didn't miss the alarm on Oaklynn's wrenched face before her expression changed. *You're good at hiding your feelings, but not from me.* He leaned closer to get a better look at the newspaper date Chloe referred to. Something about it rattled Oaklynn. "What's special about this date?"

Chloe and Oaklynn exchanged glances.

"Nothing."

Caleb wasn't buying Oaklynn's response.

A coyote howled nearby.

Another answered.

Caleb tensed and shone his flashlight on the trees at the rear of Mic's property. Eyes glistened in the beam.

What had brought the coyotes this close to the community?

Caleb eyed the blood around the doll's head. "I'm guessing that's some type of animal blood. There may be a carcass nearby and the coyotes have caught its scent."

Chloe squatted and took a healthy sample of the crimson

snow. "We'll ascertain what we're dealing with here, but I agree with your conclusion."

Briggs barked and growled as if replying to the animals, defending his territory.

"Briggs, stay." Caleb gestured toward the forensic team. "Chloe, how much longer will you be? It's not safe out here. I don't trust those hungry coyotes."

He shone his light back toward the pack, but they had vanished into the night like the perp.

The back door opened, and Mic placed one foot onto the porch. The farthest Caleb guessed she'd venture. Another step and she'd go into full panic mode.

"Caleb, you and Oaklynn need to see this." Mic gestured them inside and retreated to the comfort of her home.

So much for finding out about the newspaper date.

"You guys go. I'll help the team and we'll finish up here." Chloe hesitated. "Oaklynn, go home after and get some rest. I think you're gonna need it."

With that odd statement, Chloe left to supervise her colleagues.

"What did that mean?" Caleb cupped Oaklynn's elbow, guiding her toward the back entrance.

"Nothing. Let's go see what Mic found." She stomped up the deck's stairs.

More secrets. I hate secrets.

But yet, you have plenty of your own.

Caleb jogged ahead and opened the door for her. "You can trust me."

She pursed her lips. "I barely know you. So, no, I can't. And there's nothing to share."

The phrase *Liar, liar pants on fire* came to Caleb's mind, but he dismissed it and followed her into the heated bungalow.

His psychology experience told him she had wounds, but just how deep did they go?

A question he desperately wanted the answer to.

You can't fix everyone, bro.

An expression both of his sisters—Mic and Hayley—always said to him ever since Maxwell Greene formed his adopted family. Caleb had studied psychology in college and attempted to analyze everyone he came in contact with, including all of his siblings. They each held their own secrets and issues, leaving Caleb desperate to help them. The girls tired of his constant probing and finally told him to butt out and stop trying to fix them.

To this day, Caleb struggled with his compulsion of reading people.

"I hope you don't mind, but I fixed you both a chai rooibos tea. It's decaf, of course." She placed the steaming mugs on the kitchen's island.

Caleb pointed to the barstools. "Have a seat, Oaklynn. Take off your coat."

She obeyed.

He wiggled out of his and plunked himself down. "What did you find, sis?"

Mic opened her laptop. "I'm still working on the SD card. It's badly damaged, but I think I'll be able to salvage some. I searched the cult's name you gave me and found this." She turned the screen in their direction.

A heading appeared.

The Light Paragons—Spreading Peace to our Communities

"That's the slogan painted on the yellow van we saw in the church parking lot earlier today." Oaklynn sipped her tea. "What else does it say about them on their website?"

"The usual cult mumbo jumbo, but it's what it doesn't say that intrigued me to dive deeper. Nothing about their real beliefs. Just the fluffy stuff. I learned through Caleb that some cults hold secrets from the public." Mic turned the laptop back around and tapped the keyboard before she once again placed the screen in front of them. "This is from the dark web."

A picture of hooded figures circled around a bonfire holding spears displayed under the caption:

Join the disciples to snuff out God's Light
and cleanse the earth

Caleb hissed out a sharp breath. "So this is their actual mission. They don't want to spread light. They want to bring darkness to our community." He pounded the island.

Oaklynn startled, her tea slopping over the side of her cup. "Whoa now. Let's not jump to conclusions here." She dabbed the liquid using a napkin.

Caleb gritted his teeth. "Trust me. I know how they work, because I've been one of those disciples. I—"

Stop talking before you reveal your darkest secret. The one you haven't shared with anyone.

Mic grazed his arm. "Bro, you're safe. He's behind bars, remember?"

Oaklynn swiveled in her barstool, facing Caleb directly. "Who's she talking about?"

Caleb ignored Oaklynn's knees touching his. He stood and paced the kitchen, preparing his answer carefully. How deep did he want to go with his explanation? *I can't go back into the darkness.*

He feared if he did, he'd never return.

"Caleb, Dad told you to share with KFPD about the cult. It's why he chose you for this mission, remember?"

Caleb inhaled deeply, expelling his breath audibly. "Going back to that place is hard, Mic."

"I understand, but you know how they think. You're the only one who can expose them for what they truly are."

Oaklynn's expression softened. "You can trust me. I'll have your back. Whatever it is."

Could he trust her when she wouldn't him?

But something in her eyes told Caleb she spoke the truth. "Fine. Because it's late, I'll give you the abridged version. I can fill the team in later with more details." But not *every* detail.

Some things even his family didn't know.

"I was in and out of foster homes for most of my life. When I was fifteen, I was heavy into drinking and drugs."

Oaklynn drew in a sharp breath.

"I know. I know. Terrible to be hooked so young, but I had a rough childhood."

She held her hands up in a stop position. "I'm not judging. Just took me by surprise."

"Plus, I got into many fights. Let's just say my fists did a lot of talking in those days. Anyway, my best buddy at the time just started attending some life meetings, as he called it." Caleb air-quoted the word *life*. "I told him I was struggling with my current foster parents, so he invited me to a meeting. Thought it would help me soften my attitude or something." He harrumphed. "If only I realized Christ was the only one able to do that."

Caleb sat back down and sipped his tea to gather his thoughts. "I went to one meeting, and that was all it took. The leader, Nehemiah Love, had this unique way of luring the attendees with his talk of goodness and light. I got tricked into joining the Purity Flock. I didn't even realize it, but they had brainwashed me from the moment I walked through the door."

Oaklynn shifted on the barstool. "What happened?"

"I worshiped the ground Nehemiah walked on. Followed him around like a lost puppy, did everything he asked—good and bad."

Her eyes widened. "Like what?"

Caleb searched her dark chocolate eyes for hints of judgment, but found none. Only simple curiosity. "At first it was only helping at their meetings. Making coffee, getting snacks. That sort of thing. I had obviously proven my worth, because it soon escalated to other responsibilities. Darker tasks."

He looked away. Caleb couldn't bear to see her beautiful face turn to disgust at what he was about to say. "He told me some followers had strayed from what he'd been teaching and were threatening to leave, so he wanted me to rough them up. Threaten them. Scare them into staying." He stopped. Could he go on?

"Tell her the rest. The Light Paragons have grown to a thousand followers. Stop them before they brainwash more."

Caleb placed his hands on the island countertop and eased himself to his feet. He kissed his sister's forehead. "Oh, wise one. You're right. Again."

She winked. "Of course."

He walked to the kitchen window. Chloe's team was packing up, getting ready to leave. She carried the bagged, decapitated doll and headed toward the gate.

His sister was right. Even if this latest development had nothing to do with The Light Paragons, he *had* to stop this cult. He turned to face the women once again. "The leader showered me with job-well-done gifts. It went to my head, and I soon enjoyed carrying out his tasks. Too much."

An image of the last person he roughed up emerged. Swollen eyes. Bloody nose. Broken arm. But it wasn't those that stopped him in his tracks. It was the light in the man's eyes. Even with Caleb's beating, the darkness never returned. He told Caleb God loved him.

It was all it took to snap him out of his cult stupor. "I finally realized my enforcer tasks were wrong. In every way. I also discovered how Nehemiah's executioners were killing women who'd fought his advances. It disgusted me and I told him I wanted out." Caleb would never forget the evil that had flashed over the man's face. An evil so deep it still made Caleb shudder. "Of course, he threatened me, saying he'd leak all my wrongdoings to the cops. I said I didn't care."

"Did you get out?"

"Not without help. That's when I met Maxwell Greene. He was visiting with other members of his church on the pretense they wanted to join. They were trying to get information for the police, as the cult wouldn't allow any law enforcement on their premises. I didn't know that at the time." Caleb folded his fingers inward, gouging his palms as another memory returned.

Oaklynn rose and walked to where he stood. She cupped his hand in hers. "I know that look. What happened?"

"I didn't realize it, but Nehemiah had more enforcers at his beck and call. He ordered one of them to kill my best friend." His voice wavered as he pictured Ethan's bloody body arranged on the bed with his hands in a prayer position and lifeless eyes staring at the ceiling of the room they shared. He retreated from Oaklynn's hold. "Rage overtook me and I stormed the compound to find Nehemiah. To confront him, but—"

"That's when Dad found you," Mic interjected. "He told me he saw a knife in Nehemiah's hand and he intercepted him."

"Maxwell saved my life that day. In more ways than one." And one nobody else knew. "The police arrested Nehemiah and his enforcers. All but me."

"No one came forward and said you beat them up?"

A question Caleb had asked himself many times. "None. Maxwell said God protected me that day. Don't get me wrong. I told the police everything, but no one would corroborate my actions, so they didn't press charges. I testified against Nehemiah. It was my witness statement, along with an executioner's, that helped convict him. He's still serving time." He paused. "Mic, did you find out anything else from the dark web on this new cult?"

"Not yet. I'm still digging." She closed her laptop. "But I need to go to bed. Night all."

"Night, sis. Sleep tight."

"I'm sorry you experienced all that." Oaklynn snatched her coat from the nearby chair and put it on.

Caleb finished his tea and placed the mug in the sink. "I will never forget that time in my life or the dreadful actions I took."

Oaklynn walked to the back door and stepped into her boots. "Caleb, we all have darkness within us. We just have to choose to snuff it out."

Wise words.

But would that darkness consume him all over again?

After consulting with Chloe, Oaklynn said good night to her friend and closed the forensic van's door. Chloe would work all night. Oaklynn didn't envy her friend's absurd hours. Not that hers were any better.

Oaklynn finally arrived at her farmhouse at two in the morning. The freezing rain had switched back to snow and made her drive home even more treacherous. Thankfully, her police driving training proved helpful on the dicey roads. She opened the detached garage using her remote and drove inside.

She trudged through the crusty snow and entered the code to open her front door. She hung her key fob on a hook next to the alarm box and deactivated the system.

An eerie silence filled her home. Normally, her kittens scampered out to greet her when she arrived. "Frodo? Sam? Girls? Where are you?"

She checked the living room for their usual sleeping haunts, but none of the Bengal kittens were there. Odd.

Meow. Meow.

Their cries came from somewhere deeper in the three-bedroom farmhouse. "Where are you guys?"

Their meows intensified.

Oaklynn turned toward their howls. The basement. Had she mistakenly trapped them down there? She rushed into the kitchen and opened the door leading to the lower level.

The kittens scampered around her feet.

"There you are." Oaklynn squatted and sat cross-legged on her heated floor. The litter crawled into her lap. All five of them. "How did you get locked in the basement?"

Oaklynn scratched each of their heads as she racked her brain, trying to remember closing the basement door.

But she hadn't.

"Maybe Chloe shut you in by mistake, huh?" That must be the answer because anything else would take her through a door she didn't want to enter.

The times in her childhood when she'd failed to remember moving things around in her room. To this day, she didn't recall rearranging her toys.

Focus on the goodness in your life. Words her aunt repeated many times, and words Oaklynn now tried to live by.

She rubbed Frodo's and Sam's mitten paws. It was how she distinguished the leopard spotted boys from the three girls— Arwen, Elsa, and Anna. She named the boys appropriately for their extra "hobbit" toes. Oaklynn questioned why anyone would abandon the Bengal kittens. She knew their value. Not that she'd let any of them go. They'd stolen her heart, providing their refuge and comfort.

"How about a little treat before I head to bed, huh?"

They bounded off her lap and headed directly to the cupboard where she kept their food as if they understood the word *treat*. "Who said cats weren't smart?" She chuckled.

After feeding the gang and changing into her favorite flannel plaid jammies, Oaklynn crawled into bed. She set her alarm and spied the books on her nightstand. One drew her eye. *The Mystery of the Ivory Charm*. Oaklynn picked it up and chuckled. Did Chloe leave it here? She had shared with her friend how much she loved Nancy Drew books. Why not?

Oaklynn opened to the first chapter—Fortune Telling.

Concern crept over her like darkness in an oncoming storm. She slammed the book shut.

Was it a foreshadowing of events to come? She remembered Caleb's account of the cult he'd been immersed in. She gathered from his forlorn expressions when he retold his story that the cult stole more than his light.

It had stolen his innocence.

We all have darkness within us. We just have to choose to snuff it out. Did Oaklynn really say that to Caleb earlier? Did she believe her own words? Could she rid herself of her father's darkness?

Two of her kittens hopped up on the bed and positioned themselves on her pillow—one on each side of her head.

Hopefully, their comforting presence would lull her to sleep after today's disturbing events and talks of her serial killer father.

And whatever feelings she had about his death.

Music blared, jolting Oaklynn awake from nightmares of cults and serial killers. The kittens skittered off the bed. Her foggy, sleepy brain struggled to comprehend if the music was coming from her cell phone, but then she realized Chloe had taken the device. She checked the time on her smart speaker—4:00 a.m.

The music continued and goaded her fully awake. It finally dawned on her that the tune originated from her speaker. How was that possible?

She recognized the song and bolted upright in her bed as memories flooded her mind.

A soothing female's voice sung the lyrics.

Lullaby and good night, with roses bedight,
With lilies o'er spread is baby's wee bed.
Lay thee down now and rest, may thy slumber be blessed.
Lay thee down now and rest, may thy slumber be blessed.

Oaklynn bristled. The song played by her father while making her waltz with him during his visits. Brahms's "Lullaby."

"Alexa, stop music." Oaklynn's raspy command silenced the song.

The lullaby thrust her back to her childhood.

Where she didn't want to go.

But now had no choice.

Chapter Six

Caleb's cell phone rang through the Bluetooth in his truck as he headed into downtown Kenorapeake Falls early the next morning. Despite being plowed, the roads remained slippery after yesterday's wintery mess. He turned down a street and parked in front of the bakery before checking the caller. Maxwell Greene. Great. Caleb forgot to call him. Ouch. "Morning, Dad."

"Son, why haven't you given me an update?"

Caleb didn't miss the annoyance in the man's voice. "Sorry. The day got away from me and then the incident last night at Mic's, I—"

"Wait, what incident? Is she okay? Lilly?"

"They're fine. Lilly stayed overnight at a friend's house. Mic is okay, Dad. Don't worry." Caleb cut the engine and told his father about the decapitated doll.

"But why target you?"

Caleb had asked himself the same question when he rolled out of bed after a restless sleep. Penny's Café made strong coffee, and his system required fuel for the day. Plus, the treats went over well yesterday, so he guessed they would today too.

"I'm not exactly sure, but whoever planted the doll there must have followed me back to Mic's."

"Sloppy, son. You of all people should know to watch for a tail, being on the special ops team."

Caleb white-knuckled the steering wheel. *You don't have to remind me of my mistakes, Maxwell.*

However, his father was right. Caleb should have been more careful on his drive after the taxing day. "Won't happen again."

"Better not. I'm flying in the squad to help with this case."

Caleb bit his tongue to silence a curse word. Before he finally surrendered his heart to Christ, Caleb had a foul mouth to go along with his powerful fists. Something he wasn't proud of, so now he used his words and fists to help others. But at this moment, his frustration over his father's lack of confidence grated on his nerves. "Why? I can handle it. Mic is helping with the technology. Oaklynn and her team are quite capable."

"These deaths are getting more press, and we can't afford mistakes. Not only is the country watching CWS, but now this case."

Caleb shifted in his seat. "Wait—what are you talking about?"

"Haven't you seen the *Tribune*? Darius Wesley wrote an article stating the latest killing wasn't a suicide, but we have a Suicide Slayer copycat on our hands."

Caleb pounded the dashboard. "Where did he get that idea? Oaklynn and her team haven't made any conclusions yet or publicized anything about the death."

"Well, I have no information about his source, but the mayor is closely monitoring me and gave me a lecture this morning. That's why I'm flying in the squad. They'll all be here by suppertime. Meeting at the estate at 7:00 p.m. We'll conference in

Mic. Unless you can convince her to come out of her home. Have you made any progress?"

The secret mission Maxwell Greene had tasked Caleb with—convince his daughter to come out of hiding.

But that wasn't as easy as it sounded. "I'm afraid not, and this latest incident didn't help."

His father's forceful sigh sailed through the Bluetooth. "Keep at it. I'm counting on you. Oh, be sure Constable Brock and whoever else she wants at the meeting is here. See you tonight." He severed the call without waiting for Caleb's reply.

Caleb punched the hang-up button and stuffed his gloves on, leaving his truck to make his purchases for the team. Perhaps it would help soften the blow of this CWS meeting at his father's estate. Maxwell Greene wasn't making it easy for the KFPD to trust Caleb. Their motto is to *work alongside of* law enforcement. Not take over.

Twenty minutes later, after buying coffees and treats, Caleb walked into the Kenorapeake Falls police station. He turned the corner and halted.

Oaklynn had her nose buried in a paper copy of the newspaper.

Fortunately, Caleb noticed her before they had a typical TV-movie-coffee-catastrophe moment. "Morning. I see you're reading the *Tribune*."

Oaklynn waved it in the air. "Have you seen this article?" She crumpled the edges. "Wait till I get my hands on Darius."

"Not yet, but I just got off the phone with Maxwell. He told me about the article after reaming me out for not calling him. I guess Mayor Stevens is breathing down his neck." He held out a coffee. "Will this help?"

"Maybe. This will be my fourth." She sipped from the paper cup. "Ahh, so good. Thanks."

"Didn't sleep well?"

Her eyes clouded. "Not really." She gestured toward the briefing room. "Shall we?"

"Wait, I need to tell you about my father's request." He explained the seven o'clock meeting. "Sorry for his boldness. He can be like that."

"I'll talk to Sergeant Rollins. He may want to come too, and probably Constable Spearing, since I'm working with him on the case."

"Understood."

Caleb followed her into the room and placed the box of treats on a nearby table. "Morning everyone. Breakfast has arrived."

"Awesomesauce, Watcher. Thank you!" Spearing snatched a coffee and lifted the box lid.

Caleb swatted the constable's hand. "Eldon, those aren't for you." He brought out a bag of carrots from his coat pocket and handed them to him. "You said you were watching your waistline, remember?"

"Pfft. Hardly. None of that rabbit-food nonsense for me." He ignored the carrots and stuffed a doughnut in his mouth, mumbling between bites. "I just wanna cry. So. Good."

Caleb chuckled and slapped Spearing on the back. "Thought you'd like them."

Sergeant Rollins breezed by the group and took his place behind the KFPD podium. "Take your seats. Let's get started."

The constables scrambled to grab a coffee and doughnut before plunking themselves behind the small tables.

Caleb sat beside Oaklynn and sipped his coffee, waiting for the briefing to begin.

Rollins cleared his throat. "Okay, I'm sure you've all seen the latest article in the *Tribune*. What I want to know is how and where Darius Wesley got his information. He didn't just pluck his conclusions out of thin air. Someone leaked our conversation about the possibility of a copycat." He paused, staring at each constable individually. "Rest assured, I will find out who that was."

Spearing raised his hand. "Sarge, why do you think it was one of us?"

"Not saying that's the case, but was the reporter anywhere near the crime scene to overhear your conversations?"

Oaklynn shifted in her seat. "Sir, he was behind the caution tape. Unless he has bionic ears, there's no way he would have heard Constable Spearing, Caleb, and I chatting about the possibility. Plus, Dr. Patterson hasn't provided his observations on Missy's death. I'm not so sure there's a copycat out there."

Spearing huffed. "I beg to disagree. Why would anyone steal the body and then look for this SD card if it wasn't a homicide? And it certainly looks similar to how the Suicide Slayer killed his victims. Have you read the case files?"

"Of course. I am well-versed in working a case, Eldon."

Caleb didn't miss the slight edge in Oaklynn's voice and her closed-off body language—crossed arms and legs, compressed lips, eyebrows pinched together. He failed to understand why she was determined to dismiss the idea of Missy's death being a copycat.

"Constable Brock, did you get any information from the crowd at yesterday's crime scene?"

"Nothing substantial, Sarge."

Rollins turned to Caleb. "Did your sister get anything off the SD card yet?"

"She's still working on it, but Mic found out some information on The Light Paragons." Caleb pointed at the monitor at the front of the room. "Can I send some pics to your screen?"

"Go ahead."

Caleb stood and sent his cell phone images for all to view. "This is The Light Paragons website."

The cheery yellow page displayed across the screen.

"Looks great, right? Nice visual. Inviting. Makes most want

to check them out. But, this…" Caleb swiped to the other picture "…is what Mikaela found on the dark web."

The black page displayed the eerie group of hooded figures gathered around the fire, and the cult's real mission.

Collective murmurs filled the briefing room.

Spearing whistled. "So their 'bring peace to the community' is a front for this sinister mission. Why the secrecy?"

Caleb swiped again to the sunny image. "Because it's how they lure followers in to brainwash them into this." He flipped it back to the darker image. "Trust me, I have firsthand experience." Caleb gave the version of what he shared with Oaklynn—leaving out his enforcer role—concerning his involvement in a deadly cult. He decided they didn't need to know the messy details.

Spearing raised his hand. "Watcher, how long were you sucked in?"

"Too long." He exhaled. "Eight months, three weeks, four days."

"But who's counting, right?" Spearing chuckled. "What's the plan with this cult? We can't just go barging in."

"Very true. Once I investigate further, I'll develop a game plan with Oak—Constable Brock. We need to tread cautiously."

"Agreed. The mayor seems to think the cult is related to this case because his daughter got wrapped up in spreading the light." Rollins air-quoted *spreading the light*. "Do you concur?"

Caleb waited for Oaklynn to answer. He didn't want to appear as if he was taking over the investigation.

"Sarge, Missy had their business card, and when we spoke with Kimi, her body language screamed terror when she talked about them. And it intensified when the van came into the parking lot. So, yes, I'm convinced Missy's death is related." She nodded at Caleb. "What do you think?"

"Agree. There's definitely some sort of connection."

Chloe waltzed into the room, waving a folder. "Sergeant, got the results of the prints from the latest robbery. This one from the bank on Main Street late yesterday." She handed it to him. "Thought you'd want to see it right away."

Rollins opened the folder and read the report. He scowled before slamming it shut. "Okay. That's two this week." He cleared his throat. "Constable Dalton, you take the lead on this one." He clapped. "Okay everyone. Dismissed. Get out there and protect our community."

The constables scattered like bees from a hive ready to do their daily tasks, except for Spearing. He approached Oaklynn. "Do you want to get Wesley in here, boss?"

"Yes, please." Oaklynn's expression tautened. "And stop calling me boss. We're a team."

"Whatever. I'm on it." He meandered forward, then pivoted. "Be careful. Chloe shared the news of last night's episode. Someone is targeting you."

Oaklynn placed her hand on her chest. "Awe, you do have a heart."

"Yep. I'm not the Tin Man." He wobbled toward the doughnuts and snatched one. He bit into it and winked at Caleb.

Caleb did a thumbs-up motion. "He's a comical one, isn't he?"

"Definitely."

Caleb's cell phone buzzed in his pocket. He fished it out and read the text.

Found this tucked in one of Lilly's school books. I'm concerned. Can you speak to her? It's time she knew your past.

A picture of a brochure from The Light Paragons appeared on his screen.

Caleb flinched as memories snowballed into his mind.

He had to warn his niece to stay away from this cult—and now.

★ ★ ★

Oaklynn didn't miss Caleb's shift in demeanor. Something on his phone spooked him and his pinched expression told her it wasn't good. She understood. All this talk about a Suicide Slayer copycat weighed heavy on her chest. Ever since the news broke of her father's death, her muscles locked into a tight ball that she guessed would burst at any time. She pictured her serial killer investigation wall in her locked basement room. When she discovered her father was one of *them*, she spent most of her time studying serial killers. It was why she ultimately went into policing.

To stop killers like Aaron Crowder.

She leaned closer to Caleb. "You okay?"

He passed his phone to her.

Oaklynn read Mic's text. "Go. Call if you need me."

"Will you be okay?"

She cocked her head, flattening her lips. "I can take care of myself." *Rude, Oaklynn.* She required more sleep to squash her foul mood. If that was possible with everything happening. "Sorry, I'm on edge. Eldon and I are interrogating Darius. I'll be with Eldon most of the day going over the case." She rolled her eyes. "If I can tolerate his constant jokes and hockey talk."

"Leafs fan?"

"Habs. Through and through." She waggled her finger at Caleb. "Don't mess with his Montreal Canadiens or he'll never let you forget it."

Caleb laughed and rose. "Noted. Sounds like you have."

"Yep. Told him I wasn't a hockey fan." She stood. "You'd think I said the worst possible thing by his reaction."

Sergeant Rollins approached. "Oaklynn, why didn't you call last night?"

"It was late, and we had it handled. Besides, you have enough issues going on at home right now." Oaklynn grazed her boss's arm. "Has Isaac come home yet?"

His eyes clouded. "No." He addressed Caleb. "My eighteen-year-old has taken up with a gang and now he's more than likely helping them rob banks. Unbelievable. I raised him better than that."

"That's the print Chloe referred to earlier?" Caleb put on his coat, stuffing his cell phone in his pocket. "I'm sorry to hear that. Is this a known gang?"

"No, that's just it. We pride ourselves on the fact that we've contained most of the gangs in Kenorapeake Falls." He rubbed his temples. "This one is new."

Caleb snatched his scarf from the back of the chair. "Sergeant Rollins, do you think this could be related to the growing cult? Some commit crimes to fund their organization and compound. Has Isaac gone to any meetings recently that you know about?"

"No idea, but I'll see what my wife, Becky, knows. This latest fiasco is going to break her heart. Isaac has always been a mama's boy."

Caleb's phone buzzed. "That's probably Mic again. I gotta run." He turned to Oaklynn. "Talk to him about the meeting tonight. I'll report back later." He fished out his phone as he dashed from the room.

Oaklynn patted her empty uniform vest pocket, reminding her to check with Chloe on the status of her phone.

"What's he referring to and where's he going?"

"Sir, Maxwell Greene has called in the entire squad and wants us to meet at the estate." She folded her arms. "I'm reluctant to share information regarding this case with all these civilians. Yes, we're supposed to work alongside them, but they're not law enforcement."

"I understand your concern and echo it, but the mayor is dictating the shots now. He's met with the police board and told them to comply. They're watching us closely to see how we work with the CWS." He latched on to Oaklynn's arm.

"Go to the meeting and take Spearing. I would like to attend, but I need to calm the waters at home."

"Will do." Oaklynn gathered her notebook. "I'll find Eldon soon, but I need to speak with Chloe first. Have a good day, sir."

"Oaklynn, stop calling me sir. It's Rick."

"Sergeant Rollins, your presence is requested in the boardroom," Gracie yelled from the entranceway.

"Talk later." He hurried to follow the admin from the room.

Oaklynn snatched a treat for Chloe and meandered down the halls of KFPD's station, bypassing the group of constables hovering by the watercooler. She pushed open the door leading to Chloe's office and stuck her head in. "Okay to enter? I have treats." She waved the doughnut in the air.

"Friend, you don't need to ask."

Oaklynn entered and handed Chloe the apple fritter. "Well, I didn't want to assume that."

Chloe took off her reading glasses, setting them on top of her laptop. "You look exhausted. Didn't sleep?"

Oaklynn dropped into a chair next to her friend. "Not really. I had the strangest thing happen at four o'clock this morning."

Chloe leaned forward. "What?"

"My smart speaker flicked on, playing music. I didn't set it to do that." Oaklynn adjusted the bun at the nape of her neck. "But it's the song that spooked me. It was Brahms's 'Lullaby.'"

"I get why it coming on by itself is concerning, but why would a lullaby spook you?"

"It's the song my father played while he made me waltz with him."

Chloe cried out. "Okay, that is odd. Coincidence?"

"I don't really believe in those. Could someone get into my Wi-Fi and tamper with the device?"

"Anything is possible these days. Change your password. Just in case. That reminds me." She opened her desk drawer and removed a cell phone, sliding it toward Oaklynn. "Here's your phone back. The team didn't find any traces of a print on it."

"Thanks." Oaklynn stuffed the phone into her vest pocket, happy to once again have the feeling of security at her fingertips. "Another question, did you shut the door leading to my basement before we left for Mic's last night?"

"No, why?"

Oaklynn tapped her chin, searching her memory. "Odd. I must have. The Bengals were locked in the basement when I got home. All of this talk about dear old Dad has intensified my stressors and is playing with my mind."

Truth be told, Oaklynn's senses were still on high alert from the abrupt jarring at four. She fished out her phone and opened the home security app to check her property. "Okay, all appears clear, but I'm going to change my codes and passwords." She tapped the phone's keyboard and made the adjustments before stuffing the device back into her pocket. "Done."

"Good." Chloe put her glasses back on and wiggled her mouse. "I was actually about to go find you. We found something interesting on Missy's phone." Her fingernails clicked on her laptop keys. "There's a scary text conversation." She swiveled her screen around.

Oaklynn leaned closer for a better view.

I want out. Not safe here.

You can't. They'll kill you.

I'm leaving. Tonight.

She'll find you.

God will keep me safe.

Oaklynn's jaw dropped as fear inched up her arms and settled into her neck, knotting her muscles. God? Obviously He didn't. "Have you been able to find the owner of this number?"

"Burner phone."

Oaklynn slumped in her chair. "Figures. The text conversation refers to a 'she.' Could our killer be a woman?"

"I wondered that too. And who are they? The texter says 'they'll kill you.' Do you think they're referring to the cult?"

"Possibly. Anything on the blood found on the doll last night? Fingerprints?"

"Nothing on the prints. Still waiting for the blood analysis, but we've put a rush on it. I'll keep you updated." She templed her fingers. "I wish I had more to give you."

"I best go find Eldon." Oaklynn stood. "Keep me apprised on anything else you find."

"Will do."

Oaklynn shifted her stance. Time to get to work and find whoever was imitating her father's kills.

The Protégé pulled into the windy laneway of the Queen Bee's hive and glanced at the leader's gray, brick mansion nestled among the protection of firs and cedar trees at the compound's edge. The dead vines covering the home along with the trees hid the house's secrets not only from the outside world but from the rest of The Light Paragons followers. Even in the daylight, the building's darkness reminded him of a storybook haunted house. Snow covered the walkway and surrounding areas, adding a touch of purity to the otherwise den of wickedness.

He was on break from work and watching his Lynny. She was still inside the police station. He imagined his interference with her smart speaker had probably taken her by surprise. Aaron told him everything about his daughter's childhood, including the lullaby he played while they danced. It was the perfect tool to get inside Lynny's head.

The Protégé would let her regroup, but not for long. Right now, he'd check in with their group's leader. He climbed out of his truck.

The Queen Bee peered from the window of the enclosed widow's watchtower and waved from her perch.

She had provided him with a key because he was one of her enforcers.

Only my special disciples get one, she'd said before grazing his face using her clawlike nails.

Even though he was in her inner circle, he longed to be her "elite" disciple. According to her, the position would bring him untold riches and power. *One day soon, I'll earn the designation.*

Right now, he must do his job. He inserted his key and entered the mansion. A draft from the January air followed him and swirled in the hall. He stomped the snow from his boots. Special blinds covered all the windows, obstructing any potential prying eyes, but those inside had a perfect view of anyone approaching. But it also blocked out the daylight, adding to the eerie atmosphere.

The Bee glided down the spiral stairs. Even in the foyer's dark lighting, the raven-haired's beauty shone through. From what she'd told him, many had swooned over her and tried to win her hand, but she chose a life of mentoring a flock. It took her a few years, but she finally established a following of like-minded believers.

Incense wafted in the hallway. The flickering candles throughout the foyer and great room also added to the overpowering scent. He'd complained about the pungent smell, but she claimed it was for therapeutic reasons.

Her long black hair and dark eyes gave off an Addam's Family vibe, but she knew how to manipulate and subtly win her flock's approval.

"Good morning." Even her voice had the power to make those around her swoon. "Thank you for taking care of Missy."

She repositioned the candles on the foyer table. Her OCD wouldn't allow the perfect circle to be broken. "Have you taken care of the problem we spoke about earlier?"

"I've got it under control."

The doorbell chimed.

The Bee checked her watch. "My newest follower has arrived. This one promises protection for our group."

"Who is it?"

"None of your concern. Go check on our subjects below and then leave through the servant's entrance in the back."

"Fine." He stepped inside the kitchen, but stopped. He peeked through the crack in the door.

The person entered.

The Protégé wheezed in a breath. This was a surprise, but could give the group an advantage and strength.

He edged down the creaky wooden steps and tugged on the string at the bottom. The light flickered and came to life, creating a creepy glow to the dungeon-like basement. The dampness overpowered his body, and he tightened his jacket.

He lifted the ring of antique keys hanging from a hook and twirled them as he walked along the long corridor, checking the rooms on each side. The Bee kept followers threatening to leave in the secret part of the mansion until she deemed their brainwashing—or cleansing, as she called it—complete. Some of them were sprawled out on their beds, while others stared through the bars on their doors, eyes darting back and forth like a tennis match.

He reached the room where he'd placed Kimi. Someone had tattled that she'd been among those chatting with the police, so the Queen Bee wanted Kimi quarantined and reprogramed. Time to test her progress.

The Protégé inserted the key and opened the door. She sat on the edge of her bed in a trance.

Good, the medication was working.

He plunked himself into a nearby rocker. "How are you feeling?"

"Sleepy. Why am I so tired?"

"Don't worry, sweetie. You will feel better real soon."

Her squinting eyes surveyed the room. "This place is so pretty. Where am I?"

They had furnished the room with childlike pieces. A white canopy bed with matching vanity table and dresser. Lavender permeated the air, giving off a peaceful environment.

"Paradise." Might as well lie to her. He had to keep her contained. She had been too tight with Missy. They both were a risk to The Light Paragons. For now he'd play along with the Bee's wishes. After all, someone else on his list must be taken care of first.

Kimi smiled as she closed her eyes.

He advanced into the hall and shut the door. The dampness once again chilled his bones. A huge contrast to the warmth inside her room.

He smirked. No, not paradise.

More like the depths of hell.

Chapter Seven

Caleb rubbed his sweaty hands as he waited for his niece to finish her phone conversation, his right knee bouncing under the table. He wasn't looking forward to their talk. According to Mic, in Lilly's eyes, all of her uncles could do no wrong. Would she still feel that way toward Caleb once she discovered his past? He fingered the brochure in front of him. The cult had done a good job of concealing their true agenda with the cheerful colors, fonts, and words within the pamphlet. He'd taken time to study it as soon as he arrived back at Mic's.

"So, how's Oaklynn doing this morning after last night's incident?" Mic placed a coffee in front of Caleb and sat.

"I don't know her well yet, but I see sadness in her eyes. I get the sense something more than this case troubles her." He sipped the coffee. "Have you been able to check into her past?"

Mic frowned and leaned back in her chair. "Been kind of busy with the SD card, but, Caleb, do you really want me diving into her personal life? If you want to know, just ask her."

"Yeah, something tells me she won't willingly give up information, especially about herself."

"Well, then, take the hint. Stay out of it."

Briggs trotted into the dining room, his claws clicking on the hardwood. A quick glance wouldn't reveal the dog's injury to anyone who didn't know the K-9. His limp was mild, but enough for the German shepherd to be taken off the list of military dogs. Since the incident, Caleb had worked hard to strengthen his dog's leg and showered him with lots of love. It was his way of making amends for not listening to Briggs's instincts. Something Caleb would never do again.

Briggs sat at Caleb's side and stuck his snout in the air. He rubbed the K-9's head. "Hey, boy." Caleb pointed to the doggie bed in the corner. "Stay."

The German shepherd obeyed and settled into his cushioned comfort of rest.

Perhaps Caleb should listen to his sister's advice. Maybe he was overreacting. "Even when my gut is telling me whatever she's hiding has to do with the case, especially the date on the back of the note left by the doll?"

"What date?"

"Whoever crafted the note also left a date in the corner. After Oaklynn read it, panic flew across her face, then disappeared." Caleb withdrew a notepad from his pocket, scribbling the month, day, and year on it before ripping off the page. "I haven't had time to search on it, so maybe you could start with that."

"I will. Only to put your mind at ease." Mic stuffed it into her jeans pocket.

Footfalls shuffled along the hardwood hall. "Oaklynn? You mean the pretty cop? You have a date with her?" Lilly dropped into a chair beside Caleb.

He didn't miss the fact Lilly picked the chair farthest from her mother. Teenagers. He bit back tears. He'd give anything to see his daughter, Aiyana, in her teenage years.

But that would never happen.

"Hardly, little one, and quit eavesdropping. It's rude." Caleb pulled her into a headlock and rubbed his knuckles over his niece's brown curls before releasing her. "How was your sleepover last night?" He wanted to make small talk before diving into the issue at hand. Ease into it as he'd seen Lilly lash out at her mother when she'd asked a question his niece didn't like.

"Fine. We watched some rom-coms until three in the morning."

"Thankfully, your teachers have a PD day," Mic said.

Ahh… Caleb remembered those teachers' professional development days. He loved sleeping in and watching TV all day. If only life was that simple.

Mic reached across the table and rubbed her daughter's arm. Lilly flinched, confirming Caleb's earlier conclusion.

The thirteen-year-old wanted nothing to do with her mother.

"What did you want to talk about, Uncle Caleb?" She pointed to the brochure and turned to her mother. "Did you steal that from me, Mom?" Lilly's voice elevated and her twisted facial expression revealed her disgust.

And soon that disgust will pass to you. Tread carefully.

Mic's jaw dropped. "Caleb, I'm letting you respond so Lilly and I don't get into another fight."

He inhaled slowly, giving himself time to gather his thoughts. He had to make this appear like they wanted Lilly's help and not that they were chastising her. "Lilly, I'm working on a special assignment right now and I could really use your help. Can you do that for me?" He kept his voice's level soothing.

Her azure eyes sparkled. "You mean one of Grandpa's missions?"

"Yes."

She straightened in her chair. "Okay. What can I do?"

Caleb lifted the pamphlet. "Can you tell me where you got this brochure?"

"My friend Callie gave it to me. Why?"

He stole a quick glimpse at his sister.

Mic chewed her fingernails. Her nervous habit. She wouldn't be any help in diffusing the situation. He sensed he'd gain his niece's trust without her mother present. "Mic, can you go check on that date? I've got this."

She stopped biting her nails and sent a slight nod in his direction. "Of course. Take your time." She left the room.

Caleb waited until his sister closed her office door, then turned to Lilly. "I need to tell you something about your dear old uncle that I'm not proud of. Something that happened to me when I was just a little older than you are now."

Her eyes widened. "What?"

"This will be hard for you to hear, but I will explain why I'm telling you now." Caleb shared about the cult and how they appeared to be nice on the outside, but truly weren't. He explained how they'd brainwashed him into doing things he should never have done.

She rested her elbows on the table, cupping her chin in her palms. "What type of things, Uncle Caleb?"

He puffed out a breath, stalling to find the right words without revealing every detail. Caleb wanted to protect his niece from the horrors involved. "Let's just say I had to talk to a few people for the leader."

"By 'talking,' do you mean with your fists?"

Smart kid. Caleb pictured his last enforcer deed and cringed. "Well, something along those lines. I'm not proud of myself, but I tell you this to caution you." He pushed the pamphlet to the table's center. "These people appear good on the surface, but when you look really close, they're not as they seem."

Lilly leaned back and folded her arms. "Why are you only

telling me this now? I didn't think we kept secrets, Uncle Caleb."

"Little one, I didn't tell you because I wanted to protect you from the evil."

"Evil? I went to a meeting and the people there were so nice."

Caleb resisted the urge to pound the table. "Wait, you attended a meeting?"

"Yes, with Callie."

"When was this?"

Lilly fiddled with the tassels on her hoodie, averting his gaze.

"Last night when you were supposed to be at a sleepover?" Caleb guessed how Mic would react when she found out.

"Yes." Her eyes popped back to his. "I really was at her place. After the meeting."

Caleb tugged on her arm. "Please tell me you'll stay away from this group."

She yanked her arm away and stood. "You can't tell me what to do. You're just like Mom."

"We only want to keep you safe." He had to share one more thing to convince her to distance herself. "Lilly Beth, I almost died in that cult. Your grandfather saved me. If it wasn't for him and God, I'm not sure where I'd be right now. Probably not here. With you."

Once again, her eyes widened moments before her lips quivered. "I don't want to think...about you..." Her broken, emotional words trailed off.

He rose and reached for her hand, bringing her into an embrace. "Do you understand now why we don't want you involved?"

"Yes." She exaggerated a sigh. "Guess I'll have to decline the invite to join them."

Caleb stiffened as an idea formed. Could this be his way into the cult? He broke their hug and held her at arm's length. "What invite?"

She bit her lip. "I wasn't supposed to say anything. Callie made me promise."

"See, if this organization was legitimate, they wouldn't ask you to keep secrets. Where did the invite come from?"

"During a video game."

That's how they're getting to their flock secretly. Caleb's jaw locked, and he massaged his stubbled chin. "Listen, I need—"

Pounding footsteps silenced his words. "Caleb!" Mic raced into the dining room, skidding to a stop. "Get Oaklynn here. Now."

Briggs sprang up on all fours and barked.

Every muscle in Caleb's body locked at his sister's frantic voice. "Why? What did you find?"

Mic eyed her daughter.

"It's okay. She knows about the cult." He placed his hand on Mic's arm. "Did you find something out about the date?"

"Didn't get to that. It's what I found on the SD card." She raised a photo. "This is the mayor's daughter. Look at the figures behind her."

He leaned closer and gasped.

Followers dressed in red gowns and scary masks. But more horrifying...

Holding knives in the air.

Oaklynn drummed her nails on the steel table, waiting for Darius Wesley to answer Eldon's question. *Quit stalling. I don't have time for this.* They'd asked him to come into the station on the pretense that they required his help, but really they wanted to find out where he received the information he had reported. So far, his vague answers had only added to her frustrated state.

Eldon bolted to his feet, his chair scraping on the floor. "Answer the question, Mr. Wesley."

Seemed her colleague also had enough of the reporter's stalling.

Darius raised his hands in a stop position. "Am I a suspect here? If so, I need to call my lawyer."

"Why, did you do something wrong?" Oaklynn pushed the newspaper across the table. "Where did you get your information for this article?"

A Cheshire cat–style grin spread over the man's face and Oaklynn bit the inside of her mouth to restrain herself from wiping off his annoying expression.

Darius tapped the news article's paper copy. "I'm guessing it's true, then, or you wouldn't have trumped up a reason to get me in here. We really have a Suicide Slayer copycat on our hands, don't we?"

"We can't comment on an ongoing investigation." Eldon folded his arms across his chest, tapping his index finger on his bicep. "I'll ask again, who's your source?"

"Well, just like you can't talk about the case, I cannot reveal my source." His earlier grin turned dark. "Two can play at this game, Officers."

Clearly, they would get nowhere with this man. Time to change tactics. Oaklynn dug deep to soften her expression even though the man rubbed her the wrong way. "Mr. Wesley—"

"It's Darius to you." He moved closer. "Can I call you Oaklynn?"

Oaklynn's breakfast turned sour in her stomach. Something about this man reminded her of Aaron Crowder. She visegripped the table's edges as she fought the sudden fight-or-flight response growing inside her body.

She inhaled, counting to five to calm her nerves. "Mr. Wesley, it's Constable Brock." Another breath. "Can you tell us if you noticed anything suspicious at the scene yesterday? Anyone acting strangely?"

His eyes widened. "You think the killer was there, don't you?"

Eldon plunked back down in the chair. "Answer the constable's question."

Darius cracked his knuckles as if it would assist his mental process. "You didn't let me get close, but now that I think of it, one person seemed out of place."

"Who?" Oaklynn asked.

"A girl in the crowd. She kept moving places among those gathered."

Kimi. Not the answer Oaklynn hoped he'd give. They were aware of the young girl's situation. "Anyone else?"

"No." He hesitated, then snapped his fingers. "Wait, I saw the coroner's assistant sneak behind their van."

"That's not unusual," Eldon said. "He was probably going to retrieve supplies."

"No, he kept looking around before he disappeared and when he returned, he had nothing in his hands. I just remembered it being odd." He gestured toward the door. "That's all I've got. Am I free to go now?"

"Of course." Oaklynn extracted a business card from her pocket and slid it across the table. "If you think of anything else, or you want to give us a hint of who your source is, please call."

"Sure will." Darius stuffed the card into his pocket, winking on his way out the door.

"Well, he's an interesting guy. He certainly has taken a liking to you." Eldon nabbed his file folder from the table.

Oaklynn stood. "What's your take on what he said about the assistant coroner, Dr. Hancock?"

"Worth investigating, but I am familiar with him. He's legit."

Oaklynn's cell phone buzzed, and she retrieved it from her vest pocket. Caleb. She read his text. Finally, a concrete lead. "Looks like Caleb's sister found something on the SD card. I'm going to run over there. Tell me if you get anything from Dr. Hancock."

"Of course. I'll get Pearl and head out now."

"Pearl?"

"My cruiser."

Oaklynn tilted her head, studying the constable. "Wait, you named your cruiser?"

"Doesn't everyone?"

"Umm…no. Catch you later." She laughed and shook her head before leaving the interrogation room. At least Eldon provided their station with light entertainment in their cloudy criminal world.

Moments later, Oaklynn stepped outside their station's door. She approached her cruiser, placing her fingers under the door handle, and paused. A shudder slammed her chest. Her hand flew to her sidearm as she pivoted, studying her surroundings.

Oaklynn tucked her winter bomber coat snugly around her neck, not to shield herself from the icy wind, but to guard against the overpowering sense of someone's presence.

Watching her every move.

However, the parking lot was empty.

Was she imagining the anxious feelings consuming her nerves? Even after her father's conviction, she lived in constant fear of his retaliation over her betrayal. Especially when he yelled at her in court that he would one day get even. But—she thought she'd dealt with those eerie sensations.

She glanced over her shoulder one last time before jumping into her Charger. *Get a grip. Your past is playing tricks with your mind. Dad is dead. He can't hurt you anymore.*

If so, why couldn't she shake the feeling her father wasn't done with her yet?

Oaklynn knocked on Mikaela's front door twenty minutes later. She noticed the camera above the light. Maxwell Greene's daughter had a state-of-the-art security system. How did the perp get by her cameras last night? Before she could contemplate an answer, the door whipped open.

Lilly Cox stood in the entranceway dressed in pajama bottoms, a fluffy bright red sweatshirt, and buffalo plaid slippers. "Hi, Constable Brock. Come on in."

"Lilly, it's Oaklynn and you're looking as pretty as ever. Love your pj's. No school today?" Oaklynn entered the bungalow and stomped the snow from her boots.

The teen scrunched up her nose. "Hardly pretty. PD day." She closed the door. "Uncle Caleb and Mom are in the dining room. I'm off to my bedroom. I hear Nancy Drew calling my name."

"You love Nancy too? I devoured her books when I was a kid."

"Mom calls them 'oldies but goodies.'" She pointed to the wall hooks. "You can hang your coat there." Lilly proceeded down the hall.

Oaklynn wiggled out of her coat and hung it on the middle peg. "Thanks. Enjoy Nancy's sleuthing."

Lilly turned. "By the way, Uncle Caleb is single and handsome. Don't let his giant persona scare you." She smirked. "He's really a teddy bear."

She liked this girl's spunky demeanor even though romance was the farthest thing from Oaklynn's mind. "Aren't you a little young to be playing matchmaker?"

"Nope." She giggled and disappeared into a bedroom.

Oaklynn sauntered into the dining room.

Caleb looked up from a pile of photos, his gorgeous green eyes shining under the chandelier. "Hey there."

Oaklynn halted. Lilly was right about one thing—her uncle was definitely handsome.

Oaklynn swallowed the sudden wave of attraction clogging her throat and sat beside him. *Remember your secrets. No man would want you if they knew the truth.* "Hey, guys. Quick question. How did last night's perp get by your cameras?"

"I checked the footage. The camera's angle pointed to the

brick wall." Mic frowned. "The suspect must have knocked its vantage point."

"Interesting." Oaklynn folded her hands. "What did you find on the card, Mic?"

Mikaela picked up a photo and passed it to her. "I salvaged the pictures off the SD card and printed them."

"That's awesome." Oaklynn turned to Caleb. "You were right. She *is* good."

"Told ya." Caleb winked before folding his muscular arms.

Oaklynn's heartbeat escalated, but not from terror. For some reason, his wink didn't bother her and that realization scared her more than the criminals she'd put behind bars. She returned her gaze to the pictures.

Mic chuckled. "Well, not really. I have yet to salvage the video, but I'm working on it."

"You'll get it. I appreciate all your help."

Caleb's sister stood. "Would you like some coffee, Oaklynn?"

"Yes, thank you."

Mic nodded and left the room.

Oaklynn aligned some photos in front of her. "I'm guessing these are Light Paragons members. What do you think, Caleb?"

"I agree. Do you recognize any of them?"

Oaklynn inspected each closely. She tapped one. "That's the mayor's daughter. He was right. She was mixed up with them."

"I'm guessing that's what got her killed."

"Well, Mayor Stevens is adamant she didn't kill herself and the coroner is reopening the case. Hopefully, we'll hear more soon." Oaklynn flipped through the photos and stopped at one hidden beneath. "Oh, no."

Caleb leaned closer, his woodsy scent tickling Oaklynn's nose. "What is it?"

She tapped on a male's face. "Sergeant Rollins's son, Isaac. Rick has suspected his son of getting involved with local bank robberies."

"Right, they found his prints at the last one." Caleb picked up the photo, staring at it closely. "You called Sergeant Rollins 'Rick.' Are you two close?"

Oaklynn flinched at her slip of the tongue. Even though she'd only known the man for a few months, he'd been more of a father to her than her own. "Let's just say he took me under his wing when I first moved here six months ago. I didn't know anyone, and he's been kind to help me get up to speed with the town and introduce me to the community."

"Why did he put you as lead on this case since you're so new?"

"Probably to give me a shot to prove myself." She took the picture from Caleb. "This is going to break his heart."

Mic reentered the room and placed two mugs down.

"Thanks." Oaklynn took a sip. "Caleb, I'm wondering if the bank robberies are related."

"Perhaps. Some cults live off the land, while others need money to fund their community."

"We need to get Isaac out before anything happens to him. I'm going to see if Dalton brought Isaac into the station." She sent the text inquiring on Isaac's whereabouts. Seconds later, a reply appeared on her screen.

No sign of him. Mrs. Rollins said he hasn't been home in a couple of days.

"That's not good." She turned her screen toward Caleb.

"He could be living at the cult compound now. To keep things quiet."

Oaklynn sipped the orange-flavored coffee, letting the taste linger on her tongue. "Caleb, how do you suggest we go in? I'm sure we can't just storm their grounds. Well, especially when we don't even know where it is."

"I have an idea." Caleb tugged on his sister's arm. "You're not gonna like this, but Lilly has found favor with the group."

Mic's eyes widened. "What does 'find favor' mean?"

"Don't get mad, but Lilly went to a meeting last night and got an invite to join them through playing a video game."

Mic shot upright. "What?" She swayed from her quick movement.

Caleb hopped to his feet and brought his sister into an embrace. "It's okay, sis. She's promised me she'll stay away and I believe her. Don't get mad. She's a good kid that got tricked by the game cults play."

Oaklynn folded her arms over her chest. "So, you're telling me they're luring their flock through video games?"

Caleb released his sister. "It doesn't surprise me with all the hackers and scams going on out there these days." He raised his index finger. "But I think we can use Lilly to get an invite."

"No way. You're not involving my daughter." Mic placed her hands on her hips, her eyes glaring at her brother. "You of all people should know it's too dangerous."

"Mic, I would never put her in harm's way. I would pose as her on the video game to get—"

"I can do it, Mom."

The group turned.

Lilly had approached in stealth mode, holding her Nancy Drew book.

Mic rushed forward. "No way, Lilly Beth. I won't let you."

Lilly set the novel on the corner hutch and entered the dining room. "I'm not going anywhere. Uncle Caleb scared me from ever getting involved with this group through his story. I can help get him in."

Oaklynn finished her coffee and rose. "Wait, Lilly. Caleb said you were at a meeting last night. Where was that, and what did they say to you?"

Mic grabbed Lilly's arm. "You were supposed to be at Callie's all night."

Lilly freed herself from her mother's grip. "Mom, we went for hot chocolate and it was only an hour." She turned to Oaklynn. "Penny's Café on Main Street. They just talked about how their group loves to spread God's love to the community, but they invited me to another meeting."

Caleb added coffee to his mug. "Did they say where?"

"No, only that an official invite would come through the game."

"What video game do they use?" Oaklynn withdrew her notebook and pen from her vest pocket.

"A new one called *Parlight Warriors*. Callie told me about it."

Oaklynn scribbled the name on her page. "Did they say why they're using this method of communication? Seems odd and secretive."

"I thought that too, but the guy said they wanted to help people who were hooked on to gaming, so it was an easy way to reach out."

"Lilly, what's this guy's name?" Caleb shot Oaklynn a look.

A look that screamed caution. He didn't want his niece involved any more than necessary.

"Only said his first name—Buck." She poked at the pictures. "Wait." She pointed. "That's him."

Oaklynn stared at the man's face. "This guy looks familiar, but I can't place him. It'll come—"

Her radio squawked. "10-45 at Kenorapeake Falls Bible Chapel. All units respond."

Oaklynn tensed at Dispatch's call.

Sudden death.

"Wait, that's Chloe and Rick's church." A coincidence?

Something told Oaklynn that wasn't the case.

Chapter Eight

Caleb clung to the armrest as Oaklynn took a sharp right at an accelerated speed. Her cruiser swerved, but she compensated quickly before stepping on the gas. Her intent was clear. Get to the suicide scene as fast as possible, but the roads were still messy after last night's storm. "These conditions are dicey." They had driven together to discuss the information they'd discovered about The Light Paragons.

"We have another suicide on our hands and I'm concerned we're gonna have a crowd there with all the rumors flying about the Suicide Slayer. Thanks to Darius." Her lips flattened. "Eldon is on his way too, but I want to help contain the situation."

Caleb opened the folder sitting on his lap and lifted out one of the pictures his sister had printed. "Tell me about Sergeant Rollins's son, Isaac. What do you know about him?"

"He turned eighteen six months ago and, according to Rick, something changed almost instantly." She groaned. "Apparently, he was always a good church kid and even talked about becoming a youth pastor."

"Odd. So what happened?"

She shrugged. "Only thing Rick knows is Isaac started hanging around a different crowd than his church buddies. I'm guessing now it was The Light Paragons recruiting him since he's a huge gamer." She pointed to the picture. "That proves it has to be."

"Do you think they targeted him because he's the sergeant's son?"

She banged the steering wheel. "Possibly. They probably think his father passed down his police smarts to his kid and so he knows how to evade the force during the robberies. They also may use Isaac to keep tabs on police activity."

Caleb raised the next picture and one stuck to the back fell to the floorboard. He scooped it up and sucked in a breath.

Two evil eyes leered at him from behind a white masquerade mask, pummeling Caleb back into a dark hole.

He dropped the picture like he'd been playing a game of hot potato as the horrifying eyes flung him into a memory where the Purity Flock's Reverend had shown a flash of his true nature and the power he had over his flock. A power Caleb had wanted.

"Caleb!"

Oaklynn's loud voice filtered through the fog consuming him.

He cleared his throat. "Sorry, what did you say?" *Lord, protect me from the evil.*

A prayer he said frequently after Maxwell saved him from the Reverend. All the talk of cults had shoved him back into the darkness, where he vowed never to go again. But how could he help with this case without going there? He had to reach out to his prayer warriors for protection—the Canadian Watchers Squad.

"We're here." She parked behind another cruiser, cutting off the sirens and lights. "Where did you just go?"

"Into a black hole. Thanks for bringing me out." He reached down and picked up the photo. "I didn't see this picture before. It was stuck to another and took me back to a scene when I first joined the cult and felt the leader's evil. His power. A power I wanted." His fingers shook as he passed it to her. "Bad, I know." *Get a grip, Caleb. He can't hurt you any longer, remember?*

"I'm sorry you went through that. I'd like to hear more." Oaklynn took the photo and a pinched expression crossed over her pretty face.

One revealing to Caleb that perhaps she'd also seen the same evil.

Something they both had in common.

Caleb squeezed her shoulder. "What is it?"

Oaklynn blinked rapidly and handed him the photo. "Nothing. I need to get to the scene. Be sure to stay behind me. This is an official crime scene, and Chloe will be here shortly. Let's find out what's going on." She shoved her gloves on and left her cruiser.

"Got it." Caleb stuffed the picture into the folder. *Lord, she's suffering. Show me how I can help.*

Caleb ignored the arctic air and trudged through the snow on the chapel's front yard toward where Constable Spearing was stringing yellow caution tape. His broad frame blocked the view of the body.

"No!" Oaklynn's cry stopped Caleb in his tracks.

He picked up the pace and reached her side.

Spearing finished with the tape, pocketing the roll. "He's gone, Constable Brock. I checked for a pulse. I've called in Chloe and the coroner. They should be here soon. I'm going to ensure the folks gathered stay back." He squeezed her shoulder before walking to the parking lot.

Oaklynn stared at the victim.

Isaac Rollins—her sergeant's son.

★ ★ ★

Gone? Oaklynn hadn't really known Isaac Rollins well, but his father meant the world to her and this news would devastate him. *Oh, Isaac. What did you do to yourself?* She examined Isaac's body. He lay slumped against a tree close to the church, his bare arms positioned wide and his bloody hands facing outward. His legs were crossed at the ankles, completing the cross-like image. The body's resemblance to a crucifixion and its placement next to a church wasn't lost on Oaklynn.

Isaac's blue lips revealed he'd been deceased for hours, probably in the middle of the night. Deep cuts on his wrist told her the cause of death, but whether the manner of death was suicide remained to be seen. She'd wait for Dr. Patterson's findings before coming to conclusions. However, a picture pinned to her corkboard wall in her basement's secret room seeped into her mind. A body positioned in the same format—to the letter. Suspicion bristled the hairs at her neck and screamed one thing.

A copycat Suicide Slayer murdered Isaac. This was not self-inflicted.

Heat flushed her face even in the brisk temperatures and she clenched her gloved fingers into fists. Someone was imitating her father's kills, but the question was...

Why?

And—who?

"What are your initial thoughts?"

She startled.

Caleb's question stirred her from her observations. She didn't notice his approach.

She stood. "I hate to jump to conclusions, but I'm pretty sure this was not suicide."

Caleb walked around Isaac's body, providing a wide berth so as to not contaminate the scene. "Agree. Someone wouldn't slit their wrists and then position themselves in this precise manner. You thinking copycat?"

Eldon approached the duo. "Crime scene is secure." He eyed the body. "I believe it is indeed our copycat's work."

Oaklynn raised her hands, palms out. "Let's not be hasty in that conclusion or say it outside this circle. I don't want reporters getting wind of us thinking we have a copycat. It will cause a panic within our community. We need to wait for an official report from Dr. Patterson. Where is he, anyway?" Oaklynn searched the parking lot and the street for the coroner's van.

"On his way." Eldon raised his cell phone. "Palmer texted me earlier and said a shunting train blocked their route, but it finally passed."

Oaklynn tilted her head. "You're on a first-name basis with Dr. Hancock?"

"We play hockey together. I talked to him earlier. His alibi checks out." Eldon put on his hat.

At the mention of the coroner's team, their van pulled into the parking lot and the doctors climbed out.

Eldon gestured toward the duo. "There they are. You call the sergeant yet, Brock? Probably best he hear about his son's death from you."

Oaklynn moaned and unclipped her cell phone, ignoring the radio on her shoulder. This wasn't a conversation for the radio waves. "You're right, and I best get it over with. Eldon, who called 911?"

He gestured toward a man and woman huddled together under the church's entrance. "Pastor and his wife found the body. They're pretty shaken up." He pointed to a growing crowd and a news van that had gathered in the lot. "I'll go contain these people and stop Darius in his tracks." He left.

"Caleb, can you speak with the pastor and his wife while I call Sergeant Rollins? Your background can help."

"Sure." Caleb trudged through the snow toward the pair.

Oaklynn selected her sergeant's name from her contact list

and walked to the property line, out of anyone's earshot. She looked upward. *Give me the words.*

Not that she prayed to God anymore, but she'd take any help at this point. She willed strength into her voice and hit the button just as an overpowering feeling of being watched elevated her pulse. She straightened and scanned the property, then the street, searching in all directions. But nothing appeared out of the ordinary.

You're imagining things. Again.

A car door slammed, bringing her back to the task at hand. She shifted her gaze toward the parking lot as she waited for her sergeant to answer. Chloe exited her forensic van and waved to Oaklynn.

"I've been waiting for your call," Sergeant Rollins said. "Tell me about the scene."

Oaklynn nodded to Chloe and concentrated on her conversation. "Horrible news." More than horrible. She bit her lip, struggling with how to phrase her next words.

"Another sketchy suicide?"

Oaklynn turned toward his son's body and observed Dr. Patterson examining Isaac's wounds. "Yes. Rick, I'm not sure how to tell you this."

"Spit it out."

"I'm sorry," she whispered. "It's Isaac. He's gone." She hated to give him the news over the phone, but knew he'd hear the word before she could return to the station.

A crash penetrated the airwaves. "Sir, you there?"

Silence.

Then muffled sobs.

"I'm so sorry." Oaklynn repeated her condolences and clamped her eyes shut. She hated this part of her job. Giving news to loved ones that their family member had passed never got easy. "Tell me what I can do for you."

"Catch whoever did this. My son did not kill himself." After a sniffle, he drew in an audible breath. "I'm coming to the scene. I need to see this."

Oaklynn's eyes flung open and she glanced once again at the tree where Isaac lay. "No, sir, you don't. Go to the morgue instead. We can handle this."

An engine roared to life through the phone. "Not happening. On my way. But, Oaklynn, contain this. I don't want my wife hearing this news from anyone but me." He severed the call.

A bulldog spirit locked her limbs. The remorse in Rick's voice added to her drive to find the killer and stop him before more were hurt.

And her knowledge of a serial killer was something she knew firsthand. Only she could stop them, but first she had to go to a place she'd tried hard to avoid—her father's serial killer mind.

But to catch one, she had to become like one.

She pocketed her phone before approaching Chloe. "Just spoke with the sergeant. He's on his way. I tried to stop him, but couldn't. Not that I blame him. If it was me, I'd want to come too."

"Agreed." Chloe gestured toward the coroner team. "This hits too close to home, Oaklynn. First you're targeted with the decapitated doll, and now our sergeant's son? What's going on?"

"Not sure, but you're right." Oaklynn fisted her gloved hands at her sides. "Whoever did this will pay for attacking one of our own." Wait, did she say that out loud? *Rein it in, Oaklynn.* "Sorry, I mean, we will arrest this person." A shiver attacked her entire body. The reccurring question she'd fought when she discovered her father was a serial killer pummeled into her head.

Could I kill like Dad?

"Are we sure it's not suicide?"

Oaklynn gritted her teeth, attempting to silence her dark thoughts. *You're not like him. You're not like him.* She played her mantra in her head and refocused on Chloe's question. "Not for sure, but that's what my gut is telling me. I'm going to chat with Dr. Patterson now. Caleb is speaking with the couple who called 911."

Chloe flung her evidence bag over her shoulder before reaching into the back of her van. "I also wanted to tell you the results came back on the blood on the doll."

"What did they say?" Oaklynn's breath snagged in her throat as she waited for her friend's response.

"Pig's blood. Caleb was correct in his assumption. You need to trust his gut."

"Yeah, well, he holds secrets."

Chloe cocked her head, placing her hands on her hips. "And you don't? The Beast knows his stuff."

"The Beast?"

"The nickname the other constables gave him. Oh…and watch your back with Nika. She's out to tame the Beast."

Figures. The female constable sunk her claws into any handsome man crossing her path. Not that Oaklynn cared. She wasn't interested. "On that note, I'll leave you to collecting evidence. Catch you later."

Chloe hung her camera around her neck. "You got it."

Oaklynn approached Isaac's body, but remained outside the tape Eldon had raised. While the crime scene itself was the police's jurisdiction, the body was the coroner's. Something Dr. Patterson always repeated. "Any initial findings, gentlemen?"

The quirky coroner stood. "I hate to speculate without a thorough examination, but the deep lacerations on his wrists caused him to bleed out quickly." He circled his raised index finger around the scene. "And this positioning suggests something other than suicide."

"Agreed, but until we receive your report, we won't release any information."

Caleb returned to Oaklynn's side. "I found out something interesting from the pastor and his wife. They—"

"Dr. Patterson, look at this." Dr. Hancock raised Isaac's T-shirt at his waistline, exposing his abdomen.

The chief coroner squatted in front of the body. "Oh my."

"What is it?" Oaklynn held her breath as she waited for more bad news.

"Get pictures of this, Dr. Hancock." Dr. Patterson turned to Oaklynn and Caleb. "Definitely not suicide. Your copycat signed the body." He adjusted his position, revealing a dried blood etching on Isaac's stomach.

Oaklynn leaned closer.

Luke 22:48

Someone engraved a small "SS" in the skin beside the scripture.

Thunder ignited fire into Oaklynn's throbbing temples. Sweat flushed her body despite the frigid temperatures. The message confirmed her original fear.

Someone was indeed copying the Suicide Slayer.

The Protégé smirked and slithered his tongue across his teeth. He edged out from the hiding spot across the street from the church he'd chosen to display his latest creation and kneeled in front of a large rock, positioning his rifle on top. He peered through the scope and adjusted the sight. It would be so easy to take them all out right now, but that wasn't part of his plan. Good, they found his message. *Wait till you find the other one, Lynny. It's for you.* He wrung his gloved hands together in anticipation of her reaction. He loved toying with her emotions.

He shifted the scope and caught the pastor and his wife in his crosshairs. Kenorapeake Falls Bible Chapel and other churches were forced to face consequences for spreading lies about The Light Paragons. It was why he'd chosen churches to display his creations.

No one speaks out about their flock.

Isaac Rollins learned the lesson the hard way. The young man had taunted the Queen Bee at the supper table and claimed he'd reached his limit, warning he'd reveal their secrets.

The Protégé seized the opportunity to take Isaac out. It would bring him one step closer to the elite lead disciple position he'd been vying for. Being in the leader's inner circle was where he'd get his power. Power was what she promised those who graduated into her clique. Plus, using his mentor's positions played on Lynny's emotional state.

Made her believe her father had returned from the dead to haunt her—so to speak.

But she almost caught him earlier. *You have good instincts. Just like your father.*

Lynny had obviously sensed the Protégé's presence. She turned abruptly and nearly caught him before he ducked behind a tree.

He pounded on his leg. He needed to be more careful if his plan was going to work. His second message to Constable Oaklynn Brock would send her over the edge.

And he'd be there to catch her when she fell.

Chapter Nine

Caleb caught hold of Oaklynn's arm, preventing her from falling. The message engraved on Isaac's body solidified his death was murder and not suicide. The copycat killer no longer kept the manner of death a secret, which told Caleb he—or she—wanted to taunt the police. What did that say about this new Suicide Slayer killer?

Oaklynn's contorted expression revealed her angst, and Caleb guessed it had more to do with the message than the death of her sergeant's son. Something had shifted in her demeanor since they'd arrived.

Determination, perhaps?

"What do you make of this message, Oaklynn?"

Her eyes deviated from the body and met Caleb's, his query obviously forcing her from whatever thoughts held her captive. "The killer isn't hiding any longer. That tells me they're getting bolder. Which means they'll get sloppy. That's what I'm counting on, because I will catch this person. My scripture verse recollection is shaky. What does Luke 22:48 say?"

"Judas ushered the guards into the garden and Jesus asked him if he's there to betray him with a kiss. I'm paraphrasing, of course."

She scrunched her nose up.

A car door slammed. Sergeant Rollins flew out of his cruiser and barreled toward them.

Caleb noted the man's brokenhearted expression and slumped shoulders. His body language thrust Caleb back to the scene of his wife's car crash.

The accident that took their daughter's life and landed his wife in prison. How Paige walked away from the crash still baffled him. She'd been drinking and driving which had caused her to run a red light, killing a truck driver. Police had later charged her with dangerous driving causing death.

Oaklynn puffed out a sigh. "This is gonna be tricky. The sergeant insisted he come to see Isaac. I could use your help with him."

"Of course." Something Maxwell Greene said to him after Aiyana's funeral filtered through Caleb's head.

Son, we don't understand why, but sometimes God allows difficult circumstances in our lives to not only teach us something, but to help others.

Caleb still wrestled with the why even though it had been eighteen months since Aiyana's death, but right now he knew exactly what Sergeant Rollins was going through and could sympathize. He sent up a quick prayer, asking for guidance, and followed Oaklynn to intercept her supervisor.

She took Sergeant Rollins's hand in hers. "Rick, I really don't think you want to see Isaac in his present condition. Let us handle this and wait until Dr. Patterson is finished at the morgue."

Aiyana's twisted little body flashed in Caleb's mind. "She's right, sir. Trust me when I say this. You won't be able to forget the image of your child's death."

Oaklynn shot him a pinched look.

Time to explain about Aiyana in order to help the sergeant and make them trust his judgment. "I lost my five-year-old daughter in a car crash and I too went to the scene. I can't get the image of how I found her out of my head. It will play havoc and there's no coming back from it. Even after months of counseling, I still struggle with the sight and what my ex-wife did to our daughter."

Sergeant Rollins yanked his hand away from Oaklynn's. "But I have to see him."

"Sir, please—"

"Oaklynn, don't stop me from seeing my son." He trudged through the deep snow toward Isaac's body.

"Thanks for trying, Caleb. In the short time I've known him, I've learned when he makes his mind up, there's no stopping him." She brushed his arm. "I'm truly sorry about your daughter. I'd love to hear more about her."

"Thank you. Later." He gestured toward the crime scene. "Let's go help contain this, shall we?"

Oaklynn glanced toward the street and stiffened.

"What is it?" He looked in the same direction. "Do you see something?"

"No. I just have this uncanny feeling we're being watched." She hit her radio button. "Constable Spearing, can you check the perimeter and include the properties across the street?"

"Already did that," he replied from the other end of the parking lot.

"Please do it again. I want to ensure no one is out there. I need to attend to Sergeant Rollins or I would do it."

Even in the distance, Caleb noted Spearing's headshake. Clearly, the constable didn't like being second-guessed.

"Copy." Spearing finished his conversation with a reporter before sprinting across the street.

Oaklynn's gaze followed the constable. "He doesn't like me telling him what to do."

"How long has he been on KFPD?"

"Longer than I have, so that's why he's got his knickers in a knot over Sergeant Rollins putting me as lead on this case." She proceeded toward the sergeant who had dropped to his knees close to his son's body.

Caleb followed. "Well, in his defense, isn't it odd the sergeant would do that? Is there a specific reason Rollins put you in charge?"

She halted and turned, eyes flashing. "Why would you ask that? I already told you that he probably did it to give me a shot to prove myself."

"Just seems peculiar since you're new to the department."

"And I'm a woman?"

Ugh! He didn't mean to touch on a nerve. *Smart, Caleb.* They were getting along and he just ruined it. "I'm sorry. Not my business, and for the record, no, not because you're a woman. I've worked closely with many women while I was in the military and saw them drop a man twice their size in seconds. Just trying to look at it from Spearing's point of view."

Her fiery chocolate brown eyes softened. "Sorry for being so sensitive. I've had some unpleasant experiences at my former station. Truth be told, I'm not sure why Rick chose me."

At the mention of his name, Sergeant Rollins let out a heart-wrenching sob and Oaklynn darted to his side, dropping beside him. She gathered him into her arms.

The intimate action revealed Oaklynn and Sergeant Rollins's close relationship. Could that be why he had given her the lead or was it something more?

Caleb remained in the background as the duo spoke to the coroner. He'd give them their space. Plus, he wanted to check on Mic and Lilly. He dug his phone out of his pocket and hit Mic's number.

"Bro, what's going on? There's lots of chatter on the police band about another death." Trepidation laced Mic's tone.

Not that he blamed her. The Kenorapeake Falls community had been hit hard. Caleb explained to her as much as he could concerning Isaac's body. After all, she was the one who had uncovered the pictures that placed the sergeant's son among the cult. He checked his watch. Midafternoon. Where had the day gone? "Are you and Lilly okay? I sensed tension between you earlier."

"Just teenage growing pains." She hissed out a breath. "Dad called me about the meeting tonight. He keeps bugging me to come, but you know I can't leave my home."

Caleb squeezed his eyes shut and prayed for his sister. He'd been working with Mic, hoping to bring her out of hiding, but the decapitated doll had cowered her further into the safety of her Fort Knox home.

"Sis, I realize you've been through a lot, but until we face our fears head-on, they'll never go away. Remember, God calls us to walk through them with Him."

"You sound like Dad. It's just easier said than done."

Oh, how much Caleb knew that to be true. He had struggled— and still did—with everything he'd been through. "I know all too well, sis. Praying for you."

Caleb opened his eyes and caught Spearing trotting back across the road toward the crime scene. His tense expression told Caleb the officer had found something. "I gotta run. Talk later, okay? Love you."

"Love you more." She ended the call.

Caleb smiled at their normal banter. Of all of his siblings, he was the closest to Mic. While the others had been through rough patches, Mic related to him the best. Even though Caleb and the others got along, there still was almost a competitive rivalry between them. Something Caleb was working to end. The more well-known the team became, the more they would need to remain a powerful and united front. Caleb understood from his time with special forces, there was no room for division, or someone could be injured—or killed.

He set aside thoughts of the Canadian Watchers Squad and approached Spearing, who had reached Oaklynn and their sergeant. The pair stood.

Caleb studied their faces. "What's going on?"

"Oaklynn, you were right. Someone was out there. I found their tracks. Imprint in the snow tells me they'd been kneeling in front of a large rock, and—" Spearing eyed their sergeant, then Isaac's body.

Rollins rubbed his tears away with the back of his hand. "What is it, Constable? Don't hold back. I want answers."

"I found a long narrow impression in the snow on top of the rock." He tapped on his cell phone. "I took a picture."

Caleb leaned in for a better look. The mark, along with the indentation of what appeared to be someone kneeling, told Caleb one thing. "He watched through a riflescope."

Spearing tucked his phone back into his pocket. "But they didn't take a shot. Why?"

"Because he's toying with us." Oaklynn's words came out in a whispered, angry statement.

"And he wants us to know it." One thing Caleb guessed to be true was that this copycat excelled at manipulation.

Oaklynn fought to silence her pounding heart rate. The copycat had been watching them. Just like her father once admitted to doing after he'd been arrested and provided the police with his full confession. He'd left the bodies in different positions and observed the crime scene through his riflescope just because he wanted to relish in his accomplishments of evading law enforcement's grasp. The newspaper article had reported Aaron Crowder had also bragged about talking to the police at scenes, giving them false information. At his trial, he taunted police, stating if it hadn't been for his meddling daughter ratting him out, they never would have caught him. *I was good at deceiving everyone.*

She pushed her anger aside and turned to Eldon. "Can you work with Constables Dalton and Crabb? Get them to do a thorough search of this area and talk to the crowd. I'll stay here with Chloe to keep the scene secure. I don't want anything happening to her while she finishes her investigation."

"Copy." He pressed his shoulder radio button and walked away.

The coroners placed Isaac into a body bag, the zipping motion echoing across the property. Or at least it seemed that way. Oaklynn bit the inside of her mouth to curb the anger toward the teen's killer. The killer who appeared to be mimicking every aspect of her father's crimes. She had to remain calm for the sake of the case—and for her sergeant. But one thing was certain—she would find the person responsible.

Dr. Patterson approached the group. "Sergeant Rollins, I'm so sorry for your loss. I promise you I'll do everything in my power to find out exactly what happened to your son." He addressed Oaklynn. "Talk later." He and Dr. Hancock loaded Isaac's body into their van and left.

Rick marched into Oaklynn's personal space, waggling his finger in her face. "You catch this person. Whatever it takes, you hear me? Promise?"

She analyzed her sergeant's rugged, handsome face. His normally bright eyes turned dark and clouded, his forehead plagued with angry wrinkles.

Yes, for him and her team, she'd step into the evil abyss of her father's mind.

Oaklynn rolled her shoulders. "I promise."

His eyes pooled with unshed tears. "I understand what that means for you, Oaklynn, and I'm sorry to make you go there."

She rubbed both of his arms before bringing him into an embrace. "You're worth the risk of the darkness," she whispered, shutting her eyes to stop the tears. "You've been more of a father to me than he ever was." She kept her voice low, not wanting to reveal her background to the Watcher standing nearby.

Rick broke from her hug, holding her at arm's length. "Time for me to go home to Becky. My wife needs to hear this from me." He puffed out a ragged breath, its vapor lingering in the cold air. "God, give me strength."

"Call me if you need anything, okay? The station has your back."

The sergeant nodded, trudged across the property to his cruiser, and drove out of the lot in the opposite direction of the station.

Oaklynn turned to Caleb. "Do you think Isaac's death is connected to The Light Paragons?"

"High probability since he was in the photos Mic salvaged from the SD card. We can't say for certain without further evidence." He removed his glove and massaged his temples. "What did Rollins mean when he said, 'I know what that means for you' and that he hated to make you go there? Go where?"

Oaklynn cringed. She had hoped Caleb missed Rick's statement, because she wasn't ready to bare all with the man in front of her. His keen sense was impressive. *Think quick.* She hated to lie, but perhaps a half-truth would suffice. "Just some past cases I worked on that nearly sent me over the edge. They happened while I was on the force in Toronto and part of the reason I had to get out of a big city."

"Yeah, I imagine you witnessed lots there."

"Definitely, but I also never dreamed Kenorapeake Falls would be plagued with a serial killer. I guess anything is possible in this darkened world." She gestured toward Chloe as the investigator continued to take pictures of the tree and surrounding area where Isaac was staged. "Chloe has also helped. We hit it off quickly when I started at KFPD. The others—not so much. I'm feeling like I have to show my worth. Perhaps that's why Rick wanted me to lead this investigation. He's always been a huge encouragement to me."

Oaklynn had also guessed the sergeant had suspected something sinister was going on in his town with the suspicious suicides and realized her background would help.

An icy chill snaked down her back as coin-sized snowflakes fluttered to the ground. "Looks like more bad weather is moving into the region. I'm going to tell Chloe about the scene across the street and then how about we take a break for a coffee? Not much more we can do here."

"Sounds good."

Oaklynn turned to leave, but remembered what Caleb had said earlier. "Wait, you mentioned you found out something from the pastor and his wife. What was it?"

"Oh right. Apparently, Isaac told them last Sunday he wanted out of The Light Paragons. They were making him do things he didn't like."

"What?" She clasped Caleb's arm. "Could that have gotten him killed?"

"Possibly."

"Man, this case keeps getting stranger and stranger. Meet you in my cruiser in a minute and we'll go for that coffee. I'm frozen to the bones."

Thirty minutes later, Oaklynn sat across from Caleb and sipped her gingerbread latte. She noticed the two redheads in the corner of the café staring at the former military man. Not that she blamed them. He was eye candy, but Oaklynn still didn't trust him. That didn't stop her curiosity in wanting to find out more about his past and present. "Hey, how tall are you? Six-two?"

"Close. Six-three. Why?"

"Just wondering." She gestured toward the redheads. "Seems you have fans. They're practically frothing at the mouth." She flashed him a smile.

He repaid the gesture with a grin that not only brightened his face, but added lines beside his moss-colored eyes that deepened his appeal.

Oaklynn coughed and covered her mouth to quell the gasp from exposing how his smile had affected her in that instant. *Where did that come from?* She lifted her drink to her trembling lips and sipped, composing herself. "Did you know the constables have labeled you the Beast?"

He huffed. "Not the first time I've been called that. Beast. Giant. Bear. I've heard it all. In fact, my military nickname was Grizzly."

Oaklynn laughed. "Okay, there's got to be a story behind that name. Do tell."

His expression darkened in a split second. "Not a place I like to go to often."

"Sorry. You don't have to say. None of my business." Oaklynn related instantly to him. She was the queen of keeping her past hidden, especially from someone she barely knew.

"It's okay. Just hard to talk about and admit you're named after a bear that can rip you to shreds." He took a drink of his coffee, then ran his finger along the rim. "You see, ever since I was a teenager, I gained a reputation for fighting. I was in a terrible place, and I liked to talk with my fists. Not something I'm proud of."

She harrumphed. "Well, we all have junk in our past we'd like to change." Oops. She hadn't meant to verbalize her thought audibly.

His gaze intensified, as if his eyes burrowed into the depths of her soul. Would he see the darkness she struggled to contain?

Caleb broke their connection and finished his coffee. "I was on a mission shortly after I completed my military training. This was before Briggs. We were on patrol in a small village and we split up, working in pairs. My female partner and I came upon a group of locals attacking two women. They were attempting to kidnap their children. We called for reinforcements and intervened, but one attacker knocked out my partner. I had no choice but to protect not only her but the others. I quickly subdued them and when the rest of the team arrived, all four men lay unconscious. The women equated my protection to a bear safeguarding her cubs. After that, the team nicknamed me Grizzly."

His expression morphed into one she could only read as shame. Guilt.

She placed her hand on his. "But that's a good thing, right? You saved not only those families, but your partner. In my books, that's courage and calls for respect."

He snapped his hand back. "But what you don't know is rage consumed me. I believed God had subdued my fists, but the inner beast emerged with great intensity."

"What if he hadn't, though? Maybe you'd all be dead." Was she saying this to justify the anger brewing inside her ever since she read about her father's death? She too thought she'd dealt with the monster and his frequent visits to the childhood room she hated. A place she never wanted to see again. It held too much darkness. Too much evil.

Her cell phone buzzed, breaking her concentration. She fished it out of her pocket. Dr. Patterson's number appeared on her screen. "Coroner's calling." She hit Answer as dread wormed across her arms. "Dr. Patterson, you done already?" Oaklynn guessed the coroner wouldn't call if it wasn't important.

"Hardly, but I found something unusual you'll want to see. I took a picture. Found it in Isaac's stomach contents. Sending it now."

Her phone dinged.

A foreboding uneasiness locked her muscles as she clicked on the photo.

A crumpled piece of paper appeared with faint lettering. Oaklynn zoomed in, using her index and middle fingers.

Lynny, your secret will come out.

Spots flickered as dizziness threatened to shove her into blackness. Her cell phone slipped from her fingers, landing with a clunk on the table. A thought tumbled into her mind.

The killer knows my nickname.

But how?

Chapter Ten

Caleb tugged on Oaklynn's hand, attempting to snap her out of the trance she'd fallen into. He noted an image of a piece of paper on her cell phone's screen. He slid the device across the table and read the message. "What does this mean?"

"Constable Brock, you there?" The coroner's voice shouted through the speaker.

She straightened and snagged her phone from Caleb, not responding to his question.

Avoidance. A clear sign she was hiding something.

She put the phone back up to her ear. "Sorry, can you bag the note and I'll inform Chloe?" She paused. "Okay, thanks. Appreciate the heads-up." She clicked off, tapped on her phone, and stuffed it into her pocket before lifting her coat from the back of the chair. "We have to go. I'll take you back to Mic's."

"What's going on? Who's Lynny?" Caleb stood and snagged his coat.

"Someone I don't want to talk about."

Caleb balled his fists to curb the frustration from turning

into anything worse. "Wil was right about you. You do have secrets you hold too close and won't let anyone in."

Her eyes flashed venom. "Like you should talk. You have enough of your own. You haven't shared everything, have you, Beast?" Oaklynn pivoted and headed toward the door, thrusting it open.

Now you've gone and done it. Way to go, Grizzly.

Caleb followed the irritated constable out the door, and rushed to her Charger, climbing inside.

She sped out of the café's parking lot and turned right.

The tension inside her cruiser could be cut with a bread knife. Caleb had to right his wrong. "Listen, I'm sorry. I shouldn't have brought up Wil. I'm concerned you're keeping valuable information from me relating to this case."

Her fiery eyes shifted back to the kind ones he suddenly found hard to resist.

"I'm sorry too. I didn't mean to be so defensive." She averted her gaze to the road. "They found that message in Isaac's stomach contents. The killer must have made him swallow it."

"What?" He gathered his next words carefully. "By your reaction, I'm guessing Lynny is your nickname and one you don't like?"

She expelled an audible breath. "Good guess. My mother used to call me that years ago. It took me back to a place I didn't want to revisit."

"So the killer just made Isaac's murder even more personal."

"Yes." Oaklynn took the ramp onto the highway, heading toward Mic's place. She merged with the busy traffic and accelerated.

Caleb looked out the window at the snow-laden trees as they zipped by. The snowfall had added to the already loaded foliage, but he didn't mind. While most of his siblings hated the white stuff, he loved the snow. So did Briggs. Caleb pictured his German shepherd bouncing through the drifts along

Caleb's home an hour from Kenorapeake Falls. The pair had taken many long walks through the forest behind Caleb's four-bedroom log house. He had sold the home he'd lived in with Paige and Aiyana six months ago. He couldn't deal with the memories. His new place far exceeded the amount of space Caleb and his dog needed, but he prayed one day God would provide him with a new family. Even though the pain was still fresh and he wasn't ready for love, he still yearned for it. But his shattered heart wouldn't endure the agony.

He shifted his attention back to Oaklynn. "With all the constables on the force, why do you think the killer has focused on you?"

Her grip visibly tightened on the steering wheel. "Good question. By the way, Eldon has agreed to come to your father's meeting tonight."

Change of subject. Again. Caleb sensed she understood why the killer had targeted her, but clearly wasn't willing to share. Sometimes he hated his ability to read others. *Back down. She needs to trust you first.*

And he, her.

"Good. You live on the north end of Kenorapeake Falls, right?"

"Yes."

"How about I pick you up on my way to Dad's? Save you driving." Plus, he had ulterior motives. He wanted to see where she lived and get to know her better on the short drive to his father's.

"Sounds good. I need to have a quick bite and change out of these clothes." She pulled into his sister's home. "Why aren't you staying at the Greene mansion?"

"Too big for my liking." Truth be told, the spacious estate reminded Caleb too much of the cult compound he'd lived on for almost nine months.

Months of his life he wanted to erase.

"I bought a home about an hour from here. A secluded log house in the woods." He reached for the door handle and turned. "Text me your address. See you in a few hours."

She nodded and pointed. "Looks like you have protection."

A patrol car was parked down the street.

"I'm guessing Dad put some pressure on your sergeant earlier this morning to monitor Mic. He dotes on his little girl."

"Fathers tend to do that. Well, not all." She bit her lip. "See you later."

He left her cruiser and waved as she backed out of the driveway. Her last comment piqued his interest, making him believe she had friction with her father. Caleb wanted to know more.

He trotted up the steps and placed his thumbprint on the screen to unlock his sister's home. He opened the door and stomped the snow from his boots on the welcome mat.

A bark sounded, and seconds later Briggs bounded toward him.

Caleb squatted and let his dog plow into him. The K-9 showered his owner with sloppy kisses. "Hey, boy. Good to see you too." He hugged Briggs. *Thank You God for this amazing animal.*

Briggs had been a comfort to Caleb after Aiyana's death, even more so than the Greene family. They had all meant well, but Caleb had only wanted his furry friend around during the first few weeks after Aiyana's funeral and Paige's arrest.

And God too, of course. Caleb had spent many hours crying out to God, asking why, why, why. Why did he take his precious daughter from him? Even though Caleb didn't receive an audible answer, God finally poured a bucket of peace over him.

A peace that came through prayer warriors' petitions.

Pounding footfalls echoed on the hardwood moments before Mic appeared around the corner. "Caleb, got something for you on that date."

Her cloudy expression told him it wasn't good. "Tell me."

"According to online newspaper articles, that was the date

when Aaron Crowder—aka the Suicide Slayer—was arrested." She handed Caleb her tablet.

A picture of the serial killer appeared. Caleb scanned the article. "Okay, but why would this date terrify Oaklynn?"

Mic shrugged. "Maybe she knew one of his victims."

"Perhaps." Caleb somehow doubted that. He stared at the killer's handsome face.

The man terrified Oaklynn, and Caleb vowed to find out why.

A chill attacked Oaklynn's body even though she huddled next to the roaring fire in the cozy family room of the Greenes' estate. Today's events had not only shaken her to the core with Isaac's death but talk of the Suicide Slayer copycat's previous victims had sent her mind reeling with doubts. Butterflies gnawed at her stomach like a vulture feasting on its prized corpse. She rested her hand on her abdomen, hoping to still the beasts.

Their team now believed all the supposed suicides were the work of this new serial killer. Plaguing questions sat on the tip of Oaklynn's tongue, but she was too scared to ask them.

How were these kills linked to Aaron Crowder's? And why even copy his kills at all if the killer was no longer hiding behind the suicide angle? Oaklynn guessed the copycat had taken a grisly fixation on her father and worshiped him.

Caleb had picked Oaklynn up on time, but his previous pleasant demeanor had shifted in the few hours they'd been apart, making her wonder what happened. When she asked, he'd just explained he was pondering the case.

Oaklynn suspected something else captured his attention, but didn't press him further. Right now, Caleb sat next to her in a plush navy-and-green-plaid recliner. Close enough for her to inhale his gentle woodsy scent, but his mood had built a wall between them, distancing the pair. She thought they had turned a corner after what he'd shared earlier, even after their spat. What had changed?

The front stained-glass oak door opened and closed. Moments later, Maxwell Greene entered the room, followed by three males and one female. The Greene family minus Mikaela, who'd join them via video. Maxwell's Canadian Watchers Squad. The man himself presented a larger-than-life persona because of not only his towering height but his confident demeanor. Even though Maxwell lived in Kenorapeake Falls, Oaklynn had never met him. Time to rectify that and declare her leadership of this case.

She pushed herself upright and strode over to his location, extending her right hand. "Constable Oaklynn Brock, sir. Nice to meet you." She gestured toward Eldon, who sipped on a hot chocolate and stared out the window. "That's Constable Eldon Spearing. Sorry Sergeant Rollins couldn't attend this meeting."

Maxwell's large hand enveloped hers. "Finally nice to meet you, Oaklynn. Can I call you Oaklynn? I want us to feel comfortable together."

"Of course."

Caleb stood and walked to the group. "Oaklynn, I'd like you to meet the squad and my siblings." He slapped a blond's back. "This is Dawson Greene, the criminologist in our group. He's a superb profiler. Good to see you, bro."

Oaklynn shook Dawson's hand. "I've read about you. You used to work with the federal police, didn't you?"

"I did, but now I've joined Dad and these characters. Nice to meet you and Eldon."

Eldon nodded.

Maxwell pointed to the towering, muscular man beside Dawson. "This is Ryker. He's the firefighter in the group, but also the one who keeps us grounded in our faith."

He smiled. "Call me Preach."

"This is Kordell," Caleb said. "He's trained in survival."

"Ma'am. Nice to meet you." He hauled Oaklynn into an embrace.

"Oof." The man's quick action took her by surprise. "Well, then, nice to meet you too." She patted his back.

Caleb chuckled. "Kord is our group hugger. A real teddy bear."

The sole female in the squad stepped forward. "Let her go, Kord." She stuck out her hand. "Hi, Oaklynn. I'm Hayley."

"Pleasure to meet you." Oaklynn's gaze shifted to each CWS member, mentally rhyming off their duties, then turned back to Hayley. "So, you must be the sniper Caleb told us about?"

"Yes, but I also specialize in geographic profiling." She pointed to the gigantic TV screen. "Where's Mic?"

Caleb snatched the remote from a nearby table and pressed the power button, bringing the monitor to life. "She's here. Just forgot to turn her on. Sorry, Mic."

"No prob. Hey, everyone. Glad you all made it in safely. I've missed you so much." A tear trickled down her cheek.

Hayley grazed her finger along Mic's face on the screen as if the two were in the same room. "Sis, what's wrong?"

Oaklynn swallowed the thickening in her throat at the intimate moment between sisters. Something Oaklynn had longed for all her life. A sister.

Mic smiled and wiped her eyes. "Let's chat later tonight. What did I miss?"

"Nothing yet." Maxwell extended his arms. "Have a seat, gang. I wanted to bring us together because this case has now captured national attention, thanks to that reporter's article about a Suicide Slayer copycat. We need to get it resolved quickly. The mayor is pressuring me since he hired us to help the KFPD." He turned to Oaklynn. "Can you update us? The mayor and the police board have given our squad full clearance to all information."

"Yes, sir." She turned to Eldon. "Let's do this together."

He placed his mug on a nearby end table and stood. "You got it."

Oaklynn returned to her spot by the fireplace and lifted out a file folder from her bag. "I brought crime scene pictures." She spent the next fifteen minutes going over the case, including their suspicions of a copycat. "Eldon, anything to add?"

"Only that we're still looking into backgrounds of each victim to determine if we can find a link, but as of right now, the only thing connecting them is The Light Paragons."

"Do you know that for sure?" Dawson extended his hand to Oaklynn. "Can I see the folder?"

She complied. "Mic has found pictures linking the mayor's daughter, Missy, and Isaac to the cult. The first victim is still a mystery."

"Is there anything different about his suicide?" Dawson leafed through the pages in the folder, running his finger along each before flipping to the next.

Oaklynn caught Caleb's attention and tilted her head.

"He's speed-reading. One of his many gifts. Mic, can you bring up the pics from Missy's camera card? I want the others to see what we're dealing with concerning The Light Paragons."

"Just a sec." Mic tapped on keys. Photos displayed on one half of the screen. "Done."

Dawson raised a hand. "I want to know more about the first two victims. Oaklynn, can you give me your assessment?"

"You'll notice from the file the first male victim was a forty-eight-year-old mail carrier. Found with a bullet to his head and a suicide note on his computer." She mentally pictured the next victim's pretty face and grimaced. "Sixteen-year-old girl—the mayor's daughter—was discovered behind the high school with her wrists cut. They located a suicide note in her locker. Apparently, a boy broke her heart. Mayor and Mrs. Stevens refused to believe she killed herself. However, the coroner cited suicide as the manner of death. Case closed."

"And why the mayor called Dad." Hayley joined Dawson and looked at the file over his shoulder. "What did the other victim's note reveal?"

"That he had a gambling debt and had drained the family's finances. He couldn't bear what he'd done and begged his wife's forgiveness. Constables looked into the validity of his claims, and their bank accounts were overdrawn. His wife had no idea he gambled. Said he was the family's bookkeeper and always said they were fine."

Kordell crossed his arms. "So, you had no reason to suspect the suicides were murder. Is the coroner reopening their cases?"

"Yes."

"What about the other deaths?" Ryker asked. "Were there suicide notes?"

Oaklynn rubbed her right temple. "None that we found."

"So if the first two weren't suicides, the killer changed his MO." Dawson continued to look at the information in the folder.

"Agreed. When do you think you'll be able to provide the updated profile?"

"I'll study this tonight and give it to your team soon. Sound good?"

"Thank you." A picture caught Oaklynn's eye, and she inched closer to the screen, pointing to the one in question. "Mic, can you enlarge the photo in the bottom right corner?"

Eldon joined her and leaned in. "What do you see?"

The single picture replaced all the others. Oaklynn turned to Dawson. "Can you hand me the file?"

He complied.

She turned to the report of the first victim, drawing in a ragged breath. "Well, I'll be." She held the photo up. "Peter Ratchet, our first victim. He was also a cult follower." Oaklynn pointed to the picture of the cult gathering on the TV monitor. "There he is, next to Missy."

Eldon whistled. "Eagle eye, Brock. Good job." He nudged her.

Maxwell scowled. "Caleb, what's your take on this new cult? Any similarities to the one you were involved with?"

"Yes, but some differences. It appears as if The Light Paragons are finding their members through the video game called *Parlight Warriors*. They're reaching out to gamers."

Ryker moved to the fireplace, stabbed the poker at the coals, and added another log. "Isn't that a fairly new game?"

"It is," Mic said. "Came on the market a year ago."

"That's probably not a coincidence." Oaklynn faced Eldon. "Did the team find anything about the game's origin yet?"

"I just found out before I arrived that the game is owned by a company we've linked to Victoria Dutton. She's the sister of Kassandra Nason who is a guidance counselor at KFHS. Kassandra's van, which she said she had gifted to Victoria, was at Missy's crime scene. The van had The Light Paragons' slogan painted on it."

"Interesting. Can you talk to Victoria? Sounds more and more like she's involved."

The constable fished out his cell phone, tapping the screen. "Adding it to my notes right now."

Mic gasped. "You're not gonna believe this. Look. I found another photo in a hidden folder." Once again, the picture collage disappeared and a sole photo of another group of followers appeared. Mic used a laser beam and circled a man's face with it. "There's Peter again." She enlarged the image.

Peter kneeled in front of a group of individuals all dressed in red-hooded gowns. A white masquerade mask completed their eerie ensemble. One member had their finger on Peter's forehead and blood dripped down his face.

A shudder snaked its way up Oaklynn's spine as the evilness of the scene before her took shape, reminding her of many articles she'd read throughout the years on various cults. Why would this cult dress so creepy when they supposedly wanted to spread peace? Lies. All lies.

Caleb's expression hardened. "I'm guessing they're bringing him into the inner circle here. My cult performed similar rituals when promoting a follower. They're probably using pig's blood."

Tightness locked Oaklynn's neck muscles. "Wait. It was pig's blood on the doll in Mic's backyard. Coincidence?"

Caleb's nose wrinkled. "Hardly. Mic, can you get a time stamp on this picture?"

Fingernails clicking on a keyboard filtered through the speaker. Seconds later, Mic puffed out a breath. "This picture was taken six weeks ago."

Oaklynn's jaw dropped. "Peter was killed shortly after this ritual ceremony. Wait, why wasn't he masked?"

"I'm guessing they start wearing them directly after their ceremony," Caleb said.

"We need to find out more about The Light Paragons." Maxwell pushed himself out of his chair and placed his hand on Caleb's shoulder. "I hate to say this, but I think you know what you have to do, right, son?"

Caleb's eyes clouded. "Yes. If we want to get inside the compound and stop this cult."

Maxwell and his children mumbled simultaneously.

Oaklynn analyzed the Watchers' faces.

Their contorted expressions told her they all knew what Caleb meant. What was she missing?

"What do you mean? What does Caleb have to do?" Oaklynn held her breath.

Caleb sighed. "Go back into the darkness."

Caleb gripped his truck's steering wheel tighter as if that would help ease the angst brewing inside him. His father was right. He had to go into the minds of The Light Paragons and the only way to do that was to find out everything he could about them first. And the one person who could help him was the one person he never wanted to see ever again. Evil emanated out of Nehemiah Love like steam from cow dung on a humid day. Pungent and revolting.

"What's going on in that head of yours?" Oaklynn shifted in her seat, angling herself toward him. "You've been quiet ever since we left your dad's."

Caleb had remained silent as the team each accepted their assignments for the case. Dawson would review the files and add his observations to the current profiler's report. Mic was diving deeper into the dark web to look for more information that could help Caleb with the cult. The others would hunker down at the estate, awaiting further instructions. Ryker ended the evening in prayer and said he'd be keeping vigil. He'd also call his prayer warriors.

Hayley hugged Caleb at the front door, asking him to stay safe and said she'd be ready to act whenever he needed her. She had also planned to visit Mic in the morning. The two sisters had locked proverbial antlers when Hayley first arrived at the Greenes' home, but once they worked out their differences, their relationship deepened as if they were twins. They seemed to know each other's thoughts before they spoke.

"Caleb?" Oaklynn tapped his temple. "You in there?"

"Sorry, just a lot on my mind." He turned onto the highway connecting his father's mansion and Oaklynn's home.

The snow had finally stopped, leaving another five inches throughout the region.

"What did you mean by going into the darkness?"

The breath he expelled lit the interior for a second. "I will need to get an invitation into the group, but that's the simple part."

"And the hard part?"

"In order to find out more about this new cult, I will need to visit Nehemiah Love in prison."

"The leader you mentioned earlier."

"Yes, my cult's Reverend." The man Caleb had tried to kill, but he left that information out of the conversation. "Some cults are connected, and I'm guessing Nehemiah knows all about The Light Paragons."

"You mean they communicate with each other?"

"Possibly. Knowing Nehemiah, he's probably been reading up on them out of curiosity." Caleb let that information settle in Oaklynn's mind, then continued. "At least that's what I'm counting on, but it will be hard to see him again after all these years."

Oaklynn leaned back in her seat. "I'm sure. You want me to come—"

"No way." His response came a bit too fast, but he didn't want her anywhere near the Reverend.

"Why?"

"Because the man's charm is life-threatening. Trust me, I understand all too well how he can wheedle his way into someone's mind." Caleb swerved to avoid a sizable chunk of ice the plow had left in the middle of the road. "Whoa. That was close. Anyway, Preach will have his prayer warriors in their constant kneeling position while I go to the jail."

She huffed.

"You don't believe in the power of prayer?"

"I used to. Sort of." She stared out the window.

"What does that mean?" He ached to discover more about her background.

"My mother used to pray with me every night before I went to sleep using the same prayer. 'Father, keep Lynny safe under Your blanket of protection.'" She grunted. "Little good it did."

"How do you think our perp knew your nickname?"

Oaklynn rested her head back. "An educated guess?"

"Something tells me you don't believe that." How far should he take their conversation? "Tell me more about your mom. Where is she now?"

"She passed away when I was five."

He didn't miss the devastation in her voice. "You were close."

"Yes. I followed her around like a lost puppy."

"What about your father?"

"No comment." She leaned forward, her body language screaming something Caleb found hard to read. But one thing was abundantly clear—her father was a sore spot and Caleb just entered the no-fly zone.

Just as well. They reached her exit. Within moments Caleb drove into her long, snowy driveway. "You want me to shovel tonight?"

"My plow guy should be here soon, but thanks." Her earlier sharp tone disappeared. "You have an interesting family."

He chuckled. "That's an understatement." His truck wheels plowed through the snow, and they reached her farmhouse. "I see you also like the forest's solitude. My house is in the woods too."

The pickup's headlights caught a set of tracks leading out from a tree on the lawn up to her front window.

Caleb put the truck in Park and pointed. "I'm guessing those fresh footprints aren't yours."

She reached for her door handle. "Probably just a curious kid or something."

Did she believe her own conclusion?

He placed his hand on her arm. "Let me go first."

"You think I'm a damsel in distress and you're going to step in to win my affection?"

Somehow, he doubted that would ever happen with Oaklynn Brock. She didn't seem the type to allow any man to save her, but he'd keep that thought to himself. "Just wanted to ensure you're safe. Blame it on the gentleman in me."

"Fine. Let's go." She exited the truck.

He tracked the footsteps. "Wait, they lead to your front door along the house. Looks like they edged their way to hide their approach. That's odd."

The pair advanced to Oaklynn's entrance and climbed the four steps leading to her door.

A piece of paper wedged into the screen door flapped in the wind.

Oaklynn seized it with her gloved fingers.

Caleb snuck a peek. Black block cutout letters screamed from the page.

I KNOW WHO YOU ARE.

Oaklynn's eyes flashed fear under her front yard light.

Caleb pulled her close, a question filling his mind.

Who exactly was Oaklynn Brock?

Chapter Eleven

Oaklynn's heartbeat punched her rib cage, stealing her breath. Spots flickered in her tunneled vision. She swayed and grabbed the railing. The stalker's note sent her mind reeling. Who was this person? How did they find her home? How did they know her identity? Question upon question tumbled through her head without answers. *Breathe, Oaklynn.* She closed her eyes and counted slowly to stop a panic attack from immobilizing her body. She couldn't let Caleb see her terror or he'd insist on staying with her. Oaklynn required privacy to work through it—and she wanted to study her father's case files. There would be no sleeping tonight, especially after this person had found her home. Thankfully, it didn't appear that anyone had broken through her security system.

"What does this mean, Oaklynn? Who are you? You're hiding something from me. Let me help you."

Caleb's question broke through her foggy mind.

Oaklynn inserted her key into the lock, then punched in the code. Her double security system. No one could enter without both. She opened the door. "Let's go inside. It's freezing out." She stomped the snow from her boots before taking off her coat and hanging it on the hook by the door.

The Bengals trotted toward them, colliding together as if each wanted to be the first to greet their mama. Oaklynn laughed and squatted in front of them, sitting cross-legged.

"Well, who do we have here?" Caleb kneeled beside her and held out his hand. Frodo approached cautiously, sniffing Caleb's fingers. "I didn't realize you had kittens. They're so cute."

"They keep me sane and right now I need their love." Sam hopped up on her lap. "This is Sam." She pointed to the kitten beside him. "That's Frodo."

"Ahh…you're a *Lord of the Rings* fan, I see. Me too."

"Yep." She lifted another Bengal. "This is Arwen. The other two are Anna and Esla." The girls meowed in unison. Oaklynn laughed. "They're saying 'hi' or 'feed me.'"

Caleb raised Frodo to his face and kissed his forehead, his large hands almost covering the kitten's tiny body.

Oaklynn's heart melted at the gentleness of the giant. "Lilly was right about you. You are a teddy bear." She left off the part about her uncle being handsome. There was no denying that fact.

He tilted his head. "Oh, she did say that, did she? What else did my dear niece say?"

Oaklynn pushed herself to her feet. "That's between us girls. I need to feed them, but first I want to check the house. Just in case."

Caleb stood. "I'll help you."

Oaklynn winced as she pictured the door in the basement with multiple locks. Her secret room where she hid everything about her past. She had to come up with a quick plan to divert him from heading downstairs. "How about we split up? Get it done quicker so you can get home to Mic. I'll go downstairs. You check this level."

After they completed their search, Oaklynn brought out cat food from the cupboard and poured some into her kittens' dishes.

Caleb sat on a stool at her island, staring at the note. "You going to call this in?"

"And say what? Someone left me a note? We're both aware that unless a crime was committed, the police are unable to take any action."

"So you're not doing anything about it?"

"I didn't say that." She finished feeding the cats and stowed their food. "I'll bag it and give it to Chloe."

"Will you tell me what it means? Who do they think you are?" He draped his coat over the stool beside him.

She quelled a groan when she realized she would not get rid of him. *Might as well make the best of it.* "You want a tea? Coffee?"

"Sure, but quit stalling. Tell me your story." He tapped the counter by the note. "Or this person wouldn't be bothering you. Secret admirer? Stalker?"

She filled the teakettle and set it on the burner. "Hardly an admirer. Stalker? Maybe. The only thing coming to mind is I encountered hostility and faced threats during my time on the Toronto police force." She had rubbed some people the wrong way with her take-charge attitude. She had a couple of threats from the drug gang she helped bring down, but Oaklynn doubted they followed her and left this note.

"Well, you need to watch your back. First the doll and now this threat." He eyed the feeding kittens. "Perhaps I should bring Briggs to stay here. I doubt the Bengals will protect you."

The kettle whistled moments later, and Oaklynn filled two mugs. She set them and a selection of tea bags on the island. "Help yourself. I'm okay here with my kitties. This note doesn't scare me." Liar. Her wobbly legs told a different story, but for now, she'd stick with what she told him.

She chose a ginger flavor and dunked the tea bag into her

mug. "Let's develop a game plan. You heading to the prison soon?"

"Dad is calling the warden to arrange it. Maxwell Greene has more clout than I do and will get me in quicker." He snatched a green tea and dropped the bag into his mug. "What about you?"

"I'll get Eldon to visit Victoria Dutton. Remember, she owns The Light Paragons' van. See if he can rattle her cage. He's good at that." She sipped her tea, letting the spiced flavor linger on her tongue. "I'm going to visit the author who wrote Aaron Crowder's biography."

"You feel this new perp is following the serial killer's MO?"

"Sure looks that way." She wanted to study her crime board in her secret room. See if anything new popped. But first, she had to gently escort the teddy bear out of her home.

And she suddenly had no desire to do that.

Caleb finished his tea and took his cup to the sink. "It's getting late and you need rest after another taxing day."

"Thanks for driving me tonight. I enjoyed meeting your family." She followed him and dumped her tea, her hand grazing his. A jolt shot up her arm. What was that?

Their eyes locked and Oaklynn willed herself to look away, but couldn't. The kindness in his gentle expression held her for a few seconds. She cleared her throat and withdrew. She squared her shoulders, resolved not to be lured in by a man.

Especially this man whose gentleness almost cracked the hard shell she'd erected around her heart throughout the years. *You have too much baggage, remember?*

Caleb snatched his coat from the barstool and put it on. "Call me if you need anything, okay? And I mean anything."

"Got it. I'll touch base with you in the morning." She led him to the front door, unlocked the bolt, and tugged it open. "Drive safe."

"Lock the door behind me." He stepped outside and turned. "I'm praying for you, Oaklynn."

She sucked in a breath. The way he said her name in hushed tones melted one of her ice bricks. "Thanks. Text me when you get home."

"Yes, Mom." He saluted and trudged through the snow to his truck.

Oaklynn waved to him as he drove out to the street.

After making herself a coffee, she snatched the key for her secret room and descended the narrow stairs into her dark basement. The lights flipped on from her movement. She'd had them installed to turn on without physically hitting a light switch. Oaklynn unlocked the two dead bolts and entered the tiny room. She bypassed a round table and stood in front of a large corkboard occupying the entire white wall. Multiple pictures, placed in groupings of her father's crime scenes, filled the space.

Oaklynn sipped her coffee and stood in front of one portion of the wall. Six sets of gruesome crime scene pictures filled one half of the crime board. The Suicide Slayer's kills. Her father had taken six women's lives—well, technically eight. His first was his own mother, the second being his wife.

The only kill Oaklynn refused to put on her death wall was Jenna Crowder—her sweet mother. Oaklynn didn't want to see her mother's lifeless eyes.

It was a picture she couldn't unsee and still haunted her dreams.

Her cell phone buzzed from her back pocket. She pulled it out and glanced at the screen. Aunt Sue. Oaklynn hit Answer. "You always sense when I'm in this room, don't you?"

"Yep. God knew, so He put you heavy on my mind. Plus, I've seen the news about multiple suicides in your area and figured that would send you into your basement." Her mother's younger sister blew out a breath. "You really need to bulldoze that room, Oaklynn."

"I can't." She took a sip of her coffee before placing it on the round table behind her. "Besides, it may help me catch this new copycat."

"Someone is mimicking Aaron's kills?"

The public now knew of their suspicions—thanks to Darius. "Not one hundred percent, but it's looking that way."

"Love, why hasn't your sergeant removed you from this case? He knows your identity and you're too close to it."

"Well, we didn't know that when he first assigned me and right now, he'll be taking time off to grieve his son's death." Oaklynn observed one of the pictures of Aaron's kills. He placed the woman against the tree, arms wide.

Just like Isaac.

Oaklynn tightened her grip on her cell phone as she pictured his lifeless body.

"Well, then, you need to step down. Isn't that the right thing to do? Besides, I don't want you going back into the darkness you've worked so hard to escape."

"I can't, Aunt Sue. If anything, I'm the only person who can solve this case. I know how this copycat thinks because I know how *he* thought."

She analyzed the positioning of all the victims. Would the copycat follow her father to the letter? Her gut said yes. *Wait*— a thought rose. The killer only started mimicking her father's kills after his death. Coincidence?

"True, but it's too dangerous."

Oaklynn bristled. "I can take care of myself." She paused. "But I could use your prayers to keep Caleb, myself, and my team safe." She now asked for prayer? Caleb was rubbing off on her.

"Caleb?"

"The Watcher from the Canadian Watchers Squad the mayor hired to help us. Caleb has a cult background too, but he's too good at reading me, Aunt Sue. He's going to figure out who I am."

"Why don't you just tell him?"

"Only Rick and Chloe know. It has to stay that way." Besides, if he knew, he'd make her step aside.

And she couldn't. Not now.

Too much was at stake. She had to protect the town she loved.

Along with those in it.

The door squeaked open, and a ray of light entered her bedroom. Five-year-old Lynny cowered against her headboard, dragging her Barbie doll comforter up to her neck as if that would stop him.

Tears filled her eyes when he yanked the covers away. "Don't worry, pumpkin. I'll protect you from the dark monster."

How could he protect her from himself? He was the only monster that scared Lynny.

He pushed Play on her CD player and Brahm's "Lullaby" sounded. He scooped up her black satin shoes and held them out. "Let's dance."

God, where are You? I'm scared and need You to stop him.

She hesitated.

"Now, Lynny." His scary voice propelled Lynny into action and she scrambled to slip into her dancing shoes.

After their waltz, her father tucked her back into bed and flicked off her night-light, plunging her into the darkness as he shimmied in beside her.

No God, I need the light.

No. No. No.

Oaklynn screamed and bolted awake as she sat up in her bed, tucking her buffalo plaid cover around her neck, blocking his touch.

But his actions would never fade into the darkness, especially now with the memories of the Suicide Slayer all around, mocking her.

Oaklynn checked the clock. Five o'clock. She had studied her father's case until two in the morning in hopes of something new emerging. But only questions remained after she added the current crime scene pictures to her board. She finally gave up and went to bed.

Three short hours ago. But there would be no sleeping now. Not after that nightmare.

Oaklynn whipped off the covers, disturbing the five kittens sleeping in her king-size bed, and strode into her adjoining bathroom.

Moments later, she entered the shower and scrubbed herself, hoping to eradicate the memory of his touch from every inch of her body.

She scrubbed and scrubbed until she broke her skin, then stopped as words a counsellor had once said emerged.

Don't let him win. He's not worth the energy.

Oaklynn shut off the water and lifted her towel from the hook outside her shower door. Music caught her ear.

She stilled.

Brahm's "Lullaby" once again played through the speakers in her bedroom. Terror chilled her body, and she wrapped the towel around herself.

How was that possible?

She clenched her fists and stepped out of the shower, determination locking every muscle. No, Oaklynn would not let the darkness win.

Not again.

Caleb's cell phone buzzed, waking him from nightmares laced with the Reverend raising his knife, ready to plunge it into Caleb's heart. The man had called him Judas and claimed he had to die for taking sixty pieces of silver. The cult leader had tied him to a stone altar and was about to sacrifice him to Nehemiah's god.

Caleb snatched his phone from the nightstand, welcoming the intrusion into his dark dreams. Obviously, talk of Nehemiah Love had awakened Caleb's prior reoccurring nightmares. Ones he thought were behind him, but his pending visit to ask for help from the only man in this world that Caleb hated had resurrected the consuming horror from the past.

He swallowed to rid himself of the fright and answered without checking the caller's identity. "Greene here." His squeaky voice revealed his panicked state.

"You okay, son?" Maxwell's question held concern. "Did I wake you?"

"Yes, but thank you."

"The nightmare again?"

Caleb flipped his cover off and swung his legs over the bed's edge. "Unfortunately, yes. Talk of him must have done it."

"Well, speaking of *him*, I've secured a visit at the prison for you."

"When?" Caleb stood and stretched his tightened muscles.

"Tomorrow afternoon. Had to give twenty-four hours' notice and it was the earliest time I could get. Seems everyone is in line, wanting to speak with Nehemiah Love."

"Why?"

"I'm guessing reporters want insight on this new cult. News of its existence is reaching the community. Even got a call from Mayor Stevens this morning. He wants you to hold a town hall meeting tomorrow night. He's announcing it to the public. At 7:00 pm. Seems that reporter's article has stirred up a hornet's nest." Silence filtered through the speaker before his father continued. "Son, this is what you do best. We need to put out the fire before the town goes into a full-fledged panic."

"Understood. I was planning on contacting the mayor to address the town anyway. Has Dawson said yet when he can give the profile?"

"Yes, he's ready. How about right after the town hall tomorrow? Can you ask Oaklynn if that's okay?"

"Yes and I'm sure it will be." Caleb withdrew a green sweater from his duffel bag moments before Briggs trotted into his room and barked.

Maxwell chuckled. "Somebody else wants you up."

"He only loves me for his food."

"I highly doubt that. He saved your life, remember?"

How could Caleb forget? Guilt from that frightful day still plagued him.

"You still blame yourself, don't you?"

"Reading my mind again, Dad?" Caleb ruffled Briggs's ears.

"His accident wasn't your fault."

A lump formed in his throat. "I didn't listen to him and I got him shot when he had to drag me away from that shooter."

"Son, that's what he was trained to do."

Briggs barked.

"See, even he agrees with me."

"Funny." Caleb shook his head. "Thanks for the heads-up about the meet and the town hall. I gotta get to the precinct soon."

"You want me to go with you tomorrow?"

Caleb tapped his index finger on the back of his phone, debating his father's question. He'd love the added protection as Caleb faced the monster he never thought he'd see again.

However, Caleb also realized he must confront the man alone in order to put the Purity Flock and Nehemiah Love behind him. "I have to do this by myself, Dad. It's time." Time to face the darkness head-on.

"Understood. I'm praying. Preach has called his warriors. They'll be on their knees the entire time you're there. He can't hurt you or manipulate you any longer. You have God on your side. Remember that. Be safe." Maxwell ended the call.

Caleb punched in Oaklynn's number.

"Morning," she answered. "Just heading out the door. What's up?"

Caleb relayed the information about his prison visit, the town hall meeting, and the profile. "Would that work for your constables?"

"It should. The library is close to the station, so we can head there right after the mayor's meeting. I'm glad you called. I wanted to let you know that I'll be busy with Eldon today. How about I just see you at the meeting tomorrow night?"

"Sounds good. Stay safe."

"Will do." She ended the call.

Caleb tossed the phone on the bed, turning to his dog. "Time for breakfast, bud?"

Briggs barked and trotted from the room.

Caleb threw on his cargo pants and sweater. He snagged his Bible from the nightstand before following the K-9 into the kitchen.

He wanted to spend time with God to prepare himself for what he guessed would be a grueling few days.

He required God's armor to fight the evil encroaching Kenorapeake Falls.

The bitter January air stung Oaklynn's cheeks as she departed her home. She zipped her coat up to her neck, then adjusted her duty belt as she descended the steps and walked toward her detached garage. She loved her older home but hated that she had to store her Cherokee in the building a few meters away from her front entrance. The house's character had called out to her and she couldn't resist buying the cozy farmhouse. She planned to do some upgrades in the spring, which included the addition of an attached garage.

Oaklynn sidestepped a pile of snow the plow contractor had missed and halted in front of her door. Multiple footprints tracked from the trees to her garage. Were those her plow guy's or Caleb's from last night?

Or someone else's entirely?

They led from a group of Douglas firs on the east side of her garage. Her eyes followed the trail across her lawn to the garage door.

A bouquet of lilies sprinkled with patches of ice lay propped against the frame. A card dangled from the ribbon. Black letters held a message.

Oaklynn's pulse jackhammered, anticipating that whatever the note said would raise her blood pressure. She squatted to inspect the words.

For your grave. Appropriate, don't you think?

Her mother's favorite flower. Somehow, her stalker knew.

The card was signed, *Your personal watcher xo*

Oaklynn shot to her feet, searching for the bestower in all directions across her property.

But only ice crystals glistened on the snow.

Chapter Twelve

Caleb wrung his hands together the next afternoon, and studied the prison visitation area. Chairs lined the long counter partitioned with glass, a telephone receiver on each side. He plunked down in the small plastic chair. His muscular frame allowed for no wiggle room and he couldn't get comfortable. Dread flowed through his veins as he waited for the man who still plagued his dreams. *You've got this. God will give you strength.*

The secure door clanged open and Caleb sat straighter as he spied his former cult leader stagger into the room. Caleb choked at the sight of the man.

Not what he expected.

The formerly robust figure of Nehemiah Love had transformed into a slender, stooped man who clung to each chair as he shuffled toward the partition, reminiscent of someone in their nineties. Frail and unsteady. A scruffy beard covered his normally clean-shaven face. A snake tattoo coiled around his neck. His withdrawn eyes narrowed when he spotted Caleb.

Caleb barely recalled the man in front of him, except for his penetrating glare. Evil radiated through Nehemiah's piercing, dark eyes. Panic assaulted Caleb, sending his heart's rhythm reeling. He gripped the armrests to calm himself. *Breathe, Caleb.*

He can't hurt you or manipulate you any longer. You have God on your side.

Maxwell's words returned like a bulldozer plowing into a mound of dirt at full force. Caleb dislodged his hands and flexed his cramped fingers, releasing the panic-stricken tension. He picked up the receiver.

Nehemiah plopped into the chair and snatched his phone. "What do you want? You're the last person I expected to come see me. Didn't you do enough damage to my flock already? Here to pour salt in the wound after all these years?"

Caleb let him rant, and silently mustered courage. "Believe me, I hoped to never lay eyes on you again." He inhaled and exhaled, gathering his words. "I need your help."

A low grumble emerged deep from Nehemiah's throat, morphing into a wicked laugh. "Yeah, right. You must be pretty desperate to come to me for help."

Understatement of the year. "Trust me, I wouldn't be here if I didn't need to be."

"Heard you're part of that Watcher Squad your billionaire father formed. You people disgust me. I'm outta here." He rose to stand.

Caleb tightened his grip on the phone to keep his anger in check. "Are you aware of the recently formed group called The Light Paragons?"

His sunken eyes flashed lightning bolts, and he sat back down. "Liars. They're all liars."

"What can you tell me about them?"

Nehemiah banged his hand on the partition. "I'm not helping you with anything. You betrayed me!"

The visitor at the next station jumped at Nehemiah's actions. The guard cleared his throat and stepped forward.

Caleb raised his hands in a stop position, signaling to the guard that all was okay. Before he had the opportunity to say anything, Nehemiah inched closer and leaned his forehead on the glass.

"And I know your intent all those years ago," he whispered into the phone. "You were going to kill me. The cops wouldn't believe me and none of my flock would speak up against you. How did you silence them?"

Good question. One Caleb had asked for years, but finally guessed Maxwell had something to do with his charges being lessened. He only had to volunteer at multiple community centers to serve out the one-year sentence he received for his part in the cult. The day Maxwell found him was the day Caleb's life path had taken a one-eighty. Complete reversal and he vowed to only use his fists for good, not evil. Oh, he had failed a few times, but the military regiment—along with his faith in God—had helped tame the beast in him.

"I'm not here to talk about me. I'm aware some of your followers still keep in touch with you." Caleb guessed appealing to his narcissistic nature would grab the man's attention. "This new flock is growing and will probably take over your followers. Do you want that? Help me stop them and preserve your flock." He leaned back and tapped his thumb on the counter.

Not that Caleb wanted to help the man or his group, but he also knew some still met in private to continue on with Nehemiah's work. Caleb had kept tabs on them to prevent their growth. They weren't doing anything illegal, so authorities had no grounds to break up their circles.

Like they had done all those years ago. Not only had the Purity Flock deceived their followers with the false pretense of becoming godlike if they joined, the leaders had secretly been running a drug cookhouse. Plus, they'd killed many women. Police had caught wind of it and raided the compound the day Maxwell pulled Caleb out.

"It also appears The Light Paragons are tapping into your drug resources to fund their organization." Caleb air-quoted the word *organization*.

Nehemiah once again pounded his hand on the partition. "They wouldn't dare! She promised." He flattened his lips into an impregnable seal.

Gotcha! He was definitely connected to the cult underworld. "She? Who is 'she'?"

The man hissed out a breath. "Don't know her real name, but she wrote me a letter a few months back asking for my advice on how to grow her group. I replied with a few thoughts and tips, but told her to stay out of my territory."

"But she didn't, did she?"

Nehemiah pushed his orange sleeves farther up his arm, revealing more tattoos. A large red heart including a white cross in the middle appeared on his left forearm, with "John 13:34" written beneath. Nehemiah had multiple verses inked on his right arm in a collage. "No, my flock complained to me about how she'd been stealing some of *my* followers. I wrote her again and asked her to stop or pay a hefty price."

"Tell me about their beliefs, customs, rituals. I'm sure you've looked into them." A thought entered his mind. "You probably have a spy doing your dirty work and scoping them out."

Nehemiah smirked. "You know me too well. I researched them and discovered they recruit through a video game."

"*Parlight Warriors*. What else?"

"She has an inner circle, but no one knows who they are. They wear masks and red cloaks when they hold their meetings to hide their identities from their flock. Cowards. We never did that."

"How many are in this inner circle?"

"My spy says twelve. Mimicking the Bible, I guess." He harrumphed. "They pretend to spread peace. That's also how they get people into their circle. Treat them nicely, make them believe they're doing the community favors. Then the Queen Bee stings and steals their money by making them sign over their financials to cover living expenses."

That bit of news didn't surprise Caleb. He'd heard other cults doing the same thing. "Queen Bee?"

"That's what she calls herself and refers to her flock as her hive." He shook his head. "She's sick and needs to be stopped."

And you're not? Caleb refrained from voicing his question. He had to keep Nehemiah talking. They required additional information before dismantling the group. "Tell me more about her. How she thinks. How she would interact with her *hive*."

"She needs her followers to adore her, so she'll use her honey nature to sweeten them. Tell them if they do what she says, she'll bring them into her inner circle. Promise them the moon and power. Everyone wants power."

Caleb flinched. Yes, he did once, and that was what drew him to do Nehemiah's dirty deeds. *Thank You, Lord, for saving me from that desire.* "What else?"

Nehemiah chewed on his bottom lip. "Her sweetness will run out. If someone crosses her, watch out."

Could the Queen Bee be the copycat killer? Did the team have this all wrong? Everyone thought they were dealing with a male serial killer. "What do you mean?"

"Well, she's disciplining them because in a recent letter she asked me for advice on how to handle unruly followers."

Caleb muffled his disdain. He was well aware from previous encounters of what his idea of discipline entailed, but he never requested Caleb kill for him. Others had done the man's dirty deeds and fingered him during the raid. Now Nehemiah served a lifetime sentence for the murders he sanctioned. "Did you tell her to kill people, Nehemiah?"

The man's jaw dropped, and he averted his gaze, letting it linger on the prisoner seated beside them. "Of course not."

The man was lying. Surely, the cult leader wouldn't openly

instruct this person to kill someone. Would he? "What are you keeping from me, Nehemiah? Don't you want to stop her?"

Nehemiah drummed his fingers, stopped, then looked at the guard by the door. Nehemiah inched closer. "I can tell you someone who's helping to fund her group of blasphemers," he whispered.

"Who?"

"Promise to protect me." Once again, he stared at the guard.

Caleb slouched against the seat, a plastic edge poking into his back. The irony of the situation kicked him in the stomach. The man who stole so much from Caleb wanted his protection?

"Guess you weren't expecting that to come out of my mouth, huh? Listen, I help you. You help me."

"Who do you need protection from?"

"A group of bloodsucking guards. Perhaps your father can put pressure on the warden. Get the guards fired. If you promise to do that, I'll give you a name." He sat back and hummed the theme song from *Jeopardy*, indicating time was ticking. Seconds later, he stopped. "You don't help me. I'll send a follower to teach your new girlfriend a lesson."

"I don't have a girlfriend."

"I'm referring to the cute cop you've been hanging around. Offer expires in ten seconds."

Caleb dug his nails into his palms. How could this cult leader have seen him with Oaklynn? Were his followers watching Caleb? "Fine. I'll get Dad to help." His words came out with a hiss. He wouldn't let anything happen to Oaklynn. She had somehow wormed her way into his heart.

"You better keep your word or I will send someone after the cop."

Caleb stiffened. "Wait a minute. Have you been leaving her notes and flowers?"

"Absolutely not." The man's eye contact never wavered from Caleb's.

He told the truth. "Okay, give me the name of who's helping to fund The Light Paragons."

Nehemiah looked again in the guard's direction. "The mayor's wife."

What? No way. "How do you know that?" Is there a connection within the prison, or did one of his followers somehow discover this news?

"Let's just say the Queen has followers here." He glanced around. "That's why I need protection. I'm guessing she wants to silence me and take over my group."

"But the mayor's daughter just killed herself. Why would her mother want to fund this group?" Caleb knew the coroner hadn't reversed his original report of the suicide manner of death.

Nehemiah squinted and shook his head. "You really feel she committed suicide? Word has it she was about to leave the group, so their enforcer made it look like she killed herself."

Wow, Nehemiah Love definitely maintained his interactions in the cult circles.

"Who's their enforcer?"

"Not a clue."

Right. Too easy. "You said this woman has been sending you letters? Did she give a return address?"

"Just a post office box."

"Where's their compound?"

"No idea."

"Humor me and take an educated guess."

His expression morphed from narcissism to panic, leaving Caleb with a thought.

Nehemiah Love feared this new group. Why?

"Has she threatened you, Nehemiah?"

"Not in so many words, but my food and privileges here have dwindled. I'm done talking to you. Do what I asked or there will be consequences. I've left you alone all these years, but I can still get to you, Caleb Greene." He raised his hands to signal to the guard they were done. "My advice would be to search all the forests in the area. She's probably hiding her hives in the trees!"

Interesting idea. Caleb observed the once hard-core, get-things-done cult leader. However, a desperate man took the place of that person.

Caleb was no longer scared of his threats, but pitied him.

Forgive.

The word flashed through his mind, and Caleb knew it came from above.

Caleb placed his hand on the glass. "I forgive you for what you did to me. For what you did to all of us. Please know I'm praying for you. Praying to the only One who can help you. Surrender to the true God."

Nehemiah bolted upright. "I will never forgive you for your betrayal. Don't forget your promise." He slammed the receiver down and trudged toward the door connecting the visitors' room to the only "home" Nehemiah Love would see in his lifetime.

And the only emotion Caleb felt toward the man was sympathy.

An unexplainable peace replaced Caleb's previous angst. He hung up his phone, rose to his feet, and squared his shoulders. He could now help bring this cult down, knowing God would fight for him.

Oaklynn tightened her grip on her Charger's steering wheel as she recalled her earlier conversation with Caleb. He had shared pieces of his interview with Nehemiah Love and the news of the mayor's wife being somehow involved with the cult. Caleb and Oaklynn agreed to meet at the town hall meeting a bit earlier to give full details of both of their interviews.

Oaklynn's thoughts returned to the bouquet's note. How

did this person know her? Her pulse jackhammered in her ears, threatening to send her into a black hole. She required help to talk her off that clichéd ledge. She hit her talk button on her Charger's steering wheel. "Call Chloe."

She answered on the first ring. "Miss me already?" Chloe chuckled. "Where are you?"

"Driving to Freda Corbet's home."

"Love, what's going on?"

Oaklynn shared her assumptions about the notes. "They were meant for me, Chloe, but does this person know who I am?"

"Good question. I haven't told anyone, and the sergeant hasn't either."

Oaklynn banged the wheel. "I've stayed off social media and changed my looks. Done everything right to keep my identity hidden."

"I'm going to search for your name." Typing filtered through the Charger's Bluetooth. "Wait, that slime-ball Darius took a picture of you at Isaac's crime scene and included it with another article, calling for the police to find the copycat killer." Chloe read Darius's words, her pitch elevating with each sentence. "Unbelievable. Listen to how he ends his news report. 'Kenorapeake Falls needs to hold the KFPD accountable, specifically Constable Oaklynn Brock, and stop this serial killer before he strikes our own again.'"

Oaklynn entered the small subdivision where Freda lived. "Wait, do you think Darius knows my identity?"

"Well, he's getting information from someone."

"You think we have a leak?"

"Hope not. Have you read Freda's book of your father's memoir?"

"No." Oaklynn had refused to do that to herself. Yes, she possessed a complete wall of pictures from her father's kills, but she was unable to muster the courage to read his words.

"I did after you told me your identity. Your father shared

a lot about his life with you and your mother. He called you Lynny a few times. So anyone who read the book would have known that, or—"

"Or Freda Corbet may be our killer." She shared Caleb's conversation with Nehemiah and his suspicion of the cult leader being female.

"That's a stretch, but be careful."

"I'm about to find out more about the author now." She hit her signal light. "Hey, anything on the flowers?"

"'Fraid not. No prints on the card, ribbon, or wrapping. Also, whoever left it was smart and used their own notepaper, so there's no reference to the florist used. Eldon checked all the florists in the city. Dead end."

"Figures." Oaklynn turned left onto Freda's street. "I gotta run. See you tonight at the meeting?"

"You betcha."

Oaklynn drove into the author's driveway. "I'm here at the author's place."

"Praying for you. Love, it's time to trust Him."

Oaklynn huffed. "You sound like Aunt Sue. Catch ya later."

"Be safe."

Oaklynn ended the call and cut the engine, emerging from her cruiser. She examined the author's modest home. While Oaklynn hadn't read Freda's book of the Suicide Slayer's memoir, she investigated her personal life. Widowed. No children. Author of twenty psychological thrillers. Oaklynn chuckled at the irony. The woman sure had lots of material from Aaron Crowder's case to give her a mountain of ideas for her novels. While her books had done well and were on multiple bestseller lists, she was no Stephen King.

Oaklynn climbed the four steps to the woman's front entrance and rang the doorbell. She shook her arms by her sides to ward off the emotions plaguing her, and punched the button a second time. She hadn't called ahead as she wanted to give the element of surprise, but hoped this wasn't a wasted trip.

Thudding footsteps sounded before the door flung open. "What is it? I'm in the middle of an important scene."

Oaklynn pushed down her annoyance at the rude woman and held up her credentials. "Constable Oaklynn Brock of KFPD. Mrs. Corbet, I need a moment of your time. Can I come in?"

"I'm working."

"Ma'am, I don't mean to interrupt your writing, but this is vital police business."

The author folded her arms. "What's it about? You flag me for my research?"

Really? Oaklynn assumed most authors would love the opportunity to talk to law enforcement to help with their plot lines. After all, weren't they a valuable source of information and ideas?

"No." She might as well rip the Band-Aid off. "I want to talk to you about Aaron Crowder."

Freda's eyes widened as her mouth hung open. "Oh." She stepped aside. "Come in before my nosy neighbor sees you. I don't need him spreading rumors about me."

Oaklynn entered the foyer. An invigorating smoky scent permeated the area. "You have a fire going. I'd love to warm up." Oaklynn took off her boots.

Freda gestured down the corridor. "Fireplace is in the family room. This way." She headed in that direction.

Oaklynn studied the photos in the hallway as she followed. Framed pictures of the author's thrillers lined the walls on both sides. An image of Oaklynn's father stopped her cold. She hadn't expected to see the cover of *Inside the Suicide Slayer's Mind* so openly displayed.

Freda turned. "Yes, that's Aaron. Doesn't he have the nicest eyes?"

What? Did this woman have a fixation on Oaklynn's dead father?

If you only realized the true evil behind those eyes, you wouldn't call them nice.

Oaklynn cleared her throat to silence the words she wanted to say, as well as the shock of seeing an updated picture of her father. Someone must have taken it at the prison. "Shall we continue into your family room?"

"Of course."

The pair walked down three steps, entering the sunken cozy reading and writing room. Papers and books were stacked on a desk beside a laptop with two monitors. Freda motioned toward the reclining armchair positioned in front of the stone fireplace. "Have a seat. Would you like a coffee?"

Suspicion prickled the hairs on Oaklynn's neck. Why was the woman being so kind suddenly? Her earlier rudeness vanished after Oaklynn mentioned Aaron's name. "No, thank you." She extracted her notebook and pen, sitting while admiring the view from the bay window. "You have a beautiful backyard." A male cardinal flew by, landing on top of a feeder, its red feathers standing out against the snow-covered backdrop. Oaklynn had always loved watching birds as a child. Still did.

"Thank you." Freda took the chair on the other side of Oaklynn. "Now, how can I help you?"

"Mrs. Corbet, you—"

"Please call me Freda."

Oaklynn nodded. "Freda, you wrote Aaron Crowder's memoir. Can you tell me how you got such intricate information?"

"Well, when I had the idea to write the book, I asked my publisher, and they suggested I get the information directly from the horse's mouth, so to speak. I wrote Aaron, told him my idea of getting his story in the hands of all Canadians. Give his side of what happened. Then I asked him several questions."

Aaron?

Oaklynn jotted a note down.

On a first name basis = connection with the killer.

"How did he respond?"

She chuckled. "That's the funny part. He didn't answer my questions, but told me before he'd agree to the book, he had to meet me. In person."

Oaklynn shifted her position to hide the shock of anyone wanting to visit a serial killer. "But that's a five-hour drive from here."

"I turned it into a research trip. You know, go to the killer's hometown, drive by his house, check out the hospital where he worked and interview the staff." She smiled. "I wanted to walk where he walked, feel what he felt, get deep into his head."

Trust me, you wouldn't or his wicked nature would always haunt you.

Oaklynn waited for the author to continue.

"Then I headed to the town close to his prison and stayed at a quaint B and B for a month. I knew I'd need the time to do all this and interview him multiple times." Freda uncrossed her legs and leaned forward. "I take my research seriously."

Clearly.

"Tell me what type of information he shared? His kills? Family life? What drove him to take lives in the first place? That sort of thing." Although Oaklynn knew that information, her curiosity compelled her to discover exactly what her father had shared. Did he tell Freda his dark secrets?

"He told me everything. How his mother abused him as a little boy, called him worthless, stupid, and every bad name under the sun." Freda's lip curled, revealing her thoughts toward the woman. "How could a mother do such a horrible thing?"

How could a father do despicable things to his daughter? Oaklynn bridled at her question. "Let's move on. His first victim was his mother, and he progressed from there, attempting to make his kills look like suicide. Did he go into detail?"

"What do you mean?"

"Like, share how he killed and then positioned the bodies?"

Freda tilted her head. "You obviously haven't read the book. Yes. He gave me everything and even what he took from each victim. Pieces of hair, jewelry, that sort of thing."

Information police hadn't divulged, but it was now out in the open for all to see. The copycat killer could be anyone who had read her book.

"Why are you asking?" She gripped the armrests, leaning forward. "Wait, are you thinking someone used my book and is now killing people like Aaron? I read about those copycat suicides in the paper."

"I can't comment on an ongoing investigation."

"You don't think it was me, do you?" The woman pried out her scrunchie and fluffed her straight, sandy-brown hair.

"I'm only gathering information. You said you drove by his home. What—"

"Not only drove by, but went in. The current owner was home and friendly."

Brave woman.

Oaklynn kept her angst in check and tapped her pen on the notepad. "One last question. Did Mr. Crowder ever talk about his daughter?" The question was more for her own inquisitive mind, not for the case.

"Yes. He affectionately referred to her as his Lynny. Said he loved her deeply, but she betrayed him." The woman's expression darkened.

Was Freda the one taunting Oaklynn, taking out the Suicide Slayer's revenge?

"Shame really that I couldn't find his other daughter. The one he claimed his wife hid from them all."

Oaklynn failed to suppress her gasp. *Wait—what?*

She had a sister?

Chapter Thirteen

Oaklynn wrenched open the library's front door. The hinges squeaked, matching her frayed nerves after discovering she might have a sister. She shook the snow from her coat and headed toward the auditorium as an image from her teenage years bull-rushed her. Her mother's letter entered her mind. Was her mother's secret that Oaklynn had a sister?

Oaklynn unhooked her cell phone and scrolled through her contacts. She selected her aunt, hitting the call button.

"Hey, sweet girl."

"Aunt Sue, do I have a sister?" Oaklynn didn't have time for small talk or pleasantries.

A cry filtered through the speaker, followed by silence.

Silence revealing the truth to her question. "Why didn't you tell me?"

"Because Jenna made me swear not to. It would put you both in danger back then."

Oaklynn clamped her eyes shut. "Why? Dad was in prison."

"Aaron found out that your mother paid off the doctors to

declare their second child a stillborn. The baby was rushed away and adopted by a loving family. She didn't want Aaron doing to her what he'd done to you." She sighed. "Neither of us could stop him, Oaklynn. We tried, but he threatened to kill us both, and you, if we attempted to intervene or flee. Trust me, I did my best to get you away from him after Jenna died but failed."

And her father's random visits at night stopped when Oaklynn turned thirteen. The why still baffled Oaklynn. "But if he was in jail, how could he hurt us?"

"Aaron had many fans. Fans he bragged would do things for him if he asked. They are all sick."

One of those fans had to be the copycat Suicide Slayer. It was the only answer. She made a mental note to check into her father's visitors' logs. Something there might give them a lead on the copycat's identity.

She turned her attention back to her phone conversation. "Aunt Sue, where is my sister?"

"No idea. I don't even know what her adoptive parents named her, only that they were a loving family."

"How did Mom give her up so easily?" She tightened her grip on her cell phone, frustration surfacing toward her sweet mother.

"Oaklynn, the day your sister was born was the hardest day of Jenna's life. It broke her heart to give up her daughter, but she did it out of love." Aunt Sue paused before continuing. "How did you find out?"

Oaklynn shared about her interview with Freda Corbet and how her father had tasked the woman to find his other daughter.

Aunt Sue was right. Giving the baby up was the only way to protect her from the monster's clutches.

"I have to find her. Dad is dead, so he can no longer hurt us." Still, could she invade her sister's happy life with news of her true family? But the thought of having a sister out there trumped her question. "Do you remember anything that may help?"

"What about trying one of those ancestry kits? How long do they take to get results?"

"They only work if the person you're hoping to find also has done one. What are the chances?"

"What if she discovered she has a sister and is looking for you?"

Hope sent chills through Oaklynn's body, bringing a beacon of light to her darkened world. "It's a long shot, but I'll try anything. I've always dreamed of having a sibling."

The front door slammed, and seconds later, Caleb appeared around the corner.

"Aunt Sue, I gotta run. I'm heading into a meeting."

"Are you mad at me for keeping Jenna's secret?"

"I get it. You were only abiding by her wishes. I'm just working through the emotions of everything right now." Emotions that threatened to paralyze Oaklynn.

"If you need to talk, call me. I'm praying."

"Thanks. Love you."

"You too, baby girl." Her aunt ended the call.

Oaklynn tucked her phone away and greeted Caleb.

He smiled at her, but this time, his smile and countenance held something different.

Peace.

A desire and goal she'd had all her life, but one she could never seem to obtain.

She slanted her head, studying his brightened eyes. "What happened at the prison?"

Caleb cupped her elbow, nudging her farther down the hall, away from the steady stream of people entering the auditorium. "Apparently, the cult's leader has been corresponding with Nehemiah and it's a she, not a he."

"Wait, you think we have a female serial killer on our hands?" The odds of that were low. Most serial killers were male.

"Well, the cult leader is female. If there's a common denominator between the killings and the cult. We don't know for sure yet if she's our killer. I'm guessing someone else is doing her dirty work." He took off his gloves and stuffed them into his pockets. "At least, that's what Nehemiah did." He looked away, his peaceful expression disappearing.

She latched on to his arm. "Caleb, what is it? A minute ago, your entire body language was calm, but it has changed. Tell me what happened?"

"Lots, but the most important thing was God gave me the courage to forgive the man who stole whatever innocence I had at fifteen. I can finally move on from years of torment. I should have done this a long time ago."

Forgiveness? If it was only that easy. Oaklynn could never offer that to the monster who destroyed her life. She bit her lip. "I wish I—"

She stopped. *Don't go there, Oaklynn.* Time to steer the conversation away from God and forgiveness. "I'm glad to hear it, but you still have something eating away at you." She poked him in the chest. "Something you're keeping secret."

He crinkled up his nose. "Well, you're one to talk. Let's not go there. Unfortunately, Nehemiah said the woman never gave her name and her return address only revealed a post office box on her correspondence. I've updated Dawson to include her in the profile. He said he'd meet us at the station."

"Sounds good. Question—do cult leaders normally talk to each other?"

"Sometimes, but I'm guessing in this case her questions were twofold." He raised one finger. "One, she wanted the inside scoop on his drug resources to help fund her group. That confirms what we saw in the photos." He added another finger. "And two, she was marking her territory."

"What do you mean?"

"The Purity Flock still has active followers, but they're staying under the police radar. She wanted to tap into that, I think. I convinced Nehemiah to help us bring her down, so that's when he shared the information about the mayor's wife."

"Makes sense." Oaklynn checked her watch. "We best get inside. You ready to address the community?"

"Let's do this." Caleb opened the door and shifted to the right, allowing her to enter first.

Oaklynn moved into the room buzzing with activity. "Wow, looks like half the community has shown up."

"That's because Darius's articles have sparked their fear and curiosity. People are fascinated with serial killers."

Oaklynn pictured her wall of information in her basement room. *Yes, I know that all too well.*

Caleb tugged on her arm, bringing her closer. "I remember something Dawson told me. Our serial killer is more than likely already seated somewhere in this auditorium."

Oaklynn's breath hitched as she scanned the room, mentally assessing the group. "Yes, they like to immerse themselves in the investigation." Was the copycat killer among them?

She spotted a row of her fellow constables, her gaze connecting with Eldon.

He popped to his feet and hurried to her side, leaning close. "Tell me why you think Mrs. Stevens is involved." He dipped his head in the woman's direction.

Oaklynn gestured toward Caleb. "I'll let him explain."

"I got the information from a somewhat reliable source." Caleb shared an abridged version of his conversation with Nehemiah Love.

Eldon folded his arms and shook his head. "You're going to take a convicted felon's word on our mayor's wife's affiliation to The Light Paragons?"

"Eldon, I agree we can't trust this man, but we owe it to the residents of Kenorapeake Falls to at least look into it."

"Oaklynn's right. My sister is checking on her end."

Eldon threw his hands into the air. "So why do you need me if you have the Watchers working on it?"

Oaklynn noted her partner's hardened expression. "Eldon, I get it. This is not how we normally conduct business, but we have a serial killer on our hands. Don't you want to catch whoever is doing this and also stop this cult from brainwashing more of our residents?"

"Of course, we—"

Mayor Stevens tapped his microphone, interrupting the buzz in the room. "Folks, we need to get started. Everyone, please have a seat. We have lots to talk about."

The auditorium noise hushed.

The mayor gestured to Oaklynn. "Constable Brock, please give us an update and introduce our guest speaker."

She nudged Caleb forward and whispered. "Let's get this over with. It's been a long day and I hear my Jacuzzi calling."

Oaklynn walked up the stage's steps and stood behind the podium, taking a quick scan around the room as she prepared her words.

Once again, her neck hairs prickled, her police gut confirming one thing.

Their copycat was among the crowd.

Caleb waited for Oaklynn to begin her update, but her expression flashed a second of terror as she observed the audience. Something—or someone—rattled her. Did she see anyone suspicious among the group? He scanned the gathered residents, but nothing stood out of place to him. However, wasn't that their point? To blend in?

The auditorium remained silent as they waited for her to begin.

The mayor cleared his throat, as if urging her to speak.

Caleb leaned closer and placed his hand on her lower back, offering support.

Oaklynn shifted her stance, dipped her chin toward him in acknowledgment, and smiled at the group. "Good evening, friends." The mic squealed a reply. She leaned back. "We appreciate your attendance. While we can't divulge information on an ongoing investigation, we're devoting all resources to solve this unusual case and bring peace back to our community."

"Do we have a serial killer on our hands? That's what the newspaper said. Why has there been no communication from KFPD? Shouldn't you have warned the community?" A man bellowed his stern questions from the back of the room.

Mumbles erupted, loudening with each voice.

"How are you keeping us safe?" another asked.

"Is it true this is a Suicide Slayer copycat?"

Question after question fired at Oaklynn like a machine gun emptying its rounds.

She raised her hands. "Folks, like I mentioned, we can't comment on the investigation. Rest assured, though, we've joined forces with the Canadian Watchers Squad and will catch this person."

A female in the front row raised her hand. "Who's that?"

Oaklynn gestured toward Caleb. "This is Caleb Greene. He's a Squad member, so I'll let him answer your question. Caleb?" She stepped to the left of the microphone.

Caleb gripped the podium's edges. "Good evening. As Constable Brock mentioned, I'm a member of the Canadian Watchers Squad. We are a group devoted to assisting the local law enforcement with sensitive cases that require a unique touch such as this one. Our mission is to add a strong presence and assist in times of trouble. Each member has a unique set of skills. Mine includes military experience and a background in psychology."

A man dressed in a plaid shirt hopped to his feet and waggled his fist toward the stage. "We don't need your help. Go home."

Another man a few rows back stood. "Yes, we do. The cops ain't doin' nothin' to bring this killer to justice."

Caleb leaned closer to the mic. "Guys, please sit." He waited for them to comply.

"Yeah, Rod." The female behind him chomped on her gum. "Sit down and shut up. Let's find out what this Watcher has to say."

They obeyed.

"Friends, we won't keep you here long but just wanted to reassure you we're looking into every angle of this case." Caleb took a few minutes to offer words of comfort and encouragement, stating that the team and police department would keep their community safe. He gestured toward the door. "I will leave some business cards on that table. I want to offer my counseling services to anyone who needs to talk. Please email me." He motioned for Oaklynn to take over.

"I will also leave cards by the door, so if any of you have information regarding the recent deaths and the group called The Light Paragons, please call me or any member of KFPD."

A dark-haired woman to the right raised her hand. "Do you know who this Suicide Slayer copycat is?"

"Sorry, no comment," Oaklynn said.

The man beside the woman stood. "I read the Suicide Slayer has a daughter. Could she be taking over her father's work?"

Oaklynn let out a soft cry before clutching the podium.

Before she could answer, someone shouted from the back. "Do we even know who the daughter is?"

"I heard she's a recluse."

"Well, my aunt from Toronto said she's in a mental institution," another added.

Oaklynn's face paled, but she didn't respond.

The group continued to shout different accusations, but Oaklynn remained frozen. Caleb had to intervene. He returned to the microphone. "Folks, we know nothing about Aaron Crowder's daughter, but if she is involved, we'll find out." Caleb glanced at the mayor. "Mayor Stevens, we have no further updates. Can we adjourn the meeting?" He nudged Oaklynn aside to offer both comfort and help bring her back into the room. Something had propelled her to another time, another place.

The mayor stepped to the podium. "Friends, it's getting late, so that's it for tonight. We'll call another meeting if need be, but for now, the KFPD and the CWS will solve this. Go home, lock your doors, and stay away from The Light Paragons. Trust me, you can't believe a word they're saying."

Caleb studied Mrs. Stevens's face, but her forlorn expression revealed nothing deceitful.

"You okay?" Caleb whispered in Oaklynn's ear. "What's going on?"

She thrust her shoulders back, her lips pursing. "I'm fine. I'm just not good at public speaking and all those questions firing at me caught me off guard."

Once again, Caleb sensed she held something back, but he'd let it go. For now.

He rubbed her arm. "You did fine. Large crowds can be scary." He examined the dispersing group. "Do you think the cult leader is here?"

"Whoever is killing would want to know what we know." Oaklynn checked her watch. "It's late and I'm exhausted."

"It's been a long day." He tipped his head in the mayor's direction. "Shall we connect with him before leaving for your station?"

"Yes." Oaklynn approached Mayor Stevens and his wife. "Sir, thank you for holding this meeting. Hopefully, we assured the Kenorapeake Falls residents of our united front in apprehending the suspect."

"Any updates, Constable Brock?"

Caleb didn't miss Oaklynn's slight eye shift toward Mrs. Stevens. "A couple of leads, sir, and we're looking into them."

The mayor's face screwed into a scowl and he jerked his finger in Oaklynn's face. "I warned Rick against assigning you to this case. You're too new to our force. You better find my daughter's killer, or I'll have your badge." He took his wife's hand and hauled her off the stage.

"That was harsh." Caleb followed the mayor's abrupt exit as he pushed through the crowd and out the door.

"He's right."

Caleb turned to face Oaklynn and clasped both of her shoulders. "Don't let his anger over his loss plant doubts in your mind. You're good at your job. Did you know that was the first thing Wil said about you when he told me he had a crush on you? He was impressed with your keen sense of reading people."

She bit her lip. "He did?"

Caleb nodded.

"I'm sorry about Wil. I felt responsible for his death. I failed to see the hurt he was going through when I ended things."

He brought her into an embrace. "Oaklynn, I blamed you at first, but I don't any longer. You wouldn't intentionally hurt anyone. You're a good person."

She broke the hug, pulling back. "I wish I could believe that."

"Will you tell me what's really going on in that beautiful head of yours?"

Her eyebrows arched, revealing her surprise. "I'll meet you at the station." She didn't wait for his response, but bounded down the steps and out the door.

Good job, Caleb. Way to keep it professional.

He shook off his growing attraction, resolving to tuck his emotions away and solve this case.

★ ★ ★

He watched the Watcher, clenching his fists at his sides. Heat flushed his face. How dare the billionaire's son touch Lynny. *I see the way you look at her. You can't have her. She's mine.*

The Protégé stuck a piece of bubble gum into his mouth and bit down to curb his rage. Or he'd storm the stage and tackle the Beast. *Oh yes, you may be big, but I can still take you.*

He followed the Watcher's gaze as the man scanned the remaining residents. *You're looking for me, aren't you? Or perhaps the Queen Bee?* She had also attended the mayor's ridiculous meeting, and the Protégé caught the anger on her face when they spoke of her beloved group. He had texted her and told her to simmer down, promising her everyone would pay for their blasphemy. She relaxed in her seat after giving him a slight nod.

The Watcher's eyes rested on him. The Protégé lifted his hand in acknowledgment, playing along. Caleb dipped his chin in hello, but shifted his attention to the others leaving.

Good, he suspects nothing.

He'd keep a closer eye on the Watcher and concoct a plan to get rid of the billionaire's son.

Because Lynny was his.

Oaklynn clapped to silence the room. "Everyone, thanks for coming in on such short notice. We wanted you all to hear this together. It's been a long day, so let's get started."

The large screen displayed pictures of the victims, along with various serial killer's crime scenes shots.

Oaklynn gestured toward Dawson, who stood beside Caleb. His medium frame shrunk beside his giant brother. "Let me introduce another member of the Canadian Watchers Squad, Dawson Greene. He's a criminologist and has updated our profile." She raised her hands in a stop position. "Now, before you ask, the mayor requested Dawson look at our current working profile not because something was wrong with it, but because he wanted to ensure we were on the right track. Dawson, the floor is yours." Oaklynn stepped aside.

The blond man straightened his spine and cupped his hands together. "Thank you, Constable Brock. I just wanted to add to what she said. I agree with everything in your current profile, but I've included additional facts and characteristics I've determined from looking at updated files." He raised his index finger. "First, we now have two suspects—one male, one female. All we know about the female is she's the cult leader and loves power. She may be the one ordering these murders, but we don't feel she's the serial killer."

Dawson paced at the front of the room. "Let's move on to the serial killer. He's male, mid- to late-thirties. Doesn't have many friends. He's suffered a personal tragedy. Something drove him to kill. Something in his past made him relate to the Suicide Slayer." He paused. "He spends most of his time by himself and is meticulous."

Eldon raised his hand. "How do you know that?"

Dawson pointed to the etching on Isaac's abdomen. "Look at the detail in this engraving. He took his time." He moved to the photo of Isaac's crime scene. "The killer is highly organized as he's carefully positioned the victim and he's mirroring the Suicide Slayer. He will also insert himself somewhere at the crime scenes, so study the crowds closely."

"What about victimology?" Eldon twirled his pen.

"Good question. The only connection we can find is their age and that they were all part of The Light Paragons." He pointed to the first victim. "Except for Peter Ratchet. He was a mail carrier and the first suicide in Kenorapeake Falls. Age forty-eight. The rest were in their mid-to-late teens." Dawson returned to the front of the group. "Let's talk about the killer's MO. As we mentioned, he's following the Suicide Slayer's killings, but he's evolving. Putting his own spin on them, including the engravings. Those are his signature, and each are related to the victim." Dawson once again raised his index finger. "One more thing. We feel The Light Paragons are connected to these killings. Caleb, your thoughts on this?"

"I'm still scoping out this cult, but from my experience spending time in one, I'd speculate on two things. One, the killer is part of The Light Paragons, and, two, he's killing for whom they refer to as the Queen Bee. My guess is each of these people tried to escape the cult and paid for it with their lives." Caleb folded his muscular arms across his chest. "And the killer wants to please her. I feel he's killing for her for a specific reason. Hopefully I'll find out more when I go inside."

Oaklynn observed her coworkers scribbling in their notebooks, gathering information. "Dawson, is that everything?"

"Yes, thanks everyone for your time. Come and see me if you have questions. I'll stick around for a few minutes."

Mumblings inundated the room, raising the noise level and telling Oaklynn one thing.

KFPD's constables were nervous about this serial killer and wanted him stopped. Now.

Chapter Fourteen

Oaklynn's landline shrilled, interrupting her relaxing bubble bath. No way was she getting out to answer. She wanted to soak her weary muscles. *Leave a message. I'm unavailable.* After four rings, her machine kicked in and an unfamiliar voice sounded in the distance. She ignored it and rested her head back on her Jacuzzi pillow, digesting the horrendous town hall meeting. Oaklynn had blown it and let her personal emotions impede her job. She knew the copycat was there tonight, sensed their presence, but no one stood out to her. And when the questions fired at her concerning the Suicide Slayer's daughter taking over his work? Well, she froze. Unprofessional, she knew, but shutting down was her way of coping with past horrors. The questions had immobilized her, and she'd failed her community. Her fellow constables.

And mostly, Caleb. And why had *that* bothered her the most? Was she developing feelings for the man? He had called her beautiful.

Impossible. He couldn't see her ugliness. The evil rotting her insides. The evil her father had bestowed upon her.

"Stop it! You're not like him, Lynny!" Oaklynn smashed her fist into the water, splashing bubbles out onto the floor. Her Bengals scrambled off the plush purple bath mat and raced out of the room.

Get a grip. She had to step down from this case.

Ten minutes later, she carried her lavender tea into her bedroom and set it on her nightstand. She crawled under her comforter and grabbed her phone from her pajama pocket. Time to get this done. She scrolled through her contacts and selected her sergeant.

He answered on the second ring. "Oaklynn, you're up late. What's wrong?"

"Sir, I'm so sorry to call you with what you're going through, but I needed to talk."

"It's okay. You can call me anytime."

She picked up her cup and sipped her tea, gathering her thoughts. "I need you to replace me as lead."

"What? Why?"

She slouched and told him about tonight's meeting. "I lost it, Rick. I let my personal feelings take over and I can't do that. Kenorapeake Falls deserves better than what I can offer. Give the lead to Eldon. He's more than capable."

"He is, but your experience with serial killers trumps that."

"But, sir—"

"No buts about it. Oaklynn, you can do this." Rick emphasized her name boldly, but in a loving fashion. "Compartmentalize the fact that you're Aaron's daughter and use it to your advantage. It's obvious the copycat is imitating your father's kills. You're the only one who can put an end to this because you understand his mindset. You lived with him. I have total faith in you."

Tears escaped and flowed down her cheeks. His confidence in her abilities astounded Oaklynn. "Why are you so good to me?"

"Because you're the daughter I always wished I had." He sniffed. "And now I have no children."

Oaklynn uncurled her position and set her teacup on the nightstand. She must do this. She *had* to do this.

For Rick.

For herself.

She'd stop this person and prove to herself she was *not* her father.

"You okay?"

Rick's question broke through her mess of tears and emotions. "Thank you for believing in me. You're the father I always wanted."

"That means the world to me. Becky and I were just planning Isaac's memorial." His voice quivered.

"I'm so sorry you have to go through this. Has Dr. Patterson released his body?"

"Not yet, but we started organizing Isaac's favorite songs and passages from when he went to church." A sob filtered through the phone.

Oaklynn waited for him to continue.

Frodo and Sam jumped up on her bed, crawling on top of her as if fighting for her attention. She smiled and scratched each of their heads, proving she loved them equally.

Rick cleared his throat. "Sorry. This is so hard. I shouldn't have had to bury my only child."

"I will find out who did this and make them pay. That's my promise to you."

"I want that person to rot in jail."

"Understood." She yawned. "I'll let you go. Thank you for the pep talk."

He chuckled, then sniffed. "Remember, you've got this." He didn't wait for her reply but severed the call.

Oaklynn placed her cell phone on the nightstand and finished her tea. "Lord, if You're listening, I could use a break in this case. Help me give Rick justice." She paused. "And me some rest."

She wasn't even sure God listened to her prayers, but Caleb said He did.

Oaklynn noticed the flashing light on her landline phone sitting on her dresser and remembered the earlier call. She whipped off her comforter and headed toward the device. She pressed the button to retrieve the message and listened.

"Lynny, you looked beautiful tonight," the distorted voice said.

An elastic of panic tightened her gut, but she couldn't pull herself away from the message.

"The color of your uniform suits you." The caller chuckled. "Green is my favorite color." Silence. "By the way, I don't like how the Watcher looks at you. For that, he'll pay. Sweet dreams."

Brahm's "Lullaby" played for ten seconds before cutting off, ending the call.

Oaklynn threw the phone back on her dresser, regretting listening to the message. Now she'd never sleep.

I don't like how the Watcher looks at you. For that, he'll pay.

The caller's words echoed in her head. She had to warn Caleb. Oaklynn ran back to her bed and snatched her cell phone, selecting his number. "Please don't be asleep. Pick up. Pick—"

"What's wrong, Oaklynn?"

She released a long, audible breath before finding words. "You okay?"

"Fine."

"Mic and Lilly okay?" Oaklynn plunked onto her bed.

"Yes. What's going on? Why are you calling at midnight?"

She leaped off her bed and hurried to the dresser. "Sorry about that, but I had to check on you."

"Why?"

"Got an eerie message. Let me play it." She placed her cell phone on speaker before doing the same with her landline. She hit Playback, the hairs on her arms prickling as she forced herself to listen to the caller's creepy, distorted voice a second time.

Caleb sucked in a breath. "So, this person *was* at the town hall tonight and now he's threatening me?"

She didn't miss the anger in his voice. "That's why I had to ensure you were all safe."

"I'm irritated, but fine. You doing okay? I noticed how rattled you were at the meeting. I don't like that he's watching you. I'm coming over."

"No! I'm fine. My house is locked, and the alarm is set."

"You don't sound fine."

"Hey, any word on the video from Missy's SD card?" Oaklynn returned to her bed and snuggled under the covers.

"She's running a program on it and says it will be ready by morning."

"How about I meet you at Mic's place, then?"

Caleb yawned. "Come for breakfast at 7:30. I'll make pancakes."

She smiled. "You had me at breakfast. See you then."

"Oaklynn, get some rest…after you recheck your doors."

She saluted and rolled her eyes, even though she was aware he couldn't see her. "Yes, boss." She clicked off.

Arwen pounced on the bed, holding a ribbon in her mouth.

The same color ribbon someone had used to wrap around the lilies. Had they also somehow bypassed her security and been inside her house?

Oaklynn stiffened. "Where did you find that, Arwen?"

The kitten dropped the purple string and meowed.

Yes, Oaklynn would definitely recheck her locks.

★ ★ ★

Caleb shuffled into the kitchen at six thirty the next morning after a restless night of dreams about Nehemiah Love trying to kiss Oaklynn. Caleb had hauled the man off her, jealousy raging through him, then he kissed her instead. *Where had that dream come from?* Sure, she was beautiful, but that acknowledgment was as far as he'd take his obvious attraction. He had too much baggage and she could never love someone who had a dark secret.

"Coffee's ready."

Caleb startled, his hand flying to his chest. "Mic, I didn't see you there. Why are you sitting in the dark?" He flipped the light on and blinked at the sudden brightness. He put his thoughts of Oaklynn aside and focused on his sister.

"Because sometimes the darkness comforts me." She sipped her coffee.

Caleb swallowed the words he wanted to say. Words she didn't want to hear. *Lord, help me bring her into the light.* "I realize it's tough for you to trust after the attack on your family and Leo." He poured himself a cup of coffee and took it over to the table.

"Well, three now, counting the decapitated doll. Why is God allowing such darkness to continue in this world?"

"That's a question we'll never be able to answer, but ask Him one day when we see Him face-to-face." He leaned his elbows on the table, gripped his cup in one hand, and tapped the handle with his other thumb. "Sis, how can I help you through this? You're seeing a counselor via video, but I'm here in person. Tell me what I can do."

"It's so hard to explain the debilitating horror I go through whenever I try to step outside—and, Caleb, I *have* tried." Her lip quivered. "Lilly's friends call me a freak because of my phobia."

Caleb shifted his position and reached for her hand, his huge hand blanketing her small one. "Your struggle is real and you're not the only one who's gone through it. You are *not* a freak, Mikaela Cox."

She smiled and placed her other hand over his. "Thanks, bro. Hayley told me the same thing when she came to visit the other day. All you can do for me right now is pray and protect my daughter from this cult. I don't want her anywhere near it."

He folded his right hand on top of hers. "I promise."

She dislodged her hands from his grip. "Speaking of cults, my program salvaged some of that video. Wanna watch it together?"

He stood. "Let's wait for Oaklynn. She's coming for breakfast. I'm making pancakes."

She giggled. "You still love to cook, don't you?"

He took out a frying pan from the cupboard beneath the island. "Sure do." In truth, it was his favorite way to alleviate his anxiety.

Mic finished her coffee and brought it to the sink. "You like Oaklynn."

"Of course. Don't you?"

She nudged him. "No, I mean you *like* like her."

"It's not like that, sis. We work together, and remember Paige?"

Mic waved her finger in his face. "Liar. I see the look on your face when you mention her name. It's more than just a working relationship, and, Caleb, she's not Paige."

"Now who's psychoanalyzing?" He found ingredients from his sister's pantry and placed them on the counter. "She has too many secrets."

Mic harrumphed. "Like you don't."

"Who are we talking about?" His niece bounced into the room, Briggs at her heels.

Caleb threw his hands in the air. "Why is everyone up so early? Can't a guy have some alone time?"

Briggs barked.

"Apparently not." He ruffled the shepherd's ears. "I'll feed you in a second, bud."

"So, were you talking about the pretty constable?"

Caleb brought Lilly into a headlock, rubbing her hair with his knuckles. A gesture he knew she secretly loved. "You never mind, little one."

"Well, just in case you're thinking of asking her out, I one hundred percent approve." She wiggled out of his hold. "I think she'd be good for you."

He cocked his head, folding his arms. "What does that mean?"

"Only that you need a strong woman in your court. To tame you." She snorted, then stuck her tongue out at him. "Kidding. I love you to the moon and back." She wrapped her arms around his waist and snuggled into his chest.

"Ditto, kid." He loved Lilly as if she was his own. He released her. "Okay, these pancakes won't make themselves. Mic, do you have any maple sausages in the freezer? They go great with my famous pancakes."

"Sure do. I'll go get them and tidy up a bit before Oaklynn arrives."

A pancake or two later, Caleb observed the interaction between Mic, Lilly, and Oaklynn. *I could get used to having her around. Quit dreaming. It will never happen.*

"Lilly, you look pretty today. Green suits you." Oaklynn sliced her sausage and stuck the piece into her mouth.

Does you too. Caleb admired Oaklynn in her green uniform.

Lilly's cheeks flushed, and she poked at her pancake. "Do not."

Oaklynn placed her hand on top of Lilly's. "Yes, you do."

Lilly bit her lip but mumbled thanks.

Caleb loved Oaklynn's gentleness with his niece.

Mic cleared her throat, capturing his attention. She tilted her head toward Oaklynn and winked.

Busted.

Last night's answering machine message exploded into Caleb's mind. Yes, he had been staring at the constable. Then and now. His head told him to stop before he fell for her.

But his heart was thinking he'd like to fall.

Oaklynn chewed another bite of pancake. "Caleb, these are so good. I didn't realize you were such a good cook."

Lilly gobbled down her food and rose to her feet. "They were yummy. Thanks, Uncle Caleb. I need to finish getting ready for school. Good to see you, Oaklynn."

"You too."

Caleb took another pancake from the covered dish. "Oaklynn, you sleep after that call?"

"Barely, but Chloe is looking into it for me."

"Good." He added syrup to his pancake. "Okay, Mic, show us the video."

She opened her laptop and placed it in the middle of the table. "I haven't actually watched it yet, but the program said it was successful. Let's hope so." She wiggled her fingers over the keyboard. "Here we go." She hit Play.

Eerie chanting sounded through the speaker.

Caleb bristled, the humming reminding him of his former cult ceremonies. He pushed the sudden rush of trepidation away and leaned closer.

The camera focused in on a group of worshipers dressed head to toe in red, except for one in gold. Eyes glistened in the dimmed lighting beneath matching white masks. They were circling a stone altar holding a pig secured by ropes. The animal squirmed and screeched.

The worshipper in gold held a fist in the air.

The group silenced.

"My flock, we have gathered here to promote one of our own into the disciple circle." Some type of distortion app masked the person's voice. "Have a seat."

All sat except for the leader and one individual dressed in red who stood to the altar's right. Caleb studied the backs of the heads of those not wearing red. "Oaklynn, do you recognize anyone?"

She shifted closer just as a girl turned her head. "That's Kimi and based on her facial expression, she's terrified."

"She knows what's going to happen." Caleb knew all too well. Ritual sacrifices were common. He tapped the screen on a male's side profile. "That looks like Isaac."

"It does." Oaklynn propped her elbows on the table, cupping her chin in her hands. "They're gonna kill the pig, aren't they?"

"'Fraid so."

Mic pushed her chair back, distancing herself from the video. "I can't watch."

"It's time." The leader picked up a knife as those dressed in red once again stood and chanted as they circled the altar. One lone worshipper pounded on a drum, the sanctuary airing eeriness.

A sense of evil seeped through the screen. Caleb choked his fingers around the table edges as the leader sliced the pig's neck. It squealed before stilling.

Oaklynn drew in a ragged breath.

"Disciple, come forward." The leader pushed on the wound, the blood dripping over the side while another hooded follower held a cup beneath the flow. Moments later, he handed the chalice to the leader.

She raised it high. "Believer, drink the blood from this cup and you will become a disciple with godlike power."

Oaklynn turned to him. "Do they really believe that hogwash?"

Caleb slouched back, crossing his arms. "I'm afraid so. I'm ashamed to say I once did. I wanted the power she spoke about."

Mic sprang forward. "Wait, she? You can't tell from the voice."

"No, but according to Nehemiah Love, the leader is a woman."

Mic's mouth hung open. "So, the serial killer is female?"

Oaklynn shook her head. "Not necessarily. We may be dealing with two perps. One orders the kills while the other executes them."

"Literally." Caleb concentrated on the ceremony as the figure drank from the cup, gagged, then sipped more. Seconds later, the video stopped. "Is that all?"

Mic tapped some keys. "Appears to be."

"Can you play it again? I want to focus in on the room and not the ceremony itself." Oaklynn shoved her chair in closer.

Mic once again hit Play, then pushed herself to her feet. "I'm gonna check on Lilly. I can't watch this again."

Caleb squeezed his sister's hand as she walked by. He didn't blame her. No one in their right mind would like to watch the ghastly sacrifice.

However, the members of The Light Paragons all sat on the edges of their seats.

They needed to stop these false prophets. But how?

Get inside.

They had talked about Caleb going into the enemy's camp, but after seeing the video, terror locked his muscles. Could he put himself back into the toxic environment and risk being sucked in again?

Oaklynn stared at the screen, analyzing the room where the ceremony took place. Stone walls. Rows of wood benches were placed in a semicircle. Old-fashioned torches lined the walls, giving off an eerie glow. Chills slivered across her arms, freezing her heart mid-beat. Like Mic, she loved animals, but forced herself to watch the horrifying ritual killing again. She huffed and sat back into her chair.

Her father, as sick as he was, would never have approved of slaughtering animals. People, yes, but not animals.

"What is it?" Caleb asked.

She had to tread carefully and not divulge anything about her past. She circled her index finger around the screen. "I'm not sure the copycat killer is in the room."

"Why?"

"I've studied Aaron Crowder's files and there's no sign of him killing animals. If the copycat is obsessed with Aaron's kills like we think he—or she—is, he wouldn't approve of this kind of torture." She popped forward and froze the frame, peering at each person present for anyone familiar. "Okay, I see Kimi and Isaac. I'm assuming Missy is the one filming, do you recognize anyone else or the room?"

"Hard to tell with some cloaked and we only see the back of everyone else's heads. The crowd gathered is small, so obviously they don't let everyone attend the ceremony. It's too bad Missy didn't film more of the room. Wait, how did she even get a camera into the room? I doubt the cult leaders would allow that."

Oaklynn hunched her shoulders. "Not sure." She hit Play again. "She must have suspected the cult and wanted out, so she filmed what was really going on. But that got her killed." A shift in movement caught her attention. One follower glanced over his shoulder. "This person was in the photos. I've seen him somewhere before, but I don't remember where."

"This hits too close to home." Caleb rubbed the stubble on his chin.

She observed the habit as a pattern whenever he appeared to be either thinking or stressed. "What is it, Caleb?"

"I have to do the one thing I never wanted to do."

"What's that?"

"Go back into a cult willingly." His eyes darkened. "But these guys have to be stopped." He stood and paced. "I knew that was the plan we spoke about earlier, but seeing this just brings back too many terrible memories."

Oaklynn could definitely relate. Having to relive her childhood not only brought back her father's visits to her room, but the horror when she discovered his secret trinkets stashed behind his medical textbooks.

She took her mind off her old family home and focused on Caleb. "How do you propose we get you in? We don't even know where the compound is."

Once again, he rubbed his stubble, then his eyes brightened. "What if I tell them I want to check out their cult as if I've had a change of heart? I'll say I'm interested in joining."

"Do you really think they'll believe that?"

"I'll have to convince them it's true."

Oaklynn finished the rest of her coffee, which had turned cold like her heart ever since she'd read about her father's death. "But how?" She took her cup to the sink.

Mic and Lilly returned to the kitchen. Lilly pointed to her mother's laptop. "That's Slim—I mean Buck."

Oaklynn snapped her fingers. "That's right. Wait, I remember. They call him Slim, but his real name is Buck Smith. We busted him and his drug ring a month ago, but he was released on a technicality." She pulled out her cell phone. "We can convince him to bring you in."

"How will you do that?"

"By using his weak link. His sister is a substance abuser and has been arrested numerous times. We can use her to our advantage. Plus, having him on the inside could help convince them to let you in." Oaklynn hated to use someone so vulnerable as the man's sister, but it was the only way.

"It's a long shot, but may work. It's better than using the video game." Caleb's eyes dimmed. "Not that I really want to go back, but I have to."

Her radio blared, dispatching all available units to a church on the north side.

Another body found.

Oaklynn pictured the next victim on her father's wall of kills and cringed.

Not again.

Chapter Fifteen

Oaklynn's temples throbbed as she entered Faith Chapel and approached the body with Caleb at her heels. He arrived moments after her. Anxiety tightened her muscles at who they'd find. Why had the killer switched to targeting churches? Could the churches of Kenorapeake Falls be challenging this new cult? She made a mental note to ask Chloe if her pastor had spoken out against The Light Paragons. Her father had left none of his victims at churches, only random spots. The copycat was evolving into his own, adding to the Suicide Slayer's signature.

"Caleb, remember to stay behind the tape."

He saluted her, but smiled. "Yes, ma'am!"

Oaklynn suppressed the urge to laugh out loud. She loved that their working relationship had developed into a friendship and she enjoyed their fun banter, but now wasn't the time to show it. Someone had died by the copycat's hands. She set aside thoughts of the handsome Watcher and approached her fellow constables Eldon and Nika. "Thanks for securing the scene."

Nika spotted Caleb. "Hey, Beast. Good to see you again."

Oaklynn didn't miss the flirty tone in her voice and a stab of jealousy jabbed her heart. *Where had that come from? Focus, Oaklynn.*

"Morning all. So I hear that Beast is my new nickname." Caleb shoved his hands into his parka pockets.

Nika winked.

Oaklynn ignored Nika's unprofessionalism and entered the church sanctuary. The smell of metal combined with incense candles steamrolled Oaklynn, sending a wave of nausea crashing in her throat. Her hand flew to her mouth, subduing her queasiness. She studied the victim and gulped.

Kimi's body knelt in front of the pulpit, her fingers intertwined in a prayer position.

Just like her father's next victim.

Oaklynn's shoulders slumped as her promise to Kimi emerged.

We won't let anything happen to you.

Oaklynn had been so wrapped up in her own serial-killer-father world, she failed to save the girl. "I'm so sorry, Kimi," she whispered.

"It's not your fault, Oaklynn." Caleb squeezed her shoulder.

She turned at his touch. "How can you say that? I should have found her. Saved her. I promised." Why had she promised Kimi what she couldn't guarantee? It was something she vowed never to do on the job. She steeled her jaw, and addressed the coroner. "Let me guess. Her throat is slashed and a chunk of hair is missing."

The man looked up at her question, his fedora slipping forward. He adjusted it and grimaced. "How did you know?"

"The Suicide Slayer's third victim was found in the same position."

"But why isn't the killer trying to mask his *suicide* kills any longer?" Eldon asked.

Oaklynn cringed. "Because Aaron Crowder didn't after his

first couple of victims." She focused back on the coroner. "I'm guessing there's beads from a broken necklace somewhere at the scene."

Caleb tilted his head. "How do you know all this?"

Oaklynn caught the skepticism in his voice. "I've been studying up on the Suicide Slayer." Partial truth.

"Well, our unsub is certainly copying him," Eldon said.

Nika punched Eldon in the arm. "Dude, since when do we refer to a suspect as an unsub? This isn't the TV show *Criminal Minds*."

Eldon shrugged. "I like it."

Nika rolled her eyes.

"Well, I'll be." Dr. Patterson's expression caught their attention. "You were right, Constable Brock." He'd opened Kimi's praying hands, revealing five beads glued to her palms.

Oaklynn pictured the broken beaded necklace she'd found in her father's trinket box.

"Wait." Nika marched into Oaklynn's personal space. "How did you really know? I looked at the case too and that information wasn't included."

Stupid, Oaklynn. You just tipped your hand. Nika was correct. The police had mistakenly left that one item off the list of trinkets. Oaklynn remained oblivious to the why. *Think fast.* She rubbed her right temple. "Sorry, my eyes have gone buggy with the massive amount of paperwork, so maybe I saw it in Mrs. Corbet's memoir of the Suicide Slayer."

Nika squinted at Oaklynn, suspicion clouding her blue eyes.

Caleb inched closer. "Dr. Patterson, can you give us an approximate time of death?"

Thanks for the diversion.

"It's too soon to give a conclusive answer, but based on her lividity, I'd say approximately seven or eight hours ago. Somewhere in the wee hours of the morning."

"Thanks, Dr. Patterson." Oaklynn removed her notebook. "How is the perp subduing his victims?"

"Didn't the Suicide Slayer case files tell you that bit of information?" The sarcasm in Nika's question boomed in the small sanctuary.

Oaklynn ignored the female constable and returned her focus to Dr. Patterson.

"I was going to call you today." The coroner lifted Kimi's sleeve, revealing needle marks. "This is how. I found higher traces of benzodiazepines in the last vic's tox screen, so I went back and checked all our victims. Each had the same drug in their system. Even though I had noted it in the files, benzos are often used to treat anxiety, and we thought the first victims were suicides."

"Makes sense."

"I'm changing the manner of death to homicide on the previous victims." Dr. Patterson reached into Kimi's pocket and extracted a cell phone. "Okay, this may tell you something."

Oaklynn flinched. "How did the killer miss that here and on Missy? Unless—"

"The copycat left it on purpose." Caleb finished her thought.

"Exactly." Oaklynn spoke to Dr. Patterson. "Bag it for Chloe to get digital forensics to check."

Dr. Patterson tapped the phone, and it came to life. "Not password-protected and the last call was to…" He glanced up at Oaklynn. "You." He turned the screen in her direction.

Oaklynn's chest tightened. She'd never received a call from Kimi.

Had she? Had last night's call come from Kimi's phone?

Before Oaklynn could answer her own questions, a crash sounded from the foyer followed by a deafening whoosh. She pivoted and caught sight of flames erupting, clawing toward the sanctuary. She pointed to the side exit. "Everyone, get out!" Oaklynn tugged on Caleb's arm.

Last night's phone message invaded her mind.

I don't like how the Watcher looks at you. For that, he'll pay.

Had the copycat set the church on fire to kill her and Caleb?

Caleb covered his head as a similar scene unfolded before him in slow motion. The gunfire attack that wounded Briggs roared in Caleb's mind and a thumping rhythm clogged his throat, sending him into a desperate panic mode he thought he'd resolved. *Breathe. God's got you.* He inhaled. Exhaled. His fight-or-flight reaction lessened.

Pounding footfalls morphed into the background.

"Caleb!" Oaklynn shook him. "Did you hear me?"

Her voice jolted him out of his trance, and he turned his head.

She shook him again. "I'm going to try and contain the fire. I saw an extinguisher at the back of the sanctuary. Get the coroners and get out." Oaklynn yanked on his arm. "Can you do that?"

He nodded and nudged the doctors through the side door, stumbling behind them. Caleb gestured for the group to gather beside a nearby tree. "We'll be safe here."

Spearing darted to their sides. "Where's Oaklynn?"

"Inside, containing the flames before it gets worse." Once again, his pulse increased. "I have to help her."

"No. Firefighters are on their way."

Minutes later, Oaklynn appeared through the side door and bounded toward them. "Flames are contained. Someone tossed a Molotov cocktail into the foyer's window. How did they get by us?"

"We were canvassing the crowd to determine if anyone spotted anything." Spearing planted his fisted hands on his hips. "This is my fault. I should have been watching the entrance."

Oaklynn adjusted her duty belt. "It could happen to any of us, Eldon. Did you get any viable information from the crowd?"

Sirens blared.

"No. They all claim they didn't see anything. I'll flag the firefighters in." Spearing pivoted and sprinted to the street.

Oaklynn addressed the coroners. "You both okay?"

"Fine, but you have to see what I found just before the fire." Dr. Patterson's elevated pitch revealed his agitation.

Caleb grimaced. Not good.

"We have to wait for firefighters to give us the all clear." Oaklynn pointed to the truck as it drove into the parking lot. "I'll brief them and get us inside as quick as possible." She jogged over to the firefighter who'd jumped out of his rig.

Forty-five minutes later after getting the all clear, the group surrounded Kimi's body. Dr. Patterson eased up her shirt, exposing her lower abdomen.

Another carving.

Numbers 32:23

Caleb recalled the verse: "Your sin will find you out."

Three tiny initials were sketched beneath. *LJC.*

"Who's LJC?" Dr. Hancock asked.

Oaklynn's face paled.

"Constable Brock, can you tell us what's going on?" Darius yelled from the sanctuary's entrance.

"Ugh." Oaklynn's expression tightened. "How did you get in here?"

Caleb's cell phone rang the theme to *Happy Days*. Mic's favorite retro television show. Caleb answered, "Kind of busy right now, sis."

"I figured you'd want to know what I just found. Don't put me on speaker."

"Why?"

"Because it's about Oaklynn." His sister's tone told him whatever she found wasn't good.

Caleb squared his shoulders. He spoke to Oaklynn. "Gotta

take this outside while you deal with Darius." He left the building. "Go ahead, Mic."

"I've been searching for information on Oaklynn like you asked, but kept coming up empty on all social media, so I looked into provincial records."

"What did you find?" Caleb held his breath in anticipation.

"I searched on her name and found an Oaklynn Brock connected to a Sue Brock. Dug a little deeper and found an interesting change-of-name record." She blew out a breath. "You're not gonna believe this."

A commotion at the church's front door caught his attention.

Caleb turned back to find Oaklynn escorting Darius outside. "Spit it out, Mic."

"Name change from a Lynn Jenna Crowder to Oaklynn Brock."

Caleb whipped back around. "Wait, you said Crowder?" LJC. Could it be…? He stopped his question from stating what had just plunged into his mind.

"Apparently, Oaklynn changed her name at age eighteen and listed Sue Brock as her next of kin. Do you realize what this means? Oaklynn Brock is—or was—Lynn Jenna Crowder, and—"

"The Suicide Slayer's daughter."

What were the odds?

No wonder Oaklynn had been on an emotional roller coaster ever since someone suggested a copycat. That person was mimicking her father's kills and knew her true identity.

Slamming doors brought him back to the situation at hand. The coroners had loaded Kimi's body into their vehicle before leaving the church parking lot, just as Chloe arrived in her forensics van. The investigator rushed to Oaklynn's side.

"Bro, you there?"

Caleb observed the two women talking. "I'm here. I can't believe she didn't tell me."

"Well, she's obviously kept it a secret for a reason. Can you imagine everyone knowing she was the daughter of a serial killer?" Mic whistled.

Last night's accusations of Aaron Crowder's daughter taking over his killings entered Caleb's mind. No wonder she reacted as she had. Could it be true?

Could Oaklynn Brock have killed like her father? Who would know his case better and what he did to his victims than his own daughter?

Had she been fooling them all this time?

These questions attacked his mind like a skipping record on a never-ending annoying repeat.

He analyzed Oaklynn's countenance as the constable placed her hand on Chloe's arm in an affectionate gesture. No, he refused to believe Oaklynn was like her father. No way had Caleb misread her nature. "I gotta go, Mic. Thanks for letting me know." He ended the call without waiting for her response.

Right now, he wanted to talk to the Suicide Slayer's daughter.

And planned to get her to speak the truth. No more lies.

"Chloe, question for you. Has your pastor spoken out against The Light Paragons?" Oaklynn shifted her stance. She had deterred Darius from more false information and gave him a curt "No comment" before ordering him out of the church. The fire chief had confirmed the fire started from a Molotov cocktail and commended Oaklynn on her quick thinking to preserve the crime scene. Oaklynn's weary muscles screamed at her, and even though this late morning's scene, discussion, and message from the copycat unnerved her, she was determined to find answers. Someone definitely left the initials LJC and verse for Oaklynn, not Kimi.

"As a matter of fact, yes. I talked to him last Sunday, and he mentioned all the pastors in Kenorapeake Falls met to discuss the cult. They agreed they must warn their parishioners because the leaders of this group are sneaky. They lure them in with false pretenses."

"What does Numbers 32:23 say?"

"It talks about our sins finding us out."

Another possible message for Oaklynn?

Chloe raised the evidence bag Eldon had given her. "I heard your number is on this phone."

"Kimi didn't call me." She hauled out her cell phone and scrolled through her call logs, then turned the screen toward Chloe. "See."

"Well, hackers can mask calls easily these days." She tucked the device into her bag. "Someone is messing with your mind."

"Sure is, and it's working. I made a blunder earlier." She explained what happened with Nika.

"Ignore her. She's only out to prove you wrong in everything. I overheard her telling another constable that she hates the way Sergeant Rollins dotes on you—called you an outsider and a suck-up." Chloe rubbed Oaklynn's arm. "Don't let Nika get to you."

"She's not the one I'm worried about. Someone knows my true identity, and I'm sensing it's only a matter of time before that person exposes me."

"Why not beat them to the punch? Give Darius your story. Appeal to the community and reassure them you are not your father."

Oaklynn chewed the inside of her mouth, contemplating Chloe's suggestion. She had fought all her life to remain in the shadows. Could she now reveal the truth when she'd already been accused of taking over her father's horrific legacy? "I'm not sure."

"Why not outmaneuver this copycat? Throw him off his game?"

Chloe had a point. "I'll give it some thought."

"I'll pray for direction."

"Thanks. I'm heading to the station. Catch you later." Oaklynn trudged across the property and approached her Charger. She hit her key fob and placed her hand on the handle.

And froze.

A familiar fragrance saturated the area. Lilies.

Her mother's favorite perfume.

A tingling sensation crawled up her body like a spider creeping up on its prey, plunging her into a web of terror. Her heartbeat ratcheted up, robbing her breaths. Pressure sat on her chest and she leaned on the door to stop herself from falling, but the scent intensified. Had someone sprayed her cruiser with the perfume?

Somehow, her stalker had discovered her mother's favorite scent and flower, but how?

Her heart rate increased.

Dizziness plagued her.

Her vision tunneled.

She fought against the lightheadedness. *No, not now!* She'd never fainted from a panic attack, but the weight pressing on her chest increased.

Footfalls crunching in the snow startled her. Caleb approached with an unreadable expression, glaring darts into Oaklynn. Why?

She dropped her key fob and clutched her tightened chest with one hand, reaching toward Caleb with the other. "Can't breathe." Spots flickered. Her legs weakened.

"Oaklynn!" Caleb's cry barely registered as she dropped to the snowy ground.

Darkness called out to Oaklynn, plummeting her into its embrace.

Chapter Sixteen

Caleb crashed to the ground beside Oaklynn, whisked off his gloves, and struggled to find her pulse. A steady rhythm throbbed under his fingertip. *Thank you, Lord.* Approaching footsteps registered behind him, and he peeked over his shoulder. Chloe had seen her friend fall and charged toward them. "Call 911!" he yelled. Previous confrontational questions he had prepared flew out of his mind, Oaklynn's health trumping his need for answers.

Chloe's eyes widened, and she hit her radio button, requesting an ambulance to their location.

"Copy. EMS is five minutes out," Dispatch said.

Chloe fell to her knees. "What happened? She was fine moments ago."

"Not sure. I saw her clutch her chest and then she dropped like a rock." Caleb checked her airflow. "She's breathing and her vitals seem strong. She's young, but does she have a history of heart conditions in her family?" He noted the Charger key fob beside Oaklynn and pocketed it.

"None that she's told me." Chloe nudged her friend. "Oaklynn, wake up! Come back to me."

A scent of lilies wafted in the air. "Do you smell that?" He rubbed his nose with the back of his hand. "It's strong and smells like lilies." He scanned the area. "Odd."

Chloe's jaw dropped. "Someone left her a bouquet of them the other day. That can't be a coincidence."

Caleb rose and opened her cruiser. Only a vanilla air freshener permeated the inside of her Charger. He sniffed the car's door. "It's only on the outside and wasn't there earlier when we arrived. Did someone spray perfume while we were busy with the crime scene?"

Chloe gestured toward the group. "Could have been anyone in this crowd, but why would they do that?" She cupped Oaklynn's face in her hands. "Something made her pass out. Come on, my friend. Wake up."

Distant sirens confirmed the paramedics' approach, then grew louder.

"Stay with her. I'll wave them in." He jogged to the property's edge and waited, peering in all directions. "Come on, come on. I hear you, but I don't see you." *Lord, save Oaklynn.* His earlier anger dissipated as he willed the paramedics to hurry.

Finally, the ambulance sped around the corner. Caleb motioned for them to pull into the second driveway closer to Oaklynn's location. They parked and two paramedics hopped out. They grabbed their equipment and a gurney from the back.

"This way." Caleb waved and returned to Oaklynn.

"Step aside, please, Chloe." The brown-haired paramedic helped her to stand. "Good to see you again, but not under these circumstances."

"You too, Jayson." Chloe leaned against the cruiser. "Please help her, guys."

Jayson set his bag down and kneeled. "Tell us what happened."

Caleb gestured toward the tree he'd been leaning on while talking to Mic. "I was over there. She was by her cruiser. I headed toward her when suddenly she clutched her chest before collapsing."

Jayson checked her vitals. "Andy, vitals are strong." He spoke to Caleb and Chloe. "Are either of you aware if she's eaten today?"

"Yes, I fed her pancakes and sausage for breakfast. She had a generous helping along with a coffee and juice." Was the man thinking of food poisoning? "I ate the same thing and I'm fine."

"Any heart conditions?" Andy asked.

"Not that we know about."

Jayson and Andy continued to check her out, but Oaklynn remained unconscious. Andy stood. "Let's transport her to the hospital. Stat." He hauled the gurney closer.

Jayson unbuckled her duty belt, prying it off her waist before holding it and her radio out to Caleb. "Take these. We don't want them in the hospital."

Caleb nodded and held on to Oaklynn's police-issued weapon tightly.

The paramedics gently loaded her on the gurney.

"The medical staff will run tests and find out what's going on." Jayson spoke to Chloe. "Can you contact her family and update them?"

Chloe bit her lip. "She doesn't have any in town." She spoke to Caleb. "I'll apprise the team of the situation. Can you go to the hospital and be with her? I need to finish with the crime scene."

"Of course." Caleb retrieved the Charger key fob, handing it and Oaklynn's duty belt to Chloe. "You'll need to get someone to take her cruiser and weapon back to the station."

Chloe stuck the keys in her pocket and gripped the belt. "I will."

Andy fastened the strap, securing Oaklynn. "We can't give you any information since you're not family."

Caleb nodded. "I'm aware, but it will be good for her to have someone familiar nearby when she wakes up."

"Meet you there." Jayson pushed the gurney to the ambulance where the paramedics loaded Oaklynn into the back and roared out of the parking lot with sirens blaring.

Chloe bit her lower lip, her eyes watering. "I don't like seeing her like this. She's normally so strong, but she's had a lot on her plate lately."

"What do you mean? Besides this case?" Caleb hesitated to pry, especially with Oaklynn on her way to the hospital. But any additional information could assist Caleb in helping Oaklynn come out of whatever emotional pit she appeared to be in.

"Isn't that enough?"

"Yes, of course, but I know someone is stalking her. First, they left a note hanging on her doorknob, then the lily bouquet. Did you find out anything regarding the flowers?"

"Dead end." She unhooked her cell phone and pointed toward the church's entrance. "I've got to call the team and then get back to the crime scene. I hate not being able to go with you. She's not only a coworker but a friend." Chloe's voice hitched on the word *friend* and she fumbled to bring her phone to life.

"I understand. What do you know about her parents?"

Her eyes shot back to him. "Oaklynn is a private person, so you'll have to ask her that." She raised her phone. "Gotta make that call." She headed toward the church.

Caleb slid behind his truck's wheel and started the engine, pulling onto the street toward Kenorapeake Falls Community Hospital. He hit his signal and turned right, glancing in his rearview mirror out of habit.

The yellow Light Paragons van followed him onto the street, approaching at lightning speed.

Caleb stepped on the accelerator. He took a left into the hospital parking lot, bearing toward a police cruiser parked by the emergency entrance doors. Nika Crabb leaned against her vehicle, chatting on her phone. She turned at his abrupt arrival, her eyes widening.

Perhaps the constable would influence The Light Paragons' driver into withdrawing from Caleb, their intended target.

The van sped off in the opposite direction, disappearing around the hospital property.

Caleb blew out a ragged breath, his tightened muscles calming after the pending attack. He parked next to Nika. She approached and he hit the button to open his window. A blast of cold air burst into his cab, icing his entire body and nerves. *Keep it in check.*

Nika smiled, leaning on the frame. "What's going on, Beast? Why did you barrel in here?"

He explained what happened. "Can you alert the others to track down the van and question the driver? They were intent on ramming into me."

"Sure can. Why are you here?"

"Haven't you heard what happened to Oak—Constable Brock?" He corrected himself to keep their relationship professional.

Nika gestured toward the ER doors. "No, got called in after the fire to break up multiple fights between a few vagrants. Been kind of busy."

He explained the situation. "I'm surprised you didn't see the paramedics bring her in."

Her face twisted into an expression even Caleb found hard to read. "Like I said, been kind of busy." She pointed to another parking area. "You need to park over there, though. I'll call in the van information." She grunted and walked away, speaking into her radio.

Odd. One minute Nika was flirty and the next an ice queen. What gives?

Caleb ignored his silent question, drove to the visitors' parking area, and pressed the button for a ticket. He waited for the gate arm to raise and found a spot next to the bridge connecting the lot with the hospital.

His Bluetooth dinged with a text message.

Unknown caller appeared on his dashboard. He tensed and shut off his engine, withdrawing his cell phone from his pocket. He swiped the screen.

Next time, there won't be a cop nearby. Stay away from Nehemiah Love or you and Mic will die.

What?

Caleb strangled the steering wheel as rage emerged. *How dare this person threaten my family.*

Oaklynn gripped the sides of the hospital bed as the turmoil over the perfume incident continued to consume her. She had woken up in the ambulance confused and disorientated. Andy had reassured her she would be okay as he and Jayson rushed her into Emergency. She tried to tell them it was only a panic attack, but they wanted the doctors to check her over. That was two hours ago. After multiple tests, she still waited for a doctor's visit and assessment. The nurses had withdrawn vials of blood and said it would be quite some time before they had the results. Seemed everyone had converged through the emergency doors, expecting to be seen right away. The medical staff were filled to capacity with the recent flu season.

A slim redheaded nurse pulled the curtain back and entered the tiny bed cubical. "I want to take your blood pressure again. It was high when you first arrived."

"White coat syndrome. Hate having it taken." Oaklynn

cringed as the cuff tightened on her arm and she looked away, breathing in and out, hoping to bring the reading down. She had to get out of here. Too much was at stake.

"The doc also ordered I give you a sedative to help you relax." She dropped a couple of pills into Oaklynn's hand, then passed her a cup of water.

Oakynn took the meds against her will, but realized the quicker she complied, the quicker they'd release her. Besides, she required rest after another sleepless night.

"By the way, the triage nurse told me there's a gigantic man in the waiting room asking about you and I had to see for myself. I spoke to him, explaining we can't release any information, but he wanted us to tell you Caleb is here." She winked. "What a cutie."

Oaklynn smiled, but then remembered Caleb's expression as he charged toward her moments before she blacked out. Something had rattled him. "Can you let him come back here? He's my partner and I need to see him."

The woman wrote a couple of numbers on the back of her latex-gloved hand. "Sure can, but your blood pressure has come back down. I'm concerned he might elevate it again. Sure would mine." She whistled and walked to her nurses' station.

Five minutes later, Caleb peeked his head around her curtain. "Permission to enter?"

"Of course." Oaklynn propped herself up slightly, but dizziness spun the room and she plopped back down on the flat pillow. She closed her eyes and waited for the spinning to pass.

Caleb dragged a chair closer to the bed, the scrapping echoing throughout the emergency rooms. "How are you feeling? Has the doctor told you anything? If you want to tell me, of course."

Oaklynn opened her eyes. "They've done some tests, but I'm still waiting to hear the results from the doctor. Seems everyone has visited Emergency today."

"Yeah, the waiting room is packed. Must be a full moon. I've heard that happens."

Oaklynn fumbled with her waist. "Where's my weapon?"

"Gave it to Chloe to take to the station." Caleb grazed her arm. "Can you tell me what happened?"

How much should Oaklynn say without revealing her background? Caleb was good at reading people and she wouldn't be able to hide the anxiousness over the moment she smelled her mother's perfume. "I sometimes react to powerful smells and when I approached my cruiser, a pungent scent overpowered me." Half-truth.

"The lily perfume. I smelled it too." He leaned on his elbows. "How do you think it got there? The smell was only on the outside of your Charger."

"No idea." She fiddled with the flimsy hospital bedsheet, struggling to hide the emotions torturing her over the past few days.

"Could it be your stalker?"

Her gaze met his. "I don't have a stalker, Caleb."

He sat back in the metal chair, crossing his arms. "Call it what you want, but you do. Tell me the truth, Oaklynn. You're hiding something."

"I'm not sure who left the note or the flowers someone left outside my garage the other day and Chloe wasn't able to find anything from them."

"Constable Brock, how are you feeling?" A young male doctor, who didn't appear to be over twenty, walked into the cubical. "I'm Dr. White."

"I'm okay. Tell me what's going on."

Dr. White turned to Caleb. "And you are?"

Caleb stood and thrust out his hand. "Caleb Greene, sir."

"You family?"

"He's not, but I want him here. You can give me my results

in front of him." Oaklynn braced her muscles, expecting to hear bad news.

Dr. White removed his stethoscope from around his neck. "Lean forward, please."

She obeyed.

"Big breath." He placed the chest-piece on her back.

She winced from the coolness and breathed in.

"Again."

She took a deeper breath.

"Good. Lean back."

She complied.

He placed the chest-piece on her chest, then moments later wrapped the stethoscope back around his neck. "Your heart sounds fine, and your electrocardiogram was clear. However, the cardiac enzymes in your blood were slightly elevated earlier." He stuffed his hands inside both lab coat pockets. "Are you prone to panic attacks? Overexertion?"

"Well, my job doesn't really help. I've come close twice to having panic attacks, but the pain in my chest was intense."

"The nurse is going to draw more blood. Panic attacks don't normally lead to fainting, so we're taking all precautions and rechecking your enzymes to enable us to gain a better understanding at various time periods. For now, get some rest." He leaned closer. "Well, as much as you can in this place. I'll be back once I see the results." He spun around and marched from the room.

Caleb rubbed Oaklynn's arm. "Panic attacks can feel like a heart attack."

"That's exactly how it seemed." The image of Kimi's body entered her mind. "Seeing Kimi also didn't help. I shouldn't have promised her I'd keep her safe."

"Stop taking the responsibility for the killer on your shoulders." He reached for her hand and held it in his. "You can't save everyone. Unfortunately."

"I know."

He rubbed his thumb on her hand.

His hand in hers gave her a spark she never thought would happen, especially after all the damage her father had done. "Tell me what happened at the scene after I fell."

Caleb updated her on the situation, including his brush with The Light Paragons' van. "I gave the information to Nika, and she put the others on alert."

"Good. Eldon got nothing from Ms. Dutton. Perhaps he needs to pay her another visit."

"Possibly." Caleb cleared his throat and leaned closer. "I'm sorry to bring this up now, but I need the truth." He paused. "Are you Aaron Crowder's daughter?"

Oaklynn gasped and recoiled toward the head of the small hospital bed.

"Mic found your provincial name change, even though whoever processed it tried hard to bury it."

Her cheeks flushed as the monitor beeped her elevated heart rate. "You went behind my back and had your sister delve into my personal records?"

"Don't blame her. It's my fault, because I've sensed something off with you, especially whenever someone mentions the copycat." A hesitation. "Is it true, are you the Suicide Slayer's daughter?"

"Why does my background matter, Caleb? It's not who I am today." Or was it? Every time another victim was found, the darkness almost paralyzed her and plunged her into a pit she feared she'd never be able to escape.

"Because trust between partners is crucial."

"You're not my partner." Even though she had referred to him as being one earlier. She waggled her finger toward the curtain gap. "Please leave. Now."

"But, Oaklynn—"

"Get out before I call security."

He stood. "I'll leave, but please, we need to talk about this later." He walked to the entrance and turned. "I'm praying for you." He closed the curtain behind him.

Blocking her from the rest of the world.

Oaklynn clamped her heavy eyes shut, the meds overtaking her intent to stay awake. What had she just done? Alienated herself from the one person who could probably pluck her from the depths of her shadowy tomb. Only because he'd once been there himself. Weariness overtook her, and she surrendered to its embrace.

A crash jolted her awake, yanking her from her foggy wilderness of cults and serial killers. Thankful for the interruption, she pressed the button on her smartwatch to check the time: 5:00 pm. She'd been asleep for one hour, but it felt like an eternity while evil held her in its clutches. When would she ever be free from the claws caging her?

She eased herself up and reached for the water on the bedside table. A note propped against the cup caught her attention. Did Caleb sneak in and give her an apology? She withdrew the page from the envelope and read. A typed message piqued her curiosity.

> You look so innocent sleeping, but I know the truth. You stole my hero when you betrayed him. Time for the world to discover your identity. Sleep well because more fun is coming your way, my sweet Lynny.
> Love,
> The Protégé

Oaklynn's chest tightened and her hand flew to her heart, willing the panic to stay buried—along with her past.

Sweat beaded her forehead even though chills racked her body. She tugged the finger monitor off and swung her legs over the side of the bed. Dizziness plagued her, and she gripped the railing, allowing the room to settle before easing up. She staggered to the curtain and yanked it open, looking left and right. Only nurses scurrying to attend to patients filled the narrow corridor.

Her nurse scowled. "What are you doing up?"

Oaklynn raised the note. "Did you see who put this on the table by my bed?"

"No idea, but I've been tending to other patients." She nudged Oaklynn back toward her bed. "The doctor is coming to see you in a minute as soon as he finishes updating the nurses."

Oaklynn sighed and sat on her bed. Technically, she was now off the clock, but she mentally compiled a checklist of what she had to do before her next shift the day after tomorrow. Right now, she wanted to visit the hospital's security area and view video footage.

Dr. White bounced into her area, a smile exploding on his youthful face. "How are you feeling now?"

"Much better. Not up to chasing bandits yet, but better."

"Constable Brock, it appears you're in the clear. Your enzymes are back to normal, so I'm releasing you." He held up his index finger. "But get rest tonight and eliminate some stress from your life. Stop overexerting yourself."

Oaklynn muffled a harrumph. "Easier said than done, especially when you're a cop."

"I get it and KFPD has their hands full right now with this killer on the loose."

She bristled. "Yes, which is why I need to get out of here."

"I've already signed you out. You're free to go." Dr. White extended his hand. "Nice to meet you, Constable Brock. Please take care of yourself."

She shook his hand and squared her shoulders. "I intend to." No more panic attacks.

The young doctor dipped his chin in acknowledgment and left.

Oaklynn's cell phone buzzed on the table. She snatched it and swiped the screen. Eldon sending today's report to her and inquiring about her condition. She tapped in a reply and requested he revisit Ms. Dutton, then pocketed her phone.

The petite nurse reappeared and handed Oaklynn her jacket. "The handsome giant left this for you earlier and your ride is apparently in the waiting room."

"Thanks. Can you tell me where the security office is located?"

"Second floor." She patted Oaklynn's arm. "Take care, Officer, and don't let the giant go." She chuckled and returned to her tablet.

Well, Oaklynn was pretty sure she had ruined the likelihood of anything ever happening by the way she treated him. *You had every right. He violated your privacy.* At least, that's what she kept telling herself.

She wiggled into her coat as she made her way down the hospital corridor, and hit the red button to release the doors. She braced herself to meet Caleb, but almost collided with someone she hadn't predicted to give her a ride.

Nika.

Oaklynn halted. "Oh, I wasn't expecting you."

Nika tilted her head and tsk-tsked her. "The handsome Caleb, perhaps?"

"Listen, I need to go to the security office first." Oaklynn didn't explain why, but pointed to the side door. "How about you drive around to the visitors' entrance? I'll meet you there."

Nika frowned. "Fine. Make it fast. We're off shift and I have a pressing engagement." She headed toward the entrance but turned. "Stay away from Caleb. I want to tame the Beast." She shed the elastic holding her long sandy-brown ponytail, and stared at Oaklynn with puckered lips, as if challenging her to a duel to claim the Caleb territory.

Really? Oaklynn shook her head and burst through the door

connecting the emergency area to the rest of the hospital. She didn't have time for interoffice rivalry, or dating. *He's all yours, Nika.* She doubted Caleb would be interested—Nika didn't seem his type. Not that Oaklynn had a clear understanding of what his *type* resembled. She shrugged off the question and willed strength into her weary legs as she slugged up the steps to the second level.

Two minutes later, she approached the security door and knocked.

"Come in."

Oaklynn opened the door and stepped inside.

A single security guard sat at a desk behind multiple monitors. He raised his index finger at her as he spoke on his phone.

While Oaklynn waited for the man to finish his conversation, she tapped in a quick text to Caleb, asking him to meet her at Penny's Café tomorrow at 6 p.m. She had tomorrow off and intended to piece together this mysterious jigsaw puzzle before then. Plus, the time lapse would cool her jets and allow her to make amends for the way she reacted. He'd caught her off guard and only had the case's best interest in mind.

The guard hung up the phone. "How can I help you, miss?"

She lifted her badge. "I'm Constable Brock. You are?"

He pushed away from the desk and rose to his feet. "Head of security. Doug Speers. How can I help you, Constable?"

She explained the reason for her visit. "I can get a warrant if you want, but I need to see who visited me approximately ninety minutes ago in emergency bay number two." She paused for effect. "It's related to a high-profile case and KFPD would be eternally grateful for your assistance." She realized she was laying it on thick, but she didn't have time for a warrant.

"Let me look first. For patient privacy, of course."

She nodded and waited for him to return behind the monitors. He clicked a few buttons and checked different screens.

Moments later, he raised his hands, palms up. "I only see medical staff coming and going." He rolled back. "All yours."

She approached and leaned closer. "Take it back a bit."

He complied, then hit the play button.

Nurses, doctors, and other medical staff walked in between the corridor, housing the multiple emergency beds. Seconds later, an individual dressed in full personal protective gear stopped by Oaklynn's curtain, looked left and right before entering her area.

She pointed. "Can you pause it there?"

He obeyed.

Oaklynn studied the person's frame and body language. Average height, medium build. Hair completely covered by medical gear. Clearly, the person wanted to hide their appearance not only from Oaklynn but from everyone else. However—

Something about the individual's stance niggled at her brain. But what?

Was this person the Protégé?

And how were they able to get so close to Oaklynn undetected?

"Can you see where this person went?"

Doug fast-forwarded the footage slowly, but the person entered the medical staff lounge and never left. At least no one dressed in full garb came out. Dead end.

She thanked the guard for his help and left the office with various information, thoughts, and questions forming in her mind like one huge messy ball of expanding elastics threatening to snap.

Her cell phone dinged, and she swiped the screen. Caleb confirming he'd meet her but inquired on tomorrow's game plan. She entered a quick reply.

Off duty and plan on sleeping.

Three dots bounced on her screen.

All day?

She replied with one word.

Yep.

More bouncing dots.

Chat tomorrow. ☺

Oaklynn tucked her phone back into her pocket as appre-hension prickled her spidey senses. She glanced in all directions, but the corridor was empty.

But, once again, she couldn't escape the sensation that she wasn't alone.

The Protégé skulked around the corner where he spied Oak-lynn exiting the security office, tapping on her cell phone. He'd followed her movements from a distance, being sure to stay well hidden. She was a smart one—just like her father.

He edged out his hand, wiggling his fingers in anticipation, but drew them back. He was so close and could almost touch her. Breathe in her beautiful blond hair. He longed to discover her scent, but he'd have to wait. *Patience. Patience.* He grinned as he envisioned what he had in store for his sweet Lynny. He'd ensure their final meeting place would allow for ample time to get acquainted. Tell her all his thoughts and dreams. What he envisioned would not only surprise her, but also bring back numerous memories. Ones her father had shared with the Pro-tégé. It was the best way to give the Suicide Slayer his just re-venge for his daughter's betrayal.

Right now, he read the text messages between Lynny and

the Watcher. Yes, the Protégé had cloned her phone. Took skill and sneakiness, but he'd done it while she slept.

Keeping tabs on her through her phone helped him remain in the shadows.

A place he loved.

He clicked on a few screens, looking through her apps and chuckled. "Lynny, you should know better to keep such vital information in plain sight. Especially with techy people like me." He pocketed his phone and allowed her to leave the floor without him. Time for him to do his work for the Queen Bee, especially if he wanted the elite spot in her inner circle.

First, he would take care of the Watcher. He was tired of the man's interference. Of his superior attitude. Of his rich family. Maxwell Greene's squad would fail in their mission.

The Protégé would make sure of that.

You are not better than me, Watcher Greene. Just because you think you know everything about cults, you don't. No one knows the Queen Bee like me.

And soon he would take over everything.

Oaklynn followed Sam's cries with the other Bengals nipping at her heels. "Sam, where did you get to?" Oaklynn had arrived home after reconnecting with both Eldon and Nika at the station. Nika reported they found the Light Paragons' van abandoned in an underground garage on the north side of Kenorapeake Falls, stripped down to the framework and spray-painted with hate graffiti. Had they struck the cult's property or had Victoria done the deed herself? Eldon reported the woman mysteriously and conveniently disappeared. They issued a BOLO, but so far, nothing had surfaced. Her guidance counselor sister was frantic and demanded KFPD find her sibling.

Right now, Oaklynn was on her own mission. Find Sam. His four siblings had devoured the food she plopped into their dishes, but Sam was nowhere in sight. "Come on, boy, talk to me."

Another frantic meow came to the right of where Oaklynn stood in her hallway. She veered toward the basement and flung the door open.

Sam barreled into the kitchen.

"How do you guys keep getting locked in the basement?" Oaklynn scratched her head, racking her brain to recall if she even went downstairs early this morning. *You're losing it, girl.* Not that she didn't have lots on her mind, but she'd recall if she entered the cool lower level. Oaklynn tested the hinges, opening and closing the door. She was well aware of how the kittens chased each other. Perhaps they'd somehow shoved the door closed, locking Sam away.

Oaklynn shrugged and shut the door before returning to the kitchen. She found Sam slurping water from the bowl. She added more food. "Here you go, bud. You must be starving." She stroked the kitten's head.

Sam purred, but continued to eat.

Oaklynn stood and leaned against the counter. Her wobbly legs were done for the day, especially after her visit to the hospital. Time to take the doctor's advice and get some rest. First, she'd ensure her home was secure.

Forty-five minutes later, Oaklynn carried a hot tea and a stack of mail into her bedroom, setting them both on her nightstand. Rick had called moments ago to check in on her. Seemed Eldon had tattled about Oaklynn's trip to the hospital and Rick requested she take more time off. She refused. One day was enough. Her job took precedence over her own needs.

Oaklynn crawled into her bed and double-checked that her alarm wasn't set. Not that her internal clock wouldn't take over, but she desired a more restful sleep tonight. She grabbed her cell phone, clicked on her aunt's name in her contact list, and put her on speaker.

"Love, how was your day?"

"Interesting, Aunt Sue." Oaklynn sipped her lavender tea before giving her aunt an abridged version of what had happened.

"I'm coming to stay with you."

"No. You. Aren't." That was all Oaklynn needed. Another person to keep safe. "I'm fine. I can't put you in harm's way."

"How does this person—the Protégé—know so much about you?"

All five kittens bounded up on the bed, chasing each other.

Oaklynn jiggled her toes and Arwen pounced on top, playing with Oaklynn's foot. "No idea, but I've put in a request with the penitentiary to get Aaron's visitors' log."

"Do you believe this person paid him a visit?"

"I do. Either that or my stalker is Freda Corbet. She's the only person that would be aware of intimate case details. Details police wouldn't know." And Caleb reported the cult leader was a woman. Could Freda be involved? The woman stayed under the radar even after her book on the Suicide Slayer became a bestseller. Rumors spread throughout Hollywood suggesting turning it into a movie. Oaklynn cringed. She didn't want to see her father's kills glorified on the big screen. "There's something else that happened today. Caleb found out about my name change."

"What? How? My friend told me she buried it deep."

Oaklynn fiddled with her blanket. "Caleb's sister is a white-hat hacker. She found it and he confronted me, demanding the truth."

"What did you say?"

She clamped her eyes shut as she recalled their conversation. Not her finest moment. "Lost it on him and told him to stay out of my personal life."

"Love, why don't you just tell him the truth? I get the impression he's on your side."

She opened her eyes and stroked Elsa's fur. "But what if he believes the lies about me following in dear old Dad's footsteps?" Oaklynn couldn't bear him thinking that. She cared about what he thought of her. *You like him.*

She pounded the bed, scaring the Bengals. They dashed onto the floor.

"I honestly doubt that."

"We're only just getting to know each other. I met him when I dated Wil, but that did not go over well. I'm afraid I didn't leave the best impression."

"Sounds to me like you're crushing on the man." Aunt Sue snickered. "It's about time you showed an interest in someone. God has a strong man out there for you."

Did her aunt really believe that? "God seems to have hidden in the shadows."

"Oaklynn, that's not true. He's our light in this darkened world. Your mother had unwavering faith in her heart, even after each blow your father directed at her."

Oaklynn sipped her tea. "I find it hard to believe she could love a God that caused such pain." There. She said it out loud. Would her aunt hate her for such thoughts?

"God did not cause the pain. Yes, He allowed it and we'll never understand why until we meet Him face-to-face, but while I have life in me, I will trust in His unfailing love." Silence filtered through the speaker. "Time for you to surrender to Him. He's the only one that can give you lasting peace."

"I wish it was that simple, Aunt Sue."

"That's where the world gets it wrong. It *is* that simple."

Once again, the kittens jumped back on the bed, one by one, and circled Oaklynn's body before lying down, snuggling close as if in agreement of her aunt's assessment of God. Love and protection.

Aunt Sue yawned. "I have an early meeting tomorrow and need to get to sleep. Please think about what I said. Okay?"

"I will. Can you pray I find my sister?"

"I have been. And, Oaklynn, tell Caleb who you really are."

"Chloe thinks I should tell the entire town."

"Not a bad idea. We've tried to hide it all these years, but now that your father has passed, perhaps it's time." Another yawn. "I'll pray for direction. Night, love."

"Love you to the moon and back. Miss you." Oaklynn smiled as she pictured her sweet aunt's beautiful face.

"Love you more and miss you." She ended the call.

Oaklynn plugged her charger cord into her cell phone and dropped the device into her nightstand's drawer. She picked up her stack of mail and went through the bills, stopping at a larger envelope holding her father's penitentiary's address. The sender had written L.J. Crowder on the bubble mailer.

Suspicion coiled around Oaklynn's spine and she bolted from her bed to retrieve gloves.

Moments later, she returned with gloves on and slid her fingers under the envelope's seal, prying the flap open. Inside she found folded papers and a tiny box. Oaklynn dumped the contents onto the bed. She unfolded the paper and read.

My Dearest Lynny,
By the time you receive this letter and present, I will be gone. You see, I can't bear to live any longer. All these years, I hoped you would come and visit me. To say you're sorry for betraying me.

Didn't you love me, Lynny? I remember all our nights together cuddling in your room. Those times were special, right?

Oaklynn threw the paper down. Could she continue to read her father's rubbish? She took another sip of tea to calm her nerves and eyed the discarded letter. *Lynny.*

She could almost hear her father's voice calling her name. A shiver sliced into her, feathering over her skin. Even in death, her father held an impregnable bond over his daughter. A bond she had fought hard to break.

Her aunt's words tumbled back into her brain.

We've tried to hide it all these years, but now that your father has passed, perhaps it's time.

Maybe she's right.

Unable to resist her father's lure, Oaklynn snatched the letter and continued to read.

I loved your mother dearly, but she was about to backstab me, so I had to end her life. I'm sending you the one trophy the police never found. Her locket. She had cherished it. A friend retrieved it for me. I discovered the heirloom hidden in a secret compartment in her jewelry box, along with the secret she kept from both of us. Your sister—my other daughter. I had hoped to find her before my death, but failed.

I'm tired of this world and it's time for me to say goodbye. I love you. Lynny, you are more like me than you realize. I think you know that deep down inside. Unleash the beast and become who you're meant to be. But beware, you will pay for your betrayal. I've sent my loyal fan on a quest to find you and if you're reading this letter, it means he did. You'll never be safe from me, Lynny.

Even in death.

All my love,
Your father xo

Knots tangled her belly as her breathing shallowed. The letter slipped from her fingers and she struggled to contain the fear bubbling to the surface.

Arwen hopped on top of Oaklynn's lap and snuggled, purring loudly as if sensing her owner's terror. The kitten's action propelled Oaklynn out of her darkest thought.

She held Arwen against her cheek, letting the fur soothe her. *I am NOT you, Dad. I am NOT.*

She played the mantra over and over in her mind. The box caught her eye, and she set the kitten down. She opened the lid and found an oval gold locket with a tiny diamond sparkling from the center. Oaklynn held her breath as she opened it.

Inside was a picture of a five-year-old Lynny on one side, and a baby on the other.

Her sister.

Where are you?

Oaklynn looked upward toward her ceiling.

Lord, if You're listening, please bring my sister to me. I need to find her.

Hope washed over her as she forged her next steps. Tomorrow she would tell Caleb the truth and then all of Kenorapeake Falls. She'd outsmart the Protégé.

Catch him off guard.

Chapter Seventeen

Oaklynn shifted her cross-body bag to balance the weight and opened the door to Penny's Café at six o'clock the next evening. She had brought some of her father's case files, and his letter, to show Caleb. She mustered courage to share her past with him as she stepped inside the bustling establishment. She spied some residents she's met in her six months in Kenorapeake Falls and waved to each on her way to her reserved corner booth. It was the most secluded spot in the establishment and one facing the entrance. She slid onto the bench and wiggled out of her winter coat, exposing her purple-and-teal-plaid shirt. She loved being out of her uniform for a change. She'd been working nonstop and needed a break from the green slacks and shirt.

The owner approached, coffeepot in hand. "Hey, Oaklynn. Nice to see you again. Coffee?"

"You too, Penny." Oaklynn set her bag on the seat beside her. "Decaf?"

"Got ya covered." The fiftysomething woman filled the mug

to the three-quarter mark. "Honey and cream are in the basket. You know the drill."

"Thank you, and thanks for saving the table."

"You got a hot date?"

The bells over the door jingled, announcing a new patron. Oaklynn's eyes automatically swept to the entrance, but this time she failed to subdue a gasp.

The owner turned and whipped back around. "Oh my. Is he your date?"

Oaklynn smiled and waved at Caleb. "Not a date, Penny. A colleague."

Penny leaned closer. "Well, I sure don't look at *my* colleagues like you just looked at him."

"Shh. It's not like that." Oaklynn's previous anger toward the giant had vanished. She couldn't help but be distracted by his rugged good looks and teddy bear charm. She snatched a creamer from the basket and fumbled to open it. *Get it together. It's not a date.*

"Need help?" Caleb's deep, soothing voice only added to Oaklynn's high school girlish nerves.

"I'm good. Have a seat." Oaklynn finally found her fingers and opened the creamer, dumping it into her coffee.

Caleb removed his coat and plunked onto the bench.

Oaklynn couldn't help but stare at his muscular arms in his sage green shirt. No doubt about it, she couldn't deny her attraction any longer. *Ugh! Stop acting like a smitten teenager.*

"Would you like some coffee, sir?" Penny held the carafe over his mug.

He placed his hand on top. "Can I have tea instead?"

"Of course, handsome. I'm Penny, the owner."

"Caleb Greene, and I have to say you have the best apple fritters I've ever tasted."

"Why, thank you. Secret family recipe. Just for that, I'll bring you both one, fresh from the oven."

Caleb rubbed his hands together. "Yum. That okay, Oaklynn?"

"Absolutely. They're hard to resist." She added a teaspoon of honey to her decaf.

Penny winked and disappeared into the kitchen.

"How are you feeling?" Caleb tucked his jacket onto the window ledge.

"Still tired, but better, thanks. I slept in a bit this morning, so that helped." Even after receiving the letter and locket, Oaklynn had a solid night of rest. Perhaps because she had formulated a plan to finally reveal her identity after all these years.

"Listen—" They said simultaneously.

Caleb laughed and placed his hand over hers. "I need to say something first."

Oaklynn stilled more because she was trying hard to ignore what his touch was doing to her insides. Butterflies quivered in her tummy. "Go ahead." She squeaked the two words out.

"I'm sorry for going behind your back and getting Mic to look into your personal life." His left hand toyed with the napkin at his place mat. "It was wrong and I should have come to you first when I knew you were hiding something."

"Thank you for acknowledging that. I'm sorry for my reaction yesterday, but you caught me off guard. I wanted to meet you here and declare a truce."

"Fair enough."

She caught his gaze and held it. "You're right," she whispered, leaning in closer. "I am Aaron Crowder's daughter, Lynn Jenna." There, she said it out loud.

He yanked his hand from over hers.

She took it back. "But I am *not* my father's daughter. I went into policing to save lives, not take them." She rubbed his hand with her thumb. "And to stop as many serial killers as I can, since I kind of know how they think. Living with one gives a person a unique perspective." She gauged his expression.

He didn't flinch. Good.

"No kidding. Who all knows your real identity?"

"My former boss in Toronto, Rick, Chloe, and now you. Aunt Sue, of course." Oaklynn withdrew her hand.

"Here you go, kids." Penny placed a pot of hot water and a basket of various tea bags in front of Caleb, then set an apple fritter to his right. "Extra large one for you, big guy."

Caleb chuckled. "Are you trying to ruin my girlish figure?"

Penny set Oaklynn's fritter beside her coffee mug. "I doubt that will happen. Enjoy." She winked and left.

"She's quite the character." Caleb riffled through the tea bags and selected one. "Question, why come clean now? Is it because I found out?"

"Partly, but it's time for the real Oaklynn Brock to stand up and face her past." She took her doughnut in hand. "I want to beat the copycat and tell Darius my story. After I inform my coworkers, of course." She bit into the apple delight, enjoying the cinnamon flavor.

"So, was the first article about your father's death true? It was you who called the police on him?"

She finished her bite and took a sip of coffee. "Yes. I found his trinkets hidden in his office. I had suspected something was off after I realized he killed my mother. He just disappeared way too much throughout my life. Plus, he beat my mom. I should have figured it out long before I did."

"Well, every daughter idolizes their father."

Not really. If he only knew the entire truth, but some things Oaklynn still kept to herself.

He squeezed her hand before cradling his mug. "I'm so sorry. That must have been tough growing up in a killer's shadow."

"You have no idea." She licked her fingers before wiping them on a napkin. "This came for me yesterday." She passed her father's letter to him. "It was postmarked the day after he killed himself." She observed the Watcher as he read her father's words, his expression tightening with each sentence.

He passed the paper back to her before clenching his right fingers into a fist. "How dare he threaten you."

"He did it all throughout the trial too and reached out several times, but Aunt Sue and I moved away. We had to after all the threats I received. I started getting bullied at school too. It was terrible. I changed my name when I turned eighteen." She tapped on the letter. "He refers to a loyal fan. That's our copycat and I'm waiting for a visitors' log from the warden. I believe this person knows all about my family, even my father's cologne and mother's perfume."

"Aww, let me guess. The lily scent triggered your attack?"

"Yes. This person is following me. I can sense it."

Caleb's expression clouded. "I promise you, Oaklynn. I will keep you safe."

"No. You can't promise me that. Remember Kimi?"

He nodded. "But I'll be beside you, protecting you when we find this copycat and, mark my words, we will find him—or her."

"So you don't think the copycat is me, then?" She closed her eyes and held her breath, waiting for his response.

"Look at me." Once again, his baritone voice sent chills skittering across her arms.

She opened her eyes and stared into his beautiful green, kind eyes, which held no contempt.

"I believe you."

Should she also confess her deepest fear? "Sometimes I fear I have his tendencies. You know, 'is the evil gene hereditary?' Could I kill like he did? Those questions continually haunt me."

He placed his hand on top of hers and squeezed her fingers. "You are nothing like Aaron Crowder. I realize we're just getting to know each other, but you're kindhearted, Oaklynn." He withdrew his hand, glancing away.

"What is it?"

He sighed and faced her once again. "I need to tell *you* something. Something I'm sharing with my family tonight." He dunked the tea bag over and over in the hot water. "I too have a dark secret."

She placed her hand on his. "You can tell me. No judgment, I promise."

"Don't be too sure." He drew his hand away and sipped his tea.

Stalling for time or gathering his words?

"I told you how deep I was involved in the Purity Flock, but not everything I did in my enforcer role. Yes, I used my fists to do the talking, but once I found out Nehemiah had my best friend killed, I planned my revenge." Another sip. "The day Maxwell found me and Nehemiah fighting, he saw the knife in the leader's hand, but that's only because Nehemiah fought me for it and won."

"The knife was yours."

He nodded. "Oaklynn, I had planned to kill him that day, but Maxwell saved my life—literally and from being imprisoned. He and the police never knew that I was there to kill."

"Why didn't Nehemiah tell them?"

"He tried, but my fellow worshippers told the police how I helped them all. I wasn't just an enforcer, I was a friend to many. When they found out the truth behind Nehemiah's lies, they came forward. Not one of the flock I had beat up charged me. God had my back. I did community service for my crimes because, Oaklynn, I told them about my role even though no one came forward to lay blame." He fingered his napkin. "God brought me out of the depths of hell that day and I surrendered to Him. Don't get me wrong, it wasn't easy, especially when my sweet Aiyana was killed, but He is always there in the darkness even when I can't see His light."

"You sound like Aunt Sue. She said something similar to

me last night." Oaklynn finished her apple fritter while the two sat in silence.

Who would guess they both held such dark secrets? However, Oaklynn still hadn't told Caleb everything and right now, that portion of her story wasn't necessary to share. "I'm sorry you felt like you had to bury that part of your past." Oaklynn fingered the locket she now wore around her neck. Sure, it was a gift from her father, but more importantly, it was her mother's. She could now hold Jenna Crowder and Oaklynn's sister close to her heart.

"I was scared what my family would think and—what you would."

"Why? I barely know you." But would like to know more. The thought raced through her mind before she could stop it. "Like I said, I'm not one to judge."

"Thank you for that." He pointed at the files. "So, what's next?"

"I'm going to share my story with Darius."

"You sure?"

Was she? She fished out her cell phone, tapping a message to the reporter and asking for a meeting. It was time to bare all to the world.

She just hoped Kenorapeake Falls took the news as well as Caleb.

Caleb analyzed the gorgeous blonde's face. Even though she had shared her identity with him, he sensed she still held something back, but he would not pressure her. He made that mistake yesterday, even though in the end, it was the catalyst that urged her to speak the truth. Caleb had to admit to himself that he cared what she thought of him. His attraction hit him tonight as soon as she waved to him from her booth. Her beauty was undeniable in her police uniform, but shone in her plaid shirt and her long, straight hair out of its normal bun or ponytail. He had fought hard not to stare like a schoolboy with a crush. Was she also sensing the spark between them?

He noted her fiddling with the pendant around her neck. "Is that the locket your father referred to in his letter?"

She dropped her hand. "Yes. It seems odd to wear a gift from him, but it was my mother's, so I feel like I have a little of her with me."

"I can understand that. Are there pictures inside?"

Her eyes brightened, and she quickly opened it. "Yes. That's me on the left." She leaned closer, lifting it toward him. "This is my sister." Her voice cracked with emotion.

"You never knew about her or that your mother was pregnant?"

"No. Mom must have hid her baby bump well. She gave her second child up at birth to keep her from my father. She didn't want him—" She stopped, then closed the locket. "Let's just say she did it because she didn't want another daughter growing up in an abusive home. He hit Mom more than once."

"I'm so sorry. When did she pass away?"

"I was five and walked in on my father killing her, but he said he was trying to save her, so I believed him." Oaklynn shared how she discovered her father's secrets.

He whistled and sat back. "I can't even imagine what you must have gone through."

She raised her mug, flagging down the owner. "Now you understand the reason I kept my identity concealed from everyone. People continually ridiculed me with comments like, 'Are you like him?' 'How didn't you know?'—stuff like that. I'm glad my sister didn't have to go through that, but I need to find her."

Penny approached their booth. "I put on a fresh decaf. It will be a minute."

Oaklynn pushed her mug to the right. "No prob. Thanks Penny."

The woman nodded and retreated.

Oaklynn's phone buzzed, and she swiped the screen. "Eldon reporting he's contacted Slim, and he agreed to get you into the cult. Our plan worked." Another message. "He said tomorrow. That okay?"

Caleb's heart rate accelerated at the thought of entering another cult's lair. Could he put himself at risk again?

Oaklynn reached across the table and squeezed his forearm. "You don't have to do it, Caleb. We can find another way to get inside."

He smiled and tried hard to ignore what her soft touch did to his emotions. "Thank you for your concern, but it's the only way. We must determine for sure if these killings are related to the cult. Going inside is the only answer. I have my prayer warriors on standby. What time tomorrow?"

Oaklynn tapped in a message. The reply came seconds later. "Nine thirty. Meet Slim here in front of Penny's."

He puffed out a long breath. "Tell Eldon I'll be wearing a red hat."

Once again, Oaklynn keyed on her phone. "Tell me your game plan."

Shattering glass interrupted their conversation.

Caleb turned toward the crash. Someone had knocked into a young server. Penny placed the coffee carafe on the counter and helped the female to her feet, then bent to clean up the mess.

"I'll explain that I'm secretly interested in their organization and want to know more." He raised his finger. "I'll ask someone to show me around and go from there. I'll memorize the route, the buildings, people, armory, etc. I'll report to you after I return. I'll probably need to go back, though, to gain their trust before they'll let me in."

Her phone dinged twice. "Eldon says it's a go." She swiped her screen. "Also an email from—"

Penny appeared holding the carafe. "So sorry for the delay.

Had a little mess to deal with." She poured Oaklynn her coffee. "Anything else? More tea, Caleb?"

"I'm good."

Oaklynn added cream and honey to her cup. "Thanks, Penny."

"You're welcome. Take your time, kids. Today's treat is on the house. Thank you for your service." She smiled and pivoted, colliding with a teenager. The coffee carafe slipped from her grasp and smashed to the floor. Penny jumped backward and mumbled before throwing her hands in the air. "What's up with you teens tonight?"

The young man ducked his head. "Sorry, ma'am." He shuffled back to his table.

"Busy spot." Caleb added more hot water into his mug. "What were you saying about an email?"

"The prison warden attached a visitors' log for the past two years for my father." She set her phone down. "I'll look at it later to see if anything pops."

"Good." Caleb checked his watch. "Oh shoot. I gotta run. I promised Lilly a game of Clue before bed."

"Clue? I'm surprised this generation likes that board game. Lilly is such a cutie." Oaklynn took a few more sips of coffee, fished out a lip balm from her pocket and applied some, then nabbed her coat.

"She is." Caleb withdrew his wallet and dropped money on the table. "Tip for Penny's generosity. I'll walk you to your car." He slid out of the booth and put on his coat.

Oaklynn slipped her bag's strap over her shoulder and waved to Penny. "Thanks. See you later."

The woman saluted. "Behave yourselves now."

"What does that mean?" Caleb placed his hand on the small of Oaklynn's back, edging her toward the entrance.

"Who knows?"

Caleb opened the door. "After you."

They stepped into the brisk night. Snowflakes floated like feathers, fluttering to the ground. The evening reminded him of the TV movies Mic made him watch during the Christmas holidays, where it snowed at the end of the movie, right at the perfect romantic moment.

Had he really just thought about romance?

Oaklynn held her hands out. "Oh, I love when the snow falls like this. Winter is my favorite time of year."

He held out the crook of his elbow. "Shall we?"

She giggled and hooked her arm through his. "Yes, fine sir."

"I'm thankful we shared tonight." Caleb patted her hand. "Trust is so important to me."

"I was scared you wouldn't come after how I treated you at the hospital." Oaklynn fished out her key fob and hit the button. The lights on her red Jeep flickered.

Caleb opened her door. "You couldn't have kept me away."

A snowflake fluttered and landed on her hair. He reached and brushed it off, his fingers lingering near her face.

Their gazes locked, suspended in time as snowflakes fell in slow motion. Caleb wished he could read minds at that moment. Was she feeling their electricity?

His eyes shifted to her lips. What would it be like to kiss her and taste the flavor of her lip balm? Hold her close?

Caleb had never even considered a relationship after his divorce, but right now was a different story. He leaned closer.

She drew in a soft breath at his sudden movement, but didn't back away. Was she giving him permission?

"Oaklynn..." He caressed her soft skin.

The front café door opened and closed. Teenagers laughed and bounded toward them, breaking their moment.

She cleared her throat. "I gotta get home. I'll reconnect tomorrow, okay?" She lowered onto the driver's seat and started the engine.

"Drive safe. Night." He closed her door and retreated as she backed out of her spot.

She waved and drove out of the parking lot.

Caleb waited until her vehicle turned a corner and disappeared into the night before returning to his truck. He grinned. *That was quite the evening.*

Not how he'd planned it, but thankful they'd cleared the air. A question rose.

Had he muddied their relationship by almost kissing the beautiful daughter of a serial killer?

He banged the wheel before easing from his hidden parking spot beside the building next to the bakery. How dare Caleb touch her like a lover. Thankfully, the teens interrupted their little tête-à-tête. The Watcher almost kissed *his* Lynny. If anyone was going to kiss her, it would be the Protégé. Before he fulfilled Aaron's dying wish to make his daughter pay for her sins.

The Protégé flawlessly carried out his plan. He couldn't have asked for it to go better. He had blended into the evening café crowd nicely, pretending to be on a date with a woman he'd met on the internet. She wasn't aware of his intentions when they arrived separately. Oaklynn had even acknowledged him as she walked by their table, located close to her booth. He had the perfect view and spot to catch some of their conversation.

He'd feigned a migraine and left through the side door moments after Lynny left. Just in time to see their sickening exchange. It almost made him lose his baked treats.

Bribing those teens to create a diversion was smart. He was able to slip the right amount of drug into the coffee to get Lynny safely home, but enough for her to succumb to its effects. He smiled as he spied his bag of tricks on the passenger seat. He couldn't wait to see her expression in the morning.

And really, Lynny. You think you can beat me in telling the world who you really are? He'd seen her text to Darius. He'd send his letter to the editor as soon as he finished with her tonight.

Then the world would know the Suicide Slayer's daughter had been right under their noses all along.

And the Watcher was planning on sneaking into the compound? Well, let him come. The Queen Bee would welcome him into her hive. For now. The Protégé would let him think he was safe before striking. First, he'd make him suffer, before executing his final plan.

He smiled and turned right, following Lynny from a safe distance.

Ten minutes later, the Protégé gripped his bag and skulked between the trees, watching Lynny stumble up her doorstep. The drug was working exactly as it should.

Time for some fun.

Chapter Eighteen

Buzzing filtered through Oaklynn's foggy brain. She reached out from under the covers and slapped her alarm clock, but the constant pulsating vibration didn't stop. She eased up onto her elbows and squinted from the sun shining through her open blind. Odd. She normally closed those at night.

Wait—

She bolted into a seated position, her head struggling to clear the haze invading her mind. Oaklynn checked the time on her digital clock radio. Nine thirty? Why hadn't she set her alarm? She never slept in this late.

She flung off the covers, then froze. Why was she still wearing last night's clothes? Oaklynn rubbed her throbbing temples, racking her brain to recall what happened after she left the bakery. She remembered feeling lightheaded as she walked up to her front door, but everything after that was a complete blank. Had she been so tired that she just fell into bed?

Once again, her cell phone buzzed. She rose slowly and

snatched the device from her nightstand, swiping the screen. She gasped.

Multiple texts displayed, inquiring about her whereabouts, and why she lied. What were they referring to? Numerous missed calls also revealed her colleagues had attempted to get in touch with her, including Rick and Chloe.

Three texts from Caleb.

Morning. Hope you slept well. Getting ready to meet Slim.

Two minutes later.

You there?

Another minute.

It's now nine. Where are you? I'm worried. Calling you.

She checked her voice messages and clicked on Caleb's.

"Oaklynn, you okay? Have you read this morning's online letter to the editor yet? The Protégé beat you. Your identity is now out and the comments on the online article aren't kind. I wanted to make sure you're okay."

She sucked in a sharp breath. *No. No. No.* No wonder she received all the texts from her coworkers.

Caleb's message continued after a pause. "Call me when you get this."

She listened to messages from Chloe and Rick, each reaching out to see if she was okay. The last one from Chloe stated she was on her way to check on her.

Bile rose in her throat. Oaklynn tossed her phone on the bed and dashed to the washroom, dropping to her knees in front of the toilet. She expelled her stomach contents as her heartbeat thundered, threatening another attack. How was this happening? *Deep breaths, Oaklynn.*

In.

Out.

In.

Out.

Gradually, her heart rate slowed. She flushed the toilet and pushed herself upright, stumbling to the sink. Turning on the tap, she flushed handfuls of cool water onto her face. The freshness soothed her, but she failed to remember what had happened last night. Is this what it felt like to be drunk? She never touched alcohol because it brought back too many memories, especially the pungent whiskey smell on her father's breath when he visited her at night.

Oaklynn remembered various rape cases where perpetrators had drugged their victims. She recalled one in particular where the nineteen-year-old hadn't remembered how she was drugged, only that she woke up tied to a bed. Had someone drugged Oaklynn? How had she made it home safely?

Thankfully, Chloe was on her way and Oaklynn would ask her forensic friend what to do. They'd need to test her blood, but how had someone slipped it into her drink right under her nose? The commotions from the café entered her mind. That had to have been when her stalker had acted. It was the only answer. These perps were clever and sneaky.

Oaklynn snatched the hand towel from the hook and wiped her face, gazing into the mirror over the sink. What the—

She flicked the light on and turned her head to peer closer.

A chunk of hair was missing and replaced with a lily tattooed at her hairline. "Lynny" had been etched in black along the curved green stem.

She screamed and stumbled backward. Her shaky legs gave out, and she crashed to the floor, sobbing uncontrollably.

Oaklynn pounded the tile flooring. "Why God, why?" She

curled into a fetal position and let the tears come. She could no longer stop them. Tears over her mother's death, the years of abuse, the shame of being a serial killer's daughter, having to live in the darkness—all of it came gushing to the surface like a geyser rupturing its water volcano.

The Bengals flooded into the bathroom, circling Oaklynn and rubbing against her, as if extending their condolences.

Oaklynn's tears subsided five minutes later, and she sat up, wiping her eyes. She let out an exaggerated breath, her shoulders rising with each inhale and drooping with each exhale. She steeled her jaw, and rose to her feet. Time to put on her police uniform and face whoever invaded her privacy. She hadn't worked this hard to let a setback like this turn her into a cowering, helpless female.

The doorbell rang and she willed her weak legs toward the front door, peeking through the side panel window. Chloe. Oaklynn tugged the door open.

Chloe scanned Oaklynn's disheveled appearance head to toe, her eyes widening. "Girl, what's going on?"

Oaklynn glanced over her friend's shoulder, looking left and right. She seized Chloe's arm and hauled her inside. "I need your help. Did you see anyone on my property when you drove down the driveway?"

"No, why? You're scaring me. Why aren't you at work? You're never late. Are you sick?" Chloe's rushed speech revealed her concern for her friend.

"Because I believe someone drugged me last night and did this to me." She turned her head and pointed to her neck.

"What?" Chloe peered closer. "Was this the work of the Protégé who outed you in the letter to the editor?"

"I'm pretty sure that's the case." Her voice quivered. "I know I wouldn't have done this to myself." She gestured to her shirt and jeans. "Plus, I woke up in my bed with the same clothes on from last night."

Chloe snagged Oaklynn's arm. "Wait, you don't think—"

"No, but I need you to put your forensic hat on. What do I do?"

"Go to the hospital. Test your blood and urine. You have to get checked out. Just in case. What's the last thing you remember?"

"Driving home and walking up the front steps. I felt light-headed when I reached my door. Then nothing until I woke up this morning." Once again, she pointed to the tattoo. "How was someone able to tattoo my neck and put the film on top without me feeling any of it?"

"My guess is they gave you more drugs to keep you subdued. How did they breach your house? We need to do a thorough sweep of every room." Chloe unclipped her radio. "I'm calling this in. Put your uniform in a bag and I'll get Eldon to take you to the hospital. You can't stay here."

"Do you think whoever did this is still in the house?"

"Doubtful, but I'll get constables here and before you say anything, no, you're not clearing the house. You need to step aside this time."

Oaklynn pursed her lips, realizing her friend was right. "Are the others upset with me?"

"Let's just say I overheard some choice words at the station. Oaklynn, they'll get over it once you explain everything."

"But I wanted them to hear it from me first."

"Explain that to them. You need to stay somewhere else."

Oaklynn placed her fists on her hips. "I will not let someone drive me from my home."

"I'm pretty sure Caleb would disagree with you. He called me earlier looking for you and wanted to come here to check on you himself, but had to get to his meeting or they'd lose the opportunity to infiltrate the cult compound. He was worried. Get your stuff. Let's go." Chloe walked down the hallway, speaking into her radio, requesting a team at Oaklynn's home.

Oaklynn couldn't argue with Chloe's thinking and staggered into her bedroom, rubbing her weary muscles. *God, give me strength.* What? Now she was asking for His help? She hated her yo-yo emotions. *Get a grip.* She entered her walk-in closet, tugged her uniform off the hanger, and stuffed it into a bag, then added toiletries. Oaklynn would do as Chloe said and then get to the station.

She had fires to put out.

And a copycat killer to catch.

He smirked from his hiding place. She'd almost touched him when she reached into her closet, but the Protégé knew how to stay in the shadows. He'd done it all his life after his mother whipped him for supposedly misbehaving. She made him face the walls for hours. After she released him, he hid in her closet, watching her every move. He wanted to explore how he could unleash his revenge.

It took him five years to come up with a plan, but when he turned sixteen, he celebrated by poisoning her little by little. She wasn't aware the gradual "sickness" ending her life was orchestrated by her own son.

Even though he still loved his mom, she was the Protégé's first victim, and what sparked his lust for killing.

He waited for Oaklynn to finish packing and leave her room before he slowly emerged from the shadows. Chloe and Oaklynn talked in the kitchen, so he tiptoed down the hall in the opposite direction and exited her home through the back entrance. Years of lurking around his mother's home had honed his stealthy prowling. He crept to one tree, then another, making his way back out to the highway where he'd hidden his vehicle.

Time to put the next surprise into action.

After getting her blood and urine taken, and checked out by a doctor, Oaklynn entered the Kenorapeake Falls Police Department station two hours later. She had requested the team meet her for a quick meeting. Chloe and the constables had finished at her home, stating no one lurked anywhere, but they had found footsteps in the snow at her back entrance, leading through the trees and onto the highway. They guessed that was where her stalker had parked. Oaklynn had given Chloe the letter and locket to check for prints.

Sergeant Rollins had called the mayor to put pressure on the lab to provide results of her tests. This violation solidified Oaklynn's determination to bring this person to justice.

Time to face her coworkers. *You can do this.* She took off her coat and hung it on the rack by the door.

Chloe darted toward her, raising a document. "You're here. Good. The mayor's pressure worked. Got the results and it's what I expected. Large dosage of a benzodiazepine and *gamma hydroxybutyrate.*"

Oaklynn inhaled audibly. "Seems to be his drug of choice and why I didn't feel the tattoo needle. I was totally out of it."

"Yep." She held out the locket and passed it to her. "No prints on either this or the letter. Sorry. How are you doing?"

"Little shaky, but much better than earlier." She gestured toward the station's briefing area before pocketing her pendant. "I'm apprehensive about sharing with our team. Is everyone here?"

Eldon popped around the corner. "We are."

Chloe slapped the paper on the top of his head. "Dude, quit eavesdropping."

"Was just coming out to grab a cup of coffee and heard Oaklynn's quest—" He stopped. "Or do we call you Lynn?"

"Nope. Legally changed my name. It's Oaklynn." She addressed Chloe. "Any prints at the house?"

"Only yours. The perp obviously wore gloves."

Eldon folded his muscular arms across his chest. "How did

they gain access to your home? Did he follow you through the front door?"

"Good question." Oaklynn bit her lip as the strange circumstances happening at her home barreled into her mind. The kittens getting locked in, the lullaby. She shuddered at the thought that someone had gained access all this time. She voiced her opinions to Eldon and Chloe.

"Another reason you need to get the kitties and vacate your home," Chloe said.

"She's right, Brock." Eldon retrieved his phone from his vest pocket. "I'll arrange for cruisers to keep a continual watch on your property until you can relocate."

"I hate it has come to that, but you're right." She checked her cell phone for updates from Caleb. She had texted him on the way to the hospital, but so far he'd been silent. Not that she was surprised. He probably had to leave his phone behind when he entered the compound. *Please be safe.*

Oaklynn gestured toward the staff lunchroom. "Grab your coffee. I want to get this meeting over with."

Sergeant Rollins trudged down the corridor. "Glad to see you're okay."

"What are you doing here? I thought you were taking some personal time."

"I'm here for you." He guided her toward the front and turned to the group. "Thanks for coming, everyone. Oaklynn called this meeting, but I want to say a few words. First, I was aware of her past from the beginning, so if you want to blame anyone for the secrecy, blame me."

Murmurs erupted among the group.

He raised his hand. "Let me finish. This woman has been through more than we could ever imagine happening in our lifetime, so go easy on her. Living with a serial killer causes those around you to judge and ask questions like how didn't she know? Is she like her father? What took her so long to call the police?"

He stepped forward. "I'm here to tell you—this woman—" he pointed back at her before continuing "—Oaklynn Brock is not like Aaron Crowder. She's kindhearted, gentle, and NOT our copycat. So, if any one of you says otherwise, you will have to deal with me." He poked himself in the chest. "Got it?"

Silence filled the room.

He cupped his right hand on his ear. "Can't hear you."

"Got it, Sarge." Eldon sipped his coffee.

Others murmured their responses.

Rick turned back to Oaklynn. "Okay, go ahead."

Emotion bubbled inside Oaklynn at the man's fatherlike protection, and she struggled to keep the tears from exploding to the surface. *Keep it professional.* She smiled and moved beside him, squeezing his arm. "Thank you, sir." She inhaled a deep breath before facing her coworkers. "First, I want to apologize that you weren't informed about this by me. I had planned on revealing everything to you this morning, but the Protégé beat me to the punch. He seems to be one step ahead of us." She fisted her hands, but cemented them by her sides. "Yes, I *am* Aaron Crowder's daughter and, yes, I found his trinkets when I was fifteen." She shoved her hands in her pockets and paced, gathering her thoughts on how much to reveal. "My childhood was hard, but know this. I had no knowledge that my father was a killer until I stumbled upon a letter my mother had concealed. She had planned on taking me and running far away, but he caught her and killed her."

Stammers filled the room.

She raised her index finger. "He denied it and I believed him. Until I found that hidden letter at age fifteen. After that, I understood more about his odd behavior. At first, I thought it was just his hectic work schedule. He was a surgeon, so he was gone a lot. Left me in the company of our next-door neighbor." She puffed out a breath. "But one day when he was on a supposed trip, I looked in his study. I found the trinkets and remembered the police releasing their profile. It said the Suicide Slayer was taking chunks of hair and jewelry from his victims."

Nika whistled. "That's how you knew about the beads."

"Yes, because it was the one item the police failed to catalog. After his arrest, the police told me they had suspected my father because two witnesses came forward tying him to two different victims, but my call sealed their case. After that I went to live with my aunt Sue. She shared how my mother tried hard to leave with me, but he always found out." Oaklynn bit her lip. "And then beat her for her insubordination." She paused, thinking about how much more to share. "I started receiving death threats from the Suicide Slayer fans…and yes, serial killers have fans. Plus, kids at school taunted and bullied me. After I turned sixteen, we moved to another town. At eighteen, I changed my name legally. I had to get out of Aaron Crowder's shadow."

Eldon's hand shot up. "Sergeant Rollins, while I can appreciate everything Oaklynn has gone through, why did you put her as lead on this case? It's too personal."

The sergeant placed his hands on his hips. "Because living with a serial killer gives a person added insight, and I wanted to tap into that for this case, especially with all the talk of a copycat."

Constable Dalton stood. "So, this Protégé was a loyal fan of Aaron Crowder's? Have we checked his visitors' logs?"

"I just received the list. I didn't recognize any names. Eldon, I'm giving them to you to check into. I want fresh eyes on it." Oaklynn hoped to gain the constable's respect. "I trust your judgment and while I'm not stepping down, I want to give you more responsibility."

He nodded. "Happy to help. We need to catch this guy."

"Agreed, we should have more insight on the cult from Caleb," Rick said. "He's with them right now. Hopefully by tonight, we'll discover where their compound is so we can gather more intel and formulate an action plan. We're not moving in until we have solid evidence linking the cult with these killings. Oaklynn, anything more to add?"

"Only that again, I'm sorry, and I hope to regain your trust. I'm meeting with Darius to give him my response to the Protégé's letter to the editor as I want to assure the residents of Kenorapeake Falls I am not taking up my father's torch. I'm determined to catch the copycat."

Rick clapped. "Okay. Get back to work."

The group vacated the room seconds before the admin Gracie hurried toward Oaklynn. "There's someone at the front door asking for you."

"Okay, thanks. Tell them I'll be there in a sec." Oaklynn turned to Chloe and Rick. "Thank you for your support. You're both amazing."

Rick patted her hand. "You've got this. We're getting closer to breaking this case."

"Hope so. Gotta go see who's here." Oaklynn headed toward the station's entrance to meet her visitor. She halted, her jaw dropping as she stared into the eyes of a younger version of herself.

It couldn't be. Had her sister found Oaklynn?

Chapter Nineteen

Someone yanked his hood off and nudged Caleb out of the van. Caleb blinked to adjust his eyes to the sunlight. As he suspected, the driver had demanded he turn off his GPS and hand over his phone back at the bakery. Caleb had complied, but he hit the button of his recorder app before locking the screen and relinquishing the device. He also caught a text from Oaklynn. Her lack of response had him concerned, but Chloe had promised she'd check in on her. *Thank you, Lord, that she's okay.*

Caleb and Oaklynn had bonded last night. Revealing his secret to her had prompted him to tell his family. They took it well and his father told him after that he'd guessed something wasn't quite right with Caleb's story, but he hadn't pressed and waited for Caleb to come clean. They embraced, and Caleb felt like the elephant sitting on his chest had finally lifted—after all these years.

Thank You, God. Please protect me now as I dive into this new evil.

Once his eyes focused, he surveyed the compound and memorized details. Multiple cabins arranged in a circle surrounded a rustic large stone building that Caleb guessed to be their mess hall and meeting sanctuary. They had built the cabins among the dense forest foliage, adding to the secluded compound. Caleb noted a walkway and bridge leading over a frozen river to another area. "Impressive place you have here." Caleb had to milk the ruse to get more information. He pointed to the walkway. "What's over there?"

The driver swore and pushed him toward the main building. "None of your business." He turned to Slim. "Why did you bring this guy here? He's working with the cops, ain't he?"

Slim eyed Caleb before responding. "Said he was interested in finding out more about our organization. Coppers don't know he's here."

Caleb relaxed at Slim's answer. "That's right. I was involved with a similar organization before and loved being part of a special community." *Lord, forgive me for the lie.*

"We'll leave it to our leaders to figure out if you're telling the truth or not. Go, some disciples are waiting for you."

Caleb cringed. Was that good or bad?

Slim leaned closer. "Don't mess this up or I'm toast." He grabbed Caleb's arm. "You're gonna love it here."

The man deserved an award for his show. Seemed the drug dealer was good at deception, but had he faked Caleb's way into the compound to trap him?

Caleb prayed that wasn't the case and braced himself for confrontation as they walked up the stone steps, entering the building.

Three individuals in red-hooded robes greeted the trio. They all wore white masks. Caleb noted two had black rope belts, the other a gold one. The latter approached. "Welcome to the light. We're excited you're here, Caleb Greene."

Caleb scrutinized the trio with his former military-trained eyes. The one with the gold belt towered over the two medium-height disciples. Caleb didn't recognize the man's voice.

"Glad to be here." Caleb stuck out his hand. "I'm at a disadvantage. What's your name?"

The man placed his hands inside his robe's pockets. "I'm Disciple John and we don't shake hands here. Our leader demands cleanliness on all of her flock." He gestured toward the other two robed individuals. "These are Disciples Bart and Peter."

Caleb guessed Bart was short for Bartholomew. They were using the names of Christ's disciples. He restrained the sudden rush of anger, masking his disgust for this cult. He forced a smile. "Understood, and I respect that." He made an exaggeration of looking around. "What an impressive building. What goes on here?"

Disciple John's eyes glistened through the mask holes. "Thank you. We pride ourselves in our beautiful compound." He pointed right. "Down there we eat as a family, but first you'll see our inner sanctuary where we hold our meetings."

Disciple Bart folded his arms. "Why are you really here? I thought you were working with the police?"

His voice sounded familiar, but Caleb couldn't place the man behind the mask. "The police don't know I'm here. I've always had a fascination with groups like yours and wanted to find out more. I'm all about sharing light in our world."

Disciple John gestured to the entrance at the center of the foyer. "Come."

Caleb noted a door at the end of the corridor to the left. "What's that way?"

"Only the twelve are allowed downstairs unless otherwise instructed," John said.

Interesting. Was that where they held their sacrifices? Caleb scrambled to invent an excuse to get to the lower level, but nothing surfaced. *Show me, Lord.*

"Caleb, you have two hours and then I'll return to drive you back to town." The driver bounded down the steps and went outside.

Caleb followed the disciples through the double doors and entered a sanctuary similar to most churches. Cushioned pews lined both sides of the room. A platform holding a pulpit and twelve chairs sat center stage.

Disciple John pointed to the back row. "She's about to begin. You and Brother Buck sit here."

The duo obeyed and three others walked to the platform, sitting in what Caleb guessed were their designated chairs. He counted eleven red-robed individuals. Was one disciple missing or yet to be appointed?

Disciple John walked to the pulpit and tapped on the mic. "Greetings, flock. You're in for a treat today. Our prestigious leader is among us to extend a special message." He gestured to the right.

A figure dressed in gold with a matching hood and mask appeared through a side door. Her feminine prance across the stage revealed the leader was a woman.

John sat in a chair to the right of the pulpit.

"Welcome." The gold-robed female extended her hands out, her flowing sleeves giving off an angelic presence. "So glad you're here today."

This had to be the female Nehemiah had mentioned. Caleb listened to her voice, but guessed she used some type of distortion app as her high-pitched tone sounded digital-like. He studied the other disciples' movements. They were all masculine. A group of male disciples following a female leader. Interesting.

Caleb memorized everything while the woman spoke about love and cleansing for a solid forty-five minutes. She urged the people to reach out to their families and friends to bring them into the fold before they were cleansed from the evil plaguing their community.

Caleb stiffened in his seat. What did that mean? Various cult traditions entered his mind. Was she planning a cleansing of her flock or the residents of Kenorapeake Falls? Whatever it was, Caleb had to stop it.

Before he answered his question, a woman dressed in a white-hooded robe wearing a mask and carrying a harp walked on stage, sitting on a metal chair.

The leader raised two fingers and motioned toward the empty throne-type seat to her left. "Friends, in a few days we will announce the disciple elite replacement. The predecessor was well loved, so we will appoint someone special in his place. I will make my decision soon." She gestured to the white-robed individual. "Our sister is going to close our special time together. Then, it's lunch. You're all welcome to feast at our banquet." She moved to the front of the stage and once again held out her arms as if extending a hug to the entire room. "Be blessed, my flock." She glided off the stage and left through the side door.

Caleb dug his fingernails into the cushioned pew. He longed to follow her through the door, but that was impossible without attracting attention.

Slim leaned closer and whispered, "I can get you down there."

"How?"

"It's my job to set the tables in the mess hall. I have to slip out now."

Hope surged through Caleb at the same time as suspicion prickled his nerves. Could he trust this man? Right now, he had no other choice. "Let's do it."

Slim stood and raised his voice slightly. "Caleb, I need you to help me set the table."

"Sure. I can do that." Caleb played along.

They stopped at the entrance. A muscular member blocked the doorway, reminding Caleb of a bouncer guarding who comes and goes. The bulge at his side revealed a holstered weapon. An enforcer.

"Heading to the dining room for my duties." He slapped Caleb's back. "Showing this guy the ropes."

The expressionless man stepped aside.

Slim nudged Caleb toward the dining room, in the opposite direction from where Caleb wanted to go, but he'd follow the man's lead.

Slim turned left inside the room and pointed. "That's the kitchen. This building may look new, but it has a few old tricks since the organization rebuilt it overtop an old mansion. There's a dumbwaiter to the right of the closet. I have an idea. I'll distract the workers. Follow my lead." He raised his index finger. "You have exactly seven minutes to return. Don't get caught or I'm definitely dead."

"Why are you helping me?"

"Because Constable Spearing promised if I get you information, he'll protect my baby sister. I also want out of this place. It's a bunch of hogwash. I see that now." He headed toward the kitchen, but stopped and returned to his side. "Forgot one thing," he whispered. "Get your cop friend to look into the financials of these members. In order to become a member, they make you sign over your bank account creds, promising that you'll reap a reward for your *faithful tithing*."

"Did you?"

"I gave them one account that barely has any funds in it. The next day, it was empty. Another reason I agreed to this. You must stop them. They're bleeding these people dry right under their noses. Let's go."

Caleb shook his head in disgust and followed the man into the kitchen. Slim opened some cupboards and pulled out dishes, letting them fall to the floor.

The deafening crash caught the cook's attention. "Bro, you clumsy fool. Are you trying to get the Queen Bee to visit our kitchen again?"

Queen Bee? Same name Nehemiah had used.

"Sorry, man. I'll grab the broom and clean it up." He turned to Caleb. "Need your help."

Caleb nodded and jogged after him.

Slim opened the closet beside the dumbwaiter, making lots of noise. "Where's that broom?" He winked at Caleb. "There's no camera back here, only in the main kitchen. Seven minutes and I'll be back returning the broom."

Caleb set his watch alarm for seven minutes. "How long does the harpist strum?"

"Fifteen minutes. They chant to her music. Go. Tug on the cord when you get back in." Slim pressed the button to open the shaft. "Hurry."

Caleb hesitated.

"Don't worry, it's been updated to hold lots of weight."

Caleb ducked and entered the opening. He drew in a breath and tried hard to make himself smaller, but his enormous frame barely fit.

Slim hit the button, and the opening closed as the shaft descended.

Seconds later, the dumbwaiter stopped, and the door opened. He breathed a sigh of relief and crawled out.

Musty dampness filled his nostrils, and he placed his hands over his nose to prevent a sneeze. He glanced left and right. He didn't have enough time to investigate both, so he had to choose. *Lord, which way do I go?*

A snort sounded from the right. A pig? Caleb rushed down the corridor. The snorting increased, and he followed the noise to a door with a barred window. He peeked inside.

Two pigs grazed on straw. This is where they housed their sacrificial animals to prepare for their rituals.

Caleb advanced down the corridor and noticed flickering lights coming from a room on the left. He inched forward, hugging the stone wall, and stole a glimpse.

The room was empty, so he crept through the entrance. He

checked his watch. Four minutes left. He moved farther into the area, observing and memorizing. Stone benches circled the large altar like the video revealed. *This is where they make their sacrifices.* A row of chalices lined a table along the wall to the stone altar's right. Another door was to the left.

Ancient-styled torches hung on sconces on all the walls, creating an ominous glow. He trembled as the evil permeated off every item in the area. Six stone pillars circled the room. Caleb peered upward. Odd archaic sketches of sacrifices flooded the ceiling. The colors had faded, but one remained visible. Red blotches on top of the victims. Blood on their chests, dripping to the floor.

Caleb choked in a breath. His breathing labored as his pulse elevated, thundering in his chest. He had to escape this evil. He stumbled from the room and leaned against the wall to the right of the entrance. *Breathe, Caleb.* He drew in long breaths to slow his heartbeat, checking his watch. Two minutes. Did he have time to explore the opposite direction?

He hustled down the corridor just as a flash of gold turned the corner. The Queen Bee.

Caleb stopped and pressed against the wall, praying she hadn't seen him. After a few seconds passed without incident, he advanced toward where he'd seen her robe glimmer.

Another door. He approached and looked through the small window into an office. The Queen Bee's back faced him, and she reached up, fingering her hood.

Caleb's watch beeped a soft alarm.

The woman froze, then dropped her hands and turned her head.

He ducked. *Get out of here. Time's up.*

He hurried back to the shaft, opened the door, and climbed inside, pulling on the cord. He slowly ascended. Seconds later, Slim greeted him at the top. "The driver has returned to take you back. I told him you were in the washroom. Come on, let's go."

The duo hustled through the kitchen and into the large dining room. The cook stood behind a long table housing burner trays with food. Caleb ignored his hunger pangs and followed Slim into the foyer.

"About time you found him. You're not supposed to leave visitors unattended." The driver's narrowed eyes held accusation.

"Give me a break, man. I wasn't following him into the can." Slim pointed back into the dining room. "I have to finish my duties. You take him back and I'll catch a ride with the harpist."

"Doesn't everyone live here?" Caleb asked.

"Not everyone." Slim pushed him toward the door. "Now go."

"When can I return?"

"We'll see." Slim retreated into the dining room.

Caleb followed the driver to the van where the man thrust the hood overtop of Caleb and pushed him through the side door. "Get in."

"Okay, you don't have to be so rough." Caleb ran his hands along the seat and found the buckle.

"I just want to get rid of you." He slammed the doors closed and seconds later started the engine.

Once again, Caleb noted every bump and turn, counting sixty seconds, noting each minute it took to get back to Kenorapeake Falls.

Approximately twenty-eight minutes later, the van stopped and the driver cut the engine. He opened the side doors and guided Caleb out, yanking off the hood. "You're back."

Caleb held out his hand. "Phone, please."

"I contemplated telling you I broke it 'cause I wanted to steal it." He fished it from his pocket and slapped it into Caleb's palm. "Too fancy for me. Now get."

Caleb watched the driver screech back down Main Street before entering the code, along with his thumbprint, to bring his cell phone to life. He discovered he missed a call from his sister by ten minutes. He hit the button and played her message.

"Caleb, help me," she whispered. "Someone's in the house, he's—" Her call dropped.

No! Caleb stormed to his truck and started the engine, calling 911 as he spun out of his parking spot. He had to save his sister from whoever had breached her home.

Oaklynn sat across from the woman she believed to be her long-lost sister. She had asked to speak to Oaklynn in private, so they slipped into the staff lunchroom. "Okay, you have me alone. Tell me who you are."

"My name is Reese Waters." She drew in an overstated breath, her shoulders rising and falling. "I'm your sister, but I think by your earlier expression when you greeted me, you knew that already. We could almost be twins."

Oaklynn folded her arms over her chest. "I agree. We have a striking resemblance, but are you telling me the truth? I only found out about you recently."

"I am." A tear escaped, and she swiped it away. "My mother passed a month ago and, while on her deathbed, she revealed I was adopted."

"She never told you?"

"No. My father passed five years ago. When Mom found out she had cancer, she started cleaning out the house, getting rid of stuff." She hissed out a breath. "To make a long story short, she finally confessed. Mom was aware I had a sister. She had overheard the nursing staff talking while she visited the baby ward. They mentioned my mother's real name and that I had a sister."

"How did you find me?"

"Lots of searching. I found an article about our mother and father. That gave me your name, so I googled you." Reese fiddled with the zipper on her bag. "The only thing I found was your name in a newspaper report stating you called the police on Aaron Crowder. After that, everything went cold. No social media accounts whatsoever. Who doesn't have socials in this day and age?"

Oaklynn gritted her teeth, subduing a gust of annoyance. "Someone who's trying to stay hidden."

Reese gripped the edges of the table, leaning forward. "Our father really was a serial killer?"

"I know. It's hard to believe." Oaklynn approached the coffee machine. She required caffeine to stimulate her weary body. "Want one?"

"I'm good, thanks."

Oaklynn poured herself a cup, added honey and cream. She snatched a stir stick, blending the mixture on her way back to the table. "But, here's my question. How did you find me? I changed my name years ago."

"That was the tricky part. We actually live close. Mom, Dad, and I moved to a town an hour from here after Dad received a promotion years ago." Reese reached into her bag and retrieved a folded piece of paper. "To answer your question, I have a friend who works for the government services. She searched Lynn Crowder and found your name change." She pushed the paper across the table.

Oaklynn picked it up and read her official document. Wasn't anything private any longer?

"I had to find you. After Mom's passing, I had a sense of something being absent, like a piece of me had vanished. Call it that twin-like feeling. I don't know."

"So, how did you find me here?"

"The letter to the editor in the *KF Tribune*. I read it at five this morning and wanted to see for myself." She tapped her thumb on the table.

Oaklynn observed her body language, searching for deception, but found none. Could it be true? This was her sister?

Reese reached across the table and placed her hand on top of Oaklynn's. "I get it. I was skeptical at first too, but as soon as you came around the corner, I knew it was true. Our family resemblance is hard to deny. Even your cop mind agrees."

Oaklynn slouched in her chair and observed the woman's eyes, picturing a photo of their father. "You have his eyes."

She averted her gaze. "Not a family trait I want, now that I know the truth. You kept your identity hidden all these years?"

"I did until a copycat killer emerged. Seems our father has a *loyal fan*. You're right. I can't deny the resemblance, but I would still like a DNA test. You okay with that?"

Reese bit her lip and nodded. "I understand. Why did you go into policing? Just curious."

Oaklynn took a sip of coffee. "To stop serial killers like Aaron Crowder. Okay, we—"

Her radio squawked. "3Adam17."

Oaklynn hit her button. "3Adam17 here, go ahead."

"10-41 in progress at 387 Falcon Lane."

Oaklynn hopped to her feet. Break and enter at Mic's house. She clicked her button. "10-4. Responding." She focused on Reese. "Are you driving home or staying in Kenorapeake Falls? I would love to continue our conversation."

"I booked a B and B." Reese stood.

"I'll come and see you." She pulled out a card. "Here's my number. Text me so I have yours and tell me the B and B's address."

Reese nodded and stuffed the card into her pocket. "Stay safe."

"I will." Oaklynn hesitated, but tugged Reese into her arms. "I'm so glad you found me."

Excitement burst through Oaklynn, but as she raced from the room, one thought pummeled her mind.

She had to keep her sister a secret from the Protégé.

Chapter Twenty

Caleb eased his sister's unlocked front door open and listened for signs of movement, but the house remained silent. Where was Briggs? His German shepherd would have barked as soon as Caleb opened the door. Something was wrong. *Father, please help them be okay.* Caleb tiptoed to his sister's locked gun case, entered the code, and withdrew a shotgun, quickly inserting ammo. He crept down the hall to Mic's office. Thankfully, Lilly was at school.

Blaring sirens pierced in the distance. Help would arrive soon, but right now Caleb had to find his sister and dog. He raised the weapon and edged her office door open. "Mic, you in here?" He kept his voice low in case the intruder was still in the house.

Only silence answered his question.

Caleb entered and crashed to a halt. "No!"

His sister lay slumped in her chair, her face ashen.

Briggs lay still at her feet.

Caleb stormed forward, and leaned the shotgun against her floor-to-ceiling bookcase.

Mic's wrists each had cuts with fresh blood dripping through her fingers.

"No, no, no. God, please." Caleb placed his fingers on her neck. She was alive.

The sirens intensified and seconds later, movement sounded in the hallway. "Caleb!"

"Oaklynn, in Mic's study. Hurry!" Caleb untied Mic's scarf from her neck, ripped it in half, and fastened one on each wrist tightly. He had to stop the blood flow.

Pounding footfalls approached. Oaklynn and Eldon entered the office.

"Call for paramedics!" Caleb yelled. "She's alive."

Eldon hit his radio button, requesting EMS at their location.

Oaklynn scurried to Caleb's side. "What happened?"

"Not sure. I just got back to my truck and had a missed call from her. Her message said someone was in the house."

"Have you cleared the property?" Oaklynn asked.

"Just got here." He gestured toward Briggs. "I guessed something was wrong when Briggs didn't bark." He dropped to his knees beside his dog, then checked for a pulse. "He's alive. Thank God."

"Eldon, let's clear the house first. We don't want the suspect to still be here when the paramedics arrive." She addressed Caleb. "You okay?"

"Yes. Go."

The duo hustled from the room with weapons raised.

Caleb slid his hands along his dog's body, searching for wounds, but found none. "Bud, how did they get by you?" He performed a second cursory check, slowing his movements. His fingers grazed an object buried deep into the shepherd's fur. Caleb separated the fur, exposing a small dart. He plucked it out, anger flushing his cheeks. Someone had tranquilized his dog.

Not to kill but to subdue in order to attack Mic. Caleb got up and snatched an envelope from Mic's desk, dropping the dart inside. He'd give it to Oaklynn to pass to Chloe.

He had to get his dog to the vet and fast, but first he needed to call his father. He removed his cell phone from his back pocket.

Maxwell picked up on the first ring. "Caleb, you back from the compound with news?"

"Dad, more on that later. Listen, someone broke into Mic's house."

"What? Is she okay?"

"She's alive, but someone cut her wrists. I also found a dart embedded deep in Briggs's fur."

A seething breath hissed through the phone. "I'm on my way. My baby needs me." A door slammed in the background.

Sirens sounded outside. "Dad, paramedics are here. Meet us at the hospital instead."

"Okay, son. Don't let my daughter die. Stay with her. You know how she is about leaving her home." The quiver in his voice revealed the man fought hard to contain his emotions.

Charging footsteps brought the paramedics to the room. "Dad, I gotta go. Love you."

"You too." Maxwell ended the call.

Caleb recognized the male paramedic from Kimi's scene. "Jayson, right? This is my sister. Please save her."

"What happened?" Jayson gestured toward his partner. "This is Diane."

Caleb nodded, acknowledging the female paramedic. "I found her in here with cuts to her wrists. I applied pressure using her scarf."

"Good thinking." Jayson unwrapped one scarf and examined the cut. "Okay, they're somewhat deep, but vertical. Diane, grab the gauze. We'll get the bleeding stopped and take her to the hospital. Good thing you got here when you did, Caleb."

Diane passed Jayson the gauze and gestured toward Briggs. "Is the dog okay?"

"Alive but tranquilized."

Oaklynn appeared at the entranceway. "Is she gonna be okay, Jayson?"

"I believe so. Caleb here did a good job at applying pressure."

Oaklynn motioned toward the female paramedic. "Andy off today?"

Jayson nodded. "Yes, he requested a personal leave. Not exactly sure why, but I know his mother hasn't been well. But you're in expert hands with Diane."

"Is the house clear?" Caleb backed away from Mic, letting the paramedics finish bandaging her wrists.

"Yes. Eldon is checking the perimeter, and Chloe and her team are en route." Oaklynn pointed to the dog. "Is Briggs okay?"

Caleb raised the envelope and passed it to her. "Drugged with a dart. Give this to Chloe. I need to get Briggs to the vet."

"Let's take him in my cruiser. It will be faster." Oaklynn squatted. "Come on, boy. Be okay."

"We're ready to transport your sister. Will anyone be coming with us?" Jayson turned to Diane. "Get the gurney from the hallway."

She dashed from the room and returned within seconds.

"Wait. Oaklynn, would you be able to take Briggs to the vet? I need to go with them in case Mic wakes up in the ambulance." Caleb returned to his sister's side. "I'll call the vet and inform him you're coming. Jayson, I need to mention that Mic has agoraphobia. She will be terrified when she realizes she's not in her home."

"Understood. We can subdue her if she wakes up. Just to keep her calm." He turned to Diane. "Let's get her on the stretcher."

Caleb moved aside as they gently lifted Mic onto the gurney. *Lord, please help her be okay.* He shifted his attention to her desk. Blood had stained the papers and dripped onto the floor. A folded note with his name scribbled on top caught his interest. Not wanting to add fingerprints to anything, he lifted a letter opener from the pencil holder and carefully unfolded the paper.

And gasped.

"What is it, Caleb?" Oaklynn shifted her location to the desk.

See how close I can get to you, Watcher. Leave The Light Paragons or else, next time, I'll cut your sweet sister deeper.

Stay away from my Lynny.
The Protégé

Caleb clutched her arm. "Do you know what this means?"

Oaklynn's eyes widened before she placed her index finger on her lips, silencing him from saying anything more. "You go with Mic. I'll get Briggs to the vet. Eldon will stay here and update Chloe."

He caught her meaning. Don't discuss the case in front of the paramedics. "Thank you for looking after Briggs. I'll call the vet from the ambulance. Once I meet Maxwell, I'll text you."

"Okay, we have to go." Jayson flung his medical bag over his shoulder and helped Diane push the gurney out of the room.

"I'll carry Briggs to your cruiser on the way out." Caleb gently scooped up his German shepherd, hurrying to follow the paramedics.

Caleb had to save his dog and protect his sister from this maniac, but this attack proved one thing.

The killer just exposed his hand, revealing the connection between the cult and the Protégé.

And that would help them bring him down.

★ ★ ★

Oaklynn gently touched the sensitive tattoo on her neck as she waited for the vet's prognosis on Briggs. She didn't have the heart to leave even though she was on duty, so she monitored her cell phone and radio for updates from the constables out on patrol. It had been an hour since she'd brought Briggs in and Chloe's team were still at Mic's house. Eldon had reported he checked her father's visitors' list. Nothing out of the ordinary raised a red flag. He also spoke with the warden and the man mentioned he'd reviewed the video footage, looking for shady characters, but none stood out. More dead ends. Oaklynn was tired of those.

The front entrance door opened and Caleb slipped into the waiting area. He approached Oaklynn, his slumped shoulders and contorted expression displaying his worry. Rightfully so. The Protégé had attacked his sister and dog.

He plunked down beside her. "Any word?"

"Only that Briggs's vitals were strong. Chloe sent the dart with another worker to the lab and they put a rush on it. I'm guessing someone laced it with some type of sleeping drug." Oaklynn rubbed her sweaty hands on her uniform pants. "How's Mic?"

"Dad is with her now, trying to keep her calm. She panicked when she woke up in the ambulance, so the paramedics gave her a sedative."

"What did the ER doc say?"

"The wounds weren't deep. She'll be fine." Caleb's knee bounced. "The Protégé will pay for this. No one attacks my family and gets away with it."

Oaklynn rubbed his arm. "He's getting sloppy. The fact that he cut her wrists and left the note referring to The Light Paragons connects the killings and the cult. The question is, why is he killing these people?"

"My guess is the victims realized the evil and wanted out."

He unzipped his jacket before continuing. "What happened this morning? I was concerned when I couldn't get in touch with you." He leaned closer and placed his fingers on her chin, turning her head. "Wait. When did you get a tattoo?"

Oaklynn averted her gaze. "I have lots to tell you." She explained how she'd been drugged and woke up with the tattoo on her neck. "It was him. He got into my home. Chloe feels I need to relocate somewhere."

Caleb's eyes narrowed. "I agree. Dad told Mic the same thing. He's demanded an armed guard for her while she's in the hospital. Doc feels she'll be released soon. In the meantime, he's taking Lilly to his private cottage at the lake. He's kept it off the radar. Come with us. My family will protect you."

"I'm not sure anyone can protect me from him, especially if he learned all of my father's tricks." She bit her lip. "He must have drugged me at the coffee shop when we were there."

Caleb's furrowed brow betrayed his anger. "I should have followed you home."

Oaklynn placed her hand on top of his. "It's not your fault. This guy is good at deception and blending in with the crowds." Time to change the subject. "Tell me what you found at the compound. Any idea where it's located?"

"As I expected, they put a hood over my head. I counted and I believe it's approximately thirty minutes from Penny's Café. Give or take."

Oaklynn huffed and crossed her arms. "It could be anywhere. Any ideas?"

"Well, we drove about five minutes before moving onto a smooth highway. It's five minutes from the café to the ramp leading out of town, so let's guess it's twenty-five minutes outside of Kenorapeake Falls. The compound is deep into the forest as I couldn't hear any traffic. It contains one main building in the center of multiple cabins in the forest. There's a walkway over a bridge into what looked like a secluded area. I tried to find out where it led, but they were tight-lipped."

"What else did you learn?"

"Lots. First, all the disciples wear red robes and masks like we saw on the video. I noted one with a gold rope belt. The others wore black belts."

"What do you think it means?"

"Disciple John is in the inner circle."

"Disciple John?"

"Yes, all disciples are male and named after Christ's twelve disciples." He raised his index finger. "Except there were only eleven there." Caleb explained how the Queen Bee came on-stage, dressed in gold.

"So you're telling me these disciples take their direction from this woman cult leader? Is that normal?"

"Not really. Most are male, but it's possible." Caleb explained how Slim helped him get to the lower level where he found the inner circle sanctuary and a room containing two pigs. "I'm guessing they're getting ready for more sacrifices."

Oaklynn whistled. "Wow. Anything else?"

Caleb explained what Slim had told him about the bank accounts and Oaklynn tapped in a message to get her team to look into known members' financial records. "That everything?"

He raised his finger. "Wait, I had set my cell phone to record but haven't checked if anything came through. They made me turn off my GPS and kept my phone in the van, so I doubt I got much."

The front entrance opened and an older woman walked through, holding a Pomeranian. The small white dog's yips flooded the waiting area as the woman approached the front desk.

Oaklynn placed her hand over his cell phone. "Let's continue this conversation later." She checked her phone for updates. "Looks like Chloe has finished at Mic's and is heading back to the station."

"Good. So, you're okay with coming to the cottage? My father has increased his security there."

"Can I bring my Bengals? Will Briggs be okay with that?"

He chuckled. "He loves cats, but they may not love him. Briggs can be very protective. I'll let Dad know." He retrieved his cell phone from his side pocket in his cargo pants and tapped in a message.

"I'll head home and pack then meet you at the station." Oaklynn's cell phone buzzed with a text message from Reese.

Staying at KF B&B on Main Street.

She latched on to Caleb's arm. "Oh, I forgot to tell you. I can't believe this happened. My sister found me. What are the chances?"

"That's what I call a God-thing. I'm so happy for you."

High-pitched yelps sounded from the inner examining room.

Caleb straightened. "That's Briggs. He's awake, but I can tell he's stressed. I'm gonna see if I can get an update." He approached the reception desk.

Oaklynn tapped in a reply.

Good. So glad you found me, Reese. Can't believe I have a sister!

Three dots bounced on Oaklynn's screen.

Me too. God is good. Call me when you're free. I'm an author, so I'm working on my next book now.

Oaklynn made a mental note to google her sister's name and check out her books. She typed a quick response.

Cool! Can't wait to find out more about you. I'll be in touch. Do me a favor and don't venture far. There's a killer in Kenorapeake Falls.

Oaklynn hated to scare her sister, but she just found her and had to protect her.

More bouncing dots.

Will do. Talk later. My heroine is about to get kidnapped. Xo

Oaklynn chuckled to herself. The life of a writer's imagination.

Once again, her cell phone buzzed. Darius confirming he could meet her at the station at 6:30 p.m. She checked her smartwatch. It would be tight, but she'd make it work. She wanted this interview done. She responded before clipping her cell phone back onto her duty belt.

Kenorapeake Falls was about to find out the truth from the mouth of the Suicide Slayer's daughter, but a question hovered in her brain.

Would they believe her story?

A few hours later Oaklynn set the carrier containing her five howling Bengals on the table in a small boardroom. She stuck her finger through a hole, wiggling it around. "Simmer down. It's okay, kitties. You'll soon be at your interim home." They did not like to be caged but she couldn't leave them out in her cold Jeep. Caleb had insisted on going with her to collect her things and the kittens. She accepted his offer. No way would she go back into her home knowing the Protégé had somehow breached her farmhouse. She packed enough to stay away for an extended period until they wrapped up the case. Oaklynn struggled to contain her anxiousness over the sudden appearance of her sister and keeping her safe, so Caleb invited her to the cottage. Apparently, they had plenty of rooms. Oaklynn would pick Reese up after her interview with Darius and their meeting with law enforcement.

A knock interrupted her thoughts. "Come in."

Gracie appeared with Darius in tow. "The reporter is here." She gestured for him to enter, then backed out of the room, closing the door.

"Have a seat." Oaklynn pointed to the chair across the table. "I only have a few minutes and please keep the conversation to my story. I can't discuss an ongoing case."

He dropped into the seat and set a recorder in front of him. "Understood, Constable Brock, or should I call you Constable Crowder?"

Oaklynn dug her nails into her palms. This interview wouldn't end fast enough. "It's Brock."

He nodded and withdrew a notepad. "Constable Brock, can you confirm you're Aaron Crowder's—aka the Suicide Slayer's—daughter?"

"Yes, I was born Lynn Jenna Crowder, but legally changed my name to Oaklynn Brock at age eighteen."

"Why change your name?"

Wouldn't you? Oaklynn wanted to reply in that fashion, but she needed to portray herself in a positive light. "Number of reasons. Death threats. I was being bullied at school. You name it. We moved after the trial to get away from the Suicide Slayer. My father's fans blamed me for turning him in."

Darius whistled. "Sickening. Here's the question many are wondering. What was it like living with a serial killer?"

An obvious question. She'd be careful about her response, so she wouldn't reveal every detail of her life with Aaron Crowder. "My father was well respected within the community. Like most serial killers, he blended in with the crowd, but no one saw his other side. He was a master puppeteer, and his moods changed on a dime."

"What made you suspect him in the end?"

"Let's just say I found a letter my mother had hidden for me before he killed her."

Darius snuffed in a breath. "He killed your mother?"

"Yes, but the police were unable to prove it." Oaklynn intertwined her fingers together, wringing them over and over as she explained her story of how she found her father's trinkets.

"And that's when you called the police." Darius asked a few other questions, and Oaklynn responded with brief answers, revealing only the facts.

Darius steepled his fingers and leaned forward. "One last question. Are you the Suicide Slayer copycat?"

Another question she'd prepared for. "Of course not. I went into policing to catch serial killers like my father, not to follow in his footsteps." She'd leave out the fact that the question of whether or not she was like her father haunted her continually.

"Thank you for taking the time to set the record straight. Anything else you want to add, Constable Brock?"

"Only that we will catch the copycat."

"You mean the Protégé? That's what he's calling himself, right?"

"Yes." That much she could reveal, since the copycat had already named himself.

He gathered his belongings and stuffed them into his bag before standing. "Thanks again." He extended his hand.

His firm grip held confidence. "One request. Please send me your article before you print it. I don't want false information getting out. You understand."

He drew his hand back. "I only report the facts, but yes, I will send it to you later tonight. Please read it quickly as it will be tomorrow's front-page article."

"Of course." She opened the door and motioned him forward. "Good night, Darius."

He nodded and headed out of the station.

Oaklynn walked into the lunchroom where Caleb was waiting. "That's done."

"You feeling relieved?"

"Somewhat. Just a bit nervous on how our community will react." Her cell phone buzzed in her pocket. She fished it out and swiped the screen. Reese.

A nagging sense something was wrong snaked down Oaklynn's neck. She pressed Answer. "Reese, what's—"

"Help me, someone—" Her called dropped.

No! "Caleb, something is wrong with Reese. We need to get to her B and B." Oaklynn informed the constables on duty of the situation and demanded they get to her sister. Stat.

She asked Gracie to watch her Bengals until she returned, before racing out into the night with Caleb and the other constables at her heels.

Oaklynn just found her sister. She couldn't—and wouldn't—lose her now.

Chapter Twenty-One

Caleb leaned on Reese's doorframe, studying the constables and Chloe as they searched Reese's room. Caleb and Oaklynn had followed the constables in his truck. They found the B and B's front door open and the owners unconscious in the living room, telling them one thing. They weren't the perp's target. He was after Reese, and she had put up a struggle. Her laptop lay broken on the floor, papers strewn around the room, and her cell phone smashed against one wall. She was a fighter, like her sister.

Oaklynn slouched against the wall inside the area, biting her lip.

He moved closer and squeezed her shoulder. "We'll find her."

Chloe approached the pair and grazed Oaklynn's arm. "You shouldn't be here."

Oaklynn's attention diverted to the mess. "I can't help it. I just discovered she's my sister."

"And that's why you need to let us do this."

Dalton approached, holding a bagged note. "Constable Brock, this has your name on it." He passed it to her.

Caleb read over her shoulder.

Lynny,
I have your sister. Don't bother looking for her, you'll never find her. She'll fit perfectly in our special group.
P.

Oaklynn's hand flew to her mouth as tears pooled. "Caleb, do you think 'special group' refers to the cult? Could he have taken her there?"

"Possibly. It's deep into the forest, away from spying eyes. But would he take her to one of those cabins where the others would see her? Sounds too easy." Caleb's phone buzzed, and he fished it from his pocket. "Dad telling me everyone is at the cottage. He wants to formulate a plan for my next visit to the compound. Oaklynn, you can't do anything else here. Let's head out and get settled."

Oaklynn handed the evidence bag to Dalton. "Have you put an alert out for Reese?"

"Yes, and Nika is questioning the husband and wife downstairs as the paramedics are examining them. They're now conscious. We'll advise you if anything pops."

"Thank you. Let's go, Caleb." She shuffled from the room, shoulders slumped.

Lord, please find Reese. Keep her safe.

He followed her out to his truck. He needed his squad to develop a plan to bring down the cult and stop these killings. And fast before any other lives—especially Reese's—were taken.

Ninety minutes later, Caleb watched Briggs play with the five Bengals. Results came back indicating the dart was laced with a sleeping agent. The German shepherd was still groggy from the drug. The vet had said it would take some time to clear his system, but he'd be okay.

The kittens hissed and scrambled under the furniture.

Oaklynn slouched in the brown leather chair in front of the floor-to-ceiling stone fireplace and twirled a strand of hair, staring into the roaring fire.

Caleb guessed Reese was heavy on her mind.

Lilly bounced into the room. "Uncle Caleb, wanna play a game of pool?" She plunked herself beside him on the matching leather couch.

"Maybe later, little one. We have to talk shop for a bit. Why don't you go watch a movie in the game room?" Caleb hated to dismiss his niece, but the others were gathering to discuss the case. They all had arrived, including Mic. Maxwell had convinced the doctor to release her as she was no longer in any medical danger. And since Kordell had a medical background, the doctor finally agreed. Right now, his father was in a meeting but promised to join them soon. Mic slept in her room upstairs on the large cottage's west side.

"You're all work and no play." Lilly pivoted and her slippers scuttled on the cherry hardwood floor as she disappeared into the family rec room.

The rest of the team filed down the circular wooden staircase and found spots to sit in the cozy, rustic room.

"Guys, we have to be quiet. Mic's sleeping." Kordell leaned over the open balcony. "Or we move into another room."

Caleb looked upward at his brother and beckoned him down. "We will. Come on." Caleb received a new text message and checked the screen. Slim informing him he's been invited back. "Guys, I have another invite in two days. Slim says he caught wind of a special ceremony."

Oaklynn dropped her hair and leaned forward, coming out of her trance. "Could that be the elite disciple ceremony you spoke of?"

Caleb noted her taut shoulders. This news brought her back to the case. Good. They required her police brain right now and not the grieving sister. "Possibly. We need a plan to locate the compound."

"We'll put Bluetooth tags on you." Mic's voice echoed from the balcony.

Kordell rose to his feet. "What are you doing out of bed, sis? We were trying to be quiet."

"I'm fine, and you didn't wake me." She sat in the chair beside the railing. "I won't tackle the stairs, though."

Oaklynn tapped her chin. "She's got a point. We could track you by using the tags. Perhaps put them in your shoes. Caleb, did they check you for devices?"

"Just my phone." Caleb stood and grabbed the poker. He jabbed the coals and added another log. "I really need to get a phone inside to take pictures."

"What about an ankle holster of some kind? Hide a second one there." Hayley snatched a piece of meat from the charcuterie board on the island in the open concept area. "But you'd need a distraction to take pics, bro. These disciples will watch you closely since they're aware you're working with the police on the killings."

"She's right." Ryker popped a grape into his mouth and chewed. "You said this place is in the forest. Once we determine your location, we come in on each side and make some noise. Did you see any fencing we'd have to disable?"

"We stopped a few minutes before our final destination. The driver greeted someone, then a gate opened. When I got out of the van, we were too deep into the woods to see a fence." He rubbed his temples. "We have to assume there is one."

"I can help with that." Mic's weak voice filtered over the railing. "Did Dad bring my equipment?"

"I'll be right back." Ryker left.

Hayley moved out from behind the counter and peered up at her sister. "Of course he did."

Seconds later, Ryker wheeled in a board. "Found this in Dad's office. He'll be out in a minute. Let's draw out our game plan."

Caleb stood and nabbed the marker. "Good idea, bro."

"Once we get the coordinates, I can tap into the satellite feed. I'm sure Dad can get us access." Mic rubbed her wrists and grimaced.

"A well-placed, large donation can buy more than you'd think." Maxwell Greene raised his cell phone and approached the group. "Just got an interesting call from the mayor. Seems his wife confessed her involvement with The Light Paragons. Caleb, she's your other ticket inside as she wants out and said she'd help in any way she can. She was the one playing the harp."

The group sucked in a simultaneous breath.

"Can she tell us exactly where the compound is?" Caleb set the marker on the board's ledge.

"No. She was also blindfolded each time."

Oaklynn went to the sink and poured herself a glass of water. "Did she say why she supported them? Why did the mayor's wife agree to that, especially when these people killed her daughter?"

"Apparently, she volunteered to play music to get inside and offered a good-sized donation because she wanted to snoop around, like we are." Maxwell squeezed Oaklynn's hand. "Sorry about your sister. We'll find her."

"Thank you, and thanks for letting me stay here." One kitten clawed up the wooden stool legs and jumped onto the island. "Frodo! Get down. You're gonna get us kicked out." She snatched the kitten and dropped Frodo onto the floor.

Briggs barked and followed the cat into the rec room.

Caleb chuckled, his heart warming to the idea of Oaklynn as

part of his family. He shoved the thought aside. "Mic, can you set up a fake bank account for me? I need to prove my worth and sign over my life's savings."

"You know I can."

"Good."

Oaklynn snapped her fingers. "Caleb, didn't you say you set your cell phone to record? Have you listened to it yet?"

"No. Haven't had time and frankly I forgot. Mic, I'll email it to you. You up to checking it?"

Kordell bounded up the stairs. "Let me help, sis. I'll get your laptop. You stay there." He shuffled across the landing and walked through the open sliding doors into one side of the triple rooms. He returned seconds later and moved an end table beside his sister, placing the laptop on top. "There you go."

"A girl should get sick more often." Mic raised her wrists. "I won't be able to type fast. Send it, Caleb."

He forwarded the recording. "Done. You listen while we plan."

Maxwell reached into a drawer. "Speaking of cell phones. I picked up burner and sat phones." He handed them out to his team. "We can't risk this Protégé getting our locations."

"Good idea." Caleb tossed his cell phone into the basket on the table. "Everyone, turn off your phones and leave them here."

The group complied.

They spent the next fifteen minutes documenting their ideas and Caleb drew a rough sketch of the compound, including the bridge and a big question mark on the other side of it. He tapped the cluster of trees he drew using the marker. "I want to know what's here."

Mic let out a hissed breath. "Found something." She removed her headphones. "Listen to this. I think it's your driver talking to a friend or someone. He has him on speakerphone. That's why we can hear the entire conversation. Not the sharpest blade in the drawer." She chuckled and hit a button.

"I don't trust this Watcher guy. Just seems too convenient that he shows up today."

"Don't worry, I'm watching the Watcher." The distorted voice held disgust. "He'll be getting his reward in a few days."

"You mean like Kimi got hers?"

"Bro, I told you no names on phone calls. They've all paid their price. You just keep spying for me. That's why I pay you the big bucks." The voice chuckled. "Meeting's over. Wait a few minutes and then come for the Watcher." The call ended.

Maxwell pounded on the island. "This is too dangerous, son. I'm pulling you out."

Caleb shot to his feet. "Dad, no. This only tells us we're on the right track. We have to go through with this." He addressed Oaklynn. "Once we determine the location, your constables and our squad can be ready to move in."

"We need more to get a warrant. Mic, send Sergeant Rollins the clip. I'll call him." Oaklynn reached for her burner phone.

Mic tapped her keyboard. "Done. Heading back to bed." She meandered into her room.

Oaklynn yawned. "Me too. I'll find my Bengals and take them into my room. I'll call Rick and give him an update."

Hayley rose. "I'll help you gather the sweeties."

"Thanks. Night everyone."

"Sleep well, Oaklynn." Caleb's gaze found hers and held.

Until Hayley cleared her throat.

"You too." Oaklynn disappeared into the next room.

Hayley punched Caleb on her way past. "You're crushing on her. Remember, you have a job to do and it takes priority." She followed Oaklynn on her quest to collect her kittens.

"She's right, son." Maxwell placed his hand on Caleb's shoulder. "Case first."

Was he that obvious? Caleb hung his head, one question heavy on his mind.

Solve the case and after that...

Would he risk opening his heart again?

★ ★ ★

Buzzing vibrated nearby, forcing Oaklynn out of her jumbled thoughts of masked cult members and Caleb entering their lair in a couple of days. She woke early and was reviewing case files, not wanting to disturb the others. Caleb had insisted she stay in the bedroom on the top level at the cottage's backyard, facing the lake. He claimed the private room had the best view, but all she'd seen last night was darkness. Maxwell assured her he had placed his security guards at all entrances of his private cottage. No one would get by them. Oaklynn wasn't so sure. The Protégé had already proved he was adept at stealth. How had he found out about Reese? Through her phone? Chloe had replaced Oaklynn's phone with a burner, stating she'd be analyzing her other one. Just in case. Only her constables and the CWS had this new number. She snatched the phone and hit Answer. "Constable Brock here."

"Oaklynn. My hunch was right."

"And good morning to you too, Chloe." Arwen stretched and yawned before climbing on Oaklynn's lap.

"Sorry, morning. Sleep well in your new home?"

"Kind of. You should see this place. Absolutely gorgeous." Oaklynn had tried hard to keep her mouth closed after she'd stepped inside the Greene's family cottage. Logs made up the entire place, even the walls. Everything about the structure was rustic, right down to the wall and lighting fixtures. She breathed in the smell of a roaring fire filtering from the first level. "I could get used to this place."

"Well, don't. Once we solve this case, you'll return to your humble abode. Unless, of course, you plan on marrying into the family. I've seen the way you look at the Beast and he, you." Her friend snorted.

"Stop, Chloe." She doubted any man would want damaged goods. "What do you have for me?"

"Huh?"

"The reason you called?" Oaklynn rubbed Arwen's back. The kitten's purr intensified.

"Right. I've determined that someone cloned your cell phone. I found an app hidden deep in the files."

"What? I led him to my sister." Oaklynn fisted her hand and pounded the bed.

"Girl, it's not your fault. It's probably how the Protégé is tracking you too." Tapping of keys sailed through the phone. "We're looking into Kimi, Missy, and Isaac's financials to confirm Caleb's claim of the members signing over their bank info. We're hoping to trace it back to the cult's accounts. Oh, I also checked your landline records and the call from the other night was made from a burner phone. I'll keep you— Wait, Dispatch is calling for units to 1897 Clover Place."

Oaklynn whipped her plaid comforter off and hopped out of bed. "That's Freda Corbet's home. I'll get Caleb and meet Eldon there."

"Stay safe."

Forty-five minutes later, Oaklynn ducked under the police caution tape and entered Freda Corbet's home with Caleb at her heels. Chloe met them in the foyer, holding out personal protective equipment. "You're not going any farther without these on. Normally, I wouldn't let you go up, but you need to see this."

"Understood." Oaklynn took the PPE from her and quickly put it on.

Caleb did the same.

Eldon approached them. "Body's upstairs. It's not pretty."

"Don't worry. I know from my father's case what to expect if the Protégé is following the same pattern."

Oaklynn's heavy feet trudged up the steps. The higher they ascended, the more intense the metallic smell assaulted her nose. Not good. They reached the landing, and she turned to Caleb. "If I'm right, this will be intense."

"Don't worry. I saw intense in the military." Caleb wrinkled his nose. "You smell that?"

"Hard to miss." Oaklynn continued to the bedroom door and halted inside the room.

Freda Corbett hung on the wall in a crucifixion-style position. Nails pierced her hands and feet, fresh blood dripping down the wall. A bouquet of lilies lay at her feet, arranged meticulously in a glass vase. Someone had sprawled a caption written in blood above the woman's head.

BETRAYER

Oaklynn clamped her hand over her mouth to squash her surprise at the change from her father's MO, but also to mask the horrible stench.

Caleb stepped beside her. "Is this the same as your father's next victim?"

"The position is similar, but my father never left messages like the copycat is doing." She approached the coroners. "Any preliminary finds on how she died?"

Dr. Hancock looked up from his position. "Stab wound to the chest, but you probably already guessed that since this killer is following your father's MO."

Oaklynn noted the disgust in his voice. "Only wanted to be sure. Dr. Patterson, any messages on her abdomen?"

The chief coroner pushed his glasses farther up his nose and lifted Freda's bloody blouse. "Yep, and you're not gonna like it."

Freda failed SS. I have her.

"What do you think it means?" Dr. Patterson pointed to the flowers. "And do those have significance?"

"Freda wrote Aaron Crowder's memoir with his permission, so not a betrayal. But Freda told me she tried to find my sister. That's what the message must refer to, but she couldn't, and now the Protégé has Reese." Oaklynn gritted her teeth, fighting to keep her elevated heart rate in check. "The flowers were my mother's favorite. Those messages are all for me. My father repeatedly called me a betrayer throughout his trial, and so did his fans. That's why I had to move and change my name. I started getting death threats."

"Good golly, my dear." Dr. Patterson adjusted his bow tie. "I'm so sorry you went through that."

"Why did you keep it from all of us?" Dr. Hancock's voice once again held contempt.

Caleb situated himself beside her. "Isn't it obvious? People sometimes judge others for what family members have done. And she just told you about the threats against her life. Read the article Darius Wesley wrote. She explained everything there." He turned to Oaklynn. "Have you read it?"

"Yes. He sent it to me for approval."

"He was kind and portrayed you in a good light." Caleb waggled his finger at Dr. Hancock. "He cautions us about judging her like you're doing right now."

Dr. Patterson cleared his throat. "Okay, let's table this. Dr. Hancock, time to bring her down off the wall now that we've taken all the pictures we need."

Eldon appeared in the entrance. "Oaklynn, did your father also use benzos to subdue his victims?"

"Nope. Aaron Crowder used a muscle relaxer common in surgery to control them."

"Why deviate from his hero's methods?" Eldon rubbed his chin. "Isn't that odd, since he claimed in his letter to the editor that your father was his hero?"

"Good question. Perhaps because he wants to put his own spin on the Suicide Slayer's killings. The messages are also new. He's added that to the trinket signature." Oaklynn eyed the flowers once again and fingered the locket in her pocket. "Eldon, any word on the search for my sister?"

"We're doing everything possible, but so far, we have nothing to go on."

Oaklynn's stomach pitted into knotted coils. "We have to find her. What about Victoria Dutton?"

"She too has vanished. Trust me, constables are looking everywhere." He gestured toward Caleb. "Your trips to the compound are our only leads."

"We're working on a plan."

Chloe clapped. "Okay, everyone out."

Oaklynn saluted her friend. "Yes, ma'am. Eldon, keep me updated."

Caleb and Oaklynn removed their PPE, and exited the author's home. "Caleb, I need to go on patrol now. If I get any leads, I'll keep you updated, but Eldon's right. The cult is our strongest lead."

"Sounds good. If—"

Darius barreled up the laneway, holding his mic in their faces. A cameraman had his lens focused on them. The red button showed they were filming. "Is this another kill by your father's Protégé?"

"No comment." Oaklynn hated this part of her job. She didn't enjoy the spotlight.

"When is the KFPD going to catch this serial killer?"

Caleb placed his hand over the mic. "The constable said no comment. Please respect that."

A thought rose, and she raised her index finger. "Just a sec. I do want to say something."

Darius motioned the cameraman to follow. "Go ahead, Constable Brock."

Oaklynn hadn't okayed this move with Rick, but it might unnerve the Protégé. She looked directly into the camera and waggled her finger. "This message is for the Protégé. You can't hide forever. We will find you and put you behind bars." She dropped her hand. "To the residents of Kenorapeake Falls, we plead with you. If you have any information about this case, please contact the KFPD. We're looking for a male, mid- to late-thirties. Someone who keeps to himself, but is polite. Look closely at everyone around you. If anything is suspicious, call us. Thank you."

She approached her cruiser, speaking over her shoulder. "Caleb, I'm tired of this case. We need to find my sister. This. Has. To. End." She forced out her words.

"Agree. Listen, I'm going to head back to the cottage and find out if Mic has discovered anything else. You know the restaurant just off the highway heading toward the cottage?"

"I saw it all lit up last night."

"Wanna go there for supper after your shift?"

"You mean like a date?"

He tilted his head, his lips turning upward into a captivating smile. "You want it to be a date?"

Did she? Yes. Would she? No. "No comment. Six thirty good?"

"See you then. Stay safe." He winked before jogging to his truck.

Oaklynn sighed. *Grizzly, if I was up for a relationship, it would definitely be with you.*

Handsome, kindhearted, protective, amazing teddy bear hugs. What more could she ask for in a man?

Shouts caught her attention, and she pivoted, placing her hand on her sidearm.

A growing crowd had formed in front of Freda's home. Was the Protégé among the group? Dawson's profile said the killer would want to watch the scene. She studied each intently, but none stood out.

However, she guessed he was there.

Watching. Waiting.

★ ★ ★

Caleb parked close to the restaurant's door at 6:20 p.m. and placed a foot onto the fresh blanket of snow. The sun had disappeared midafternoon, snowflakes replacing the clear day. He didn't mind. It made for a more romantic dinner with a beautiful woman. *Not a date. Not a date.* The three words echoed in his mind with each step he took toward the Italian restaurant's entrance, reminding himself to keep his feelings in check. He entered the quaint, elegant restaurant.

"Mr. Greene, so nice to see you again. It's been a while." The fortyish blonde picked up a menu. "For one?"

"Good evening, Helena. No, two please, and can I have the table in the corner with the splendid view?"

She gathered a second menu. "Of course. This way."

He followed her through the dimly lit restaurant to the back, where the table overlooked the rear of the property and the frozen pond and bridge. Clear lights illuminated the pathway, leading to the bridge and small patio. The large snowflakes only added to the romantic atmosphere.

Not that this was a date. "Thanks, Helena."

The hostess placed the menus at both place settings. "Take your coat?"

Caleb took off his jacket and passed it to her.

"My, you're looking rather dapper tonight. Special occasion?"

Caleb glanced at his black button-down shirt and gray slacks. Had he overdressed? His brothers had teased him, but he couldn't help it. He was tired of cargo pants. "Just supper with a friend."

Bells jangled, indicating another patron had entered the restaurant.

Caleb turned and spotted Oaklynn. He waved. "There she is now."

Helena dipped her chin and backed away. "Have a nice evening. Your server will be with you shortly."

"Am I late?" Oaklynn approached and removed her coat. Caleb choked in a breath.

She too had changed. The baby pink angora sweater and black slacks hugged her figure nicely. The tiny diamond in her newly acquired locket glistened in the dimmed lighting.

Stop staring. He was a blundering fool. He tore himself out of his trance and pulled out the chair. "Just in time." He breathed in her lavender scent. "You look lovely this evening, Constable Brock."

"Thank you. You look dashing, Watcher Greene." She draped her jacket on the chair to her right and sat.

Caleb seated himself and clasped his hands in front of him. "How was your day?"

The server appeared and filled their glasses with ice water. "I'll give you a few more moments to look over the menu." She retreated.

"Well, after discovering Freda's body, my day was uneventful. I would normally say that's a good thing in a cop's life, but no new leads. My sister is still missing." She fingered the locket.

"Nothing new from Mic either."

"Dead ends." She picked up the menu. "Enough talk of work. What's good here?"

"Everything. The salmon is my favorite, so that's what I'm ordering."

"You come here often?"

"I used to."

Their server approached. "You ready to order?"

Caleb waved toward Oaklynn. "Ladies first."

Oaklynn pointed to her menu. "I'll have the red pepper and mushroom gnocchi."

"Good choice. It's excellent." Her eyes shifted to Caleb, widening. "Wait, you're that billionaire's son, aren't you?"

Oaklynn chuckled, then clamped her hand over her mouth.

Caleb found it hard to ignore the glimmer in Oaklynn's dark

brown eyes, as well as the amusement at his expense. "I am and I'll have the salmon, please." He handed her the menu without averting his gaze from Oaklynn.

"I'll get that started for you." The server left.

"You found that funny, huh?"

"I was just expecting her to repeat what I heard all day about my father. Clearly, she only had eyes for you." She slouched back. "Not that I blame her."

He loved her playful banter. In the short time they'd been together, her teasing demeanor rarely made an appearance. He liked the change. Caleb picked up his glass and drank his water, attempting to curb his crush.

"New topic. I'm curious about something. What happened between you and your ex-wife? Only if you want to tell me, of course."

He gulped in air, gathering his words. "To make a long story short. I met Paige at a mutual friend's party and we connected instantly. We dated. I proposed within three months. We married fast and then had our daughter a year later. I was smitten from the first time I held Aiyana in my arms." He withdrew a picture from his wallet and stared at his daughter's sweet face. He swallowed the thickening in his throat and pushed the photo across the table. "This is Aiyana."

Oaklynn lifted the picture and smiled. "She's beautiful. I'm so sorry you lost her." She passed it back to him.

He tucked it into his wallet and sipped his water to keep his tears at bay. "I didn't realize Paige was an alcoholic. Once I discovered that, I asked her to get help. She ended up going into rehab and was on the road to recovery. Or so I thought. The day after her release, she got drunk and took Aiyana in her car." Caleb's knuckles burned from the fists he'd formed without realizing it. He flexed his fingers. "Paige ran a red light and swerved into an oncoming truck. She survived. Aiyana didn't.

Paige was convicted of dangerous driving causing death." He stared out the window.

"I'm so sorry you had to endure that. I knew about your daughter passing, but not the circumstances, or that Paige went to jail."

"I've been told she's changed in prison. Maybe that's true." He looked back at Oaklynn. "I preach forgiveness to anyone I counsel, but honestly, she's the one person I haven't been able to forgive. I've forgiven Nehemiah, but why not Paige? I'm terrible."

"Hardly. You're the kindest person I've ever met, even though you hide behind your grizzly image." She caressed his hand. "Trust me, I don't say that lightly."

Forgive.

The one word Caleb had heard often from his father. His memory returned to his conversation a couple days ago, where he confessed his dark secret to his family. They all had forgiven him.

He gripped the table's edges and once again glanced out the window into the dark, snowy night.

He'd failed not only their daughter, but his family and God.

God had forgiven Caleb for his grisly past. Why couldn't Caleb forgive Paige?

A shadow flashed to the right of the lit walkway, revealing a hooded figure standing midway on the bridge, staring in Caleb's direction. Something about the person's stance caught Caleb's attention.

He bolted out of his chair. "Someone's watching us."

Chapter Twenty-Two

Oaklynn parked beside Caleb's truck at the cottage and climbed out of her Jeep, pondering their evening. The conversation had taken a turn when Caleb spotted a hooded figure spying on them, but when they hustled outside—whoever had been there—was gone. The tracks in the fresh-fallen snow led to the road where a vehicle had been parked. Despite the interruption, Caleb and Oaklynn both refused to let it impede their dinner. Her gnocchi dish was delightful, and they topped their meal off by sharing a piece of mouthwatering tiramisu.

The snow stopped, and the moon peeked through the clouds. The clear patio lights strung along the pathway and out to the dock illuminated the beauty of the area. *I could get used to this.*

"Penny for your thoughts."

Oaklynn had failed to hear Caleb's approach. "The view here is spectacular. How is it possible you don't live here all year round?" She pictured each season in all its splendor.

"We spend a lot of time together here as a family. It's our

place to decompress." He gestured to the dock. "Want to take a stroll down there? Are you warm enough?"

"I was just thinking I didn't want our evening to end." Plus, a notion niggled at her. He had shared more about his life. Dare she share her darkest secret?

Caleb held out his arm. "Shall we?"

She hooked her hand in the crook of his arm as he led her down to the frozen lake.

They stepped onto the dock. Shivers seized Oaklynn's muscles, and she hugged herself.

"You cold?" Caleb enveloped her into an enormous embrace. "This place is my oasis. You should see it in the summer and the fall. Beautiful. When I sit here on the dock on summer mornings with a coffee, I marvel at the stillness and God's creations."

She stiffened.

"Why don't you believe? Is it because of your father?"

Was this the segue she needed to tell him everything? She left the safety of his arms and moved to the right, close to the edge.

"Oaklynn, what is it? I sense there's something you're keeping close to your chest. Something big." He rubbed her back. "You can trust me."

She whirled around. "Can I? Most of the men in my life have treated me poorly. My father, childhood buddies, colleagues. I'm not sure I have anything left to give."

"I'm not most men." He took off his glove and grazed her cheek. "I hope you can see that now after our rocky start."

She lifted her chin. He was right. He was definitely not her father or the other men she'd met along her rough journey. Her eyes shifted to his lips. What would it be like to kiss him—and why was she even thinking of kissing him?

A wolf howled in the distance, sending chills bushwhacking Oaklynn's body. She eased closer to Caleb for both protection and warmth.

He dipped his head and inched forward. "Oaklynn, I—"

His lips met hers. The softness of his lips surprised her while his minty breath tasted refreshing.

The howling wolf faded into the background, along with thoughts of serial killers, her father, and her worries.

Stop, Oaklynn. He needs the truth. After that, he'll never want you.

She severed their closeness. "I can't." He deserved the truth.

"Please tell me what's going on. I know you sense our electricity."

She looked away and lifted her gaze to the sky. The clouds had parted and stars twinkled. "You won't feel the same after I tell you."

"Remember my secret. I won't judge you after everything I've done."

"Don't be so sure." Oaklynn bit her lip to extinguish the flames he left there. She inhaled and stared out over the frozen lake, letting the stillness prepare her for what she wanted to say. "No man would ever want me after what I'm about to tell you." The darkness from her father's touch sent tremors coursing through her body. She clamped her eyes shut, blocking out the images of him. Images still plaguing her after years of torture.

She turned back to Caleb. "My father not only killed people, but was abusive."

"To your mother. You told me that."

Oaklynn fisted her gloved fingers and stuffed them into her coat pocket. "I was five when it first started. He came into my room and made me dance with him before he crawled into my bed. I figured he was going to read a story to me, but then he—" Could she go on? "Well, you can guess what happened next."

Caleb drew in a sharp, ragged breath. "How long did it go on?"

"Until I was thirteen. I guess I didn't serve his needs any longer. I told my mother about it once, but he beat her when she confronted him. After that, he threatened to hurt me if I said anything." She kept her eyes on the wooden planks. She couldn't bear to see any disgust on his face. "That's the entire reason I went into policing. To stop people like my father from hurting others."

She walked back to the edge, being careful not to get too close. "And ultimately, why I was so quick to call the police when I found his trinkets. I hated him. Still do, even though he's gone. Years of therapy never stopped my hatred." She spun around. "And why I have doubts. How could a loving God allow such evil in this world?"

"I don't know the answer to that, Oaklynn, only that humanity is sinful, and that sin has perverted our world. God doesn't want that. God is the only light in the blackness."

"But why allow such darkness?"

"Maxwell once told me our lights shine the brightest in the darkness."

Similar words Aunt Sue had spoken often. Could Oaklynn believe her aunt and Caleb?

"I have baggage that won't allow me to be in a relationship with a man." She analyzed his expression.

The moon's rays caught the whiteness in his eyes, revealing the one thing she feared.

Disgust.

He looked away, but it was too late. She caught his repulsion.

"See, I said you'd hate me when you discovered my secret. Disgust is written all over your face." Oaklynn pivoted and stormed off the dock, distancing herself from the man she'd fallen for.

"Oaklynn! No…"

His words faded into the night as she stumbled into the cottage, tears streaming down her face.

Tears she now feared would never stop.

★ ★ ★

He'd blown everything. First the kiss, then Caleb failed to contain his disgust. However, Oaklynn misread him. His disgust wasn't for her, but for Aaron Crowder. He had to tell her. He couldn't end their lovely evening with her thinking he loathed her. Caleb fled down the dock and up the snow-covered stone walkway, slipping a few times. When he opened the patio doors, Oaklynn was nowhere to be seen.

Hayley sat reading by the fire.

He chucked his coat and gloves onto a nearby chair.

"She's gone to bed. What did you do, bro?" Hayley closed her book. "Oaklynn doesn't strike me as the crying type, but whatever you did brought her to tears."

"I have to right a wrong." He hurried to the spiral stairway.

"Stop, Grizzly." Hayley's voice boomed. "Give her time."

Caleb pivoted from the first step. His sister was right. Oaklynn needed time and God. Not him.

He meandered back to the fireplace and gently ran his fingers along the pictures sitting on the stone mantel. "I blew it."

"What happened?"

"We had a lovely dinner. We even talked about Paige." He lifted the picture of Aiyana his father kept. "I'm struggling to forgive my ex."

"Caleb, it's hard. Trust me, I still wrestle with forgiving my biological father, but the hurt is slowly dissipating."

Caleb set Aiyana's kindergarten picture down and plunked onto the couch. He reached for Hayley's hand. "How were you able to do that after what your father did to you? Tell me, so I can help Oaklynn."

His sister yanked her hand away. "Wait. Oaklynn's serial killer father also abused her?"

Oops. He hadn't meant for that to slip out so easily. "Please don't tell anyone. I guess it started when she was five."

Hayley hissed out a breath through her teeth, revealing the

same disgust Oaklynn had read on Caleb's face. "Same as my dad. Oaklynn has gone through so much. Not only living with a serial killer—but a father who turned his horrifying advances on her—has got to be devastating. That's hard to come back from."

"I want to help her."

Hayley placed her hand on top of his. "It has to start with Oaklynn. She has to want to get over her father's betrayal. I've learned through counseling that some people hold on to the hurt as some weird sort of comfort. They lack the understanding of how to accept love when it is given. I should know. Give her time."

"I'm afraid that's not the only thing I blew tonight. I kissed her out on the dock." Caleb slouched farther into the couch.

"You what? Remember the rules. No relationships while on a case. Dad will have your head if he finds out."

"I know, I know, but I've never felt this strongly so quickly for someone before." He paused. "Not even Paige, and you're familiar with that outcome. I vowed never to make the same mistake twice."

"Bro, when true love comes your way, it's not easily controllable. Pray for guidance."

Love? Not possible that fast.

Could it be?

He slipped off the couch and rose. "I'm heading to bed. See you in the morning."

She threw her arms around Caleb. "Night, bro. God will keep you safe and work out everything with Oaklynn."

Caleb squeezed his sister, setting his chin on top of her head. "I hope so." He released her and kissed her forehead. "Thanks for the pep talk. Love you."

"You too."

Caleb trudged up the stairs and stopped at Oaklynn's door, lifting his hand to knock, but stopped.

Time, Caleb, time. His shoulders drooped as he walked away from her room with one thought in his mind.

He must right his wrong.

Tomorrow.

The wind whistled outside Oaklynn's window. Why didn't Caleb come after her? She wasn't ready to face him yet, but didn't he care enough to make amends? She hissed out her frustration. They had a case to finish. After that, they'd go their separate ways. She threw off the covers and moved to the window, her fingers grazing her lips. Unfortunately, she'd never forget his kiss.

But had to, or she'd never survive. He snuck in and stole her heart without her even realizing.

But she also couldn't forget the look on his face after she'd shared her secret.

Letting go of what she'd bottled up inside herself for so long brought her relief. But had it been worth the risk?

Oaklynn leaned her forehead against the cool glass window and gazed at the dock.

Briggs barked from the lower level.

Movement under the moon's rays caught her attention. She straightened. Who was out there? Caleb?

Briggs's barking intensified.

An explosion blasted, and pieces of wood flew into the air, destroying the dock. Caleb!

Oaklynn stepped back into her shoes, racing out of the room and down the stairs. Pounding footfalls revealed the others followed. Someone called 911, but it didn't register who in her brain. One person occupied her mind.

Caleb.

She yanked open the door and stormed down the stone pathway, ignoring the chill biting into her skin. "Caleb!"

She fell to her knees at the lakeshore. The explosion obliterated the landing connecting the shore to the dock. The small wharf where they'd just stood was gone—all of it.

"Oaklynn!" Caleb's voice cut through the wind.

She rose and pivoted.

He ran down the steps holding a fire extinguisher and pointed the device at the broken plank, spraying the liquid over the flames. "You okay?"

"Yes. I thought you were still out there."

The entire family stumbled to the shoreline and gawked at the demolished dock.

"I called 911." Hayley grabbed her father's arm. "How did someone get past your guard?"

The man's eyes narrowed under the dock's lighting. "Good question. I need to check on them." He tapped in a message on his cell phone.

Caleb finished putting out the fire and set the extinguisher down.

Fire still raged on the severed dock, but they couldn't reach it. Not without risking falling through the ice to get to there.

He approached. "Oaklynn, what happened?"

"I noticed someone in the trees and thought it was you still out here." She pounded on his chest. "You scared me."

"I'm okay. Where did you see someone?"

She pointed to the clusters of trees near the cottage's east side.

A flash of white flapping in the wind caught her attention. "What's that?" She darted toward the tree, Caleb at her heels.

Someone had nailed a piece of paper to the tree trunk. The moon's rays cast light on the message.

YOU CAN'T HIDE FROM ME, LYNNY.

Oaklynn dropped into the snow. "No!" Her presence had put everyone at risk, but how did the Protégé find her behind the cottage's fortress walls?

Chapter Twenty-Three

Oaklynn plodded down the stairs, following the smell of bacon cooking and coffee brewing. After the late and exhausting night, her body required caffeine. Firefighters had contained the flames while police combed the woods for the suspect. As expected, the Protégé had slipped through their fingers. Again. This copycat not only found her, but walked the property without their knowledge. Maxwell had discovered the guard at the east gate out cold. He'd been knocked over the head. This had to end. Now.

She plunked her duty belt on the counter. Briggs brushed up against her leg. She bent down and petted the German shepherd. "Morning, bud. How are you feeling?" The fact that the dog only alerted to an intruder right before the explosion revealed the drug had still been in his system.

Briggs barked and wagged his tail.

"He's more spry this morning, so hopefully he's back to normal. Coffee?" Hayley hit the espresso machine button and returned to the stove. "I'm cooking bacon and eggs."

"It smells wonderful." Oaklynn waited beside the coffee machine to finish hissing out her double caffeine delight. She removed the mug from under the spout and added a pinch of creamer, not wanting to water down the caffeine. She required fuel for her day. "Where's everyone?"

"Still sleeping, but I figured you had an early shift, so I wanted to make you something. I'm aware of what a cop's day looks like and you need energy. I also prepared a bag of granola bars and fruit for you." She retrieved a plate and added two eggs along with several slices of bacon before handing it to her. "There are fresh croissants on the table."

"Wow. You're amazing. Let me guess. You're also the resident cook on the squad?" She carried her plate and sat at the round log, knight-style table.

"Caleb is too, and we share the cooking duties." She filled her plate and walked over. "You mind if I join you?"

"Not at all."

"I'll say grace." She bowed her head and prayed over the food, asking God to keep them all safe today. "Amen."

"Amen." Oaklynn sipped her coffee before diving into her bacon and eggs. "These are delicious." She took another bite before continuing. "Caleb seems to be a man of many talents. He made me pancakes the other day. So good."

Hayley jabbed her eggs. "Go easy on him. He's been through a lot."

"Haven't we all?" Oaklynn gobbled down her food. She had to get to the station in a little less than an hour.

Hayley placed her hand on Oaklynn's. "My father also abused me. I know what you went through. If you ever want to talk, I'm here."

Oaklynn jerked her hand away and jumped to her feet. "He told you that?"

"Not in so many words. He was upset last night." She stood. "He cares for you."

"I gotta get to work. Eldon is meeting me at the gate to escort me into town. Thanks for breakfast." She grabbed her duty belt and the lunch bag from the counter before rushing to the coatrack.

"You off to work so early?" Caleb bounded down the stairs and stopped in front of the door.

Oaklynn put on her coat and marched into his personal space, jabbing her finger into his chest. "How could you tell Hayley about my father? That wasn't meant for any other ears."

"Oaklynn, I said little to her. She's been through it and guessed." He held her finger. "Stop poking. I'm sorry. Can we talk about last night? I need—"

She wrenched her hand away. "You're like all the other men in my life. I have to get to work." She thrust the door open and jogged to her Jeep, resisting the urge to turn around.

Oaklynn hated the two-year-old-like tantrum she allowed to take over her actions. She'd apologize later. Right now, she had a job to do.

Catch the Protégé before he kills again.

Gothic music filled the sanctuary as Caleb approached The Light Paragons' meeting. Slim had contacted him just after Oaklynn had left for the station, indicating his appointment with the leader had been rescheduled to today. Caleb regretted the way he and Oaklynn had parted, but she failed to respond to any of his texts. She was angry, and had every right to be. He never should have said anything to Hayley.

By the time Caleb had reached the station, Oaklynn had left to go out on patrol. Chloe had provided Bluetooth tags and helped him hide them in his socks. That was an hour ago. Slim had left him alone at the sanctuary's entrance, claiming he had to help in the kitchen.

Caleb shuffled toward the last row as a follower dressed in

a white robe bumped into him, placing an object firmly in his hand. "Sorry, sir. Didn't see you."

He gripped the cell phone and nodded. "No worries." The mayor's wife had made contact. Good. Now he could document everything. If only he could peruse the grounds on his own. He'd find a way. The case depended on it.

After their morning meeting concluded, the gold-robed leader approached. "Glad to have you join us, Mr. Greene." She pointed to the side door. "Let's chat in the boardroom."

Moments later, he sat across from the masked leader. He had to keep her talking. Even though he determined she was disguising her voice, her tone held a familiarity. "I have to ask. Why are you and all the disciples wearing masks? Why hide?"

She steepled her fingers. "We don't call it hiding, but preserving ourselves from pride. We don't want the others to feel unworthy, so we don't reveal our identities. You understand."

Not really. "I would like to join your group. I'm impressed." Perhaps if he played along, they'd let him walk around the grounds like one of them.

She rolled to a small cabinet, opened a drawer, and removed a stack of papers. Then rolled back. "We were hoping you would. We could use someone with your talents. Just as long as you're not here to deceive us." She leaned closer. "Because we will know if you are."

Caleb raised his hands. "I promise. I'm here to shine my light." Not a lie.

"Good." She slid a paper across the table and placed a pen on top of the document. "All members must sign their consent and banking information. We charge a minimal donation tithing fee for you to stay here. Tax deductible, of course."

Doubtful. "Well, your grounds are beautiful. I can't wait to explore it."

"Sign first."

He jotted the bank account Mic had set up for him in the required spot, then added his signature. "Done."

She picked up the document and stood. "Wait here. We just have to verify things. We've had some individuals scam us in the past, so we always confirm." She left and closed the door. A click sounded.

She'd locked him in.

He tapped his thumb on the table. They really took things seriously. He noted the camera hanging from the ceiling in the corner and squashed the idea of texting Mic. He refused to expose the forbidden cell phone hidden in his sock.

Five minutes later, the leader returned. "You're good. Welcome to The Light Paragons." She handed him a thick packet. "Our administrator will assign you a cabin. Just so you know, you can only leave with a vested member."

"And who are the vested members? The ones in red?"

"No. Those are the disciples. Vested members are ones we've deemed fit and those who have proven their loyalty. You'll find out more in the next few days." She beckoned him to come. "Sister Angela requested she be assigned to you."

Good. If the mayor's wife truly wanted out, she would help him get the information he needed to dismantle this group.

The leader led him down the hall and back out to the front of the sanctuary, where the mayor's wife waited. She approached and stuck out her hand. "Mr. Greene, I'm honored to be assigned to you. Welcome to our family."

"I'll leave you to it." The masked leader placed her hands in her pockets before disappearing back into the hallway.

Caleb leaned in, keeping his voice low. "Thanks for the phone, Mrs. Stevens."

"Come." She lifted her coat from a rack inside the main doors. "Call me Sister Angela. I'll show you around the property."

He followed her outside and down the steps to the front yard.

"Okay, we're somewhat safe to talk here, but keep your voice low. Be careful in the buildings. There could be hidden cameras." Angela glanced in all directions. "We have to act fast. Apparently there's a big event happening today. The elite disciple is being chosen."

"Are we allowed to watch?"

"Nope. Only for the disciples and a select few. Where do you want to go first?"

He tilted his head toward the bridge. "I'd like to see what's beyond the walkway."

"That will be tricky, but I know another way not using the bridge." She gestured him forward. "Let's go."

Over the next two hours, Caleb carefully took pictures of everything he could, including the eerie stone house hidden deep in the woods. Angela mentioned she'd been in the foyer once, but after her initial meeting, the leader cut off her access.

Caleb noted the guards patrolling the home, increasing his curiosity about what secrets were housed behind the old stone walls. Something valuable to warrant the heavy security. A man emerged from another building at the property's rear, pushing a dolly filled with boxes down the plowed walkway. "What's in there?"

"Something interesting I was going to tell you about. I think it's how they're helping to fund their cult. Come, we'll go through the woods to the back of the building. There's a blind spot there." She looked around before moving to the next tree.

He followed. "What made you go undercover? Your daughter's death?"

"Before that. When Emily hadn't returned one night, I was frantic. I noticed a large withdrawal from her checking account. The account she'd promised not to touch as she was saving it for university tuition. I was able to get into her laptop and discovered she was involved with the cult."

"But how did you know where to come? They stuck a hood over my head to bring me here."

"I contacted them through the video game like Emily did. Apparently, they started blindfolding after some members tried to leave."

He read the sadness in her eyes. "You mean Emily?"

She nodded. "This way." She slipped between two trees and pointed to the back of the building. "Take a quick peek through the window, but hurry. We don't have much time."

Caleb crouch-walked, scanning the area before approaching the building. He peeked inside the dirty window. Despite the obscured view, Caleb noticed something on a corner table.

Beakers, petri dishes, and burners. They were cooking drugs, confirming what Caleb suspected from the pictures Missy took.

Caleb snapped a few photos and returned to Angela's side. "You're right. My guess is they're cooking meth. Clearly, draining people's bank accounts isn't enough for this group. These pics should help with a warrant."

He tapped in a quick message to Mic and Chloe before emailing them both the pictures.

A bell rang from the main building.

"Lunchtime. We have to go," Angela said. "Be sure to tell everyone how impressed you are with this place. Keep up the ruse."

"Got it. Just a sec." Caleb tapped in a quick text to Mic.

Got my location yet from the tags?

Seconds later, the device buzzed a response.

Still working on it. Hold tight and stay safe.

He bent to tie his laces, hid the phone in his sock, and rose to follow Angela into the building. They joined the lineup for the dining room. "I appreciate the tour, Sister Angela."

"My pleasure. So glad to have you here." She introduced him to a few waiting in line.

Slim greeted them at the door. "Friends, I have a special table for you."

They followed him to the far corner to the right of the kitchen entrance. "Here we go." He leaned close to Caleb. "Word has it a ritual is happening in fifteen minutes. You want help getting down there again?"

"Sure do."

"Get your food and I'll be back. Follow my lead."

Slim returned ten minutes later, holding a wrench. "Brother, didn't you say you were good at faucet leaks? We have a bad one in the kitchen."

Caleb threw down his napkin and stood. "I can look."

"Well, I found a hair in my lasagna. I'm going to have a word with the cook." Angela took her plate and marched back to the food table.

Good cover. Caleb followed Slim into the kitchen and around the corner to the dumbwaiter.

"Get what you need and get back." Slim opened the door and Caleb climbed inside.

Once again, the dumbwaiter transported him to the lower level. Caleb exited and inched his way to the room he found at his last visit. He stole a glimpse around the corner. The occupants sat on the benches. Caleb slipped inside, staying hidden behind a stone pillar.

Chanting filled the corridor, but this time the steady beat of a drum accompanied the chanting. The pairing created an eeriness, and the flickering torches intensified the evil permeating from the room. He prayed a prayer for protection.

The disciples gathered around the stone altar. The sacrificial pig screeched.

"Folks, we're gathered here to welcome Disciple Bart into

the elite circle." The woman in gold raised a knife and the chanting-drum combination increased.

Blood swooshed in Caleb's ears, his heart pounding dangerously fast. He fished out his cell phone and aimed the device at the sacrifice. He hit the video record button.

"We offer this willing animal to give power to Disciple Bart." She drove the knife into the pig.

Another disciple held the chalice under the pig's blood flow, then handed it to the leader.

She moved to Disciple Bart, whose robe now adorned a gold belt. "Drink, my brother, and obtain the Paragons' power." She held it to his lips.

He choked, but continued to drink.

Caleb stopped the video and quickly sent the footage to Mic. He had to return to the kitchen before anyone caught him spying. He replaced the phone and rose. Footsteps sounded behind him seconds before a blunt object hit his head.

The room spun. White spots invaded his vision. He fought the growing murkiness and reached for the pillar to steady himself but missed.

His knees buckled. *Lord, help me.*

Evil opened its arms as Caleb battled to stay in the light, but the lure was too great.

He crumpled to the floor and succumbed to the darkness.

Fools. Every single one of them. The Canadian Watchers Squad was a joke. How could they save Canada when they couldn't even keep their own safe? He'd easily snuck onto the property last night. He faked his reason for being there and took the guard by surprise, but didn't kill him. He wasn't there for him but Lynny. To play with her emotions.

The Protégé chuckled as their bouncer apprehended the Watcher observing their ritual sacrifice. The Protégé's induction into the elite. Now Caleb Greene would pay for his snooping. The Queen Bee placed him in the room where they kept the pigs. How fitting. This pig will be their next sacrifice if he had anything to say about it.

He remembered the kiss Caleb and Lynny shared last night after their dinner. Disgusting. He had monitored from the tree line at a safe distance to maintain his hidden position from the group and the shepherd.

Raised voices from around the corner stilled him in his tracks. Something had agitated the Queen Bee.

He inched along the wall and crept to her office deep in the dungeon, putting his ear against the door. "We need to get rid of her." The Queen Bee's high-pitched tone betrayed her current emotional state.

A muffled reply from an unknown source.

"I'll do it, then. You need to stay hidden."

Another mumbled reply.

"I'll contact Constable Brock and tell her I have information about The Light Paragons she needs to hear and ask her to come to my home. That will bring her running and then I'll take her out. She needs to die today. I'll leave now."

What? The Protégé's hand flew over his mouth.

Change of plans. *No, Queen Bee, you won't kill Lynny. That's my job.*

He raced out of the dungeon to the pig's room. He wanted what the bouncer had found hidden in the Watcher's socks. Caleb's fate would have to wait, but he would get his just reward. Right now, the Protégé had to get to the Queen Bee's home before she did.

"All units, possible 10-45 at 872 Watercross Lane." Dispatch's call blared through the Charger's speaker. Oaklynn grabbed the radio. "3Adam17 responding." She hit the sirens and lights, glancing at Eldon sitting in the passenger seat. "Not another one."

Eight minutes later, Oaklynn and Eldon arrived at the scene. "Let's use extreme caution. We don't know if the suspect is still on-site." Oaklynn shuffled from the cruiser and rested her gloved hand on her sidearm.

A woman paced the porch, rubbing her arms.

"I'm guessing she called it in." Eldon gestured toward the fiftyish salt-and-pepper-haired woman.

"We'll soon find out." Oaklynn approached. "Ma'am, did you call 911?"

Her teeth chattered. "Yes. She's—in—bedroom." Her words came out mumbled. "I—think—dead."

"It's freezing out," Oaklynn said. "Where's your coat?"

"Inside. I came to clean. Found her. Ran outside."

"Who lives here?"

"Kassandra Nason."

That's why the address sounded familiar. "Constable Spearing, grab her coat and take her to the cruiser for now until we clear the home."

After placing the woman in the heated cruiser, Oaklynn and Eldon went room by room, checking for intruders. But found none. One more room to clear.

Oaklynn raised her Glock and turned to Eldon, gesturing him to go right.

He dipped his chin in agreement.

Oaklynn nudged the door open and steered to the left. Eldon to the right.

"Clear," he said.

"Clear." Oaklynn spied Kassandra lying on her bed, hands and feet tied to the bedposts. A gold robe wrapped around her neck.

"Is she—"

Oaklynn holstered her weapon, flew to the bed, and removed her right glove, placing two fingers on Kassandra's neck. "She's gone." She eased the robe down, noting the ligature marks. "It appears someone strangled her using the robe."

Kassandra wore a white cloak, and Oaklynn guessed the blood on her abdomen came from some sort of carving.

Eldon whistled. "This another one of your father's masterpieces?"

"No. This one is new. The Protégé is evolving into his own."

"Why do you think that is?"

"To prove himself, perhaps. I'll wait for Dr. Patterson to show us the stomach. Don't touch her body." Oaklynn stuffed her glove back on, studying the message written in blood above the headboard.

The Light Paragons now have a new leader. This one failed her flock.

Oaklynn's jaw dropped. "Kassandra was the cult leader?" She pointed to the initials written in tiny letters below the message. "It appears the Protégé is taking over."

"This guy is sick."

"Sure is." Sirens sounded, and Oaklynn looked out the window. "EMS is here. You update them. I'll call Chloe."

"Copy that." Eldon left the room.

Oaklynn punched in Chloe's number.

She answered on the first ring. "You at the house on Watercross Lane?"

"Yep, and it's not good." She described the situation. "How far out are you?"

"Arriving now and, Oaklynn, I need to tell you something."

Oaklynn didn't like the sound of her friend's voice. "What?"

"Caleb failed to return at his scheduled time. Mic is studying what he emailed her, hoping to find some sort of lead."

The harsh words Oaklynn spoke to him earlier returned

tenfold. "We have to find him. I said something I need to take back." He wasn't like the other men in her life. Not at all.

"We will, love." A car door slammed in the background. "I'm here and so are the coroners. Be right there."

Pounding footsteps resounded up the staircase. Seconds later, Chloe entered, followed by the coroners.

She rushed forward. "We'll find him."

Oaklynn nodded. She didn't trust herself to speak right now. Her nerves were on the brink of going somewhere she never wanted to go.

Outbursts like her father confessed to having during the trial. It was what sent him on a killing spree.

You're not like him. You're not like him. She swallowed the mantra and focused on the scene before her. "Doctors, I had to touch her neck to check for a pulse. That's why the robe is down a bit."

"Understood, Constable." Dr. Patterson addressed his partner. "Dr. Hancock, take lots of pictures."

He nodded and pressed the camera button over and over as he focused the lens on Kassandra's body.

Oaklynn jumped at each shutter click.

"You okay?" Chloe whispered.

Oaklynn chewed on her bottom lip and shook her head. "I need to find this killer. I feel like I'm about to explode and do something I shouldn't."

"You're not him. Remember that." Chloe extracted her camera from her bag and hung it around her neck. "Leave now, love. Time to process the scene."

"Oh my." Dr Patterson's frenzied two words boomed in the small room.

Oaklynn stilled. "What is it?"

He raised the white robe higher, revealing the crudely carved message.

Judas the betrayer.

Two round items smeared in blood lay on each side of the message.

"What are those?" Oaklynn inched closer, pointing.

"Dr. Hancock. Take a picture of them."

The assistant coroner obeyed. Then Dr. Patterson picked one up. "Appears to be a Bluetooth tag."

Oaklynn flicked her gaze to Chloe. "Were these the ones you put on Caleb?"

The investigator examined them. "Yes, so this is—"

"Another message for me. They have Caleb." Oaklynn's heart drummed louder, her panicked state increasing. "I need to get back to CWS and help Mic locate Caleb."

Oaklynn had to find him to tell him her true feelings before it was too late.

Chapter Twenty-Four

Oaklynn paced the cottage's family room floor, her Bengals nipping at her heels as if they sensed the trepidation flowing through her body. It was now eight thirty and Caleb still hadn't returned or contacted them. Eldon, KFPD's Emergency Response Unit, Ryker, and Kordell remained in close proximity of the compound, waiting for the order to breach. The rest of them had gathered at the cottage. Mic had shared all the pictures Caleb had sent her and attached them to their rolling board. Oaklynn cringed at the disturbing video of the sacrificial ceremony. This cult embodied the stigma of evil that had emanated from Aaron Crowder. The same evil Oaklynn was petrified flowed through her own veins. She dug her fingernails into her palms. *Stop, Oaklynn. Focus.* She picked up Arwen and held her close to her face, soaking up the kitten's warmth and love as if that would eliminate her paralyzing fear. She needed to move on and concentrate on the case. Caleb's life depended on it—and her.

Despite Sergeant Rollins ordering her to stay put, Oaklynn

was on the verge of defying a direct order if they didn't hear from Caleb soon. Mic had obtained the coordinates from the tags before someone took them and placed them on Kassandra's body. Rick requested a warrant because of the pictures of their meth lab. Oaklynn had the sickening feeling something terrible was about to happen and her helplessness now consumed her body. They required probable cause to storm into the compound. Plus, many innocent lives were at stake behind the gate.

Wait—she spun around. "Mic, silly question, but have you pinged the cell phone Caleb sent the pictures and video from?"

"We're triangulating off cell towers, but we lost the signal just after he sent the video. I'm guessing someone destroyed it, so hopefully between the two, we can get close to his location. The compound is huge, but we now know which gate is closest to Caleb. It's five kilometers east of here. I'm checking satellite imaging now."

"I can't believe they were so close and we had no idea." Maxwell Greene dropped into a chair and held his head in his hands. "I shouldn't have insisted he go into the cult."

Dawson plunked beside his father and rubbed his back. "Dad, it's not your fault. God's got Caleb in His hands."

"It's just hard knowing what he went through with Nehemiah Love."

Briggs whined and also paced the room, his keen senses back on track and detecting an issue.

Hayley bent down and hugged the K-9. "We'll find him, bud." She glanced over her shoulder. "Have we tried contacting the mayor's wife or this Slim guy to see what's going on inside the compound?"

"Yes, but no answer. Hopefully, they're okay and not caught in the cross fire." Mic clicked on a few more keys. "Wait. I got a hit off the fake bank account. Someone just withdrew the money we deposited. Let me try something." Her fingers once again flew across her keyboard. Seconds later, she smiled. "Interesting." A few more clicks. "Got you."

Oaklynn let Arwen go and moved to peer over Mic's shoulder. "What is it?"

"Bank account linked to The Light Paragons' charity, which is owned by none other than… Kassandra Nason."

Oaklynn's jaw dropped. "Wait, she's dead. How did she transfer it?"

"Didn't you say her sister was still missing?"

"Yes, and she was driving the van. Send the information to Chloe and Sergeant Rollins. This will help expedite things." Now it was only a matter of time before they got the warrant. But would it come too late?

Oaklynn held her Glock in the ready position, pointing it downward in a firm grip. She waited for the ERU team leader's command. The warrant had come through an hour later, after Rick had gotten the mayor involved. Briggs whined and struggled to free himself from the cage inside the vehicle. The dog wanted to save his partner and friend too. *God, if You're listening, please help us save Caleb and the other innocents.*

ERU's armed vehicle sat ready to plow through the front gate, but also waited for the command.

"Okay, everyone. Listen up." The leader stepped beside Oaklynn. "We've strategically placed the team around the property. It's large and has a few entrances to breach, but now that we have the warrant, we're ready." He clicked his radio button. "Leads, confirm you're in position."

One by one, the leads radioed their confirmation.

"Breaching in three. Get ready." The leader waited.

Oaklynn and Eldon each hopped onto the running board of the vehicle that would take them through the gate and down the driveway, deep into the woods. "Ready."

The team leader nodded. "One…"

"Two…"

Oaklynn raised her weapon.

"Three. Breach. Breach. Breach."

The armed vehicle shot toward the gate and bulldozed into the structure at full speed, creating an opening. The impact boomed through the night air, as the convoy of vehicles followed with their spotlights shining. They sped toward the compound.

They stopped near a large building, and ERU hopped down, raising their weapons. Everyone else followed.

Hayley unleashed Briggs. "Briggs, seek!"

The dog ran across the yard with the team, including Oaklynn, Eldon, and the members of CWS. The animal ran with amazing speed—even with his old injury.

Two guards raised their rifles and fired, but the team evaded their bullets and neutralized them before they could get any more shots off.

Oaklynn darted after Briggs as she guessed he'd be the one to catch Caleb's scent. He charged up the steps and stopped at the door, barking.

"He's in here, isn't he, bud?" Oaklynn turned to Hayley. "Go right. I'll go left. Ready?"

She nodded.

Oaklynn opened the door and Briggs advanced. Hayley and Oaklynn divided, clearing the foyer. Briggs scampered through a door. The duo followed and entered the mess hall.

Oaklynn surveyed the empty room. "Where has Briggs gone?"

"Caleb trained Briggs in many aspects for a military dog. He's caught his handler's scent." Hayley crept farther into the room. "Where is everyone?"

Briggs barked.

Hayley gestured toward the kitchen. "He went that way. Let's go."

They followed and found Briggs barking by a strange access panel on the wall.

"What is that?" Oaklynn spotted a button and pressed it. The door opened. "It's a dumbwaiter."

"Wait, would Grizzly fit in there?"

"It's commercial size, so it would hold his muscular frame, but it would have been a tight squeeze." Oaklynn radioed their location and described what the dog had alerted to, indicating they were following Briggs's lead.

"Constable Brock, wait for backup." Eldon's voice boomed through the radio waves.

"I have backup. Hayley and Briggs. This dumbwaiter probably leads to a lower level. See if you can find another entrance on the west side of the main building." Oaklynn adjusted her duty belt. "I'm going down." She clicked off and turned to Hayley. "I'll send it back up. You and Briggs follow."

Hayley gripped Oaklynn's arm. "Be careful."

"I will." Oaklynn shimmied inside. "Okay, hit the button."

Hayley obeyed, and the dumbwaiter descended, opening at the bottom.

Oaklynn raised her Glock and climbed out. Her radio squawked. Eldon. She fumbled to turn the volume down. "Go ahead."

"Found second entrance. Breaching now."

"Copy that. Hurry."

Oaklynn pointed her weapon left and right. The corridor was empty, but a beating drum and chanting sounded to the right. She suppressed the urge to investigate immediately, but hit the button to send the dumbwaiter to Hayley and Briggs.

She wouldn't risk Caleb's life by proceeding without backup.

Caleb shivered. What happened? His pounding head answered his question. Someone had hit him over the head with a blunt object. Dampness settled into his back. He fingered the smooth surface beneath him, and gulped in a breath, silencing his fear. Someone had fastened him to the stone altar where they held the pig's sacrifice. He wiggled his hands and feet, but his tight restraints didn't budge. *God, help me!* His abductors were going to sacrifice him and he'd never be able to tell Oaklynn his feelings. He was falling in love. A fact he could no longer deny.

He wiggled again, but it was of no use.

Heated whispers to his right stilled Caleb.

"Where is she?" one hushed voice said.

"Your sister is dead." The male's whisper sounded familiar. "She betrayed us."

Was this the Protégé?

Dialogue to his left revealed other disciples stood nearby in the sacrificial sanctuary. He was surrounded.

"What do you mean, Disciple Bart?"

Caleb fought his foggy brain. He needed to make sense of their conversation. The male mentioned a sister.

"You know of what I speak. Take that gold robe off now. You'll never follow in your sister's footsteps. I'm the new leader of The Light Paragons. Kassandra's hive is now mine."

Wait? That's why the leader's voice had sounded familiar earlier. Kassandra Nason was the Queen Bee, and this woman was the missing sister, Victoria Dutton.

But who was the Protégé?

"How could you?" This time Victoria didn't lower her voice. "She was everything to me and promised we'd cleanse the world together."

"Stick with me, and we'll do the same. She was going to kill Lynny and I couldn't let that happen. Constable Brock is mine to kill. She will pay for betraying her father." A pause. "But right now, we have another sacrifice to perform. You do it. Earn your keep under my leadership and I'll promote you. The Watcher will die."

God, no. Help me get out of here, so I can save Oaklynn!

A dog barked in the distance.

Briggs!

The team had found him.

"Police, stop!" Oaklynn yelled, charging into the room. Briggs's bark had revealed their presence and they couldn't wait any longer.

Hayley followed with Briggs at her side.

Pounding footfalls down the hall told her the rest of the team was almost there.

Oaklynn scanned the room. Red-robed figures turned from their huddle in the corner.

Caleb lay tied to the stone altar. A gold-robed figure stood over him, knife raised.

"I said stop!" She took aim. With Kassandra's death, she guessed the figure was the Protégé. Finally, she would end his killing spree.

"He has to die." The stampede of officers and the Canadian Watchers Squad almost silenced the muffled words.

Hayley moved beside Oaklynn, rifle poised. "You kill him. I kill you."

Briggs barked, his teeth baring as he advanced from the right.

The figure raised the knife higher before lowering it.

Both Oaklynn and Hayley fired multiple shots.

The gold-robed figure dropped, the knife clanging on the stone floor.

Hayley stormed forward and kicked it away before approaching her brother. "You're alive! We were so scared."

"Oaklynn—"

"Don't talk. Oaklynn's okay." Hayley leaned her rifle against the table and unclipped a jackknife from her belt. She cut his restraints and pulled him into a hug. Briggs leaped up onto the table, licking his handler—and friend.

Oaklynn would let them have their moment. She'd have hers soon and tell him her feelings. She turned her attention to the team subduing the other disciples and leaned against the column as realization dawned on her.

The copycat was finally dead.

A pinprick pierced her neck.

She gasped.

She tried to yell, but her cries for help only squeaked out like a mouse. Never to be heard over the flurry of movement masking her attacker.

The room spun.

The torches on the walls flickered.

Evil called out.

Darkness plunged her into the abyss.

Chapter Twenty-Five

He placed her on the queen-size bed and adjusted her blond hair so the curls sat on her shoulders. He shifted another lock to a precise spot. *There, perfect.* Leaning down, he drew in a deep breath, relishing her scent. Finally, time alone with his prize.

She stirred but only shifted in the bed.

He'd give her another shot to ensure she stayed subdued. He retrieved the syringe from his pocket and raised the comforter, plunging the needle into her vein.

He brushed his fingertips down her arms. "You're beautiful. I think even more than your sister."

If that was possible.

"We'll have lots of time later." The Protégé tucked the comforter snug to her neck and walked around the bed, approaching the gift for the Suicide Slayer. His first daughter. He'd brought her to the spot Aaron Crowder spoke about.

The place the Protégé now owned and visited enough to keep suspicion away from the building. The neighbors believed him to be a traveling salesperson. If they only knew the Suicide Slayer's legacy lived next door.

Thunder boomed outside. The weather had turned, bringing a winter storm. So be it.

He rose and meandered to the dresser, picking up the bouquet he'd bought along their journey. He placed flowers in the vase, arranging each meticulously. Everything had to be perfect for his girls.

He set them on the nightstand and studied the blonde sisters. They could have been twins.

Shame your father never met you, Reese. He'd be proud.

He lifted the locket he'd found in Lynny's uniform pocket and placed it around her neck. A final gift from her father, but also from him. Aaron had given the necklace and his letter for his daughter to him the day before he took his life. The Protégé opened the pendant, fingering five-year-old Lynny's face. Such a cutie. However, she never guessed what lay beneath, hidden from prying eyes. He'd placed the tiny item underneath, well concealed from even a constable. Then mailed it from the post office near the penitentiary after he'd found her.

This is how I tracked you. Lynny, it's almost time for you to wake up.

The drug he'd given her would wear off within the hour. The Protégé wrung his hands together and licked his lips, his heart somersaulting.

Then the fun would begin.

"Where is she?" Caleb paced the sacrificial sanctuary's floor, his pulse amplifying with each step. "Where is Oaklynn?"

Briggs whined at his owner's barked question.

Hayley latched on to his arm. "She was right beside me. We'll find her. What happened?"

Caleb stared at the gold-robed disciple—Victoria Dutton. "I was videoing their ceremony. Shortly after that, someone hit me from behind. Knocked me out cold. I woke up to Victoria talking. I presumed to the Protégé. He confessed to killing her sister and said he was taking control. He ordered her to kill me. Then I heard Briggs." He embraced his sister again. "Thank you for saving me."

"It was a team effort, bro."

Spearing approached and gestured toward the group of red-robed men. "We unmasked all the disciples. Can you identify the Protégé by his voice?"

"Perhaps. His voice sounded familiar, but I still can't place it."

"We'll get each to talk. Come."

Caleb followed Spearing.

One by one, each disciple spoke.

Caleb shook his head, then clenched his jaw. "He's not here. He's taken her somewhere. That's the only answer to why she's missing. She wouldn't just up and leave a crime scene." His heartbeat intensified. If he didn't contain his fury, he'd explode into his full-fledged grizzly state.

Chloe bounded into the room and approached. "I heard over the radio that Oaklynn is missing. How did that happen?"

"I'm guessing the perp took advantage of the chaos once we breached the room." Spearing pointed to the pillars. "Maybe hid behind one of those. It's shadowy in here. Easy place for him to conceal himself."

Hayley snapped her fingers. "That's it. I remember when I hugged Caleb, out of the corner of my eye, I saw her lean against one."

"And he's used drugs on her before." Chloe grimaced. "That's probably how he subdued her." She pointed to the side door. "And exited through there. Unseen."

Caleb took several deep breaths, silencing the panic. *Clear your thoughts.* "Wait. What about the creepy house across the bridge? Has anyone checked there?"

"They just arrived at the house," Spearing said. "They found the meth lab."

"We have to check the house. Briggs, come." Caleb raced into the night and across the bridge, the shepherd at his heels.

Spearing, Chloe, and Hayley followed.

Other constables met them in front of the stone house. Constable Dalton approached. "We've found something interesting in the basement." He beckoned them forward.

Caleb peered up at the lit widow's walk and shuddered. Something about this house sent eerie chills racing up his spine. *Lord, protect us from evil.* He followed the others down into a dungeon-like basement. Torchlights adorned the stone walls, illuminating the haunting area. Cells lined each side and held people like caged birds.

Chloe whistled. "What is this place?"

Briggs whined.

Caleb petted his dog. "It's okay, boy. I'm guessing this is where they brainwash some who have strayed. The Purity Flock used a similar area for that purpose. They do it in private so the other followers won't see what really goes on."

Spearing frowned. "Creepy. Dalton, any sign of Oaklynn in this house?"

The constable shook his head. "I thought she may be held down here, but she's not in any of these rooms. I've called for EMS to check these people out."

Hayley looked into a room. "Good plan. They probably drugged them." She turned to the group. "So if Oaklynn isn't being held here, any ideas of where she was taken?"

Caleb paced. "We have to consider the possibilities. The Protégé worshipped her father. Knows everything about him and seems to know about Oaklynn's childhood. Where would he take her?"

"No idea." Chloe's eyes brightened, and she unclipped her cell phone. "But I know someone who might."

"Her aunt." Hope surged through Caleb. "Can you give me her number and your phone?"

Chloe scrolled through her contacts. "Oaklynn gave it to me after she shared her story. Here it is. Sue Brock." She handed him the phone.

"Thank you." Caleb hit the icon to connect him to Oaklynn's aunt as he left the spooky dungeon. "Pick up. Pick up."

"Chloe?"

"No. This is Caleb Greene. Is this Sue Brock?"

"Yes. You're the Watcher working with Oaklynn…" Her pitch elevated at the end. "What's wrong? Where's my niece?"

Caleb explained the situation. "I know this is hard and we're doing everything to find her. Where do you believe the Protégé would take her? Somewhere from her childhood, perhaps?"

Silence sailed through the speaker.

"Ms. Brock?"

"I'm thinking and praying." Another moment of silence. "Wait. The only thing that makes any sense, and this is a long shot—her childhood home near Elora. I heard someone bought it, so I'm not sure if that's right."

"What's the address?"

She rhymed it off. "Find her, Caleb. Is there any word on her sister?"

"None, but I'm guessing the Protégé has her, too. Thank you. We'll keep you updated. Please pray."

"I'm calling my prayer chain now and getting on my knees."

"We have the local authorities searching and my father will ensure we have all the means to find her. I promise." Panic corded his neck muscles.

"Thank you. She means everything to me. Bye." She ended the call.

Me too.

He rushed back to the group who had relocated to the house's kitchen. "She guesses Oaklynn's childhood home. Got a location. I'm calling my sister. She'll find out everything about the property, and fast." He called Mic's number.

"What's going on, bro? I've been sitting on pins and needles. Dad too. I'm putting you on speaker." A commotion sounded in the background.

"Son, what's happening?"

He explained the situation. "Mic, can you find out who owns the house?"

"Let me do my work." Fingers tapping on a keyboard seeped through the silence as he waited for information. "Okay. Found something. A Bartholomew Johnson bought the house."

Disciple Bart. "That has to be the Protégé."

More tapping. "Yep. Can't find anything on him. It's obviously an alias."

"The house is just outside of Elora, son. That's over a two-hour drive."

"And he's had a head start. Dad, can you arrange for a chopper?" His father had multiple contacts at his disposal.

"My jet would be quicker. Get the team to the tarmac. I'll arrange everything."

"Thanks, Dad." He punched off and shared the information. "The team is gathering. Spearing, you want to come?"

He slapped Caleb's back. "A chance to fly in a jet? Dumb question, Watcher. And besides, Oaklynn is one of our own and we need to save her."

Twenty minutes later, Caleb, Hayley, Ryker, Spearing, and Briggs sat in Maxwell Greene's luxurious jet as it ascended to seven thousand feet. Spearing had apprised Sergeant Rollins of the situation, and the sergeant arranged for local law enforcement officers to meet the team at the airport. They'd travel from there to the Protégé's home.

Caleb leaned back in the leather seat and prayed. *Father, I beg You. Help us get there before it's too late. I can't imagine life without Oaklynn in it now. She's Your child. Save her. I need You.*

Thoughts of his hatred for Nehemiah Love and Paige entered his mind, followed by a single word.

Forgive.

Where had that come from? *God, what are You telling me?* A verse flashed.

Forgive them, for they know not what they do.

Jesus begging His Father to spare those who had betrayed Him.

It was time. Time for Caleb to truly leave all of his baggage in the past—and to forgive those who wronged him. *Lord, I'm sorry for the animosity I've had for Nehemiah and Paige. I don't understand why they did what they did, but You do. You've forgiven me for my wrongs. It's my turn. I forgive them and release them and my past to You. I see now how my bitterness has held me back, but I want to be Your light.*

Peace washed over him, and his tensed shoulders relaxed. *Thank You.*

God had obviously wanted him to deal with what still plagued him. It was done.

Now it was time to save Oaklynn.

Oaklynn's hand flew to her neck to stop the ache. She fluttered her eyes open, but her vision remained blurred. Where was she? How long had she been out? The scent of lilies permeated her space. Her chest constricted as heat set her face on fire. That smell only meant one thing. The Protégé wasn't dead.

And he held her captive.

But where?

She blinked her eyes until the shadowy room came into view. She turned her head to the right to figure out her location, then left.

Her sister slept beside her, her curls positioned in perfect order around her face and down her shoulders. *Reese, I'm so sorry.*

She eased herself into a seated position to study the rest of the room.

And cried out.

Every muscle in her body locked as thunder exploded outside and in her temples.

She was in the one place she never wanted to see again.

Her childhood bedroom.

Her ankle was handcuffed to the metal footboard.

No escape.

Reese slept peacefully. Oaklynn leaned closer, peering at her sister's feet. Why wasn't she restrained?

Oaklynn shook her sister's shoulders. "Reese, wake up!" She shook her again.

But no response.

She whipped off the comforter and examined her sister's arms. Pinpricks on the inside of her elbow. He had drugged her to keep her sedated.

Oaklynn flopped back onto the pillow, her mind racing for ways to escape her old bedroom. Memories blasted through her head, raging a war with her childhood and adult fears. Fear of her father's visits. Fear of his evil mind overtaking hers. Fear of never leaving this room again. Fear of losing the sister she just found. And mostly—

Fear of never telling Caleb she was sorry.

A flash of lightning brightened the darkened room, providing a ray of hope. A verse her aunt liked to recite emerged.

"I am the light of the world. Whoever follows me will never walk in darkness, but will have the light of life."

Aunt Sue explained that Jesus had been speaking in the temple. Was He the light she needed to shine in the darkness?

Her mind recalled the last Christmas Eve she'd spent with her mother. They had gone to a candlelight service, and they sang "Silent Night" as the pastor lit a candle. Then lit the woman's candle beside him, and she lit the next person's. The process continued and, one by one, the single flames turned the total darkness into an explosion of light.

Was He telling her she was that single light? And her light would extinguish the evil?

Something her aunt said during her father's trial, after Oaklynn had confessed her fears, came to mind.

God will meet you in the darkest corner and provide the light for you to escape. You just have to let Him in.

Tears flowed like a waterfall, running along both sides of her neck.

Yes, it was time.

Time to surrender to the One she'd been fighting all these years.

Not her father. Not the copycat. Not herself.

God.

She wiped her tears and sat back up, the cuffs pinching her ankle. She ignored the biting pain, clamped her eyes shut, and folded her hands.

Lord, I see now. I see You in the darkness. In the evil. Not because You like the dark, but because You're the only light shining when all other lights extinguish. You're there right beside me, behind me, before me. Everywhere. Just like Mama and Aunt Sue said You'd be. I'm sorry for not seeing it. I'm sorry for not truly listening to You. You've been speaking, but I created too much noise around me to hear. Please forgive me and my wrongdoings. My dark thoughts. I surrender them and my entire being to You. Take my life and use it for Your glory, even if I'm only alive for another few minutes. Use me to shine for You. I want to be Your light in this darkened world. Provide a way for me and Reese to escape. Protect Caleb and the others. I surrender all this to You. In Your name, amen.

She opened her eyes. Fresh tears flowed, bringing a moment of peace before fear once again consumed her. Why? She'd surrendered to God. What else was there?

Forgive him.

She stiffened at the two words that tumbled into her mind. Forgive her father? She balled her hands into fists. *No, I can't. Not after everything he's done.* Tears slipped down her cheeks.

Forgive him.

No! Oaklynn covered her ears as if blocking out her thoughts. *I won't!*

Even as Christ forgave you, so also do ye.

Another verse Aunt Sue used to quote barreled into Oaklynn's mind. *It's the only way to be truly free of him*, she had said. Was that true?

Childhood memories tumbled through her thoughts. Every touch. Every lie. Every betrayal.

More tears cascaded and Oaklynn squeezed her eyes shut.

Forgive him.

Her pulse pounded, her breathing labored. *You can do this.*

"Dad, I forgive you. I release you." She whooshed out an audible breath.

She opened her eyes and scanned the room that once held her captive, but now only peace flowed through her. A peace she recognized as only coming from God.

Thumping footfalls approached, and the door creaked open.

Oaklynn braced herself to meet the Protégé face-to-face.

A hand reached inside the room and flicked on the switch, flooding the room with light.

Oaklynn blinked until her eyes adjusted to the brightness and she stared at her father's copycat.

"You!"

Caleb and the team landed at the airport thirty minutes later and met with the local authorities. Spearing conversed with them and introduced everyone. Their team leader had shaken their hands and mentioned Maxwell Greene had apprised them of the situation, ordering them to allow his squad to help. Their chief had agreed, but the team lead had a few choice words to say on the matter. However, Spearing explained their background, indicating how they'd been working together to stop a serial killer, vouching for their expertise.

The man pursed his lips, but nodded.

The group now sat in their vehicles a few houses down from Oaklynn's childhood home, mapping out a plan of attack. Thankfully, Maxwell had Sergeant Rollins contact a local judge to get a warrant. They were still waiting.

"This is taking too long." Caleb opened his door. "I'm going to check things out. Take Briggs for a stroll. No harm in that, right?"

"Caleb, not a good idea." Hayley checked her riflescope.

"I can't sit here and wait for him to kill her. I'm simply a civilian out for a stroll."

Spearing handed him a radio. "Take this. Radio us if you see any signs of a threatening situation. Then we can breach."

Caleb nodded, stuffed the radio into his coat pocket, and climbed out, racing around to the vehicle's back. He opened the tailgate. "Briggs, come."

The dog jumped down.

Caleb attached the leash, and they headed toward the Protégé's lair.

Time to save the woman he loved.

Oaklynn inched closer to her sister in a protective mode. "Let her go. It's me you want." She studied the man's face. "How can you take lives? You're in the job of saving them. You disgust me."

The Protégé—aka paramedic Jayson Scott—stepped to the foot of the bed. "That's only my day job. I've taken over your father's work. I'm cleansing the province's riffraff. Didn't you hear? I'm now the leader of The Light Paragons and have the power I need." He flexed his biceps.

"You really think drinking pig's blood will give you power?

You're dumber than I thought." She hated to antagonize him, but she needed to stall. Buy Reese and her time. She had to devise a plan to get the cuffs off her ankle.

His lips turned into a crooked smile. "That's all for show. The Queen Bee believed a lie Nehemiah Love told her. That to get power, she had to drink blood." He cursed. "The only way to truly obtain power is to be the leader. That's what I wanted, but first I had to take out the flock who either got in my way or who threatened to expose our little group. I started with the first elite disciple."

"Peter Ratchet. You followed my father's methods and posed the victims in the same manner, but how did you pick the others?"

He rubbed his hands together. "I love this talk. Okay, after Peter I had to take care of the mayor's daughter. She threatened to leave and tell everyone about us." He raised his index finger. "But that was a bit of an oopsy. The mayor called in that Watcher group and Caleb. I saw that kiss. Disgusting."

"You were watching us? How did you keep finding me and get into my farmhouse?"

"I watched you at your home and figured out your code. Did you like how I shut your kittens in the basement? I also cloned your phone while we took you to the hospital. Messed with your Wi-Fi and smart device to play the lullaby. Aaron told me all about your past, including the special dance. His cologne. Your mother's perfume. Everything. Even how he drugged you as a child. You never knew that was the cause of your memory loss."

What?

He pointed to her neck. "Do you like your special tattoo? Drugging you at the bakery was easier than I realized when I bribed those teenagers to make a commotion. I knew how much of the drug to give you to keep you lucid until you got home where I gave you my special cocktail."

He truly was evil. Perhaps even more than the Suicide Slayer. "How did you find me at the cottage?"

"You're a cop. I thought you'd figure that one out." He moved back around to her side and bent close.

She flinched.

He lifted the locket. "Your father had me insert your pictures, and I added a small tracker behind yours." He tapped his right temple. "Smart, huh? Of course, we didn't know where you were, but I knew I'd find you eventually. I couldn't believe it when we met at Missy's crime scene."

Oaklynn chewed the inside of her mouth, at a loss for words. She had to keep him talking and pictured KFPD's leaderboard. "Why Missy?"

He contorted his face. "She got too nosy and smuggled in a camera. She paid for her mistake. Don't you love how I chose the churches to display my victims? Your father didn't do that, but I wanted to add my own special touch. Or *signature*, as you cops like to call it. I'm good at what I do, don't you think?"

Did he expect her to smile and agree? "What about Isaac Rollins? Why did he have to die?"

"He was useful at first. Helping to rob banks for us. That gave us the money to set up our meth lab. But then he—" he raised his fingers and air-quoted "—'went back to God' and wanted out. Nope. Once you're in, you stay. Kimi found that out too." He tapped his chin. "Who's next? Oh yeah, that author. She failed my hero. He'd tasked her to find your sister. I decided she had to pay for her failure. Funny that sweet Reese did the work and found you."

Oaklynn eyed her sister. Her steady breathing told her she was okay, only sedated. "What did you give her?"

"Never mind. Back to my story. When I heard Kassandra plotting to kill you, I had to take action. We found your boyfriend spying on us, so I added his tags to Kassandra. Don't you think that was a nice touch? Aaron would be so proud of me."

"You're sick like my father. Why would you worship such an evil man?"

He stormed toward her.

She recoiled, the cuff banging on the metal railing. Pain shot up her leg.

Jayson got in her space, inches away from her face. "Don't you ever call Aaron Crowder sick. He's a hero."

His saliva sprayed her face. The smell of whiskey and stale smoke reeked on his breath. She fought to suppress the rising nausea.

He pulled out a knife and ran the blade's tip down her cheek. "I could make you pay for betraying him right now. Mess up that beautiful face."

God, help me! "Tell me how you met him."

He grinned and backed away. "Through the medical profession, originally at a conference. Something about him intrigued me. Of course, I didn't realize he was the Suicide Slayer until you called the cops on him, but I'd been following his kills." Jayson set the knife on the tall dresser and approached the side of the bed where Reese lay. He bent over her and adjusted one of her curls. "Your father and I had lots in common. You see, my mother also treated me like dirt. Beat me when I wet the bed. She made me do unbelievable things just for kicks. Kids bullied me at school because they found out about them." Tears pooled and his lip quivered. "Despite everything she did, I still loved her, but she had to die. I poisoned her, bit by bit."

Oaklynn softened at the man's obvious pain. "I'm sorry she treated you poorly. Parents can be cruel."

He grazed Reese's arm.

Oaklynn tensed at how the man touched her sister, her disgust returning. It reminded her too much of her father. "Please let her go. I'll do anything you ask."

He rose. "Would you kill for me? You know you have it in you just like your dear old dad."

Lies. All lies. "I used to believe that, but it's not true. I have God's light inside me now."

Jayson swore. "God? Hardly." He caressed Reese's shoulder, his fingers lingering. "I'm going to mold her into your father. She'll do as I say." He turned his gaze to Oaklynn, eyes flashing. "It's too late for you. I see that now. You must pay for your betrayal."

"Why did you bring me here to my old bedroom?"

"It's a fitting place for you to die. I bought the house years ago. I'm quitting my job in Kenorapeake Falls and moving here. Thought I'd start my cult here since I know KFPD have stormed the compound." He paced. "I'll stop killing for a bit, but I'll condition your sweet sister and we'll pick up where your father left off in this area."

"Reese will never kill for you."

He folded his arms across his chest, tapping his index finger on top. "Perhaps you're right. Maybe you both deserve to die. I'll sacrifice you for your father. Just like Abraham was about to do to Isaac." He removed keys from his pocket, fiddling with them as he walked back to Oaklynn's side.

She spied the key to her cuffs among them.

A pounding knock sounded below.

Jayson jolted from the sudden noise, dropping the keys.

More pounding. "Hello, anyone home?" A dog barked.

Oaklynn sucked in a breath.

Caleb and Briggs.

Jayson swore and seized the knife. "Time to finish the Watcher." He stomped from the room.

"Caleb, run!" She screamed as loud as she could.

Oaklynn's scream sent Briggs into a frenzy, barking and baring his teeth. Caleb yanked out the radio and hit the button. "She's inside. Get here. Now!"

"Team. Move in," the local constable yelled into the radio.

Doors slammed and rushed movements sounded behind Caleb. Some circled around the back.

Caleb positioned himself and Briggs beside the door, holding the dog's leash. It wasn't time to let him go, and he also had to compensate for his dog's injury. He wouldn't put him at further risk.

The group bolted up the laneway, weapons raised.

One constable carried a battering ram and stood to the left side of the door, waiting for the order.

Their team leader lifted his hand in a hold position and waited until the others were ready. "Breach."

The constable plowed the battering ram into the door, the wood shattering on impact.

The leader motioned them forward. "Go. Go. Go."

They breached the Protégé's residence with a clear mission. Save Oaklynn.

Oaklynn adjusted her position and reached for the keys that had slipped under the bed. "Come on, girl!" She had to free herself before Jayson returned. She stretched farther and her fingers grazed the ring. "Almost there." She snagged the keys and ignored the flickering spots from her sudden movement. Reaching for her foot, she fumbled to insert the key and finally unlocked the cuffs. She wiggled out of them and flew to her sister's side of the bed. She shook Reese, but the woman didn't wake. "What did he give you?" Could she carry her? *You can do it.* She placed one arm under Reese's waist and another under her knees.

Pounding footfalls announced an intruder. Oaklynn set her sister back on the bed.

Jayson reappeared and ran into the room, slamming it closed before locking them in. "How did you—" He hit his forehead with the back of the hand holding a knife. "Stupid. Stupid. I dropped the keys." He cursed.

Movement sounded below.

"It's over, Jayson. Give it up." She stepped closer, hoping to distract him and get his weapon. "There's too many of them."

"Get on the bed." He placed the knife on the dresser and hauled out a gun from the back of his waistline, pointing it at Reese. "Or she dies now."

Shouts came from the hallway.

Oaklynn inched closer.

More shouts followed by doors opening and closing.

Jayson turned.

Enough for Oaklynn to act. She dove for him and knocked him into the wall. The gun clattered onto the hardwood floor.

She snatched it up and pointed it at him. "No. *You* die."

He sneered. "Do it. Maybe this was always the intended outcome. You have it in you. Just like your father."

Her hand shook as the thought of ridding this man from the world surfaced. Her earlier peace faltered and fear threatened to send her careening back toward the darkness.

Beckoning her to return.

"Come on. You know you want to." Jayson cocked his head, then opened his arms wide. "I'm ready."

Another flash of lightning glowed under the window blinds.

Light in the darkness.

No. She was God's light. "No. More. Darkness." She kept the weapon trained on Jayson and dashed to the door, unlocking it and whipping it open. "In here!"

"Oaklynn?" Caleb hurried across the threshold with Briggs. "Are you okay?"

She nodded, turning her attention to the man she'd fallen for. "He egged me on to kill him, but it didn't work. This is finally over."

Caleb squeezed her shoulder. "It is."

More footfalls approached.

Briggs growled, alerting them to increased danger.

Jayson reached for the knife, but before Oaklynn could respond, Caleb grabbed the gun and fired multiple shots.

The Protégé dropped.

Eldon and the rest of the team entered, taking over the scene and calling for EMS.

Caleb handed Eldon the gun and nudged Oaklynn to the corner of the room. "Are you okay? Is Reese?"

Oaklynn stole a glance at her sleeping sister. "She will be." She faced him and stared into his gorgeous eyes. "Me too. Are you okay?"

"I am now." He caressed her face. "I thought I lost you."

She stepped closer. "Caleb, I have to tell you—"

He smothered her words with his lips, stealing her breath. Oaklynn ignored the snickers in the background and got lost in the moment, letting his kiss eradicate the darkness from the room. Darkness she could now put behind her.

And move forward. With him.

Caleb broke the embrace. "I know. I'm sorry too. And the disgust you saw on my face when you told me about your father wasn't toward you. It was toward him." He ran both hands down each of her arms. "Oaklynn, I want you in my life."

"Even with all my baggage?"

"If you'll accept mine."

She failed to stop the tears from forming. "I've never met anyone like you in my life. I'm falling in love with you, Caleb Greene."

"The feeling is mutual." Once again, he claimed her lips with another kiss.

A kiss promising a future together.

Epilogue

Oaklynn cupped her hands around her coffee mug, staring into the lake's stillness. She loved the early mornings out on the rebuilt dock at the Greene family cottage. It was now her favorite place, even in the October coolness. A loon called out in the distance as if beckoning the others to begin the day. Mist rose from the water as the sun peeked over the horizon in a wondrous mixture of red, yellow, and orange. The fall display was breathtaking. She loved how God painted the trees this time of year. Even though winter was her favorite season, the autumn leaves fought to compete. She smiled and sipped her orange-chocolate-flavored coffee. *Be still and know that I am God*. She now recited the verse often. After years of torment, peace finally washed over her. Thanks to her Heavenly Father.

The family had gathered for a huge Thanksgiving feast and invited Oaklynn, Reese, and her aunt Sue. Oaklynn and Reese had both undergone a DNA test and discovered they were indeed sisters. Even though Reese fought the darkness from their father's past, Oaklynn promised they'd win the battle—

together. Reese moved to Kenorapeake Falls and was working on another bestseller.

The community was shocked when they'd discovered the Protégé's identity—especially his paramedic partner, Andy, who had returned to work after his mother's funeral. Jayson's colleagues claimed he was the nicest person, which fit Dawson's profile. It had been nine months since Caleb snatched the gun from her hand and killed the copycat killer. He said he'd done it so she didn't have to. He knew. Knew what she had fought only moments before in the dark.

The darkness still reared its ugly head, but the light always reemerged, shining brighter.

Whistling exposed Caleb's approach. He set his coffee down on the table and wrapped a plush plaid blanket around her shoulders before kissing her cheek. "Good morning, my love."

"Morning, my handsome Grizzly." She giggled and reached up, pulling him toward her. She kissed him, warmth spreading throughout her body. "How'd you sleep?"

"Fine." He hauled the heavy Adirondack chair closer, then sat and grabbed her hand. "Look at those colors. It's going to be a beautiful Thanksgiving this year. Even more with you here by my side."

"I'm so happy. Your family has been kind to allow my aunt and sister to join them."

"You're all part of our family now. You know that, right?"

"I do."

Caleb and Oaklynn went out on their first official date a couple of weeks after the Protégé frenzy settled. However, she still wrestled with insecurities about herself. She'd gone back to counseling, and that had helped, but Caleb's reassurance of their lasting relationship had convinced her.

He released her hand and rose. "Well, I have something to ask you, and this is the best place to do it. It was where we had our first kiss."

"Yes, before the dock was blown to smithereens."

He chuckled. "True, but now it's larger and even nicer. Dad knows how to go all out."

"That he does."

Caleb removed an object from his pocket and knelt in front of her.

She gasped.

"Oaklynn Brock, I think I fell in love with you the night at the bakery out in the parking lot when we almost kissed. You stole my heart. I love you." He held the small jewelry box in front of her and opened the lid. "Will you marry me?"

Both hands flew to her mouth as tears formed.

"Please."

Oaklynn yanked her hands down. "Yes! Yes!"

He took the ring, placed it on her finger, and rose to his feet, hauling her up with him. "You scared me for a minute."

She gazed at the sparkling ring. "I love you, Caleb Greene." She stepped into his open arms and kissed him before resting in his teddy bear embrace.

The sun crested and the light burst over the lake, reminding Oaklynn of God's love and His mission for her.

To be His light in the darkness.

★ ★ ★ ★ ★